LM 1288031 0   S

KT-478-500

To Judy Shephard

Praise for OLIVIA DARLING

'Packed with passionate encounters and saucy flings,
as well as fraud, death threats and revenge'
**** *Heat* on *Priceless*

'Another top bonkbuster from Ms Darling'
Closer on *Priceless*

'Settle back with a glass of wine and enjoy'
Daily Express on *Priceless*

'This frisky novel has something for everyone'
**** *Star* magazine on *Priceless*

'I giggled my way through this tongue-in-cheek saga of power,
revenge and lust ... this 21st-century bonkbuster is a great
excuse to hole up with a glass of bubbly'
Eve on *Vintage*

'A bonkbuster with bubbles'
**** *Daily Mirror* on *Vintage*

'A great, no-morals romp!'
**** *Hot Stars* on *Vintage*

'Hugely enjoyable, definitely a novel
to grace your beach bag this summer'
Daily Mail on *Vintage*

'Dazzling ... Prepare for lust, betrayal and
strictly no moral fibre' *Heat* on *Vintage*

Withdrawn from
Lambeth Libraries

Also by Olivia Darling

Vintage
Priceless

About the Author

Having grown up in the west of England, Olivia Darling now lives in London with her fiancé. She enjoys dancing, wine and music. Doesn't everybody?

Temptation

OLIVIA DARLING

HODDER

First published in Great Britain in 2010 by Hodder & Stoughton
An Hachette UK company

First published in paperback in 2010

1

Copyright © Olivia Darling 2010

The right of Olivia Darling to be identified as the Author of the Work has been asserted by
her in accordance with the Copyright, Designs and Patents Act 1988.

All rights reserved. No part of this publication may be reproduced,
stored in a retrieval system, or transmitted, in any form or by any means
without the prior written permission of the publisher, nor be otherwise circulated in any form
of binding or cover other than that in which it is published and without a similar condition
being imposed on the subsequent purchaser.

All characters in this publication are fictitious and any resemblance
to real persons, living or dead is purely coincidental.

A CIP catalogue record for this title is available from the British Library

B format paperback ISBN 978 0 340 99274 6
A format paperback ISBN 978 0 340 99286 9

Typeset in Adobe Jenson by Hewer Text UK Ltd, Edinburgh

Printed and bound by Clays Ltd, St Ives plc

Hodder & Stoughton policy is to use papers that are natural, renewable
and recyclable products and made from wood grown in sustainable forests.
The logging and manufacturing processes are expected to conform
to the environmental regulations of the country of origin.

Hodder & Stoughton Ltd
338 Euston Road
London NW1 3BH

www.hodder.co.uk

Overture

Chapter One

Milan, Italy.

Everyone who saw Cosima Esposito sing at La Scala that night knew that they had witnessed something truly special. The little American soprano with the enormous voice had given a performance that would go down in opera history. She had sung a Tosca to rival that of any of the great divas: Maria Callas, Joan Sutherland, Montserrat Caballé. Now Cosima Esposito had established herself firmly in their ranks. But even as the audience, stunned for just a moment by the drop of the curtain on such magic, erupted into rapturous applause, Cosima could not enjoy her triumph.

'Someone help me up, for fuck's sake.'

While the audience had seen Tosca jump hundreds of feet from the forbidding walls of Rome's Castel Sant'Angelo,

Cosima had actually fallen just four feet from some cardboard-clad scaffolding onto a very big crash mat, had landed awkwardly and somehow managed to get tangled up in the voluminous skirts of her late-eighteenth-century costume. Eventually, two stagehands had to haul her to her feet, at which point her co-star, Nolan O'Connor, who was looking considerably more composed despite being covered in blood, joined her. He'd had a little more time to gather himself since he met his stage death ten minutes earlier in front of a firing squad as Tosca's ill-fated lover, Mario Cavaradossi.

Nolan offered Cosima his arm.

'Fuck you.' She refused his offer of gentlemanly assistance and stormed ahead of him to the front of the stage. The chorus had already taken their bow. It was time for the principals to step forward. Out in the auditorium, the audience were wild with appreciation.

'Come on, Cosi.' This time Nolan grabbed for her hand.

'Get off.' She shook herself free again.

'We're supposed to be lovers,' said Nolan.

'We're supposed to be *married*,' Cosima hissed. She had married Nolan O'Connor at the tender age of twenty-one, full of youthful conviction. Seven years later, it appeared that he was getting the itch. Earlier that day, Nolan had failed to meet Cosima for lunch after she finished a morning of interviews for an Italian press eager to know more about this beautiful rising star, with young Liz Taylor looks, who had a voice like syrup onstage and a heavy Noo Yoik accent when she was off it. Nolan didn't get her message, he said. He claimed he was in the gym with his phone switched off. Cosima was certain she knew otherwise.

'Where the fuck were you this afternoon? Where were you, Nolan? Admit it. You were with that violinist, weren't you? The one with the pierced tongue and the very bad taste in other women's husbands.'

'I told you I was working out.'

'And I'm telling you, you were fucking the fiddler.'

'Just smile and take your fucking bow,' said Nolan, squeezing Cosima's hand so tightly that she winced as the big green stone on the engagement ring he had bought her cut into her hand.

When the curtain rose on that evening's principals, the audience saw nothing but love and magic, but as the curtain closed again, Cosima returned the favour of Nolan's horribly hard squeeze by slapping him right across the face with her free hand, not caring that the entire company was assembled behind them watching with prurient interest. Though she was only five feet two inches tall, the force of the unexpected blow had Nolan reeling.

'You're a bitch,' said the horrified tenor.

'And you're a total shit,' Cosima responded. 'You just can't keep your dick in your pants for one minute! You ought to be castrated!'

'I'd still sing better than you if I *were* a castrato,' Nolan retorted. 'You sing like a fucking crow.'

'Oh!'

It was the worst thing he had ever said to her. Cosima's voice was her life. To hear Nolan tell her she couldn't sing onstage and in front of so many people was worse than his constant infidelities.

'How dare you!' Cosima flew at her husband and co-star, fists flailing.

The other members of the company backed away discreetly

while the stage manager signalled that the curtains should not be opened again though the audience were far from finished with their standing ovation. The poor conductor had to scuttle on in front of the closed drapes to take his bow alone.

'That's it,' said Cosima as she flounced from the stage. 'I want a fucking divorce.'

Chapter Two

JULIET Hunter was in the audience at La Scala that same evening. But while Cosima Esposito and Nolan O'Connor's marriage fell apart behind the sumptuous velvet curtains, Juliet's big romance was only just beginning.

Juliet was in Milan on business. She was accompanying Christopher Wilde, her new boss in the private banking division of the Anglo-Italian Bank. The visit to La Scala was business too. Anglo-Italian had a permanent box at the opera where it entertained important clients with the best seats in the house and all the champagne they could drink. A night at the opera had exactly the kind of top-class cachet that impressed the bank's high-net-worth clientele. It suggested a degree of sophistication that would hopefully be attributed to the bank's investment strategies as well.

That evening, Juliet and Christopher were hosting Russian billionaire Evgeny Belanov and his young wife Nadezdha. Nadezdha Belanov was a genuine fan of the opera and was quite delighted to have the chance to see Cosima Esposito sing. She explained to Juliet that she had followed the diva's progress from the very beginning, when New Yorker Cosima made her debut at the Met as Mimi in *La Bohème* and the critics announced that a star had been born. Evgeny Belanov had never been anywhere near an opera house until he met the stunningly attractive Nadezdha, but since then he too had become quite fanatical. Cosima Esposito was one of his favourites as well. Seeing the hard-man Belanov so transported by Esposito's stellar performance as Tosca, Juliet and Christopher were both pleased and relieved. The Belanovs thanked them profusely for the opportunity to see such a wonderful singer in action.

Client entertainment usually made for a long evening, as customers tried to claw back something of the vast fees they paid the bank by eating their body weight in caviar and steak. To that end, Juliet had booked one of the best restaurants in Milan for after the performance, but Nadezdha Belanov begged off. She said she had an early start. She had to fly to Romania to visit an orphanage endowed by her charitable trust. Her husband said he would escort her home. The Belanovs took their entourage of eight assorted cronies and bodyguards with them.

'Well, she is quite a *new* wife,' said Christopher, when Juliet expressed surprise that *everyone* had bailed out of dinner because Nadezdha had made her excuses. In fact Nadezdha was Belanov's fourth wife, coming after his childhood sweetheart (left behind in a Moscow slum the minute the Soviet Union crumbled), the Aeroflot stewardess and the former lap-dancer from Kent, who was now one of the wealthiest women in the world thanks to her record-breaking divorce settlement. Unlike her predecessors,

Nadezdha had money of her own. She was the daughter of one of Russia's richest families, thirty years Belanov's junior and educated in England and the United States. She had model looks and rocket scientist intelligence. Belanov was clearly head over heels. He was proud to tell everyone that his new wife had real class.

Juliet shook her head. 'All those divorces. Expensive business. It's a wonder he's got any money left at all.'

'Ah yes,' said Christopher. 'But Belanov's a true romantic, you see. And who wouldn't render themselves penniless for a shot at real love?'

Juliet was surprised to hear Christopher say that. He had always seemed such a pragmatic sort of man. She was even more surprised later that evening when he told her he thought he might be falling in love with *her*.

When she heard his declaration, Juliet gave an astonished little laugh. Christopher studied her face anxiously as he waited for her more considered response.

He need not have worried. Christopher Wilde had enchanted Juliet on her very first day at Anglo-Italian.

Juliet had been head-hunted to join Anglo-Italian from another private bank, where it was widely thought that she had the potential to reach the top. Though she shared her former colleagues' belief in her abilities, Juliet couldn't help but be nervous as she joined the Anglo-Italian team. She knew there would be those among her new co-workers who wondered whether she merited her big 'transfer fee'. After all, she was still in her twenties and looked younger still with her boyishly short blond hair and perfect peachy skin. She was used to having to show ID when she tried to buy a bottle of wine. She knew that it would take a while to convince her new workmates that there was steel behind her soft exterior, so she had gone the power suit route for her first morning at Anglo-Italian. She'd followed all the usual advice about firm handshakes, looking people straight in the eye, projecting ultimate confidence and then ...

Christopher strolled in. Christopher Wilde. The mysterious 'CW' who had been copied in on all the correspondence regarding Juliet's appointment but who had been too busy to attend any of her interviews. She had envisaged him as yet another middle-aged man of distinctly middling appeal, but he looked like a model in his charcoal Zegna suit and Bulgari tie. He was the kind of guy you see in an ad for Patek Philippe watches with his thick hair greying so elegantly at the temples and his broad, perfect smile. He had great teeth of course. He was in his late thirties then. At the top of his game.

But even as she was taking in his indisputable good looks, Juliet had also clocked his wedding ring and determined just as quickly to turn off the tap of attraction. They were to be colleagues. He was married. It could be no more than that. Despite that resolve, she couldn't help blushing whenever he complimented her on anything, even though he was more likely to compliment her on a spreadsheet than her hair or her outfit.

One glass of champagne more and Juliet might have admitted there and then that she had long since fallen in love with Christopher too. Instead she gathered what sense she had left and said, 'Oh, Christopher. Don't be silly.' The worst thing she could do was admit to sharing feelings he would deny when he sobered up.

'I'm not being silly,' he said, reaching across the table and taking her hand between both of his. 'I was attracted to you the moment I saw you. I can still remember what you were wearing on your very first day at Anglo-Italian.'

'Tell me,' she said.

'That red suit. With the sleeves that don't look long enough.'

He was right.

Juliet laughed. 'Bracelet sleeves is what they're called.'

'Quite daring, I thought. The red. Marked you out at the very beginning as someone who would prove to be a force to be reckoned with.'

'Really?'

'Oh yes. And it made your bum look magnificent too.'

Juliet tutted but it was a playful tut, encouraging him to carry on.

She looked at her hand, sandwiched between Christopher's. She found she liked the contrast between them. Her hand small and fine and manicured, with polished nails like the inside of shells from a Caribbean beach. His hands so large and undeniably masculine. A bear's paws by comparison.

'I thought you were going to be a ball-breaker,' Christopher smiled. 'But there's so much more to you than that, right? I quickly came to realise you're not just a talented business-woman, you're a truly kind person as well.'

'Thank you,' said Juliet.

She thought that perhaps she should pull her hand away, but at the same time she wanted him to go on. It had been a long time since anyone had properly flirted with her. Even if he was someone else's husband, she could enjoy the compliments, couldn't she? Things didn't have to go any further.

The restaurant staff was circling the room. They were too professional and polite to interrupt the romantic moment by announcing that they wanted to close, but no matter how quietly they went about their business, Juliet and Christopher couldn't ignore the fact that it was getting late and the waiters just wanted to go home.

'Can I get you anything else?' asked the waiter who had been looking after them that night. Christopher shook his head and the look of relief on the waiter's face was unmistakeable.

'I suppose we should leave,' said Juliet, finally wriggling free of Christopher's grip so that he could put the bill on his company credit card.

They were staying in the same hotel, of course, though their rooms were on different floors and Christopher's was slightly bigger as befitted his higher status in the bank. Still Juliet had been happy enough with hers. Back in London she lived in the tiny flat she'd bought five years earlier. Every thing about her first home was beige. Tentative. Beige carpet, beige walls, beige upholstery. Not tasteless but definitely without taste. It didn't reflect the woman she felt she was becoming. She was secretly fond of the swagged curtains and gilded mirrors that the Italians did so well.

However Christopher was not about to let Juliet retire to her comfortable boudoir. He insisted they had another drink in the hotel bar, stringing the evening out for as long as they could. But soon it was two in the morning and even the barman was yawning.

'Time for bed,' said Juliet.

Christopher grinned at her. Juliet shook her head.

Since leaving the restaurant, they had not continued with the conversation about their attraction for each other. They'd spoken of everything but . . . however the unspoken subject had coloured every sentence, until the atmosphere between them was soft pink with the beginnings of love.

'Just one more drink,' Christopher pleaded. 'And then I promise I will let you go.'

'The barman wants to close his till.'

'The mini-bar in my room is always open.'

Christopher's hand crept along the zinc rail and sought out Juliet's fingers again.

Before she knew it, Juliet had agreed to one more drink, a nightcap, from the mini-bar in Christopher's room. He poured a mini-bottle of brandy into a glass for her. He had a whisky. He turned on the stereo. Low and atmospheric. The hotel made much of the music that was played in its bar. There were frequent guest spots by famous DJs and a compilation CD was found in every bedroom. It was the kind of music that encouraged slow-dancing, long looks, making love . . .

On agreeing to go to Christopher's room, Juliet had told herself that she would leave within half an hour but now she knew that a kiss was inevitable. And she wanted it. She watched Christopher's lips move as he recounted a childhood memory for her. She had never felt so attracted to anyone. She had long since put aside the fact that he was her boss, and a man with a wife and two children. Her body had taken control.

And god, it felt good to surrender. It had been a while since Juliet went to bed with anyone. Ages since she'd even shared a passionate kiss. Concentrating on her career had left her with little time for love. In the past few years she'd had only a couple of short-term flings with fellow bankers who ultimately found her drive intimidating and even unattractive. Christopher wasn't threatened by Juliet's success in the least. His lips were soft and gentle as he pressed his mouth against hers. How could she possibly resist?

Giving in to the moment, Juliet closed her eyes and parted her lips.

The kiss quickly became more passionate. They were hungry for each other – ravenous – and now that their appetite had been unleashed, there was to be no holding back. Christopher's hands roamed the beautiful curves of Juliet's body. She did not protest as his hands soon moved beneath her clothes. Within moments she was helping him to unfasten the zipper on the blue dress she suddenly realised she had picked out with the subconscious hope of impressing him. As she lifted her arms to pull the dress off over her head, Christopher was already kissing her flat, toned stomach. His tongue traced the edge of her white silk knickers. His fingers sought out the clasp of the lace-trimmed bra that showcased her bosom so perfectly and unleashed it to find that Juliet's nipples were already puckering and hardening with undeniable arousal.

While Christopher devoured her neck with kisses, Juliet worked at getting him out of his clothes, desperate to feel his bare skin upon hers. Christopher stripped off his trousers and soon they were both completely naked. Juliet pressed her body against his, luxuriating in the feel of skin on skin.

The new lovers looked deep into each other's eyes, eager to read permission to take this all the way. Juliet gave a tiny nod and a smile that made Christopher break into a grin. He kissed her again, while his fingers tiptoed down to the place where her fine long legs came together. He found her clitoris and stroked it carefully. Juliet moved her pelvis up to meet his hand, willing his fingers to stray inside her. She knew she was already wet. He smiled more broadly when he felt it.

When the teasing of Christopher's fingers became too much to bear, Juliet begged him to enter her. She knew that he was ready. She could already feel his penis pressing hard against her thigh. All she wanted now was to have him inside her. Juliet wriggled her hand down between their hot bodies and sought out her lover's erection.

Juliet guided Christopher towards her pussy. Their eyes remained locked on each other's as he gently pushed into her and began to move. With each thrust she felt herself opening up to him, pulling him deeper. He never took his eyes off hers, so that she felt as though their minds were making love as well as their bodies. Juliet abandoned herself to the sensations he aroused in her, feeling an orgasm build inside her like the unfurling of a long-dormant flower. As Christopher came, he begged her to hold him more tightly and called out her name.

Next morning, waking early next to Christopher, her boss and now her lover, Juliet was too dazed to be regretful. Still she was grateful when he rolled over and gave her a squeeze that reassured her he wasn't horrified to find her in his bed.

'Good morning, beautiful,' he murmured.

And back in London, in the taxi, all the way from Heathrow to the bank's office in the City, Christopher held Juliet's hand. From time to time he cupped her face and kissed her. Juliet felt sure that everyone would know what they had been doing. Christopher's kisses had left her pink. His lips were darker than she had ever seen them, but as they walked into the lobby of the Anglo-Italian building Christopher was cool and unruffled as ever. He nodded at the receptionist and ushered Juliet into the waiting lift.

'One last kiss,' he said, as they were between floors.

Juliet obliged him.

'I have to see you again,' he told her. 'Outside the office. What are you doing tomorrow night?'

'Nothing,' she said. She hardly bothered to make plans with her friends anymore. Her career took up so much of her time.

'Then you're "working late" with me. All right if we go back to your place?'

Juliet hesitated. But before her brain could kick in with all the obvious objections, they had reached their floor – the sixteenth – and Christopher was striding ahead towards his office, tossing greetings and instructions to his underlings as he went.

'You're all red,' said Juliet's PA, Michaela. 'You must have caught the sun in Italy.'

'Yes,' said Juliet, as she watched Christopher pause by the water-cooler. 'Forgot to pack my sunscreen. Silly me.'

It was silly to say the least, getting involved with a married man. Juliet knew that. But she hadn't felt anything so strongly in a long time and that throwaway line as they left the opera house, about people rendering themselves penniless for a shot at real love, had stuck with her. Maybe, she convinced herself, just maybe, Christopher Wilde might turn out to be every bit as foolishly romantic as Evgeny Belanov.

Chapter Three

𝒜 YEAR after Cosima's astounding performance at La Scala, the official recording of the evening was still riding high in the classical music charts. John Heywood, head of music (in fact the only teacher of music) at The Downey Road School in South London, had ordered the CD for the school's paltry music library. And that was where Mercy Campbell found it.

That week's assignment for the GCSE music class was for the pupils to listen to a piece of music they had never heard before and write about how it made them feel. Most of the class cheated, writing five hundred words on the latest single by the kind of rap stars who sang about sex, money and death and left their listeners feeling strangely inadequate and angry. Only Mercy did something genuinely different.

Mercy wasn't exactly what you would call academic. Most of her written work was returned to her covered in pencil scribbles (the school having decided that red ink was too demotivating), but in music Mercy Campbell excelled.

Singing was in her blood. Her mother, aptly named Melody, told Mercy that she had musical talent even in the womb.

'All through my pregnancy, I felt driven to turn the radio on the moment I woke up. And then you would start bouncing around. I thought you were going to be a dancer.' She gave Mercy an affectionate up and down, taking in her daughter's generously rounded figure. 'But I guess your lungs are too big.'

Mercy laughed. It wasn't meant as an insult, she knew. She was the image of her mother at the same age.

And what her mother said was true. Mercy couldn't remember a time when she didn't have music in her head and in her heart. When just a toddler, her mother would dress her up in a white dress and matching crocheted cardigan and carry her proudly into church, where Mercy would be passed like a rugby ball from mother to aunt to grandfather and cousin yet still remain perfectly content so long as she could hear the singing. What the infant Mercy liked best was to lay her baby head against her grandmother's chest and feel the vibrations as Connie hit the high notes. Her grandmother could have been a star, everyone told her. She had been approached by one of Phil Spector's people back in the 1960s. But Connie sensed that the road to stardom would also be the road to ruin and remained instead an anonymous mother of five with a voice that could lift the whole congregation up to heaven.

Mercy soon developed a voice of her own. As soon as she could stand she joined the other children at the front of the church and sang out as hard as she could. By the age of twelve she was a regular soloist.

The school she attended might have been the end of it all. There wasn't much inspiration to be found at the Downey Road comprehensive, though brave and idealistic rookie teachers kept turning up and trying, imagining themselves like Michelle Pfeiffer in *Dangerous Minds* or Hilary Swank in *Freedom Writers*. And one of them got through to Mercy at least.

Mr Heywood recruited Mercy for the school choir as soon as he heard her sing. And he was endlessly encouraging. So when he announced the new music assignment, Mercy headed straight for the music library to find something that was truly new to her.

She had never heard Puccini's *Tosca*. She knew nothing whatsoever about it. If she was honest, what really attracted her to this new recording, made at La Scala, was the photograph on the CD case. Looking every bit the diva, Cosima Esposito gazed into the middle distance. Her beautiful dark eyes and the dignity of her expression intrigued Mercy Campbell, who had no idea that Cosima's expression was actually one of despair as the soprano considered her upcoming divorce proceedings. Mercy signed the CD out.

Mr Heywood nodded approvingly when Mercy told him the name of the piece of music she planned to write about.

'You ever listened to Puccini before?' he asked her.

'I heard that song about football,' she replied.

Mr Heywood smiled. '"Nessun Dorma". Well, I would advise you to listen to this piece a couple of times before you make your judgement. First listen to the music. See if you can guess what's going on. Then read the libretto.'

Mercy raised her eyebrows questioningly.

'The words,' Mr Heywood explained. 'They've got the Italian and the English translation inside.'

'It's in Italian?' Now Mercy was nervous.

'You'll cope,' said Mr Heywood.

Back at home, Mercy slipped the CD into her mother's player and listened. It was hard to find a time to listen to the whole thing at once. Interruptions were frequent. Her mother wanted to do the vacuuming. Her little brother Francis, just ten years old, wanted to watch something on TV. But eventually, Mercy was able to hear the whole thing and found herself transported by the story of the talented but jealous singer Floria Tosca, her lover, the principled artist Mario Cavaradossi and their doom at the hands of the evil Baron Scarpia.

Love, jealousy, intrigue. It wasn't hard at all to write the assignment.

At the end of the year, Mercy won the school music prize. She was given a voucher with which to buy herself a suitable gift to be presented at the annual prize-giving ceremony. Mercy chose a CD of Cosima Esposito's performance of *Tosca*.

The following Christmas, when it was clear that her daughter was developing a passion for opera, Melody presented her with a pair of tickets to see *Tosca* at the Royal Opera House in Covent Garden. They were the best she could afford on her income support but still Melody was horrified to discover that she had inadvertently bought standing places in the amphitheatre. She had to lean against the wall, unable to look down on the stage for fear that vertigo might overcome her. Mercy wasn't all that keen to spend a few hours in such a precipitous position either, but it didn't matter so much to her. She didn't need to look. The music and the singing sounded just as good with her eyes shut. Though when she could bring herself to open her eyes, what she saw was even more magical.

Mercy knew in that moment what she wanted to be. And when it came to her interview with a careers officer four months or so later, just ahead of Mercy's GCSEs, she did not hesitate to name her dream job.

'I want to sing opera. I want to be a soprano.'

A soprano? Mrs Andrews, the careers officer had never heard anything like it. Certainly not at a school like Downey Road. She looked at her file on Mercy Campbell. She looked at the poor marks in English and Maths. The laughable grades in the sciences. The E in history. The school hadn't even bothered to enter Mercy for a GCSE in French or in Spanish – the two languages available to the brightest kids. A large coffee stain obscured the music teacher's glowing report. She closed the file and met Mercy's soft brown eyes in that sweetly pretty face.

'Well, singing is a lovely hobby,' Mrs Andrews said. 'I imagine you get a lot of pleasure out of it. Now I see you've had a Saturday job at McDonalds for the past two years. You know they have a management training scheme ...'

Act One

Chapter Four

ϑ

$\mathcal{F}$IVE years had passed since that night at La Scala when Cosima Esposito finally gave up on her marriage to Nolan O'Connor. The subsequent divorce had been relatively speedy. There were no children involved, thank goodness. Not much property either, since she and Nolan had both been living the peripatetic lives of professional performers when they met and had not had time to put down proper roots since their wedding, so busy were both their careers. It was really just a matter of undoing the ceremony so that Cosima could take back her own name on her bank statements and credit cards. Fortunately, she had not changed her name for stage purposes.

So, Cosima stepped away from her marriage relatively unscathed in material terms, but Nolan's endless infidelities had not done much for her self-esteem.

Why had it gone so wrong? Perhaps they had married too young. Cosima had been just twenty-one; Nolan only two years older. Cosima's mother had warned her that people change a great deal in their twenties. Was that what had happened? Had they simply grown apart?

Nolan is just an idiot, said her friends. Any man should be proud to be with Cosima Esposito. Already in her short career she was one of the world's greatest divas, and destined to go on to greater things.

'But he told me I sing like a crow,' said Cosima whenever Nolan cropped up in conversation. She would never forgive him for that. It wasn't just the throwaway comment her friends imagined. When he made that analogy Nolan knew he was striking right at Cosima's heart. Only a few days earlier, she had shared with him her concern about her ability to hold the top notes in her range. 'I can hear a croak in my voice,' she had told him. 'Like a magpie's call. Or,' she shuddered, 'like a crow's.' After seven years during which they had practised together and in front of one another almost every day, she had trusted Nolan to tell her the truth about her fears absolutely. He had assured her that nothing was wrong with her voice. His careless retraction of that assurance – onstage and using her own frightened analogy – was more significant to Cosima than if a thousand musical directors had told her the opposite was true. That moment saw the death of her trust in him.

Five years on, Cosima still heard that vicious comment in her head at least twice a day. Her friends had come to recognise the look that passed over her face when it happened and stopped trying to convince her to forget it. Maybe, thought some of them, the horror of the 'crow' comment had actually spurred Cosima on to greater things. Her career had certainly gone from strength to strength since Nolan made that stupid jibe.

But Cosima swore she would never forgive him. It hadn't helped that a year ago, four years after the divorce, she discovered that another guy had been cheating her too. This time, however, the material damage was much much worse. It transpired that Cosima's financial manager had been channelling money from her accounts, leaving her almost penniless and with an enormous outstanding tax bill to boot. The accountant had robbed half his clients and gone on the run. He'd been evading the police for months; it was thought that he was probably in Costa Rica. He had met, through Cosima ironically, a beautiful Costa Rican ballerina, who had stolen his heart. It was almost certain he had stolen Cosima's money to impress that very girl. Such were the stupid things that men would do for love.

And thus Cosima was near financial ruin. But if she thought about it properly, she would have to admit that the rest of her life was on the up. At last she stepped out of her self-imposed purdah and had recently become romantically involved – albeit tentatively – with a new man. A good man. Though he was also a very successful tenor, Andrew Fleetwood had none of Nolan O'Connor's notorious 'artistic' tendencies towards drinking and fucking too much. And then there was work. The critics still loved her. The audiences loved her. The world's opera houses were clamouring to have her heading up the bill. All she needed was to get the IRS off her back ...

Cosima was thinking about exactly that when the phone rang.

'Cosima!' It was Duncan Strange, Cosima's exceedingly camp English agent.

'Hello, Duncan,' she said.

Cosima loved her agent. He had recently managed to

secure a very nice little deal for Cosima to promote a top French jewellery line – Martin et Fils, part of the Domaine Randon group of luxury goods companies. Though the fee itself wasn't incredible, Cosima had been delighted with the job, which involved a day-long photo shoot and the promise of the most fabulous jewels in the world on loan to wear whenever she made a public appearance.

'Mr Randon is very pleased with the way the photo shoot turned out,' Duncan reassured her now. 'I have to say, Miss Esposito, you do look especially beautiful in diamonds.'

'Thank you.'

'And emeralds and pearls,' Duncan continued. 'And the shots of you in those ruby chandelier earrings!' He gasped. 'With your ebony hair. Sweetheart, you look like a goddess! Simply ravishing. I don't know how they'll chose which shot to use in the ad campaign when every one is just so wonderful.'

By the time Duncan had finished singing Cosima's praises, she was practically purring, which, of course, had been Duncan's intention. Because what he had to say to her next might not go down so well. Not at all.

'Sooooo,' he drawled.

Cosima knew from that one, drawn-out word, that he was about to ask her something that might be considered a favour and that it was probably the kind of favour that costs the giver dear.

'What is it, Duncan?' Cosima's tone of voice was intended to let him know that while she was open-minded and would do whatever she could to accommodate him, she was not to be taken advantage of. 'Are you going to ask me to do a charity gig for that cats' home you've been getting involved with?'

'Gosh, no,' said Duncan. 'It's a paying job.'

'OK. Let me have it.'

Cosima sat down and made herself comfortable. She had high hopes for what would come next. She knew of several opera stars who had been asked to do private performances in the Middle East for eye-bleeding sums of money. Millions for just an hour or so's work. Was she about to be offered a gig like that? She would do it in a heartbeat, even if it meant a week in the desert, risking her voice with the heat and the dust.

'The good news is, I've had a call asking you to do a six-week tour of the opera houses of Europe, reprising your fabulous Tosca. I know there's no role you like better. And the money is sensational,' he assured her. 'As befits a sensational singer like you.'

'So what's the downside?' Cosima cut to the chase.

Duncan took a deep breath. He knew of no two words that could make Cosima Esposito lose her poise more quickly and he was about to utter both of them. He muttered them at high speed. 'The downside is they've already signed Nolan O'Connor ...'

'What?'

Duncan was right. The mere mention of the Irish tenor was enough to send Cosima ballistic. She unleashed a string of four-letter words that made her agent hold the phone away from his ear. Cosima railed on O'Connor for what seemed like an hour. Then she railed on the concert promoters for signing him. She was particularly upset that they had approached her ex-husband before they approached her. She then railed on Duncan. She was mortally offended that Duncan had not told them where to stick their offer to her from the start. For heaven's sake! They had asked Nolan first? Didn't Duncan agree that Cosima was by far the bigger star?

'Of course I do. Darling, darling...' he tried to break into her rant. He didn't dare tell her that her arch-rival, another soprano, Judith 'Judy' Shephard, had originally been cast in the role she'd just been offered. Especially since Judy had coined Cosima's nickname: 'Miss Piggy', while they were appearing opposite each other as Mimi and Musetta in a particularly fraught production of *La Bohème*. 'These people...' Duncan sighed. 'What can I say? They don't know how opera works. They went to O'Connor ahead of you because he's the man, I suppose. They thought it was important to cast the male lead first. It's straightforward sexism.'

That sent Cosima into another rant. 'The opera is called *Tosca*, Duncan. *Tosca!* Floria Tosca is the leading role.'

Half an hour later, she was still shouting and Duncan was no nearer to knowing whether he could go back to the tour organisers and tell them Cosima was on-board or not. Eventually, when she had settled into quiet sobbing, he tried once more.

'The money is really very good.'

He finally named the figure. And while it wasn't quite as much as Cosima might have anticipated for a sheikh's birthday party, it was enough to make her pause and ask, 'Say that again?'

'For six weeks,' Duncan reminded her. 'Just six weeks when you've got absolutely nothing else in the diary.'

'Those six weeks are my vacation time,' she pouted into the phone. 'I thought we agreed I deserve a good rest. I've had a busy year.'

'You'll be doing a maximum of two performances a week. If you take this job,' said Duncan, 'it will be like a six-week holiday in Europe, with the added advantage that at the end of it, you'll be able to pay off the IRS and rent yourself a lovely little place in the South of France next time you have some time off.'

'Hmmm,' said Cosima.

Duncan could tell she was thinking about the whole thing more seriously.

'Tell me who else is on-board.'

Duncan ran through the provisional cast list the touring company had given him. Cosima murmured approvingly at most of the names. The respected baritone Donald Law would be singing Baron Scarpia. And Karl Strindberg, the musical director, was someone for whom Cosima had a great deal of time. If Nolan hadn't been involved, she would have given her consent in a heartbeat. But Cosima hadn't seen Nolan in the flesh since the day their divorce came through, six months after the night she told him she wanted out of their marriage. The thought of seeing his smug, fat face again was not a pleasant one. It was so unpleasant that she wasn't even sure several hundred thousand pounds could sweeten the pain.

'Meet me for lunch at Da Silvano,' Duncan suggested, naming Cosima's favourite Italian restaurant. 'We can talk about it properly there.'

Over lunch he played up the positives. Wouldn't Cosima love to spend some time in London and Paris? A night at La Fenice in Venice had been planned. Hadn't she always wanted to sing at La Fenice? Wasn't Venice Cosima's favourite city?

'In the summer?' She wrinkled her nose as though she could already smell the dirty brown water.

'I will get you a suite at the Cipriani. With air-conditioning.'

Duncan continued. He talked rhapsodically about summer nights in Verona, where Romeo and Juliet played out their tragic love. Cosima had never sung in the amphitheatre there.

'It's really something,' Duncan told her.

Cosima had to agree. She had visited Verona several times. But still she wasn't persuaded that the tour was worth her while.

'I promise you five-star luxury all the way. Hell, I promise you six-star!' he laughed.

Cosima pushed a last mouthful of panna cotta around her dish.

'I want to be in a different hotel from Nolan in every single town,' she said. 'I don't want to have to see his face unless we're onstage together.'

'Your wish is my command. Does this mean you're saying yes?'

'Duncan,' said Cosima. 'I have no choice. You know I need the money.'

She knew that Duncan needed his twenty per cent too. The vet's bills for his three rescue cats were ridiculous. It would have been cheaper to send three children to private school.

'You won't regret it, I promise,' Duncan told her. 'You are going to have the summer of a lifetime.'

'You can stop the BS,' Cosima told him. 'I'm just doing it for the money. Full stop.'

That evening, Cosima had a date with Andrew Fleetwood, who had an evening off from his critically acclaimed run in *La Bohème* at the Met. She told him about her summer plans. If he was jealous at the thought that she was going to spend most of July and August with her ex-husband, he didn't show it. Instead, just as Duncan had done, he played up the positives. All the best theatres in Europe. The best hotels. The best people turning out to watch. It would be wonderful.

'And I can come with you for most of it,' he said. 'I'm free from the fifteenth of July. Won't that be great?'

Cosima nodded. Andrew's presence had certainly made New York more fun of late. But that night, as she tried and failed to go to sleep, Cosima wondered whether she had made a big mistake. She needed the money, no question. But was she ready to take the stage with Nolan again? After all the heartache he had caused her, she so wanted to believe that she was over him and yet, five years after the end of their brief but tempestuous marriage, she still thought about him every day. At some point every twenty-four hours she would find herself having an imaginary conversation with him, berating him, screaming at him, or, more often lately, simply quietly begging to know what had gone wrong. It didn't matter how many times she tied to convince herself that theirs had been a 'starter marriage' and would certainly not be her last chance to get love right.

In the bed beside her, Andrew stirred. Cosima propped herself up on one elbow and looked down into his sleeping face. Andrew Fleetwood was a good man. She knew that he loved her and she cared for him deeply in return. He was handsome, funny and kind. He had already told her that he would never be unfaithful, having divorced his wife after she had had an affair. Cosima could trust Andrew Fleetwood implicitly. She should have been glad that he would be able to accompany her to Europe and yet . . .

'Stupid girl,' Cosima berated herself under her breath. Of course she should be happy that she had this tour to take care of her money worries and that Andrew was planning to go to Europe with her. She knew she would appreciate his support. Nolan would inevitably have a woman in tow after all, if not a different girl in every town. Andrew's presence wouldn't be a problem. Why should it be? It wasn't as though she and Nolan ever had a snowflake's chance in hell of getting back together again. Five years should have been enough to put him behind her. Cosima just had to approach the tour as a job. That's what it was. Just a singing job. With her ex-husband.

The man she was absolutely *not* still in love with.

Chapter Five

*F*IVE years at the Anglo-Italian Bank passed by in a flash. Juliet had risen effortlessly through the ranks by working hard and giving her job one hundred and fifty per cent. She was satisfied that her success had nothing to do with her continuing extra-curricular relationship with Christopher Wilde. Though they had been together for five years, their affair was still as secret as it had been the day they consummated their feelings for each other in Milan. However Juliet was confident now that it wouldn't always be that way.

Juliet was often able to spend a couple of nights a week with her lover. Conveniently, the fact that the bank's headquarters were in Milan meant that she and Christopher were often expected to be in Italy on a Wednesday morning to brief their Italian counterparts on business in the London office. That meant flying out to Milan on a Tuesday evening, where they would book into the hotel (separate rooms of course, though only one bed was ever slept in), then go for dinner and chat like any couple who had been together for five long years before going back to the hotel to make wild passionate love like a couple who had known each other for less than a month.

If Christopher's wife Caroline had guessed that her husband was having an affair, she gave no hint of it to him. Perhaps she knew but didn't care. From time to time Christopher even joked that his wife might be having a Tuesday night affair of her own. He wouldn't know. They led increasingly separate lives, he told Juliet. He claimed that Caroline only bothered to speak to him when she wanted money for gym membership, or new shoes or the endless lunches she took with her hideous Botox-fiend friends. Their fifteen-year marriage, which had started in haste when Caroline became accidentally pregnant, was over in all but name. Christopher was just waiting until the children were a little older. As soon as the youngest was in secondary school, he would tell Caroline he was leaving. The youngest was in his final year at prep school now. Juliet looked forward to the very near future with excitement and some trepidation when she considered the inevitable fall-out of Christopher's divorce.

It would be tough but Juliet was sure they would make it. She had helped Christopher through one catastrophe already, when his older brother Nat, an auctioneer, was jailed for manslaughter. What a horrible affair that was. Nat had been fighting with a business associate on Hammersmith Bridge and, after throwing a few well-aimed punches, he had tossed the hapless bloke over the barrier and into the drink. Problem was the poor bloke couldn't swim. And even if he had been able to swim, his busted ribcage would have made it difficult to beat the Thames at high tide.

Temptation

Christopher was devastated when Nat was sent to prison. He worshipped his charismatic big brother who stood up for him during his horrible early years at Eton. They had drawn closer still after the death of their father. When Christopher left Oxford with a first class degree in PPE, he moved to London and into Nat's flat.

'I got lucky far more often than I should have done, thanks to Nat,' Christopher confided to his mistress. 'The flat was always full of girls mooning over my bro. Some of them had to console themselves with me.'

Nat Wilde's natural charm had helped him to stratospheric success in the auction houses, where he regularly persuaded people to part with the equivalent of a small country's GNP for exquisite old masters or potato prints by the darlings of contemporary art. But his personal life had not gone so well. His wife Miranda stripped him to the bone in their divorce, leaving Nat pining for the lifestyle he had once enjoyed and willing to do anything to raise his living standards again. It was that which had led him to indulge in a spot of fraud with the chap he eventually tipped off Hammersmith Bridge.

After the court case and Nat's subsequent imprisonment, the rest of the family had cut off the former golden boy. Christopher, however, visited his beloved brother in jail every week. Religiously. He told Juliet that the only appointments he would never break were his nights with Juliet and his visits to Nat in Wandsworth. Juliet was intrigued by the thought of Christopher's brother. Apparently, he was doing very well behind bars.

'It can't be any worse than school,' Christopher assured her.

*   *   *

That weekend saw Juliet turn thirty-three. Since her birthday was on a Saturday, and Saturdays were when Christopher had to take his sons to their various sporting practices, she was unable to see him. But he had sent roses from Moyses Stevens, the smart London florist. Five dozen of them. Juliet didn't have enough vases in her house for all the blooms. And he had promised her that when they went to Milan for the next board meeting, he had a very special surprise in store.

He certainly pulled out all the stops. He booked the restaurant where he first declared his love for her. He'd ordered champagne. Vintage Clos Des Larmes by Champagne Arsenault. 1996. The very best of recent years. And then he had pulled out her real birthday gift. Juliet's heart leaped as she recognised the thick white cartridge paper and blood red wax seal that whispered 'Cartier'. She unwrapped the gift carefully, not wanting to ruin the paper. She would keep it all; she kept everything Christopher gave her. She still had a daisy he'd plucked from the grass of Ludgate Circus, during an impromptu picnic shortly after they confessed their love. She'd pressed it between the pages of her diary. But this was more significant than a daisy. Inside the paper was the red box trimmed with gold. And inside the box . . .

Juliet gasped when she saw the bracelet inside. It was from Cartier's Trinity collection. Three interlocking bangles in three colours of gold with the centre bangle glittering with pavé set diamonds. Christopher lifted it out of the box and told her the significance of each differently coloured circle.

'White for friendship. Yellow for faithfulness,' he gave a rueful smile. 'Well, you know that you are the only one in my heart . . . And finally, pink for love.'

Juliet held out her hand so that he could slip the bracelet onto her wrist.

'I wish that this could be a ring,' he said. 'But I promise it won't be long now. Jamie will be moving schools in September. I'll make sure he's settled in and ... well, I'll have to wait until after Christmas of course but ...'

Juliet put her finger to Christopher's lips.

'Let's not talk about this now,' she said. 'We're celebrating my birthday. I just want to be happy tonight. And I am happy, here, right now, with you.'

Christopher looked relieved to change the subject.

'Do you like your present?' he asked her.

'I love it,' she assured him. 'I will wear it every day.'

All through the rest of dinner, they had held hands across the table. They walked back to the hotel with their arms around each other and stopped to kiss a dozen times, like a pair of teenagers unable to do anything more. Inside the hotel room, Christopher took Juliet by the hands again and led her to the bed. They lay down upon it together, still kissing as they started to undress. Juliet ran her hands appreciatively over Christopher's chest. She caressed the smooth skin of his shoulders and his back as they pressed their bodies together and kissed some more. He tasted so good to her and she had the sensation that she grew more beautiful with every kiss.

Juliet was naked except for the bracelet. The secret lovers paused to admire the glitter of the diamonds against her peach-white skin.

'I can't believe someone as beautiful as you could love me,' said Christopher.

'Believe it,' said Juliet.

That night, they made love with such passion that Juliet

couldn't possibly have believed anything other than that they would spend the rest of their lives as one. Their bodies fitted together so perfectly. Never had Juliet felt so fulfilled by making love. They had shared so much pleasure and so many secrets over the past five years. Theirs was more than just a run-of-the-mill affair.

'You're my soulmate,' Christopher told her, as they lay curled around one another in the darkness. 'I promise we'll be together one day.'

Chapter Six

𝒜 COUPLE of days later, back in London, Christopher went to visit his brother in prison. Christopher was surprised to see that Nat looked somewhat better than he, Christopher, was feeling. Nat was even sporting a light tan.

'Exercise yard is a sun trap,' Nat explained.

'You look like you've been to bloody St Tropez,' said Christopher.

'And you look like you've been to hell and back,' Nat observed. 'What's the matter with you? Why the long face? Wife making demands? Mistress been giving you hell?'

Christopher sighed. Nat was the only person he had told about his clandestine relationship with Juliet. It seemed safe enough. Nat was tucked away inside one of Britain's most high-security prisons. He wasn't going to get drunk at a family barbecue and spill his little brother's secrets for a long while yet. And Christopher desperately wanted someone to confide in. There were times when he felt he was going mad, juggling his family life and this much greater passion.

'The market has been all over the place in the past three days,' was Christopher's answer to Nat's latest question, however.

'I thought your investment method was foolproof?' said Nat.

Christopher frowned. He knew that while he had always worshipped Nat, Nat was also a little jealous of him. Before Nat went to prison, even when times were good, Christopher had netted at least five times as much a year.

'It's serious,' said Christopher. 'My bonus is going to be half what I expected. I'm having a difficult year.'

'You mean you're down to your last Jag?'

'It's not quite so serious that I would ever swap the Aston for a Jag,' Christopher managed a smile. 'But I need to pull some money from somewhere and quickly.'

'Before the mistress moves on to a bigger fish.'

'It's not like that. Juliet ... she ... she's not in it for the money. That much I do know.'

Christopher's mind drifted to a picture of Juliet on the bed in the hotel in Milan, with that bracelet around her wrist. That bracelet had cost him more than twenty grand. It hadn't seemed like too great an extravagance at the time, but when he got back to London the following day, his wife had greeted him with some very unwelcome news. News that could cost him a fortune.

'Look,' said Nat. 'There's someone I think you should meet. He was here with me last week. He was on a murder charge but managed to get out thanks to some police cock-up over the evidence. I only wish the plod had been as sloppy when they were investigating me. Anyway, I helped him get through his time here and he said that I should look him up if I ever needed a favour. Or if there was a favour I could do for him. He's a businessman. Got all sorts of investments. I think you might be able to help one another.'

'Who is he?'

Checking that the screws were occupied elsewhere, Nat leaned forward and whispered a name to his brother.

'James Dean.'

'Like the actor? That's a made-up name, right?'

'I didn't ask. He seemed a little tetchy on the subject. Anyway, give him a call and tell him that I sent you. His company is called Foxtrot Oscar.'

'You mean FO, for fuck off? Sounds like he was pulling your leg, Nat.'

'No. He's the real deal, all right. Look, give him a call. I said I would make sure you did.'

'Thanks.' But Christopher had no intention of following up Nat's hot tip. In the recent past, Nat hadn't exactly shown himself to be a good judge of character when it came to choosing business associates. It was a supposedly foolproof scam that had led to the fight that landed him in jail. But Christopher could see that Nat was enjoying the feeling that he might be able to help his little brother out and there were few pleasures to be had within the walls of HMP Wandsworth.

Visiting time was almost over. Christopher handed over the cigarettes that he brought along every week. Nat didn't smoke but the cigarettes helped him keep on the right side of the hardest men on his block. Nat took them gratefully.

'Next time I want to hear more about that mistress of yours.'

'Sure,' said Christopher. Though he didn't know how much longer she would be on the scene. And that made him sad.

Christopher was still preoccupied when he got back to the family home in Wimbledon that evening. As he pulled into the drive of the six-bedroomed, common-side mansion, he sighed to see that a light was burning in every window. Naturally, every window was clad with curtains costing thousands of pounds. And of course Caroline had gone ahead and bought herself that new Porsche Cayenne. It was sitting on the drive, next to the Mercedes estate she had yet to get rid of, meaning that Christopher had to park his Aston Martin on the street. He was not best pleased. He didn't see why his wife needed the Porsche. Not yet. But Caroline Wilde did not know the meaning of economy. And when she was in the mood to shop ... Jesus. That woman got personally signed birthday cards from a grateful Al Fayed.

'Oh. You're back,' she said when Christopher walked into the kitchen. It wasn't much of a greeting. Not even a 'hello'. 'I suppose you've been to see that ridiculous brother of yours again. While I have been trying to cook supper for the boys without retching into the pan.'

'I'm sorry,' said Christopher reflexively.

'But that's you all over, isn't it, Christopher? Thoughtless.'

'I didn't know you weren't feeling well,' said Christopher.

'Jesus, Christopher. Don't you remember how bad it was the last time?'

Christopher hadn't thought about it.

'Well, you'll just have to cook for yourself because I need to lie down before I fall down.'

'Is there anything I can do?' Christopher asked. 'For you? Massage your shoulders?' he suggested.

Caroline snorted.

'Empty the dishwasher,' she said.

Chapter Seven

𝒯ʜᴇ best laid plans ... Having found her inspiration in Cosima Esposito, Mercy Campbell had believed that everything was possible, especially as she learned more about the soprano's life. Contrary to what Mercy expected, Cosima had not grown up in a world of privilege where visits to the opera were as common as a visit to the flicks. According to her website, Cosima had hardly known her father and she hadn't had a formal music lesson until she hit fifteen. Everything Mercy read about Cosima made her dream seem a little easier to achieve, but now she decided that Cosima must have had something extra. A better support network. More luck.

After the careers interview in which the careers officer pooh-poohed her ambition and instead flagged up the management opportunities in the fast-food sector, Mercy felt her bubble begin to deflate. And unfortunately, pretty much everyone she encountered from that moment on was similarly sceptical about her chances of achieving her ambition. Everyone except Mr Heywood, that is. But alas, when Mr Heywood told Mercy about the colleges that could help her to hone her talent for music it didn't take much research to reveal that the cost would be beyond her family's means. Even staying on at school to take a music A Level was out of the question. Mercy's father had left home before she was born, coming back into her life only for the three weeks it took for him to father Francis and clear out Melody's savings. Mercy's mother had raised her children on benefits and the proceeds from the occasional badly paid cleaning position. Mercy knew she had to shoulder her family responsibilities and get a full-time job.

And so, four years on, Mercy was no nearer to being an opera diva than she had been when she accepted the school music prize. Instead she had followed the careers officer's advice and parlayed her Saturday job experience at McDonald's into a place on their management-training scheme. She gave up on that scheme after a row with her supervisor and since then she had drifted from job to job, taking whatever work she could get. She had stacked shelves in all the local supermarkets. She had collected money in a multi-storey car park until she was held up at knifepoint and quit. She had handed out newspapers outside tube stations, a particularly terrible job. The people she tried to hand the papers to were rarely grateful. Sometimes they were downright rude, shoving the paper back at her so hard, you might have thought she had tried to hand them a turd. When a particularly charming member of the public, pressed his chewing gum into her hand, Mercy decided she wanted a job that involved a great deal less contact with the public.

But with just one GCSE, in music, unskilled work was all that was available to her. And that was how she ended up at City Clean Stars.

This must be what it's like to be a ghost, thought Mercy on her first day in her new job. In the pale blue overall with the gold-stitched 'City Clean Stars' logo on the back, Mercy was invisible. She had arrived five minutes early to be signed in and given her instructions by Hazel, who headed up the City Clean Stars team at the Anglo-Italian Bank. Hazel hadn't been what you could call friendly. She had barely looked at the new girl – the fifth new girl in a fortnight, as it happened – just handed her a clipboard and a locker key.

'Your overalls are in there. What's your name again?' she asked.

Mercy was used to repeating her name. 'Mercy. As in kindness and compassion.' She trotted out the line her mother had repeated to her all through school.

'Mercy it is,' said Hazel, with a nod. 'And tonight you're on toilets, level fifteen.'

Toilets. But it wasn't all bad. As the bank worked on Central European time, the offices of the Anglo-Italian bank were mostly empty at seven in the evening, which was when Mercy's working day began. It was so quiet you could hear the hum of the strip lighting overhead. There was no one around to care if Mercy listened to her iPod.

Mercy still had the opera. Though her dream of taking to the stage seemed further away than ever, she could still listen to her heroes and heroines sing. Who would have guessed that while she was mopping the floor of the Gents, her melancholy expression was not due to the thankless and grinding nature of her task but to African-American diva Jessye Norman's heartbreaking rendition of 'Dido's Lament' from Purcell's *Dido and Aeneas*?

Mercy could still sing too. She was still the star of the church choir and now her voice rang out loud and clear in the perfect acoustics of the tiled executive bathroom. As she vacuumed and dusted, she would sing along to Maria Callas and Cosima Esposito. In reality she was in a toilet stall but in her dreams she was on the stage at La Scala. No one could ever take that away from her. Her dreams.

Chapter Eight

Tʜᴇ corporate department at the Royal Opera House in London was on a fund-raising blitz. Though the recession had hit charitable giving badly, at last green shoots really were starting to appear and several corporations had recently made very good donations. In return, the most generous companies were assured that a good box in the grand tier would always be available for their directors and clients and several times a year, when a particularly special singer was in town, the Royal Opera would hold a dinner, where important donors and their clients could meet their opera heroes face to face.

That evening, the opera house was holding a special donors' dinner in honour of Nolan O'Connor, the world-renowned Irish tenor many believed would eventually eclipse his own hero Placido Domingo. He had flown in to London from his recently acquired bachelor apartment in Milan to begin rehearsals for a new touring production of *Tosca*.

Nolan O'Connor loved his job. Onstage and off, he

played the part of the romantic hero to the full, as many an aspiring soprano could attest.

'I need to get up,' he said, gently lifting the petite blond girl off his chest.

'Will I see you later?' she asked, hoping that he would invite her to stay and relax in his sumptuous hotel room until he returned from the corporate dinner he had been complaining about all afternoon.

'I don't think so,' he said. 'These things always go on for half the night and tomorrow morning I've got a whole round of radio interviews.'

'How about Tuesday?' asked the blonde.

'Let me call you,' he said, with a gentle smile. 'Write your number on that pad by the telephone. Now you must go so I can get ready.'

The young blonde scribbled her number on the pad and dutifully retrieved her clothes from where Nolan had thrown them. As Nolan had hoped she would, she seemed comforted by his asking her to leave her number and didn't push for a firm date. As she left, a chambermaid was hovering just outside the door, blushing furiously at the thought of having interrupted a tryst.

'Is it OK for me to make up the room?' she asked.

Nolan, who was wearing a dressing gown and knew he looked as though he had been making love all day, waved her on in. 'Why not? You can make a start in here while I have a shower.'

Of course, he sang in the shower. As he did so, he liked to imagine the effect it was having on the young woman now tidying his bedroom. Assuming that she, like most people her age, didn't know her *Aida* from her elbow, he treated her to a blast from *Porgy and Bess*.

When Nolan emerged from the shower, the chamber-maid was still in the room, emptying the waste-paper basket into the grey binbag that hung from the back of her trolley.

'I'll er . . . I'll come back,' the girl muttered as Nolan paced the room in nothing but a towel.

'No need,' he grinned. 'I don't mind if you don't.'

He used a smaller towel to dry off his dirty blond hair. He knew that he looked good. He'd been working out with a personal trainer for the past five months. 'You don't mind if I start my scales?' he asked. 'I need to warm up.'

'Of course,' the girl stuttered. She was wiping a duster across the dressing table now, her back towards him. That had probably seemed the safest way. But when she glanced into the mirror on the dressing table, Nolan was looking straight at her reflection. Their eyes met.

'You're that famous opera singer, aren't you?' the girl ventured.

Bingo, thought Nolan.

'It's Nolan O'Connor, isn't it?'

'That's right.'

'My grandmother is a big fan of the opera.'

That wasn't quite so good, but still . . .

'Really?' said Nolan.

'Yes. She listens to opera all the time. Used to drive my grandfather crazy. He preferred jazz. Gosh,' she put her hand to her mouth. 'I hope you don't mind me saying that.'

'Not at all. Different music for different emotions,' Nolan said graciously. 'I like a spot of jazz myself. But what do you like? What's your name?'

The girl blushed again. 'Irina.'

'What do you like, Irina?'

'Well, I like to listen to opera sometimes. But it's so expensive to see it live here in England.'

Nolan nodded understandingly. He sat down on the edge of the bed, with his legs open so that the white towel just about covered his modesty. He knew that his pose was provocative. Irina glanced involuntarily towards his knees then averted her gaze again.

'Perhaps I should give you a private concert,' he said. 'Why don't you sit down here,' he patted the mattress beside him. 'And I'll sing to you.'

'Oh, I couldn't,' said Irina.

'Of course you can.'

'I've got work to do.'

'You'll be making this VIP hotel guest very happy.'

Irina did as he asked.

'What shall it be?' asked Nolan, looking deep into her eyes. 'I know. Let's have a love song. How about this one . . .'

Nolan chose 'Nessun Dorma' from *Turandot*. It wasn't a particular favourite of his but, thanks to the World Cup campaign of 1990, it was well known and he hoped that would help his cause. And indeed, though she had been but a twinkle in her father's eye in 1990, sweet Irina quivered like a wine glass about to shatter as Nolan hit his big notes.

Nolan stopped singing and looked at his little audience of one. So transported had Irina been by his performance that she had closed her eyes in order to be able to savour the sound more completely. Her eyes were still shut. Nolan decided it was time to take advantage. He was ninety-nine per cent certain now that he wouldn't be rebuffed. While the last note of his song to her was still reverberating inside Irina's angelic head, Nolan silently leaned forward and placed a kiss on her soft rose petal lips.

'Oh!' Irina opened her eyes at once. Before she could complain, Nolan took her head in both her hands and continued to kiss her hungrily and passionately, until she wrapped her thin arms around his neck and he was sure that she wouldn't protest if he went further.

Soon she was on her back on the freshly made bed. Nolan loosened her chocolate-coloured hair from its tidy little ponytail and set to work getting her out of her overalls. His bath-towel quickly found itself on the floor, releasing the manhood that was as impressive as his voice. Actually, perhaps even more remarkable than his voice.

'Wow!' Irina was suitably awed as Nolan guided her hand to his prick. Five minutes later, she had altogether forgotten to be shy and retiring. She had her legs wrapped around his waist and the headboard was banging against the wall so loudly and violently (for the third time in two hours) that the people in the room next door called reception and asked to be moved.

'Nnnnnnngggghh,' the noise that Nolan made as he came was far from musical.

Irina looked a little shocked. She struggled to sit up against the cushions. Her skin was flushed a very pretty pink.

'I . . . I . . .' she stuttered. 'I didn't mean for that to happen. I'm not usually . . . I don't know what you must think of me.' She began to justify her behaviour. Nolan, feeling both relieved that she had taken the blame upon herself and magnanimous, stroked her hair.

'I would never judge you for following your passion,' he said. 'Sometimes in life you have to go after what you want. You have to push aside convention and go for what will make you happy. Never let that little voice in your head object when you find something that gives you pleasure. We made love, my little Irina. There's nothing wrong. That's life-affirming and wonderful. It is nothing to be ashamed of.'

Snuggling close into his side, Irina looked up at him. Her expression was rapt and grateful as Nolan pressed a tender kiss on her mouth. After a moment in which he looked into her eyes as though there were no other girl in the world. Nolan turned his attention to the clock. Half an hour had passed since he came out of the shower. If he did not pull himself together pretty sharpish, he would be late for that dinner at the opera house.

'I have to get ready to go out,' he said. 'When you arrived to clean the room, I had just sent my *secretary* away, thinking that it was getting late. Now it *is* late. I have to attend a fund-raising dinner in my honour. I'm sure you understand.'

Irina nodded at him. He stood up and looked about for his towel.

'I can get you a fresh one,' Irina suggested. 'From my trolley.'

She jumped up, eager to please. She handed him two fluffy white bath sheets. Nolan couldn't help but wish he didn't have to leave when he looked at her standing there. Naked but for her white ankle socks, her dark hair messy around her shoulders. Apart from anything else, he would have enjoyed a little snooze in her arms. But he'd already wasted enough time and he couldn't waste a moment longer. The charity reception beckoned. He knew how important it was for him to be there, encouraging the punters to donate generously so that younger, less fortunate singers might have a chance to make it to the top.

'Thank you.' He kissed Irina on top of her head.

'I suppose I should get dressed too,' she said. 'I've got the rest of this floor to do.'

'OK. Just one more thing,' Nolan said. 'Perhaps you could remake the bed while I'm in the shower.'

As Nolan stepped out of the hotel half an hour later, he knew he should have felt like a million dollars. He was on his way to a reception in his honour, fresh from making love to not one but two beautiful girls. And yet ... He caught a glimpse of himself in a shop window. The face he saw there reflected how he truly felt. The frown that reflection wore didn't belong to Nolan O'Connor the celebrity, but to Nolan O'Connor the human being: the man who worried about his voice letting him down. Who worried that one day all the praise would be turned against him. The man who believed he really wasn't *all that*. The man who woke up in the middle of the night fearing that he might never be loved for the vulnerable, honest, ordinary part of himself again.

'Chin up,' Nolan told his mirror image. 'The show must go on.'

Chapter Nine

𝒮INCE returning from celebrating her birthday in Milan, Juliet had been on Cloud Nine. She wore the bracelet that Christopher had given her every day. When it drew compliments in the office, she said that she had bought it for herself with her bonus. Anneli, who was in charge of the secretarial team but made it her mission to interfere in the private lives of everyone in the department, told Juliet that she was far too young and beautiful to be buying herself diamonds.

'I don't understand why you haven't got a boyfriend,' Anneli lamented. 'A lovely girl like you with a good job and your own home and such a pretty figure.'

'Maybe I'm happy with my life the way it is,' said Juliet.

'Ah, but you're not,' said Anneli. 'I can tell. You want to try Internet dating.'

Christopher, who overheard the conversation on his way to the coffee machine, shared a conspiratorial glance with Juliet over Anneli's head.

Juliet was not about to start trawling for dates on the Internet, but she did admit to Anneli, in the interest of throwing her off the scent and changing the subject, that she had recently signed on to Facebook.

'I always thought it was stupid but I came to realise it's the only way I can keep up with my friends,' she said. 'Nobody actually calls anybody anymore. They just post their news online. I was really missing out. Though I could do without knowing what my old flatmate had for breakfast.'

It was true that Juliet was surprisingly addicted to Facebook. Her job left her very little time to connect with her friends in a real way, but the networking site was a brilliant method for making sure that she didn't forget birthdays, especially important now that she had four godchildren. It meant that she got to see news and photographs from people she would otherwise not have heard a peep out of from one year to the next. And it meant that she got the odd, very pleasant, surprise.

David Stevenson had sent her a 'friend request'.

David Stevenson! A smile spread over Juliet's face at the very thought of him. And it definitely was him, because in the message attached to his request he had written, 'Is that you, Goldilocks?' Goldilocks had been his nickname for her at college.

Juliet responded at once.

'Indeed it is! How the devil are you?'

This was a blast from the past that made her very happy indeed.

'All the better for tracking you down,' David responded.

Juliet often thought of David. It was strange and sad how they'd drifted apart. They'd been tutorial partners at

Oxford, enduring three years of academic hell together. They became very close and Juliet's other friends liked to tease that there must be more to their closeness than a shared interest in very complicated equations. But Juliet could tell her girlfriends quite honestly that she and David had never progressed beyond the odd hug after a particularly gruelling exam. Though she would have to admit that she had often wondered what would have happened if they had gone further. David was good-looking. Athletic. Funny. At least, he had been.

They saw a little of each other when they both moved up to London, but soon both their jobs were taking over their lives. Juliet in banking; David doing something for the civil service. They would make arrangements to see each other but someone always had to drop out at the last moment due to a work-related crisis.

Then David quit his job and went travelling in South America. There were a couple of postcards but then nothing. Juliet wondered if he ever received her note about moving house, sent to a poste restante address in Uruguay. This was before most people carried mobile phones and thus numbers were easily lost. And so was the friendship. But now he was back.

Now that she had access to David's profile, Juliet was disappointed to discover no real gossip. He had used a picture of a dog as his profile picture. He'd always liked dogs. But further investigation revealed nothing more. There was no information about his marital status or his job. No personal email address to give the name of his employer away. No pictures of children. No holiday snaps to reveal how good or otherwise he looked now. Juliet didn't even know if the dog belonged to him.

'Is that it?' Juliet asked in a message. 'Are you not going to tell me what's going on in your life?'

'It's a long story,' he said. 'Let's meet up so I can tell you in person.'

'Can't wait. Isn't technology wonderful,' wrote Juliet.

Yes, the Internet had made it very easy for people to track other people down.

Though Christopher had made an instant and very easy decision not to meet Nat's prison associate, it seemed that wasn't to be the end of the story. Three days after Nat suggested that his friend could solve all Christopher's financial problems, Christopher got a call on his mobile. It was a Sunday afternoon. Christopher and Caroline were sitting on the lawn, reading newspapers and doing their best not to argue (at least, Christopher was doing his best not to provoke one). Caroline rolled her eyes when the phone rang and so Christopher went back into the house to take the call.

'Mr Dean would like to meet you,' said the voice on the other end of the line. It was a voice that suggested a shaven-headed thug, leaning on the bonnet of his top of the range Freelander as he called.

Though Christopher was very senior in his office and often got his personal assistant Lucy to make calls for him so that he didn't have to wait on hold, he was disturbed to be called by Mr Dean's goon. Who was this bloke, so recently out of prison, that he couldn't pick up the phone himself?

'Who is this?' Christopher asked.

The phone was handed over. 'My name is James Dean,' said the guy.

'Your real name?' Christopher snorted.

'It is my real name,' said Mr Dean indignantly. 'My mother was a fan. You got a problem with that, dipshit?'

'Of course not,' said Christopher. But 'dipshit'? How had it happened that this thug had disturbed his Sunday afternoon and the conversation was already going so badly?

'Now, your brother says you're something of a genius when it comes to handling investments,' James Dean got straight to the point.

Christopher mumbled a modest rebuttal.

'I hope you are,' Dean continued. 'Because I'd like to do some business with you.'

Christopher felt the skin on the back of his neck begin to prickle. During his years in banking, he had come to be able to read people remarkably well and just the sound of James Dean's voice told him that this would be a tricky customer.

'It's not quite that simple,' said Christopher.

'What? You're saying you don't want to make some money? Come out and have a drink with me. I'll tell you exactly what I'm thinking.'

'Why don't you call my assistant on Monday,' said Christopher. 'And we'll arrange a time to meet in my office.' Christopher had no intention of meeting Dean at all but he would let Lucy handle the fallout. She was a tough cookie. She even scared Christopher from time to time.

'Can't wait till Monday. How about now?' asked Dean.

'I'm with my family,' Christopher explained.

'Your sons are both out,' said Dean. 'Your wife will be grateful for a bit of peace and quiet.'

'What? How do you–'

'Know that? Because I'm right outside your house,' said Dean. 'Now put your jacket on. We're going for a ride.'

*   *   *

All Christopher's instincts about his brother's prison friend were confirmed when he saw the two men waiting in the car outside. They were driving a top of the line Range Rover. It was matt black with blacked-out windows. The sight of the car parked across his driveway in that quiet suburban street sent an injection of adrenalin into Christopher's brain. It was the kind of car that always seemed to be involved in fatal road rage incidents and gangland shootings. The two men were leaning on the bonnet. As Christopher emerged from the house, they straightened up and fixed him with their best smiles. One of the guys had three gold teeth. The other, who was Mr James Dean himself, had his collar turned up to partially obscure a tattoo of barbed wire around his neck.

What the fuck had Nat got him into this time?

'Greetings,' said Dean.

The other guy opened the rear passenger door and motioned Christopher inside.

'Now look,' Christopher said right away. 'I think you're taking a right bloody liberty turning up unannounced like this on a Sunday afternoon. I won't be going anywhere with you. Not today. Not any day.'

James Dean shook his head. 'That's a pity. Because your brother was rather relying on you to help him make amends for some debts he's been racking up on the inside.'

'What are you talking about?'

Of course Nat hadn't told him the whole truth. The bit about Nat helping Dean on the inside was bullshit. They had been gambling buddies and Nat had made and lost some big bets. How was it possible that not even being sent to prison could keep Nat Wilde out of trouble?

* * *

So Christopher found himself spending the rest of the afternoon with James Dean and his associates, listening to them outlining a scheme so outlandish in its scale, Christopher began to wonder whether this was an elaborate set-up. Afterwards Christopher tried patiently to explain to them why their scheme would never work, knowing that his reasoning was falling on deaf ears. The likes of James Dean didn't see rules or regulations as any kind of barrier. That much was quickly evident.

And having let Christopher put forward all the reasons why he couldn't be involved, James Dean finally delivered the single, most compelling reason why he would come on-board whether he wanted to or not. Dean's colleague reached into his laptop case and pulled out a large manila envelope. Christopher knew almost at once what it would contain.

'Your brother really isn't very discreet, is he?' said Dean. 'Still there isn't a lot to talk about in prison so I suppose you can't really blame him. And he was right. She is a hot little piece of skirt, your girlfriend. I wouldn't have said no myself, vows or no vows. And I'm a *very* happily married man . . .'

Christopher opened the envelope and looked at the pictures inside. There he was, standing on the doorstep of Juliet's flat. And there she was, letting him in, dressed in the La Perla nightgown he had bought for her on one of their trips to Milan. How beautiful she looked, with her freshly washed blond hair falling around her shoulders and not a scrap of make-up on her face. Despite the horror of the situation in which he currently found himself, he couldn't help but be uplifted by the sight of the face that he loved. And the body . . .

The next photograph was one of the two of them in bed together. Naked. He was lying on his back, a big Cheshire cat grin on his face, while Juliet straddled him. She was arching backwards, lifting up her hair, perfectly posed, as though she knew that the camera was upon them. There were several more pictures of Juliet naked but alone. Gratuitous pics.

'How the fuck?' said Christopher.

'As you come to know me, little Chrissie, you'll discover that there is very little I can't do,' said Dean. 'As I said, your girlfriend is one hot little piece of tail. And if you don't want to be my friend, then I might have a go at her myself. I know where she lives, after all.'

Christopher felt hot and cold. His vision seemed to blur. The thought of that dickhead's hands on Juliet was far more frightening to him than the thought of Caroline finding out about the affair. And God knows that was bad enough. He knew that Caroline would not hesitate to take him to the cleaners. He remembered how she had left a divorce lawyer's card on the kitchen table one afternoon the previous summer. When he asked her about it, she had claimed the card belonged to one of her girlfriends, who had come over for lunch and *accidentally* left the card behind, but Christopher knew better. He had checked the lawyer out and discovered that she was notorious for eviscerating city boys on behalf of their starter wives.

Christopher was between a rock and a hard place. Though he planned to divorce Caroline at some point, this wasn't the right time to do it. And the thought of Juliet coming to harm . . .

'Don't even think about touching her,' Christopher warned.

'Nobody tells me what not to do,' said Dean. 'I have what I want, when I want it, unless there's a reason not to. For example, if the man in question is a valued colleague.'

What choice did Christopher have? If he refused then three of the most important people in his world would be affected. In all probability, Caroline would get over it. She would get her pound of flesh and move to Sunningdale, which is what she'd always wanted to do. But Juliet . . . And Nat. What would happen to Nat? Though Christopher didn't especially have much love for his brother in that moment, he did not want him to be hurt.

'I need to think about it,' said Christopher. 'I need to work out how it can be done. There's not much point in my saying I'll be on-board if I can't do anything for you, is there?'

James Dean smiled. 'It sounds like you're coming round to my way of thinking. Marks you out as a very intelligent man that does. And, trust me, if you can help me out, you will be very well rewarded. You might even be able to move out of this shitty area to somewhere really nice,' Dean added, waving his arm at the houses on Christopher's street. There wasn't a single home in that postcode worth less than six million.

'That's just great.' Christopher nodded tightly. 'Now if you don't mind, I'd like to go home. My wife will be wondering what has become of me.'

'Where the fuck have you been?' Caroline barked at him.

'I just went for a drink, with an old friend.'

'And you thought it was OK to just fuck off to the pub without telling me? For crying out loud, Christopher. What if I needed you? What if something had gone wrong?'

Christopher didn't have the heart to tell her that in all probability, things were about to go very wrong indeed.

Chapter Ten

'ARE you singing Puccini?'

For a moment, Mercy didn't realise that it was she who was being addressed. She was singing along to *Turandot* again, taking for herself the part of Liu, a devoted slave girl, who gives her life to save her princely master from death at the hands of the cruel Princess Turandot who has vowed to take his life if she can guess his name before dawn. Mercy carried on, hitting Liu's final note. At the moment when Liu kills herself to protect her prince, Mercy slumped against a desk, imagining herself centre stage, the lights on her and her alone as her last breath left her body. The ultimate sacrifice to love.

Edward Taylor, twenty-five year old graduate trainee in the private banking department, rushed to her side, terrified that she was having some kind of fit. Having no proper first aid training, he frantically fanned her face with a document. When Mercy snapped out of her trance and realised that she hadn't been alone after all, she almost passed out for real in embarrassment.

'Oh no.' She sat up, her face burning with shame.

'Are you all right?' Edward asked.

Mercy got to her feet quickly.

'Yes, yes,' she said, desperately trying to stuff pens back into a desk tidy she'd upended in the course of her dramatic death scene. 'I was just . . .'

'Singing. Liu's final aria from *Turandot*, right? I love that opera. And Liu. What a trooper! I don't think the prince deserved her sacrifice at all.'

Mercy was unsure for a moment whether she was hearing things. He knew what she was singing. This sharp-suited guy who crunched numbers for a living knew about opera.

'You knew I was singing from *Turandot*?'

'Of course. I heard you from right down the corridor. Thought someone was playing a CD. A bit loudly.'

Mercy put her hands to her face.

'Did I distract you?' she asked.

A curious soft expression crossed Ed's face as he looked into her eyes and told her, 'You're distracting me now . . . In a good way.'

Mercy wasn't sure what he meant. She looked away from his friendly blue eyes, put the last of the pencils back in the pot and reached for the handle of her trolley.

'I'd better get on with my work,' she said. 'Er, thanks for worrying about me. I'll try not to make any more noise.'

'That would be a pity,' said Edward. 'Your voice is very beautiful, you know.'

Mercy just stared at him, unable to find the words to respond.

'Ed!' came a shout from the corridor. 'Ed? Where the fuck are you? Conference call in two minutes.'

'I'd better go,' he said. 'No peace for the wicked!' He tipped an imaginary hat at her. 'Good night.'

After the young banker had gone, Mercy sat down on the desk she had practically dismantled with her impromptu performance. She put her hands to her face again. Her cheeks were still burning. Having had her earphones on as she sang, she had no idea how loudly she had been singing, but if that guy had heard her then inevitably other people had heard her too. It was all too embarrassing.

She was certain she would get the sack. But then again, that guy hadn't seemed pissed off. He had talked to her in a friendly way. He had known what she was singing.

And she had acted like a dumb fool. She looked down at her blue overalls and for the first time since she had started working as a cleaner, it mattered to her that someone might see her in those overalls and make the wrong assumptions about her. Had she met that guy under any other circumstances, she wouldn't have acted so coy. She would have asked him what he thought of *Turandot*. Maybe he had seen it.

Hazel interrupted her reverie.

'What's the matter with you?' she asked. 'You look like you don't feel well. You're not going to go bloody sick on me, are you?'

Such was the extent of Hazel's concern.

'I'm fine,' said Mercy. 'I was just catching my breath.'

'I see,' said Hazel. '*Just catching your breath*. Not on my watch you don't.'

Mercy felt oddly nervous when she returned to work the following day. Part of her was still mortified about her encounter with the opera-loving banker and wanted to avoid his floor. Another part of her was actually very keen to see him again. She felt a mixture of delight and horror when Hazel told her she would be on floor fifteen as ever. And the theme of half hope, half horror continued as Mercy tidied herself up in the staff restroom. It wasn't going to be easy to look attractive in her overalls but she made a good stab at it, unbuttoning her top two buttons to reveal a hint of her fabulous cleavage. Perhaps just a little flash of bra? She decided against that. The ultimate way to attract attention to herself again would have been to sing, of course, but she didn't want to be so obvious. And what if the banker was only being polite in responding to a woman who appeared to be in some distress and hadn't actually enjoyed her voice at all.

Still she was delighted when he found her again. The wave and smile he gave her when he spotted her in the corridor left her in no doubt that he was pleased to see her too.

'I'm glad I caught up with you,' said Ed. 'My name's Edward Taylor, by the way.' He stuck out his hand. 'Everyone calls me Ed.'

'Mercy Campbell,' said Mercy. 'But everyone calls me Mercy.'

What a stupid thing to say, she thought immediately afterwards.

'As in compassion and kindness?' asked Ed. 'That's pretty. Pretty name. Pretty . . .'

Mercy looked at her shoes.

'I heard you singing again,' he continued. 'That's how I found you. I followed the voice.'

'Was I singing?'

'Of course you were.'

'I tried not to. But I can't help myself,' said Mercy. 'I put my headphones on to get through the work and tell myself that I'm not going to sing along but . . .'

'Don't apologise. You've got a fantastic voice. And your repertoire is right up my street. I'm a big fan of Puccini. Have you heard this? I dug it out for you when I got home last night.'

He handed her a CD of *Turandot*, recorded at the Met in New York.

'I think it's the best version I've ever heard.'

'Is it?' said Mercy.

'You can borrow it, if you like.'

'No. I can't do that.' She tried to hand it back to him but Ed insisted. He pressed it back into her hands.

'It's OK. I've heard it a thousand times. You can bring it back next week,' he said. 'You will be around next week, I hope.'

'Unless I win the lottery,' Mercy laughed.

After that, Ed seemed to find an excuse to see Mercy every evening. In the course of a week, he lent her six CDs. Mercy was embarrassed that she didn't have anything much to offer except her precious Esposito recording of *Tosca*, the school music prize.

'Oh, I've got that one at home,' he said, when she offered him the disc. 'It was one of the first versions of *Tosca* I ever listened to.'

Of course it was, Mercy thought.

'My grandmother was a keen opera buff,' Ed explained. 'She told me that Esposito would turn out to be something special long before she became famous. Granny was right. I saw her singing *Norma* at the Met only last year. Spectacular.'

Norma? Mercy didn't know that opera at all. She hadn't even heard of it. She felt herself shrinking, but Ed didn't seem to mind that their conversation was so unbalanced. In fact, that night he asked if he could buy Mercy a coffee when she finished her shift.

'Don't you need to go home?' Mercy asked him. 'You must have been here since the crack of dawn.'

'Ha. My boss would be quite happy if I slept here,' said Ed. 'Trust me, I'll be skiving off to have a coffee with you.'

So Mercy joined Ed in Caffè Nero at the end of her shift. They continued their conversation about Cosima Esposito. Then Ed told Mercy more about his grandmother.

'Always claimed she could have been a diva herself but her father, who was practically Victorian, simply wouldn't have it. So she poured all her love of music into my mother and her sister. My mother is a very talented pianist and my aunt teaches singing in her spare time. One of my cousins is a pretty good baritone but I can't sing a note. Hopeless. I spent three years at Oxford, trying to get a part in the student operas but I was relegated to doing their accounts. How about you?'

Ed seemed genuinely interest when she told him about Mr Heywood and the music lesson that changed her life.

'He recognised raw talent,' said Ed. 'Tell me. Have you thought about having professional training? Perhaps I could ask my aunt to put you through your paces.'

While Ed talked, Mercy was mesmerised. He knew so much. In the space of half an hour with him, she learned more about opera than she had managed to work out for herself over the space of five years. Not only that, he was so good-looking. God had made no mistakes with him. Blue eyes, straight nose and a mouth that was generous but not too feminine. His face was so kind and open. And he didn't seem to care at all that they were attracting curious looks as they shared their coffee: him in his Saville Row suit and her still in her overalls. Eventually Mercy allowed herself to relax.

Eight days after their first conversation, Ed found Mercy in the corridor and said, 'I've been wondering . . .'

'Yes.'

'It's a bit forward of me . . . I mean, we haven't known each other very long. But . . .'

Mercy gave him a smile that was intended to make him believe that whatever he was about to ask he could trust her not to reject him.

'I've got tickets for a special performance at the Royal Opera House next Thursday. The bank is sponsoring it. Cosima Esposito is singing in it. Should be a good party afterwards. Would you like to come?'

'Would I like to? You know I would *love* to.' Mercy would have given her right arm to see her heroine sing, but she said, 'I'm supposed to be working that night.'

'Take the night off.'

'I might lose my job.'

'I'll make sure you don't,' Ed insisted. 'You have to come. This performance is made for you.'

Mercy laughed.

'It's going to be fantastic,' said Ed. 'And it's pretty clear to me you would enjoy it. And I would very much enjoy taking you.'

It was that last line that meant the most.

Chapter Eleven

𝒯HE following day was the first day of rehearsals for the star-studded European tour of *Tosca*. There was no danger that Cosima would be late. She had lain awake for most of the night, tossing and turning as though sleep were an aerobic exercise. She could hardly believe that the next morning she would see Nolan O'Connor again. She hadn't laid eyes on him since they passed each other on the street outside her lawyer's office on the day their divorce was finally settled. Their last words to each other had been a pair of emphatic '*fuck you*'s. Since then, she had assiduously avoided reading about his career. Her friends had been instructed that unless Cosima initiated the conversation, they must not talk about him at all, unless it was to tell her that he had died. She had no idea whether he had found himself another woman. Actually, she was certain that he had found several.

'This is ridiculous,' Cosima had exclaimed the previous afternoon, when she found herself in Harvey Nichols looking for an outfit to wear for that first rehearsal. A special outfit for a rehearsal! For heaven's sake! Ordinarily, Cosima would turn up in a Juicy Couture tracksuit, practical and comfortable. Why then was she shopping for a summer dress with a small floral print that she could cinch with a big red belt to show off her curves? Why had she bought a pair of Christian Louboutin espadrille wedges to go with it? Why was she going straight from Harvey Nicks to Hari's on the Fulham Road to have her thick dark hair blown into submission and thence to get a manicure and pedicure?

'I'm arming myself,' Cosima thought. She didn't want to give Nolan any ammunition, any reason to be snide.

And so on the day of the rehearsal she rose at seven and dressed with as much care as she had done on the day she married Nolan O'Connor at New York's City Hall. The results were suitably impressive. Almost twelve years may have passed since that fateful day but Cosima was certain she actually looked better with age.

She spent the next two hours doing her vocal exercises. She had no doubt that the musical director would want to lead the whole cast in exercises when they were gathered together for the first time, but she wanted to be warmed up ahead of them. Her physical appearance was taken care of. All that remained was to ensure that Nolan O'Connor had no reason to accuse her of sounding like a crow.

Though Cosima would never have guessed it, Nolan was also nervous about their meeting for the first time in five years. So nervous, in fact, that when the girl he had taken to bed the night before asked him if he was interested in a demonstration her special 'wake-up' methods, he told her that he wasn't.

'First day of any new project,' he explained. 'I get preoccupied. Need to conserve my energy.'

The girl understood. She had once dated a premiership footballer.

Nolan shuffled her out of the room as quickly as he could. He did a few press-ups and gargled some scales in the shower. He got dressed, changing three times before he settled on a pair of black jeans and a billowy white shirt combo that was at once casual and dramatic. But it was still only half seven in the morning. There was an hour and a half to spare. So Nolan logged on and read the emails that had been sent to his website. The previous evening's one-night stand had convinced him of his physical attractiveness. He hoped that the emails to his website would convince him that he was the world's greatest living tenor. They didn't disappoint. There were five new fan mails to read that morning. All on the theme of Nolan's magnificence as a singer. Except for the last one, which also rhapsodised about his good looks and sparkling personality.

'Dear old Florence,' said Nolan as he clicked on an email from his most devoted fan. Florence Carter wrote to Nolan via his website at least four times a week. She also sent occasional handwritten letters via his manager's office and never failed to send a card and gift for Nolan's birthday and Christmas. The gifts had started out quite modestly. One year she sent a cake she had baked herself. Nolan didn't eat the cake, of course. It would be madness to eat food sent by a stranger. But for that year's birthday, Florence had sent him a pair of Cartier (Cartier!) cufflinks. A quick visit to the nearest branch of the jeweller confirmed that the cufflinks had cost many thousands of pounds. It was the most extravagant gift Nolan had ever received from someone he didn't know, and so, softie that he was, he broke his own strict rule about responding to fan mail. Rather than sending Florence a signed photograph of himself in his latest role (in any case, she must have had enough of those to paper her apartment), Nolan pushed the boat out and bought a nice thank you card into which he scribbled a note.

I was absolutely bowled over by your generous birthday gift. I shall wear them and think of you.

Nolan's manager Karen was unimpressed. 'It's way over the top, Nolan, and you know it. Guessing from her address, that woman just spent her life savings on those cufflinks for you. That is outright wrong. You should have sent them back so she could get a refund and pay her rent.'

Nolan examined the links of which he was already rather fond.

Karen shook her head. 'No good can come of it.'

'But how many times in a tenor's career does a fan send him a gift he actually wants to keep?' Nolan asked. 'Besides, I think it's bad manners to send back a gift. I imagine she will take great pleasure in knowing that I am enjoying them.'

Indeed it seemed that she was. In her latest email to Nolan, Florence wrote that she noticed he was wearing the cufflinks she sent in his new publicity shot.

It makes me very happy indeed to know that in some small way I can be with you even when I can't make it to your performances. Of course, my dear Nolan, I shall do my very best to be with you in person too. I was so excited when I heard about your new European tour of

Tosca. I have downloaded the itinerary and given it to my travel agent who is doing his best to ensure that I can be with you for as much of the tour as possible. Of course, I will not be able to take the full six weeks off from work, but I am owed some time off in lieu, so should be able to be with you for at least three weeks. Which three weeks would be best, my dear? Would it help you to have me there at the beginning or towards the end?

Nolan didn't care. He dashed off a response.

Still loving those cufflinks! Hope you can join us in Europe. If you do, make sure you wave!

At half past eight, Nolan shut his laptop and finished dressing. Standing in front of the mirror, he practised his most winning smile.

'Cosi!' he stepped forward as though to embrace her. Too effusive? Too familiar?

'Cosima.' He offered his hand.

'*Cosima*.' Just a curt nod of his head perhaps?

Once upon a time it would not have been so difficult. He would have thrown his arms around her and lifted all five feet two of her cuddly curves right off the floor. That's how it was from the day they met until the last year of their marriage when her career really started taking off and Nolan reacted like a spoiled child when she didn't have so much time for him. And then that girl in the orchestra started to look at him in the way Cosima used to and it was all downhill from there.

'Forget it,' Nolan told himself.

Then he put on the cufflinks and checked his reflection one last time before he headed for the rehearsal studio and his first meeting in half a decade with the only woman who had ever really touched his heart.

The cufflinks were one of the first things Cosima noticed. She had an eye for fine jewellery. Especially when it came to Nolan, since he didn't ordinarily wear the stuff. Her first and immediate thought was, 'Cartier! Who on earth bought him those?'

Karl Strindberg, the musical director, was expecting trouble. He had begged his producers not to cast Cosima after Judy Shephard dropped out to spend the summer with a sheikh in St-Tropez but Cosima was the only available soprano who was a big enough draw for the prestigious venues the tour would be taking in. Now Cosima had arrived early and Nolan was late. By the time Nolan arrived, Karl was a wreck. He was so agitated that he jumped to his feet and said, without thinking, 'Cosima Esposito, this is Nolan O'Connor.'

'We have met before,' said Cosima icily. 'Hello, Nolan.'

Karl wished that the earth would open up and swallow him. Of course he knew that. Of course, of course. He had been wondering how on earth one introduces ex-lovers all week. And now he'd made the most monumental cock-up of introducing one of opera's most notorious pairings to each other as though they were total strangers.

But Nolan too had been practising this moment and he went through his routine exactly as planned. He placed his hands lightly on the tops of Cosima's arms and leaned in to blow two air-kisses, one straight past each side of her face. No actual cheek-to-cheek contact at all, but close enough for the former lovers to discover that neither had changed their signature scent. Acqua Di Parma's delicate Iris Nobile for her; Chanel's Egoiste for him.

To anyone regarding her – and of course, every member of

the company was watching the moment intently – Cosima seemed to retain her cool. While Karl led Nolan around the rest of the assembled musicians and singers, Cosima returned to her seat and made a show of intently studying the libretto she already knew by heart in Italian, English and Flemish (boy, had that version sounded weird). When he had finished his meet and greet, Nolan took the seat directly across the circle from her. Cosima managed to keep her eyes firmly averted until Karl announced the beginning of the rehearsal and gave her something else to focus on.

Cosima had managed to get past that first dreaded moment: the greeting. Next up, the first note.

After a series of warm-up exercises, Karl suggested that the cast sing through the score from the very beginning. Though she thought her heart might burst out of her chest with anxiety as she waited through Nolan's first musical exchanges as Mario Cavaradossi with the political refugee Angelotti and then the sacristan, Cosima's first note came out as clear and perfect as a note on a tuning fork.

'Mario!'

She had done it.

She sang like a bird and this time Nolan O'Connor could definitely not call it a crow.

The company whizzed through the first sing through. Karl was relieved beyond belief that the collection of people he had pulled together at such short notice seemed to have a remarkable synergy. By the end of the day, Karl had almost forgotten his introductory gaff and the reservations he had about working with Cosima and Nolan on the same production were all but gone. Like everyone else in the cast, he had heard the recording made at La Scala five years earlier and been transported. To hear these two singers he loved and admired singing live in the same room was far better than he had ever imagined.

'Are we doing OK?' Cosima asked.

'You're doing beautifully,' Karl could say in all honesty.

He began to feel that he had been right to take the risk. If anything, both Cosima and Nolan's voices had matured and improved since La Scala. What a coup it would be to direct them in a performance that knocked spots off that legendary recording. Perhaps this tour would make Karl's name after all.

'So,' said Karl, high on the early signs of success. 'I think we can say we've had a very successful day's rehearsal. Now, who would like to come to Café Des Amis for a celebratory drink?'

The younger company members twittered their excited agreement. Karl turned to Nolan.

'I'll come for one,' he said. 'Cosi?' Nolan turned to his former wife. It seemed safe to ask her to join them.

'It's Cosima,' she said.

OK, thought Nolan. She'd stopped him from using the diminutive by which he'd always known her on first try. Perhaps it wasn't quite so safe after all.

'And much as I would love to join you all,' she added in a way that left Nolan in no doubt she didn't include him in that 'all', 'I'm afraid that I have a prior engagement.'

'For dinner?' said Nolan. 'It's only half past five. You can join us for a swift one first.'

'Actually, I have to get back to my hotel as soon as possible. My *boyfriend* has just arrived from New York.'

Cosima got a little satisfaction from seeing Nolan's eyebrows raised in query.

'I'm seeing Andrew Fleetwood,' she said triumphantly.

'What?' Nolan couldn't help himself. 'That amateur?'

The company held its breath for Cosima's reaction.

'Amateur? I think you'll find the review in yesterday's *New York Times* suggests otherwise,' Cosima bristled.

'Yes. Well, if you can find me a reviewer from the *NYT* who doesn't need a hearing aid, I'll find you a virgin at Stringfellows.'

'I know it's next to impossible for you to believe it, but there are other tenors out there, that people want to hear from just as much as you.'

'Any fan of Andrew Fleetwood is no fan of opera. I've heard better singers in the chorus of *Joseph*.'

'I don't have to listen to this.'

'You'll have to listen to it all the time if you insist on dating a man who hits one note in three.'

Karl, who had worked with Cosima before, saw the telltale signs of trouble brewing. Miss Piggy was now in the building. If Nolan didn't wind his neck in pronto, he was in danger of getting a 'hi-ya!' chop to the windpipe.

'I do not have to listen to this,' Cosima insisted. 'Karl, tell him to wind his neck in or I will be leaving the tour.'

With that she grabbed her coat and left.

Andrew was waiting in the hotel room when Cosima returned. He was fast asleep on the bed, having had a late night before his long flight, but she noticed that he had made himself at home. His clothes were hanging in the wardrobe next to hers. His toiletries were in the bathroom. The sight of his contact lens solution by the basin made her feel strangely claustrophobic.

But it wasn't that she didn't want Andrew to be there. Of course not. She was delighted to have him with her on this tour. As soon as she got used to having to deal with Nolan again, she would be fine. She would be able to relax and enjoy having her lover with her in some of the world's most beautiful cities.

Nolan was wrong about Andrew Fleetwood. Andrew was a fantastic singer. Every bit as good as Nolan considered himself to be. The *New York Times* had confirmed it.

Still, she couldn't help looking at Andrew critically now. He looked older than Nolan, didn't he? Even though he was two years or so younger. How did Nolan still look so fantastic? In such good shape for a man who used to think that donuts were one of the basic food groups? And still singing so very well. Cosima couldn't believe Nolan had come through their time apart unscathed. The only word for it was 'unfair'.

On the bed, Andrew stirred. Cosima rearranged her critical features into a big, welcoming smile.

'Oh, hello, darling,' she said. 'It's so good to have you here.'

In a bar with the rest of the company, Nolan hid his own frown behind a vodka tonic. Perhaps this tour was going to be harder than he'd expected.

Chapter Twelve

AFTER that unwelcome Sunday visit from James Dean, Christopher Wilde made an unscheduled trip to see his brother in prison to ask him what the hell he thought he was getting them into. He had decided to tell Dean to stuff his scheme, but he wanted to gauge the reality of Nat's situation first. He hoped that on this visit Nat would reassure him that he would be fine no matter what Christopher wanted to do. After all, Nat was in a high-security prison. There were guards everywhere. There was no way that someone could get away with attacking his brother in that kind of environment surely.

But Christopher soon came to realise that his view of the situation was somewhat naïve. Nat was definitely not his usual chipper self when he entered the visitor's room. For entered, let's say 'limped'. Not only was he having difficultly walking, his left arm was in a sling and his devilishly handsome face was bruised and puffy.

'What the hell happened?' Christopher asked.

'I take it that you weren't too impressed by James Dean's money-making scheme.'

Christopher's mouth dropped open.

'He has eyes, ears and *fists* absolutely everywhere,' said Nat. 'I do hope you'll reconsider your position, little bro. They told me that next time they'd break my wanking arm.'

'Jesus Christ, Nat. Didn't the guards try to break it up?'

'When it comes to James Dean and his associates, the guards have adopted a biblical approach. See no evil . . .'

'But this is ridiculous. This is outright assault. How can they ignore a bloody black eye?'

'What are they going to? Lock them up for it? This is the reality of prison, Chris.'

'You need to file a report.'

'And get another beating? And god knows what would happen to the people I care about on the outside.'

'Like whom?'

'My nephews. You.'

'I can look after myself,' said Christopher.

'You think so?'

'I'll call the police as soon as I get out of here and make sure he doesn't come within ten miles of me again.'

'I don't think that would be such a great idea, little bro. In James Dean, you're not dealing with an ordinary man, you're dealing with a psychopath. What's more, you're dealing with a psychopath who has a whole network of other like-minded psychopaths, willing to do his bidding night and day, behind bars and even out there in leafy, lovely Wimbledon. God knows I will never forgive myself for getting you involved in this, Christopher. But I have and now you are the only person who can get us back out.'

'What? By getting involved with his scheme? What did he tell you about it? It's crazy, Nat. He has no idea how the banking system works. He tells me he's got some IT wizard on his team but I've already met his right-hand man, Nat, and I don't think he's bright enough to tie his own shoelaces. I have no faith that he'll have picked a better computer guy. And that means the whole thing is doomed from the start. If I get involved, I'll end up behind bars with you quicker than you can say "profit share". And he won't get the money he wants and you'll still be in trouble. If what you're saying is true.'

Nat reached across the table and took his brother's hand. It was an uncharacteristic gesture. Nat and Christopher had not been raised in an especially affectionate family. Nat sometimes blamed the fact that he had spent most of his adult life chasing tail on that lack of early affection. It wasn't about sex at all; he just wanted someone to cuddle him. And right then, he needed reassurance from his brother. Christopher could see it in his eyes. He had seen that look just a couple of times before. The first time was when Nat had to have his appendix out, shortly after the death of their father. The next time was when he appeared in the dock at his trial for murder. Though he wished he could deny it, Christopher knew that Nat was terrified.

One of the guards was already wandering in their direction to check that nothing untoward was going on.

Nat squeezed Christopher's fingers. Christopher squeezed back.

'I am scared,' Nat admitted. 'Hell, Chris, you know me. I'm not a wimp. I boxed for my college. It was my fists that ended me up in here. But there are no Queensberry Rules with these guys and I'm afraid that next time could be much much worse. And I'm afraid for you too.'

Christopher wanted to say, 'It's a little too late for that,' but the words stayed in his head. He could see that his brother wasn't kidding and understood how hard it must be for him to admit his weakness.

'OK. I'll agree to meet the IT guy,' Christopher said. 'And then I'll persuade your friend Mr Dean that he really is wasting his time and hope that is the last we hear of it.'

'Thank you.' Nat's eyes were swimming in tears. Christopher pretended not to notice. That was what Nat would have wanted.

Christopher didn't have to track James Dean down. By the time he got outside the prison, feeling more relieved than usual to be on the right side of the bars, Christopher's phone had already registered three calls from unknown numbers. A fourth came minutes later.

'You saw your brother?' said Dean.

Christopher confirmed that he had.

'We thought you might. How's he getting on in there?'

'I'm sure you've already had a detailed progress report.'

Dean sniggered.

'My brother is a good guy,' said Christopher. 'And a tough one. Don't think that roughing him up is going to have him begging me to get into bed with you. He can take it.'

'I heard he was practically crying.'

Christopher decided that this was a double bluff. There was no way Dean could have heard the details of Christopher's conversation with Nat so quickly. Unless Nat's claim that Dean had eyes and ears everywhere was true.

'Anyway, I do believe you're not worried about Nat. He'll survive. He's tough as old boots. The women in your life, however . . .'

'Don't think that threatening me is going to make any difference.'

'Why don't you think about the incentives instead? I understand you're sailing into dire straits, financially. Expensive business, infidelity. Especially once the missus files for divorce.'

Christopher was not ready for Caroline to find out about Juliet yet. Not now everything was so up in the air while they waited for the hospital results. It was going to be easier to give in for the moment. He was coming to understand that Dean would not stop harassing him until he was properly convinced that Christopher couldn't help him.

'Christ, all right,' he said. 'I'll meet you.'

Dean gave Christopher the address of a service station on the road to Essex.

'A service station?'

'Just park up and wait.'

Like his brother, Christopher Wilde prided himself on the fact that he was not a wimpish kind of man. All the same, he felt his stomach churning with anxiety as he pulled into the service station as he had been told. As he waited for Dean and his friends to arrive, Christopher called Juliet.

'Are you OK?' she asked. She knew at once that something was wrong. Juliet's sensitivity to his moods was one of the reasons Christopher loved her. Caroline had long since stopped caring whether her husband was happy or sad. If she ever had cared at all.

'I'm fine,' he said. 'Just a bit tired. And Nat wasn't in the best shape this evening.'

'It's lovely the way you care about your brother,' said Juliet. 'But from time to time you need to care about yourself more. Don't let it get to you. Do you want to come over?'

'I can't. Caroline is expecting me,' he lied. For once, it wasn't his wife who was keeping him from Juliet's side.

'Then I'll just have to blow you a kiss down the phone. Sleep tight, sweetheart. I'll see you in the office tomorrow.'

Just as Christopher was turning off his phone, Dean and his sidekick appeared.

'I didn't see you,' he said. How could he have missed the biggest Range Rover in the south of England?

'We came in a different car,' Dean explained. He indicated a plain-looking Ford Mondeo. 'Jump in. We're going for a ride.'

It was a classic intimidation tactic, of course. Away from his own car, Christopher felt horribly vulnerable.

They drove to another service station to meet the third man there. He didn't look like the others. He was dressed in a checked shirt, a blue sweater and khakis. Classic ex-public schoolboy casual gear. He said his name was David Sullivan. Christopher was relieved to be introduced to someone who had an RP accent and no visible tattoos. On first appearances, David Sullivan seemed like a nice enough guy. But how crazy must he be to join forces with a thug like Dean? Then again, Christopher considered, perhaps he too had felt like he didn't have a choice. Christopher wondered what dirt Dean had on this mild-mannered man.

Anyway, David Sullivan was to be the brain behind the scheme that Dean was bankrolling. The idea was simple. David was an IT whiz who had worked on security applications for many of the big name banks during his career. Now he was gamekeeper turned poacher. He felt he hadn't benefited from the boom times in banking and now the fat cats were trying to pay him less than he considered himself worth. James Dean, he said, recognised his true value.

So, David had developed, 'With Mr Dean's generous sponsorship', a programme that, once inserted into Anglo-Italian's system, would choose bank accounts at random and siphon off small, random amounts into an offshore account that could be accessed by Dean and his team.

'You'd be surprised how few people check their bank statements,' David told Christopher. 'A few quid here or there is easily overlooked. I've worked in security. I've seen situations where cards have been cloned and people have lost hundreds of thousands before they realised anything was amiss. There are people out there with so much money they could lose the cost of a Gulfstream without feeling the pain. Look at those guys in the City a few years back. Their secretary took them for millions just a few quid at a time. It took them years to cotton on.'

David had a point and Christopher was impressed by his verbal CV. If he really had worked in the finance departments he claimed to have worked for, then he had been at the cutting edge of security technology.

'There's nothing I can't get round,' David assured him. 'Sure, there are new developments all the time, but the guys who do security in these places are anyone's for hire. They're not dedicated to the protection of the banks they work for. They don't care about the customers. They don't care if selling the bank's security secrets ultimately ends up costing some granny her home. What matters to them is the thrill of setting up a wall and challenging their peers to knock it down and vice versa. It's all a game.'

Christopher nodded. Though when he thought about

the grey-faced security team at Anglo-Italian, he couldn't say they seemed to be having an awful lot of fun.

Next David outlined Christopher's part in the scheme. It seemed easy enough. All he had to do was get hold of a number of passwords that would in turn give David's team access to innumerable accounts. He could do that by getting David a job in the IT department there.

'Not going to happen,' said Christopher. 'There's a hiring freeze.'

'We've thought that might be the case so have come up with a Plan B. You'll just have to collect the passwords with some key-logger software and install the main programme yourself. I'll show you exactly what to do. It's really very simple.'

Christopher found that very hard to believe.

'I don't think—' he began.

They were interrupted by David's BlackBerry. He pulled it out of his pocket at once and told his colleagues that he had to reply to an email as a matter of urgency.

'Addicted to that thing he is,' said James Dean, sounding almost like an indulgent father.

'You know,' Christopher tried to persuade the big man of the stupidity of his plan one more time. 'Anglo-Italian has a whole floor full of people looking out for exactly this kind of scam. I just don't think it will work.'

'I need you to have more faith,' said James Dean. 'Because we can't have you backing out right now. Especially since we've named this little project in your honour.'

Christopher narrowed his eyes. 'What do you mean?'

'David's calling the scheme "Juliet".'

* * *

Temptation

While Christopher was waiting for David Sullivan to get off his BlackBerry in a car park somewhere in Essex, Juliet was safely tucked up at home, emailing her old college friend David Stevenson. They arranged to meet for lunch at a small Italian restaurant in Mayfair the following afternoon.

Chapter Thirteen

Juliet was surprised at how her heart seemed to race as she got nearer to the site of their rendezvous. Had it really been ten years since the friends last saw each other? She remembered the 'going away' party David had thrown before his trip to South America. She'd stayed at his house that night, in his room, and they had almost, but not quite, made love. It was the first and only time they went to bed together. And the last time she saw him.

Now here he was again. It was a cliché but a true one when the old friends told each other, 'You haven't changed at all!'

'We must have changed,' Juliet told him later. 'It's just that we've got short-sighted at the same rate.'

Once seated in the restaurant, she had a chance to look at him closely. She could see that though he still had as much hair as she remembered, it was a little grey in places and there was no denying either that the blue eyes that always seemed to be smiling were framed by a few more laughter lines. Still, it wasn't unattractive. In fact, she might have said he was growing into his looks.

'What have you been doing all this time?' Juliet asked him.

'I don't know where to start. When did we last see each other?'

'Was it really at the party you threw to celebrate going to South America?'

David nodded. 'I'm embarrassed to have to say yes. But I wrote to you. When I didn't hear anything in return, I assumed that you had found yourself a nice boyfriend. Perhaps even got married and had twins.'

'Do you think I would have got married without inviting you?'

'Then you're not married,' David said, with a big smile on his face.

'I'm still auditioning for the first Mr Hunter,' Juliet said. 'And you?'

'There have been a couple of girls since we last met but no one special. My job has made it a bit difficult to settle down. I've been moving around a lot.'

'Where have you been?'

'I stayed in South America for a while. Then I was in the States for a couple of years. Then Nigeria.'

'Nigeria?' Juliet was surprised.

'A government project,' he replied.

'What kind of project?'

'I got into IT security,' David explained. 'Just at the right time. And now I'm back in London.'

'How long are you here for?'

'Who knows,' said David. 'For a while, I hope. Certainly long enough to get to know you again.'

Juliet was delighted. She clapped her hands at the news. 'I'm very happy to hear that. We're going to have great fun.'

It was so easy to be with David. It took just a few minutes, really, for the old friends to slip back into the easy way they had with one another. There was plenty to talk about. Lots of gossip about people that Juliet had kept in touch with since college. David admitted that he really hadn't kept up with many people at all.

'I can't say I ever really think about any of them. Except you.'

Juliet felt herself blush. She was pleased to hear that but she hoped it didn't show.

'I'm glad to find you looking so well,' David continued. 'And happy. And so successful in your career. Remind me whom you're working for these days. Are you still at Barclays?'

'No,' said Juliet. 'Really, we have been out of touch for too long. I left that job about three months after you buggered off to Peru. I went to Coutts right after that. And about five and a half years ago I joined the private banking sector of Anglo-Italian.'

'Anglo-Italian? Seriously? Who are you working with? I have a former colleague who works for them.'

'My direct boss is called Christopher Wilde.'

Juliet felt a peculiar frisson as she said her lover's name out loud to her friend. It was as though in saying his name, she was admitting to their ongoing affair at the same time. She studied David's face for a reaction, as if she expected a reaction to the news of the infidelity.

'Nope,' said David. 'I've never heard of him. My former colleague was called Joe Previn. Have you come across him?'

'No,' said Juliet. 'Though it's a big company. There are two separate office buildings in London. He might be in the other one.'

'Well, I wouldn't bother seeking him out,' said David. 'He's one of the most boring people I've ever worked with. Talks about nothing but golf.'

'Then he would get on well with my boss,' said Juliet, covering up for the secret she hadn't revealed by affecting disinterest in Christopher.

The end of the lunch came far too quickly.

'Let's not leave it so long next time,' said Juliet.

'You're right,' said David. 'How about later this week?'

Juliet grinned. 'Why not,' she said. 'Thursday?'

'I'll cook for you. You can come and see my new gaff.'

Juliet said that she would be delighted.

When she got back to the office, Christopher was soon by her desk, ostensibly with a pile of papers he wanted her to look at but really, Juliet guessed, to find out more about her mystery lunch companion. She told him everything.

'He's just moved back to London.'

'And got in touch with you just like that? After almost ten years of nothing? Are you sure you didn't sleep with him?'

'Of course I'm sure,' Juliet responded testily.

'Then he must want to sleep with you now.'

'Why do you have to be so cynical, Chris? There doesn't necessarily have to be an ulterior motive behind him getting back in touch. We were very important to each other at a certain point in our lives. That's all. I'm glad he tracked me down. I'm having dinner with him later this week.'

'Dinner?' Christopher harrumphed. Juliet had the feeling that he would have liked to ask her not to go to dinner with David but, of course, he couldn't. Not since he would be spending the evening with his wife and children. And then the conversation had to end anyway. Christopher had an appointment in Mayfair.

'Client?' Juliet asked.

'Personal,' said Christopher.

Juliet rolled her eyes. Christopher probably thought he was getting is own back by acting all mysterious but Juliet merely assumed he was doing something really exciting like getting his prostate checked.

'OK,' she said. 'See you later.'

Chapter Fourteen

MERCY'S younger brother Francis had returned from his holiday with their father in Jamaica with more than a couple of shell-covered ornaments for his sister and mother.

'What is up with your accent?' Mercy asked.

Francis had come back from his holiday sounding like a yardie.

'Francis, you are not a hard man,' his sister told him. 'You are fifteen years old. You are applying for an NVQ in catering.'

Francis sucked his teeth. 'Not no more,' he said.

'What?'

'I ain't going to no college.'

'You're what?'

'No use to me. Spending three days a week learning how to make pasta. For what? So I can get me some dumb minimum wage job when I leave? I need money now. I ain't hanging round.'

Mercy shook her head at him. 'You're nuts, Francis Campbell, if you think it's going to be better for you to give up on college and get a job without an NVQ. Stay on. That's what I should have done. Get your qualifications and then look for a job. The whole world will be open to you then.'

'Yeah. Right,' said Francis.

Before Mercy could try to convince her little brother further, the ringing of his phone interrupted them. Seeing the number on the screen, Francis sloped off into the hallway to take the call. And when the call was over, he shouted to his mother and sister that he was going out.

'But I just put your food on the table!' Melody protested.

'It's OK, Mum. I'll get something when I'm out,' said Francis, missing the point altogether.

Melody looked at the three plates on the table with a frown. She picked up the plate heaped highest and took it back into the kitchen where she lovingly wrapped it with aluminium foil.

'Mum,' Mercy berated her mother, 'you shouldn't bother. You should put it straight in the bin. Who does he think he is? Expecting you to cook for him and then not even bothering to stay and eat when one of his mates calls.'

'He's young,' said Melody. 'And most of the time he's a good boy. I don't want to lose him, like Mrs Hale did her youngest.'

Mercy laid a comforting hand on her mother's shoulder. She knew the story and understood why it affected her mother so much. After a monumental row of the type that would be familiar to anyone living with teenagers, Xavier Hale (Zav to his mates) had walked out of his mother's house to live with some of his friends. He'd got involved with gangs and next time his mother saw him, he was on a slab in a mortuary. Melody Campbell was convinced that if she knew where her son was sleeping, if she just kept doing his washing (and turning his pockets out before she did so), she would know at once if anything was wrong and save her son from Xavier Hale's fate.

Mercy was less convinced by her mother's strategy.

'He needs to learn how to act like a man,' she said. 'And real men do not disrespect their mothers.'

Melody glanced at the shell-covered ornament on the sideboard. It bore the message: 'I Love My Mum.'

'I'm sure he'll apologise when he gets home.'

Mercy rolled her eyes. Francis definitely got cut more slack than she had ever done at the same age. Mercy could have complained about it for hours, but that evening she had more interesting things to talk about than her reprobate brother. She was delighted to see the smile return to her mother's face when she told her about the date.

'I'm going to the Royal Opera House!'

Of course Mercy had allowed Ed to persuade her to go to the reception. How could she refuse? It was as though Christmas had come early. But as soon as she told him she'd be delighted to accept, the real problems started to emerge. Getting an evening off work was one thing – Hazel moaned so much you might have thought she would have to clean the toilets herself in Mercy's absence. But what to wear? Mercy had a feeling that Ed didn't have two standing tickets for the amphitheatre and she wanted him to be proud when they walked into the auditorium together.

However, there was nothing in Mercy's wardrobe that would do the job and she didn't exactly have money to spend on something new. She shared her frustration with her mother.

'What were you wearing when you first met Dad?' she asked.

'Not enough,' sighed Melody.

Mercy told her mother all about Ed, about how much she enjoyed talking to him and how much she wanted the first time he saw her without her overalls to be special. Melody could see Mercy's point but she wasn't able to help her with some money for a new dress.

Later that evening, however, Melody had a big surprise for her daughter.

'You can wear this,' she said. She handed Mercy a box. It was old. The lid, which was falling apart, carried the name of a store that Mercy didn't recognise.

'What is it?'

'It belonged to your grandmother,' Melody explained. 'She left it to me. I haven't ever worn it because my sister, your aunt, would wrestle me to the ground for it if she ever found out that I had it.'

Mercy carefully took the lid off the box.

Inside was a dark blue velvet dress, the colour of a clear midnight sky. Mercy lifted it out of its ancient, rustling tissue paper and held it up. It was from the 1950s with a fitted boned bodice and a generous flared skirt.

'It was her pride and joy. She wore it when she married your grandfather. She told me she got a velvet dress instead of a white one because she didn't know when she would next be able to afford something new and she wanted to get lots of wear out of it. Not that she did. I never saw her wear it except in her wedding photos.'

'It's beautiful,' said Mercy.

'Try it on.'

'But it's so delicate. I can't. It'll tear.'

'Try it on,' Melody insisted. 'I know that you'll be careful. And she would have loved to see you in it.'

It was the perfect dress for Mercy's figure. A little tight around the ribs perhaps. People were so much smaller back in the day, her mother explained. But the full skirt was wonderfully forgiving. The bodice and the skirt combined gave Mercy the perfect hourglass shape. The velvet was as sumptuous as it had been the day Connie Campbell walked up the aisle.

'Can I really wear it?'

'Of course,' said Melody. 'I want you to knock that boy's socks off.'

'It's not like that,' said Mercy. 'I mean, we're just friends. We just talk about music.'

Melody raised an eyebrow.

Mercy felt a little silly. Naturally her enthusiasm about Ed, her rhapsodising about how interested and generous and good-looking he was had made it obvious to her mother that Mercy's excitement was about more than a free opera ticket. She went back to regarding her reflection in the mirror.

'Thank you, Mum. I promise I'll bring it back in one piece.'

'You will go to the ball,' smiled Melody.

Chapter Fifteen

AFTER the spat between Nolan and Cosima over Andrew Fleetwood, the rehearsals continued in a similar vein for a week. When Cosima and Nolan first encountered each other in the morning, they would grunt in acknowledgement. After that, they would keep to opposite sides of the room until the last possible moment, when Karl called them into their positions to begin the rehearsal proper. As soon as the music started, hostilities were off. Cosima was Floria Tosca and Nolan was Mario Cavaradossi again: once more the love of her life. Boy, were they convincing with their flashing glances and heartfelt sighs. Anyone who didn't know their history as a couple would have been utterly convinced that they were simply crazy about each other. As soon as the music stopped, however, they were back on opposite sides of the room. Cosima surrounded herself with a clique of serious-minded young women who wanted to emulate her success. Nolan drew the pretty ones who quite fancied the idea of marrying into success instead.

Though Cosima pretended not to notice, of course she quickly worked out which of the girls in the company Nolan would try to seduce first. And of course Nolan was always subtly watching to see if Cosima was watching him. And every time he caught her regarding him out of the corner of her eye, his heart leaped a little. She still cared. He wasn't sure why that meant so much to him when, if he felt like it, he could wine, dine and inevitably bed girls far younger, prettier and infinitely sweeter every night of the week. But it did.

Perhaps, he thought to himself, if he and Cosima could just catch up properly, the mystique, and thus the urge to know what was going on behind those dark eyes, would be gone. A week and a half into rehearsals, he dared ask her if she would care to join him for supper. She could even bring that loser Fleetwood if she wanted. Though of course, Nolan didn't actually use the word 'loser'.

'We're busy,' Cosima told him.

Nolan was horrified to discover that the thought of how Andrew Fleetwood might be keeping his ex-wife busy put him off the idea of going out at all that night. Instead he slunk back to his hotel room and ordered room service. He was in such a bad mood that he didn't even think about giving the girl who delivered his BLT sandwich anything other than a monetary tip. He ate his sandwich in front of *Top Gear* but the thought of a new car did not lift his mood at all either. Then he made the mistake of googling Andrew Fleetwood.

It didn't help. Fleetwood's personal website was full of

ridiculous photos of the idiot in costume accompanied by toe-curling extracts from his reviews. Apparently, one tone-deaf critic had acclaimed Fleetwood the 'greatest tenor of his generation'.

'My arse,' said Nolan, but he couldn't help but compare the type of reviews he'd got from the same guy, which had always been lukewarm by comparison.

Nolan checked his own fan mail to boost his flagging spirits. 'Mr O'Connor, you are a star ... blah blah blah.' 'Nolan O'Connor, you *are* opera,' was a particularly good one. He saved Florence Carter's email until last in the desperate hope that she might at least make him laugh. She could always be relied upon for some effusive praise.

Good news! I've been made redundant. How can that be good news? You ask. Well, because I had been at the plant for so long, my boss couldn't let me go without a huge severance package. It's almost a whole year's money! Which means I won't feel in the least bit guilty or worried about taking all of the summer off and seeing every single show on your European tour! I am so excited. I can't wait to see you again. But, tell me, how are rehearsals going? It must be hard for you, working alongside your ex-wife. Still, keep your chin up, dear Nolan. Know that there is at least one woman in your life who truly appreciates you and your magnificent talents. Oh, I am so happy tonight. Six weeks in Europe, hearing you sing night after night. I will be in heaven. Do say you're delighted too.

Had Nolan been in a better mood, he might not have written back at all. But he was feeling tired and lonely and looking for approval and, right then, Florence Carter was the only person likely to provide him with that at short notice. So he hit reply and tapped out an email back to her.

> I'm glad that you're taking your sudden redundancy so well. It's true that every cloud has a silver lining, I suppose. Now that I know you're going to be in the audience, I will have to make sure I sing my heart out. As for rehearsals with my ex-wife, they are going as well as can be expected. She hasn't changed at all . . .

It wasn't much but Nolan had no idea of the effect his careless words would have on the woman in New Jersey who read them later that night with her heart pounding and her imagination firing on nearly all cylinders.

Florence Carter printed out Nolan O'Connor's email and read it fifty-four times. She could hardly believe it. Sure, Nolan had emailed her before, but his responses to her carefully crafted messages were always so short that, on bad days, she found herself thinking that perhaps he didn't write them at all. Perhaps he had some secretary employed specifically for the purpose of responding to the mail that arrived via his website. Perhaps, she thought with real horror, though he wore the cufflinks she had bought for him in his new publicity shot, he didn't even actually know they were from her.

This email changed all that. Although it comprised only six sentences, this email was twice as long as anything Florence had received from Nolan's fan-site before. A mere assistant would not have bothered to write such a long and interesting message and as Florence read the words out loud, she could hear Nolan's voice in her head. The written words reflected his speech patterns, as heard in the interviews that Florence had found on YouTube. She knew his voice and the way he spoke as well as she knew the voices of her parents and her closest friends (if you could still call Helen and Maria close friends when she hadn't seen them in five years). This email was definitely from Nolan's own hand. And, by definition, from his heart.

Florence was ecstatic. Ever since she had first seen Nolan sing at the Lincoln Centre, she had known that he would play an important part in her life and she in his. At first, she had merely sought out his recordings. Then she did her best to make sure that she saw him whenever he was in New York. When she sold her car to fly to see him in Los Angeles, it was Helen who suggested that this 'Nolan O'Connor thing' might be getting a little out of hand.

'Florence, you need a car,' said Helen.

'I'll buy a old wreck when I get back from California.'

'Why don't you just keep the car you've got? I don't understand it. You don't have the money to follow this guy all over the country. Why don't you just see him when he comes to the East Coast and get recordings of the other stuff? You must be able to get a DVD.'

'But I want to be able to see him in the flesh. And I need him to be able to see me. To know that I'm there to support him.'

Helen sneered. 'He can't see you,' she said. 'The performers can't see anyone in the audience because of the stage lights. They always say that.'

'I want a chance to wait for him by the stage door.'

'You're going to fly all the way to Los Angeles for an autograph?'

'Haven't you ever had someone important in your life?

Haven't you ever met someone you would do anything for? A flight to LA isn't such a big deal.'

'I agree. But we're not talking about a proper relationship here, are we? You haven't met this Nolan guy. He's a celebrity. And you're just a fan.'

A fan? Florence bristled at the word. She was so much more than a fan. She considered herself a friend, at least, and hoped for more. She told Helen what she believed. She and Nolan had a special connection. She thought they might even have been together in a past life.

'I think you're nuts,' said Helen.

The former best friends hadn't seen each other since.

Florence didn't need Helen's approval. She would continue her crazy pursuit of Nolan O'Connor regardless of what anybody thought. Not only did she sell her car to fly to California to see him at the Disney Hall in LA, she eventually sold her apartment and moved back in with her parents. She told them that she was worried about job security and a downturn in house prices. In reality, she needed the cash from her house to see Nolan in DC and Seattle and again and again in New York and to buy him a very special birthday gift to prove just how serious she was. She spent most of the proceeds of the sale on those Cartier cufflinks.

Florence was delighted when Nolan finally got his act together and set up a website. Now she had a way to contact him whenever she wanted and at last he had reached out to her in return!

Being laid off now seemed like part of a higher plan. At last, at forty years old, she was destined to go to Europe for the first time. She was sure now that Nolan would seek her out in the crowd and after all the years of waiting they would be together.

She wrote back to him.

Don't worry, dear Nolan. Soon the tour will be underway and you won't have to see that nasty ex-wife of yours except when you are onstage together. Think of the fun you can have during the daytime. So many wonderful cities to explore.

Florence stopped short of saying, 'We can explore them together.' But she did send him an updated photograph of herself so that he would be sure to recognise her when she arrived at the first date of the tour in London, England.

Chapter Sixteen

As promised, just a few days after their first meeting in ten years, Juliet and David saw each other again. Juliet took a cab straight from the office after work to David's new flat in South Kensington. It was a corporate let, he said to excuse the fact that it was so sparsely decorated, but what little he had brought with him on his return from his travels was fascinating. The mantelpiece was arrayed with interesting pieces of bric-a-brac bought back from South America and Africa.

'I like this,' said Juliet, picking up a little beaded figure playing a miniature guitar.

'How funny,' said David. 'I must have known that you would. Would you believe that I bought that little fellow for you in Chile and have carried him round for the past decade, sure in the knowledge that one day I would see you again?'

'Really?'

'Absolutely. As I recall you used to love that kind of crap before you started working for an Italian bank and got all sophisticated. You can take it with you.'

'I don't know if I want it! Got all sophisticated, eh? Is that what you think happened?'

'Yes, and it suits you,' David grinned.

Dinner was great. David had certainly expanded his cooking repertoire while they'd been apart. The last time he cooked for Juliet and a bunch of their friends, he'd made a potato curry but didn't cook it for long enough, so that the potatoes were like stones in a yellow-grey sludge. This time he made a Moroccan dish in a real tagine.

'I learned to cook this in Marrakech,' he said. 'I brought the tagine back on my head, like a hat, to save excess baggage charges.'

'Nice idea,' laughed Juliet. 'Were you there on holiday?'

'I was there for a couple of months. On a job.'

'God, your job sounds glamorous. You go all over the place.'

'I go to some of the world's worst shit holes. Your job is the glamorous one. You're working in banking in London and Italy. You must meet some real characters.'

'I do. But I can't tell you about any of them, so don't ask. I've signed a confidentiality agreement.'

'Of course,' said David, with a wink. 'But you can change the names.'

'Oh, if you insist.' And so Juliet launched into the story about one client – codename Mrs Pooch – who insisted on bringing her four pet pugs to every meeting.

'Since it's their financial future we're discussing,' Mrs Pooch would explain. The pugs were the four main beneficiaries of her last will and testament.

'Of course none of them were toilet-trained,' Juliet explained. 'The carpet in the board room, which cost more per square inch than gold leaf, was always a mess but we didn't dare put down polythene in case the pugs were offended and the client withdrew her cash. She's richer than the average small African nation.'

'I'm sure you handled the situation with your usual sang-froid,' said David.

'Oh no, I spent the whole time struggling not to laugh. Every time I looked up, Christopher, my boss—'

'Your boss . . .'

'Was so obviously trying not to laugh too. It was next to impossible to keep a straight face. But someone with that much money has to be taken seriously no matter how cuckoo they are.'

'Are all of your clients that crazy?'

'To be honest,' said Juliet. 'Some of them are plain frightening. Especially the ones who turn up with bodyguards. I've always thought that life must actually feel a lot less safe if you have a bodyguard, like a huge shadow, scowling all the time, carrying a gun that could just as easily be used against you as for you. I'd hate to live like that, no matter how much money I had tied up in offshore accounts. I'd rather be penniless and free.'

David nodded in agreement. 'I know what you mean.'

'There's this one guy,' Juliet continued. 'A Russian, who has to send his children to school under armed guard in case they are kidnapped by one of his rivals. Christopher and I went to his London house once. I couldn't wait to leave. Except we couldn't leave when we wanted to because there was a power cut and the electric gate got stuck.'

'A Russian? Was it Belanov?' asked David. 'He just bought my football team.'

'I told you I'm not supposed to name names,' said Juliet, hoping the rush of blood to her cheeks wouldn't give the game away. Perhaps David had just made a lucky guess. Belanov was the name on everyone's lips, thanks to his sudden entry into the football world. Christopher had been angling, without success, for a seat in the directors' box.

David asked a lot of questions about Juliet's work that evening. She felt flattered and was glad, since it struck her halfway into the evening that she didn't have a whole lot else to talk about. She was reminded of the last time she had managed to squeeze a night with the girls into her diary. Their lives were so full now: careers, husbands and babies. Though they complained bitterly about being tired and feeling stretched in all directions, Juliet couldn't help but envy them their funny anecdotes about family life. Thinking about that made her wistful. It must have shown on her face.

'So how come there is no Mr Hunter?' David asked.

'Oh, you know . . .' said Juliet. 'I guess the right guy hasn't come along.'

'Really? No one close? Not even so much as a kiss?'

'I've been a nun,' she said, with a little snort.

Juliet found herself on the verge of telling him about Christopher. On the one hand, she wanted so much to have David's opinion. She had spent five years loving that man and even her best friends had no idea. She felt as though David wouldn't be judgemental and it would be so wonderful to be able to speak her love out loud. On the other hand, something made her hold her secret closer to her heart than ever before. Was she subconsciously trying to pass herself off as available?

'Well,' concluded David. 'The men of Great Britain are clearly nuts.'

'Oh, you're too kind,' said Juliet, giving David a playful shove.

Juliet went home at midnight. She had a busy day ahead. And besides, though she owed Christopher no loyalty at all, she loved him enough to feel that she did and a late night spent drinking with a handsome single man seemed somewhat dodgy under the circumstances.

After that odd call when he seemed so unhappy, Juliet had been quite worried about Christopher. She longed to talk to him properly, but for the rest of the week it had been impossible. There was simply never a moment when the two lovers found themselves alone together. And there wouldn't be for another fortnight. That week's meeting in Milan had been cancelled. Instead, the senior staff of Anglo-Italian would be holding their weekly briefing in London. The reason for the change was that all the senior staff was assembling in London for Anglo-Italian's annual bash, held this year at the Royal Opera House. The evening would comprise a champagne reception, followed by a short concert of opera favourites, picked to appeal to the philistines among Anglo-Italian's staff and clientele, followed by yet more champagne in the Crush Room.

That year, Juliet and her PA had been in charge of putting together the guest list and sending out the invitations. Juliet's department would be hosting the event, with her in the position of official hostess. It was important to be on top form.

Chapter Seventeen

AFTER much teasing, Mercy had admitted to her mother that she hoped that tonight's date with Ed would lead to something more. As she got ready for the evening at Covent Garden, she imagined that this would be the first of many such evenings. Ed danced through her mind in his smart suit and shiny shoes, singing a slightly flat accompaniment to Mercy's favourite arias. He seemed to like her well enough already, talking as he did about the possibility of introducing her to his singing teacher aunt. What would happen when she was out of her overalls and he was out of the office? As she carefully applied another layer of lipstick, Mercy had the feeling that everything would go wonderfully right.

To get to her date with Ed, Mercy had to take the tube to Covent Garden. She carried her high heels – bought especially for the occasion from New Look – in her bag and changed into them on Floral Street, just around the corner from the opera house. Ed had already sent a text to say that he was waiting for her outside the main entrance and now Mercy wanted to make a big entrance of her own. Checking her make-up in the tiny mirror on her compact, she took a couple of deep breaths and practised her very warmest smile. She took off her denim jacket and folded it into the bag that now contained her flat shoes. It wasn't all that hot but Mercy figured she had just a few metres to walk and she would rather be a little chilly than turn up with such a scrappy garment over her grandmother's beautiful velvet dress. Meanwhile, her new shoes pinched her toes and rubbed at her bare heels even after a couple of steps.

Her sacrifice was well rewarded, however. As she strutted the last few feet to the opera house door, Mercy caught several admiring glances and Ed's face was the most appreciative of all.

'You look marvellous!' he said.

'Bet you were afraid I'd turn up in my overalls,' said Mercy.

'Not for a moment,' he assured her. 'I always knew you would look wonderful. That dress is so fantastic. It fits you . . .' Ed opened his hands and unconsciously echoed the shape of Mercy's curves in the air. 'Like a second skin. Mercy Campbell,' he breathed with something approaching reverence. 'You are a bombshell.'

Warm from the glow of Ed's compliments, Mercy tucked her arm through his and allowed him to escort her into the building.

The reception was being held in the Crush Room, one of the opera house's restaurants. It was a jewel box of a room lined with gilt-framed mirrors. Mercy had only peeked into this room on her last visit to the house, as though someone might shoo her away before she was spotted by the glamorous people dining there. On Ed's arm, she walked into that room as though she truly belonged there. Ed seemed to know everyone. Mercy was thrilled to be with someone so very popular. She was even more thrilled when Ed introduced her to his colleagues and friends and a real live countess, one of the private banking department's clients.

'Mercy is an aspiring opera singer,' Ed told the elderly woman whose crabbed fingers were covered in jewels the size of bumblebees. She leaned forward to hear more clearly and smiled indulgently.

'An aspiring singer, eh?'

'Oh, I wouldn't say that,' said Mercy.

'Why not?' Ed asked her. 'Countess, let me tell you, Mercy has a voice that would silence an angelic choir. I couldn't believe it when I first heard her singing in the office. I thought someone was playing a CD of a young Angela Gheorghiu.'

'Oh don't,' Mercy squirmed at the comparison to one of her all-time favourites. 'I'm really not that good.'

'I'm not joking,' Ed assured his audience. 'Angela Gheorghiu had better look to her laurels.'

'So you work at Anglo-Italian, dear,' said the countess. 'Will I have the pleasure of hearing you sing out the figures on one of this whipper-snapper's abominable spreadsheets next time I'm in your office?'

'Oh no,' said Mercy. 'Ed and I met at Anglo-Italian but we don't work together. I don't actually work in banking at all.' Mercy put her hands up to her face and whispered through the gap. 'I'm just a cleaner.'

The countess looked a little confused for a moment, then she laid her hand on Mercy's arm and beamed as she said to

Ed. 'Oh, you have such a funny girlfriend, dear! A cleaner!' she laughed. 'Such a funny girl.'

The countess shuffled off in the direction of her much younger beau. Mercy bit her lip as she turned back to Ed, anxious to see if he had been embarrassed by her explaining her job to his client. He didn't look very bothered. He was gazing at her again.

'I can't get over how beautiful you look tonight,' he said. He pinched another two glasses of champagne from a passing waiter and handed Mercy's glass to her as though he was presenting her with a long-stemmed rose.

'Let's drink to you,' he said.

Mercy smoothed down the navy velvet skirt of her grandmother's dress. This evening was going to be wonderful.

Chapter Eighteen

♪

Juliet also looked especially elegant that evening in Covent Garden. She had pulled out an old favourite: an LBD in chiffon by Oscar de la Renta. It was the perfect dress for this type of event. Perhaps not as eye-poppingly gorgeous as a Herve Leger bandage dress (Juliet spotted five skin-tight Leger numbers within three minutes of walking into the opera house that night) but perfect for her. She didn't want to have to worry about flashing her knickers or looking like mutton dressed as lamb. She felt comfortable in her old Oscar dress and that was very important, given the guest list, which boasted one person in particular that Juliet wanted to impress with her cool elegance.

Christopher would be there. With his wife.

Juliet had met Christopher's wife several times over her five years as his colleague at Anglo-Italian. She'd studied her rival quite closely. Caroline was exactly how Juliet had imagined her to be. Exactly like all the other bankers' wives, in fact. Her complexion suggested she had once been a brunette, but had opted for that ubiquitous toffee blond that covers early traces of grey. She could have been any age between thirty-seven and fifty. Like her hair, her figure was perfect, honed through hours of Pilates with a personal trainer who probably cost almost as much per hour as her dermatologist. Botox was essential for any self-respecting Yummy Mummy these days.

That night Caroline arrived without Christopher. As the reception started, he was still in a meeting, making plans to hide money for a wealthy client who was about to file for divorce. Still, even without her husband in tow, Caroline Wilde walked in as though she owned the place. She was dressed in a cream Chanel suit that proclaimed her as a woman who didn't have to worry about getting filthy on public transport. She could wear satin Manolos because she rarely had to walk. Juliet hated her and was fascinated by her all at once. She held her breath as though to make herself invisible but still Caroline caught Juliet's eye and made a beeline for her.

'No Christopher?' was the first thing Caroline said.

'He's in a meeting,' said Juliet. 'But he'll be here before the performance starts, I'm sure.'

'Always in a meeting,' Caroline sighed. 'Tell me, Juliet, does he really work so hard or is he actually off tapping one of the secretaries?'

Juliet felt hot with fear but she need not have worried. Caroline's question was rhetorical. She was already looking about the room again, trying to catch the eye of a waiter. But when she succeeded, Caroline waved the champagne away and instead asked if she could have a glass of sparkling water. Having made her order, she turned back to Juliet with a conspiratorial smile on her face. Juliet understood at once that she was supposed to make some comment on Caroline's temperance. It took just a couple of seconds before the penny dropped with a resounding clunk.

'We've just had the twelve-week scan,' said Caroline.

Juliet felt the blood rush to her face, then, just as quickly, rush away again. While her body flushed hot and cold, she edged her way to the nearest table and leaned against it heavily.

'You're pregnant?' She tried to make it sound casual.

Caroline laid her hands over her belly.

'Not exactly planned. We were playing Vatican roulette,' she said with a laugh.

Juliet forced a laugh too. But of course, the implications were far from funny. Christopher had told her that he and his wife had not had sex since the birth of their youngest child and now here she was, smug as Angelina Jolie, cradling a very new bump. Juliet couldn't help doing the maths. If Caroline had just had her twelve-week scan then Christopher must have known his wife was pregnant when he presented Juliet with her birthday present and promised eternity four weeks earlier.

Subconsciously, Juliet touched the bangle that hadn't left her wrist since Christopher put it there. Suddenly it felt quite tight. Caroline noticed.

'Oooh, lovely,' she said. 'Isn't that Cartier? Christopher gave me a ring from the same collection for my birthday but I've had to take it off. My fingers are swollen already. I tell you, being pregnant is a nightmare. I am so angry with him for not being more careful!'

She wasn't the only one.

'Will you excuse me,' said Juliet. 'I've just seen an important client arrive.'

*   *   *

In reality, Juliet fled the Crush Room and headed straight for the Ladies. She shut herself in a cubicle and sat down on the closed toilet seat, shaking like a newborn lamb and trying her damnedest not to cry. Caroline. Pregnant! All Juliet's dreams crashed to the floor and shattered. Was Christopher going to have to stay in his marriage until this new child was eighteen? But it wasn't just that. Juliet knew that men didn't have to be *in love* to make love, but he had sworn to her that his marriage was dead in all but name. He had told her that he hadn't even seen Caroline naked in the best part of a decade.

Juliet knew now she had been stupid. She knew she had no one but herself to blame for the way her heart was breaking. Christopher had turned out to be like all the others. He hadn't fallen in love with her. He was just one more married man looking for a bit on the side and prepared to say whatever it took to get it.

Bastard. And to think he let her find out like this? Tonight, when she had to be on her best form, when she couldn't just cut her losses and go home.

It was half an hour before Juliet felt ready to come out of the cubicle. When she walked back into the reception – still feeling like her legs might buckle under her – Christopher was upon her in seconds.

'Where have you been?' he said. 'You're supposed to be the hostess. I've been looking for you for ages.'

Noticing that they were being watched by a couple of clients, Juliet forced a smile. 'I just had to have some air. Felt a bit light-headed. Maybe it was something I ate.'

'Well, you're back, thank goodness. Have I told you how sexy you look in that dress,' he drew her close and whispered. 'You're like a Hitchcock blonde. God, I wish we could be together tonight.'

Juliet looked straight towards Caroline, who was holding court with a bunch of bank colleagues' wives, hands still resting on her stomach.

'If you hadn't already spent so much time gone AWOL, I would suggest that we find somewhere to have a quickie,' he said in her ear.

'And I'm afraid I would have said no,' said Juliet.

'Is something the matter?' Christopher asked.

'I'm fine,' Juliet clenched her jaw.

She was so close to telling him exactly what was the matter, but fortunately for Christopher, they were interrupted by one of the most senior executives from Anglo-Italian, who had flown in from Milan specifically for the occasion.

'Christopher,' he said, saying the word in such a way that imbued it with extra syllables and a lot of romance. 'I need to pull you away from this beautiful woman for just a moment. I have someone I want you to meet.'

Christopher gave a little shrug in Juliet's direction as he allowed himself to be pulled away. Then a bell rang to announce the beginning of the performance. Juliet would have to wait.

The concert itself was agony to endure. It wasn't that the singing wasn't beautiful. It was just that every piece seemed to have been chosen to snatch up a handful of Juliet's heartstrings and tie them in a bow. Here was Mimi dying in *La Bohème*. Here was Liu sacrificing herself in *Turandot*. Here was bloody Tosca, trying and failing to save her lover's life and giving up her own. Juliet identified with every one of the doomed women but she could not and would not give in to tears right then. Three rows ahead, Christopher and his pregnant wife sat side by side, but in the seat beside Juliet was the global head of the Anglo-Italian banking group. She could not cry in front of him.

After the performance, the audience returned to the Crush Room for yet more drinks and small talk. Juliet circled the room. There were plenty of people she could and should have stopped to speak to, but she really wasn't sure how much longer she could hold it together. And so she just kept moving. Pausing and smiling before moving on as quickly as she could, pretending that there was always someone else she needed to find. And that worked perfectly well, until she found herself passing by the group of women where Caroline was holding court and, to her horror, one of the women grabbed her by the arm and pulled her into the circle.

'We need you to settle a question,' she said.

'Who has Ed Taylor brought along tonight?' asked one of the wives. 'I don't think I recognise her. Does she work at Anglo-Italian?'

Juliet shook her head. 'I don't know,' she said. 'I haven't had a chance to meet her properly.'

'I told you,' said Caroline, drawing them all closer. 'She definitely works at AI. But you'll never guess in what department.' Her brown eyes glittered maliciously. The other wives were intrigued. Caroline made sure she had everyone's attention before she delivered the punchline. 'I overheard her telling one of the clients. Are you ready for this?'

The women pleaded to be put out of their misery.

'Ed – our dear old Etonian Ed – has only gone and brought along one of the cleaners!'

The women erupted in shock and mirth.

'Oh my God!'

'That's crazy!'

'Couldn't he find a proper date?'

'A cleaner!' crowed Caroline. 'Can you imagine it? How low can you go? It's not even as though the girl's pretty! I've always thought Ed must be gay. Or maybe he has a thing about screwing a bit of rough? Perhaps she reminds him of the servants at his parents' stately home! An Anglo-Italian banker actually going out with a *cleaner*. Isn't that the most ridiculous thing you ever heard?'

The other women agreed. All except Juliet. Juliet didn't think it was ridiculous at all. And she said so. She'd heard plenty of sexist, racist and classist rubbish at this sort of gathering before. Ordinarily, she would have pretended she hadn't heard. In general, the guests at any Anglo-Italian bash were too valuable to offend by calling them out on their rudeness. But that night, Juliet didn't care. She let Caroline have it with both barrels.

'I don't see what your problem is, Caroline,' she said. 'At least Ed's date works for a living.'

Caroline raised her eyebrows. She must have known what Juliet was digging at. Caroline hadn't worked since her eldest son was born fifteen years earlier, despite having a full-time nanny and several other part time staff to help run the family home in Wimbledon.

'And I don't see what's low class about doing an honest day's work,' Juliet continued. 'To me, the only low-class thing I've seen in this room is the way you all reacted to Caroline's gossip.' She turned her sights on the other women. 'Thank goodness Ed has the sense to be able to see beyond job titles.'

The rest of the wives fell silent at Juliet's outburst but not Caroline. She wasn't in the least bit moved to contrition.

'I don't know why you're so defensive of her, Juliet. Is

there something in your CV you're not telling us? Did you start with a stint at the AI loos as well?'

The other women laughed, relieved that Caroline did not seem mortally wounded by Juliet's ticking off. Far from it. Her ego hadn't even sustained a graze.

'If I had, it wouldn't be something I would be ashamed of,' Juliet responded. 'I admire women who support them-selves, no matter how they do it.'

But Caroline wasn't listening any more. She just turned her back on Juliet, physically edging her out of the smug coven. Juliet was only too pleased to go.

She passed Christopher on the way out of the room.

'Where are you going?' he asked, grabbing her by the elbow as she tried to get by.

'I already told you. I'm not feeling great,' she said. 'I'm going home.'

Part of her wanted to tell him the truth but still she didn't dare. Not then, in a room full of her colleagues and her most important clients. Surely he would work it out in any case.

'Can I see you tomorrow night?' Christopher whispered urgently.

'I don't think so,' said Juliet, shaking her head. 'Why don't you go and talk to your wife?'

One final look back across the room found Caroline staring straight at her. If Caroline hadn't guessed before that Juliet and her husband had been having an affair, then in all certainty she had cottoned on now. But the look she gave Juliet was not murderous, as one might expect. Far from it, Caroline smiled with the smug assurance of a woman who knows she has won. She had the ring. She had the baby. She would have her husband back.

Chapter Nineteen

𝄞

𝓘F Caroline's intention had been to humiliate Mercy, she had succeeded.

Mercy had heard everything. She could tell that Ed had too. They had been standing not ten feet away and Caroline's coven was full of women who had the kind of cut-glass upper-class voices bred to carry over battlefields. Mercy and Ed had subconsciously fallen silent while Christopher's wife and her hideous friends laughed and then while Juliet upbraided her. Mercy didn't know what to do. Had she been in her comfort zone, she could have held her own. She would have waded in and told those witches that she was not ashamed of anything about her life, thank you very much. But she was definitely not in her comfort zone in a room full of uniformly middle- and upper-class white professionals and their trophy spouses. And so she just stood there, nursing her champagne glass, pretending she couldn't hear what was being said, while every word pierced her like another small, poisonous dart.

'It's not even as though the girl's pretty! A bit of rough!'

What could Mercy do except pretend it wasn't happening?

Unfortunately, Ed, dear Ed, chose the same plan of action too. He just stood there, fiddling nervously with his cufflinks just like the Prince of Wales.

Later, Mercy would wonder why he hadn't defended her. Had her grandfather heard someone talking that kind of shit about her grandmother, he would have waded in fists flying. But Ed chose to pretend that nothing was happening. He just smiled at Mercy and attempted to make more small talk about opera. Had she ever seen *Adriana Lecouvreur*?

Of course not, she wanted to shout at him. She had only ever seen *Tosca* and the performance they'd witnessed that evening. That was all the live opera she had ever seen. She never had the money to see anything else. Ed knew that. She'd told him on at least three occasions. Had he not paid attention to anything she said?

'I haven't seen it,' she half-whispered, as she struggled to keep the rising anger out of her voice. 'Look, Ed,' she glanced at her watch. 'It's late now. I should be going home.'

'It's early,' Ed protested.

'If I don't go soon, I'll have to get a night bus and they only come every half hour.'

'But I was going to ask you to join me for dinner. I've got a table booked just around the corner. An Italian place. I know you'll like it.'

'Dinner? At this time of night?'

'It's not so late.'

'I've got to go. I have to work tomorrow.'

'So do I. And I've got a six o'clock start. And that's six o'clock in the morning!'

'I want to go,' said Mercy firmly.

'Then I'll put you in a cab,' said Ed.

'I don't want to waste any money on a cab.'

'I'll take care of it,' Ed insisted. He seemed to reach for his wallet.

'No. Really. I don't want you to.'

Mercy didn't want anything from him. She especially didn't want that bitchy woman or any of her friends to see Ed handing over a twenty-pound note. She could well imagine the kind of response that might engender.

'Mercy,' said Ed, more assertively this time. 'I do not want you going home on public transport.'

'We'll talk about it in a minute,' she said, excusing herself to the Ladies'. But that wasn't her destination. Instead, she slipped straight out of the opera house and into the Covent Garden piazza, where she changed from her high-heeled shoes into a pair of flatties for the walk to the tube. For once she was grateful for the anonymity of the crowds of tourists who thronged the night-time streets.

How different she felt three hours earlier.

Ed had seemed so pleased to be with her. He had introduced her to lots of his colleagues and when she managed the odd joke that made someone laugh, Ed had seemed delighted and proud. Mercy allowed herself to think that evening might be the first of many such occasions.

Three hours later, however, reeling from the fact that he hadn't defended her from that awful bitch, it struck Mercy that Ed might have taken her along for her novelty value. Perhaps, to someone like him, a date with a black girl from south London was something to talk about. Maybe he felt it would give him kudos in the eyes of his colleagues. Well, that had backfired. They obviously thought Mercy was well beneath them.

Ed tried to find her, of course. Mercy's phone rang as she waited for the lift at Covent Garden. She didn't take the call. As she sat on the Victoria line, that vile woman's amused exclamation was still playing over and over in her head. Ignorant though that woman may have been, she was right. Mercy told herself that she had to stop pretending she an opera diva in embryo. She was a cleaner. She was a cleaner who liked opera. That was all.

As Mercy emerged from the tube station, her phone buzzed again. Ed had sent her a text.

'What happened to you, sneaking off like that? I wish you'd come for a drink at least,' he said. 'I hope you enjoyed tonight?'

What a question? Was he joking? Still . . .

'I enjoyed it very much,' she assured him in her reply, knowing that she would never find herself stepping out on Ed's arm again. And then she felt doubly sad for the girl who had stepped out that evening with so much excitement and hope and was now walking home in her tatty flat shoes like a Cinderella whose prince would never try to find her.

Act Two

Chapter Twenty

THOUGH Duncan had promised Cosima it would be otherwise, he had not managed to ensure that she and Nolan stayed in separate hotels. So when Cosima got up early the morning after the benefit to take a massage in the hotel spa, she had to walk past Nolan's room, and almost bumped into the girl coming out of it.

'See you later,' Nolan's voice called after his latest conquest.

Meeting Cosima's eyes at that moment, the girl did not return Nolan's cheery farewell but scuttled away shame-faced. Cosima pursed her lips and shook her head. She thought she recognised the girl as one of the violinists from their orchestra. Would Nolan never learn not to dip his pen in company ink? Cosima could already see how this would pan out. After a week or so the girl would begin to think she was in love; that it was the real thing. Meanwhile, Nolan would begin to feel claustrophobic. He would try to let her down gently, but in the end she would probably find out their fling was over from the girl who replaced her. And then there would be tears and tantrums and the orchestra would be a violinist down when the poor girl flew home with nothing but bad memories of Milan, or Venice or wherever the big bust-up finally happened. At least, thought Cosima cruelly, a violinist was relatively easily replaced.

As she enjoyed her massage, Cosima decided that it was time to make a pact with herself. If she was going to allow herself to be upset or even interested every time Nolan copped off with one of the chorus girls, it would make for an excruciatingly long and painful six weeks. She had to let go. Andrew, who had dabbled in Buddhism, had often told her that letting go was the real secret of happiness. She was beginning to think he was right. Certainly, Andrew seemed extremely chilled out and managed a very friendly relationship with his ex-wife. He was even godfather to her second son.

Cosima thought she wanted that kind of relationship with Nolan. From now on, whatever Nolan O'Connor did was none of her business. He was just a colleague. Perhaps at some point in the future he would also be a friend. First she had to get past her residual anger towards him. Later that day, she found herself an elastic band. She slipped it around her wrist with the intention of snapping it against her skin every time something Nolan did or said upset her. The same method had worked when she was trying to give up coffee. Every time she thought she fancied a cup of Joe, she would snap the band and keep on snapping until she reached for the herbal tea instead.

While Cosima had her massage, Nolan was definitely feeling in need of one. Contrary to Cosima's assumption, Nolan had not spent the night making love to the violinist in his enormous double bed. Instead he had snatched just fifteen minutes of shut-eye on the suite's over-stuffed and surprisingly uncomfortable sofa, while Chelsea the violinist lay on his bed as though it were a psychiatrist's couch and regaled him with endless tales of her most recent ex-boyfriend.

It wasn't even as though Nolan had *wanted* to spend the night with Chelsea. When she asked if she could come back to his room for a nightcap, he tried to put her off. He reminded her that everyone in the company needed to be on top form for the first night of the tour which was coming up fast. That meant getting lots of sleep. But tears had glittered in the corners of Chelsea's eyes and Nolan had been powerless to resist her plea to have just one drink and a very short chat about her woeful love life.

'I won't keep you long at all. I promise. It's just that you seem to understand how women feel,' Chelsea told him.

'Tell Cosima that,' Nolan thought to himself.

So, Chelsea had inveigled her way into Nolan's suite and settled down for a long session of free psychoanalysis. Having listened to her for two hours, Nolan told her it was clear her ex didn't care for her and it was time to start moving on. That prompted such a torrent of tears that Nolan had to listen to the whole tale again until she calmed down, lest someone see her leaving his room all red-eyed and think the worst.

Chelsea really didn't seem to see how hopeless her situation with this bloke of hers was at all. She seemed so naïve. So young. Just twenty-one. Nolan couldn't help thinking how different Cosima had been at that age. As Chelsea went back over the promise of her early dates with her worthless ex, Nolan remembered his own first date with Cosima. At the time, he could hardly believe that she'd agreed to go out with him at all. Cosima was a goddess. A serious cut above his previous girlfriends. He'd been so nervous when he approached her that his voice had squeaked halfway through his invitation, as though he were fourteen years old and just hitting puberty again. Still, Cosima had said yes and so Nolan spent a whole month's rent money on taking her to La Grenouille, the ridiculously over-the-top old school French restaurant in Manhattan, because he knew he had competition and he wanted her to be impressed. (As it turned out, it wasn't her first time there). At the end of the evening, he escorted her home in a cab. At the door to her apartment building she told him, 'Nolan O'Connor, you call me tomorrow or you never call me again.'

How could he disobey? Though the evening had bankrupted him and he had to walk fifty-three blocks in the rain back to the tiny place he was sub-letting from a friend for the duration of his stay in NYC, Nolan could not have been more delighted. He was besotted. Cosima wanted to see him again. He called her the next day and the next and the next and the next. He begged to be allowed to fill every moment of her spare time. He would have walked fifty blocks in the rain any night of the week for Cosima.

'I would have walked over broken glass for her. That is what someone will do when they love you,' he tried to explain to Chelsea when finally she paused for breath.

'But you were unfaithful to her, right?' Chelsea pointed out. 'At least that's what I heard.'

Nolan turned to look out of the window, which was open because Chelsea was a smoker – another reason why Nolan would not have considered bedding her.

'I was unfaithful,' said Nolan. 'And it may well have been the biggest mistake I ever made.'

'Why did you do it?' Chelsea asked. 'I want to know. It might help me work out what I did to push John away.'

Nolan shook his head. 'You can't extrapolate how John feels from what I did. Every relationship is different. But I think I cheated on Cosima because I wanted her to pay more attention to me. Her career was just taking off. Everyone wanted to cast her in their opera. Whenever the phone rang in our apartment it was her agent, asking her to sing for the calibre of directors I wanted to be begging for me. I tried to be happy for her but I started to feel like her secretary, taking messages from so-and-so at La Scala and what's-his-name at Glyndebourne. I thought it was turning her head. I thought that one day soon she might start to think she had made a mistake in getting married to me, because her talent was so much bigger than mine. So I acted like a spoiled child. I didn't care if she found out I'd been unfaithful, because having her scream and yell at me was almost as good as having her hang on my every word again. It was attention.'

'Sounds like an explanation your shrink might have suggested,' said Chelsea. 'Sounds pathetic.'

Nolan nodded. 'You're right.'

Cosima began her elastic band treatment at the very next rehearsal. At first, Nolan said something that made her hackles rise at least once a minute on average. But about two days into the rubber-band project, she decided that she was feeling a little better. It was like that time when she was a child, when her mother suggested to her that she should always count to three before walloping her older brother in response to some silly tease. Cosima had practised her mother's advice religiously for several weeks. The results were good. Though Cosima didn't stop walloping her brother when he teased her, the three-second pause gave her time to take proper aim.

Pinging the elastic band had a similar effect, giving Cosima time to hone her barbs rather than react willy-nilly. She knew that her colleagues all called her 'Miss Piggy' behind her back, thanks to that witch Judy Shephard. If she was going to be remembered for her temper, she wanted it to be for the sophistication of her rapier wit, not because she had the self-control of a Muppet.

It seemed to work. It wasn't long before Nolan began to notice that something was different about the woman who had once been his wife. Her hair-trigger temper seemed slightly less, well, hair-trigger. Now, she was as serene as a novice nun. Karl and the rest of the company were also relieved. The first performance of *Tosca* was just a day away. Karl dared to believe it might actually happen.

Chapter Twenty-One

WHILE Karl congratulated his team on their dress rehearsal, Florence Carter's plane was just touching down at Heathrow. What a journey it had been. Though she had filled the long nights of her childhood reading books about Italy and France and the kings and queens of England, Florence had never been outside the United States in her life. To leave her home for a six-week tour of Europe was a surprisingly stressful endeavour.

Still, the British Airways staff had gone some way to making her feel comfortable with their lovely accents and their great manners and the guy in the seat next to hers had been very kind, allowing her to grip his arm on take-off – Florence hated take-off and landing. He had listened to her talk about her trip for a little while too and professed himself to be a fan of Puccini. But three hours into the flight he had taken a sleeping pill and slept until the bumpy landing in London. When he woke to find Florence gripping his arm again, he had looked a little surprised.

She lost him in the terminal. He, being British, was allowed to enter the country through the EU Nationals channel. Florence had to go elsewhere and wait longer while the immigration officer checked her visa waiver. But thankfully, all was in order and Florence was finally on British soil. Her enormous suitcase had made it too, despite the reputation of Terminal Five's baggage handling. She dragged it through the terminal in search of the tube station, and thence on the Piccadilly line to Caledonian Road station. The travel agent had chosen a hotel there for its alleged proximity to Covent Garden, according to the Internet search engine he used.

The tube journey was long. Really long. More than an hour. Feeling horribly jet-lagged, Florence fell asleep a couple of times. Once a young man who was concerned for her purse jogged her awake. He seemed to be trying to tuck it out of sight for her but she made it to Caledonian Road with her purse still on her shoulder. In any case, her real valuables, her passport and her traveller's cheques, were in a secret pochette wrapped around her waist and concealed by her red fleecy sweater. Florence wasn't a fool. She'd heard from her mother's best friend that London was full of pickpockets. It was practically a national sport.

'You'll need water purification tablets too,' the same helpful woman had told her.

At the Caledonian Road tube station, she asked for directions. The Underground worker raised an eyebrow when she told him the name of the hotel, but confirmed that it was indeed a short walk from the tube stop. 'Towards the prison.'

The prison? 'Oh.'

That was Florence's first clue that she hadn't exactly lighted upon the best address in town. Indeed, even the hotel receptionist seemed surprised to have a booking.

'You sure you haven't been referred,' she asked, 'by the council?'

'No,' said Florence. 'I'm visiting from the United States.'

'Well,' said the receptionist. 'I'll show you to your room. It's shared bathroom.'

'I'd rather have en suite.'

'There are no en suite bathrooms here.'

'That's not what it said on the website.'

'I don't know nothing about any website.'

The receptionist showed Florence to a room that was smaller than the closet she had back home. It was furnished with a narrow single bed covered in a grey blanket, a bedside table and a dining chair. There was no wardrobe. Just a few hooks that bore wire coat hangers. There was a little basin in one corner. The tap dribbled a sad trickle of rust-red water.

'You don't have a better room?' Florence asked.

'This *is* the best room,' the receptionist claimed.

Florence was horrified. She called her travel agent at once, hoping he would tell her there had been a mix-up. There hadn't.

'It was the only hotel within your price range,' the travel agent reminded her. 'London isn't cheap.'

The trip had been so carefully budgeted, choosing the least expensive hotels possible so that she would have enough money over for one of the very best seats at each of Nolan's performances. Florence momentarily shut her eyes on the horrible scene and told herself she would just have to get on with it. After all, it was just a couple of nights. She only had to sleep there. She would be out all day sightseeing.

As it happened, she soon discovered she had no choice about being out all day.

'Guests have to vacate their rooms between nine in the morning and six in the evening,' the receptionist told her.

'What?'

'Those are the rules of the hostel. But you can leave your stuff here. I have to keep the key though.'

As Florence headed out onto the street again, wistful for the nap she so desperately needed, a pair of policemen was heading into the hotel. Florence glanced behind her to see them talking to the receptionist. The girl shrugged and gave them a handful of keys. That was why keys had to be left at reception. So the police could easily get inside a room for a search.

Florence found a call box and telephoned her mother to confirm that she had arrived safely.

'And how's your hotel, dear?' her mother asked.

'Oh, it's great,' Florence lied. 'Just like you'd imagine a London hotel to be.'

Florence determined to make the best of it. Seeing Nolan would make everything worthwhile.

Chapter Twenty-Two

JULIET knew that she had to end her affair with Christopher. All weekend she turned the events of that evening at the opera over in her mind, but there was no way to put a positive spin on it. She had been engaged in a five-year affair with a married man. Given that he had lied to his wife for that long, it should have come as no surprise to find out that he had lied to her too. And yet . . . It was going to be hard to let that man go.

After all, Juliet had no one else in her life. She was an only child. She didn't speak to either of her parents. She'd never been especially close to either of them. She was a forces child, moving from country to country according to where her father was posted; spending half the year in boarding schools where she never quite fitted in among the girls whose parents, rather than the army, were paying for their education. Her father had practically disowned her when she chose to stay with her mother after the divorce (though really, an eleven-year-old should never have been asked to make the decision). Her relationship with her mother had deteriorated more slowly. Clare Hunter never quite recovered from the stigma of losing her husband. She started drinking in an effort to forget all about it. She filled her evenings with a succession of awful, equally alcoholic men. Once Juliet left for university, she never moved back home again.

It just didn't seem fair that a woman like Caroline, who seemed so careless of other people and their feelings, should have everything that Juliet wanted.

Christopher had always claimed that Caroline had trapped him. Apparently, she had announced that she was pregnant with their first child after they had been dating for just over three months. Her father told Christopher that they were getting married before it arrived and Christopher agreed. Caroline's father was not a man you disagreed with. *Fait accompli*.

From time to time, Juliet hated Christopher for being so weak that he would just give in like that when he might have kept himself free for the day he met her. Who got married after three months these days, even if the girl got pregnant? On other occasions, she admired him for doing the right thing by his child. Unfortunately for Juliet, that was why she could be certain that he would do the 'right thing' by Caroline again.

Immediately after that night at the opera, Christopher left London for a week-long banking conference in Florida. The original intention was that Juliet should go with him but Juliet had decided right before the opera night that there was too much to be done in London. And so Christopher went alone and Juliet stayed behind to stew on what she had learned from Caroline.

When David called up and asked her if she would like to go out for dinner, she gratefully accepted the chance to be distracted.

After dinner, David insisted that they share a taxi and that Juliet be dropped off first. It seemed only natural to invite him in.

'Have you just moved in?' he asked, looking around her apartment.

Juliet was embarrassed by the lack of furniture and decoration.

'Seven years,' she said apologetically. 'I've been meaning to buy some paintings and things but I never seem to get round to it. There's always something that needs to be done more urgently. Something to do with work.' She shrugged her shoulders.

'I know that feeling,' said David.

'But I've got a week's holiday coming up. I'll go to John Lewis and do a blitz.'

'What? And get some mass produced prints? You can do better than that.'

'Says the man who had that poster of a girl on a tennis court scratching her bum on his wall at college.'

'It was a classic,' David laughed.

'Coffee?'

'I'd prefer something stronger,' said David.

'Me too,' said Juliet. 'I think I might have some Calvados somewhere.'

Juliet poured the golden liquid out into her best glasses: a pair of enormous hand-blown brandy bowls. They had been a gift from Christopher to make up for a rendezvous missed, a rare occasion. She had only ever used them with him. Whenever Christopher was able to spend the night at her place, Juliet pulled out all the stops and made him a sumptuous dinner, which they followed with brandy as they snuggled on the sofa. It was the only time Juliet ever bothered to cook at home.

David had already installed himself on the rug in front of the 'living flame' gas fire. He'd taken up Christopher's usual position.

'I've got chairs,' she said. There had been a point when she lived in a flat furnished only with beanbags but that was long gone.

'I'm more comfortable down here,' said David. He was fiddling about with the fire, working out how to turn it on. He succeeded. 'Why don't you join me?'

'It's nearly August,' said Juliet, nodding towards the fire.

'But it is bloody cold,' David observed. She couldn't disagree. She joined him on the floor. The gas made a 'whompfing' noise as the fire burst into life.

'Tell me about the job you're working on,' Juliet asked David as they sipped their Calvados and watched the flames flicker over fake logs.

'It's dull,' David assured her. 'I spend my days looking at data.'

'Who are you working with?'

'A bunch of morons who have very unrealistic expectations of my abilities,' he told her. 'Who think that throwing their weight around from time to time will persuade me to split the atom, which is the equivalent of what they expect me to be able to do with a piece of banking software.'

'What's the name of the company you're working for?' Juliet persisted.

'Like you,' said David. 'I have signed a confidentiality agreement.'

'Touché.'

'Besides, I don't want to talk about work. Do you remember that time we rented a cottage in Wales one summer?'

'How could I forget?'

Along with four other students, David and Juliet had paid for a week's self-catering near Dolgellau. None of them could afford to go abroad. Wales was cheap and they hoped that they would have some luck with the weather, it being August. But they had been badly caught out. Torrential rain that, thanks to the driving wind, was sometimes horizontal. They soon understood why Welsh mountain sheep always look so miserable. So much for the picnics on the beach they had planned. They'd spent pretty much the whole week playing cards indoors. They had to light a fire.

More than a decade later, David told Juliet, 'Seeing you sitting in front of this fire takes me right back. I remember how lovely you looked as you gazed into the flames like some heroine from a Victorian painting. You haven't changed. Still beautiful.'

Juliet batted the compliment away.

'And I still want to kiss you.'

He leaned towards her. Not knowing what else to do, Juliet put down her glass. He kissed her. He took her head in both hands and pulled her towards him and kissed her right on the mouth. Before she knew it, she was kissing him back. She felt a rush of heat through the centre of her body like the gas flame leaping into life moments earlier. But as he tried to pull her down onto the rug beside him, she pushed him off. Lightly but firmly.

'Did I do the wrong thing?' he asked.

'Yes. No. I mean, I don't know,' Juliet told him. 'It's bad timing. I've got a lot of things going on. I can't explain.'

David told her he needed no explanation.

'You can't blame me for seizing the opportunity,' he said. 'You're beautiful, Juliet, and every bit as wonderful as I remember.'

'Oh, David.'

'I'll leave you for now,' he added. 'But you know that you can call me whenever you want. I'll always be there for you.'

He opened his arms. Juliet stepped into them for a hug.

'Thank you,' she said. 'Thanks for understanding.'

After David was gone, Juliet found a text on her BlackBerry from Christopher. He wanted to know if she would see him at the weekend. Caroline was taking the boys to see her parents in Shropshire. Juliet texted 'yes'. Better to get Christopher out of her life sooner rather than later. Sitting on her bed, she glanced at the Cartier bangle on her dressing table. She'd taken it off the day she found out Caroline was pregnant and hadn't put it back on since. She wondered what Christopher was thinking. Did he think that Caroline's being away would give him the chance to spend a whole weekend in bed with his mistress? And then she thought about David and what it would be like to have him in her bed instead.

Chapter Twenty-Three

𝄞

MERCY did not want to go back to Anglo-Italian. The conversation she had overheard at the opera reception had lodged itself in her mind far more firmly than Cosima Esposito's fabulous voice. What a hellish evening that had been. It was bad enough to have that memory. To risk seeing Ed every day would only exaggerate the pain.

'I need to be put onto another job,' she told Hazel.

'Why?' Hazel asked, her already small eyes narrowing further as she waited for some juicy gossip.

'It's just that getting there is such a pain,' Mercy lied. 'There are engineering works on the tube line all the time and the bus trip takes over an hour each way. Haven't you got something nearer my home?'

'Mercy,' said Hazel. 'We're a City cleaner. We specialise in jobs in the City. The clue is in our name. City Clean Stars. We don't have contracts anywhere else.'

'Nothing?'

'Nothing. And there's nothing I can move you onto in any case. Do you know how many people would step up and take your job?'

'I'm not complaining about the job itself,' said Mercy.

'Then what's happened?' Hazel probed. 'Has someone had a go at you? Tell me who it was. I'll sort them out.'

It was on the tip of Mercy's tongue to tell Hazel exactly what had happened. But she wouldn't understand. Or perhaps it was that Mercy could imagine Hazel's response only too well. She would tell her that she had been foolish to think that she could ever cross over into that world. Ed was public-school educated. He came from a wealthy and important family. He was of the Brahmin class. Mercy had grown up in a council house. She knew the postman better than she knew own father. People like Mercy and her City Clean Star colleagues had to know their place.

'I'll go back to Anglo-Italian,' she said. 'But can you put me on a different floor?'

Hazel rolled her eyes and turned her attention to her clipboard. 'I'll put you on the sixteenth. OK?'

'I'm really grateful,' said Mercy. 'Really, really grateful. Thanks.'

'You won't be,' said Hazel. 'They're a right bunch of pigs up there.'

Mercy thought she would be safe, working on a different floor, but just a day later, as she stepped out of the lift pushing her overloaded trolley, Mercy bumped into Ed. It was as though he had been waiting for her.

'I've been waiting for you,' he confirmed.

Mercy tried to get past him.

'Why haven't you answered any of my calls?' he asked. 'I

thought you'd quit. I had to ask one of the other girls to tell me where you'd gone to.'

'I've got work to do,' she said.

'It can wait. Look, Mercy, I think I've worked out what went wrong. I know you heard what that stupid woman said about us in the Crush Room and it made you feel embarrassed. I hope you know that I don't care what she thinks.'

If you meant that, thought Mercy, then you might have stood up for me when it happened. Ed didn't seem to understand that his reaction – or rather his lack of reaction – had made the whole situation worse. Mercy longed for him to wake up to that and tell her that he was sorry but he didn't.

He denigrated the woman a little. ' I really don't know who she thinks she is anyway,' he continued. 'As far as I know, she's never done a day's work in her life.'

But he didn't get anywhere near suggesting he should have done anything differently. As she listened to his speech, Mercy almost began to dislike him. He hadn't stood up for her at the opera. He would be no good if she ever really needed his support. Finally, Mercy could stand it no longer.

'It's not because of that stupid woman. It's because . . . it's because I've already got a boyfriend,' Mercy lied.

Ed's mouth opened in surprise.

'I should have told you but I really wanted to go to the opera. I didn't think you would take me if you knew. I'm sorry.'

Ed's shoulders drooped. Mercy was surprised to see him react quite so openly. She could tell she had scored a direct hit on his heart. Or rather on his pride, she corrected herself. What man wanted to think that a girl had gone out with him solely because he had tickets to a benefit? She felt sad and ashamed. But not, she reminded herself, as sad and ashamed as Ed should have felt for failing to stick up for her!

'In that case,' said Ed, his expression changing like a shop sign flipping from 'open' to 'closed', 'I won't waste any more of your time.'

He walked away without looking back. Mercy remained where she was, looking skywards in an attempt to keep from crying. She couldn't cry. She had heard Hazel's voice in the corridor behind her. Now Hazel drew level with her.

'Was that him?' Hazel asked. 'Your problem. What did he say to you? He doesn't look like a sex pest. You could snap him over your knee.'

'He's not a sex pest,' said Mercy. 'And he didn't say anything.' Which was true in a sense.

'All right,' said Hazel, giving Mercy a little squeeze. 'I'm not going to push you. How about you get us a couple of teas from the machine and we have a little sit down.'

As she went to fetch tea, Mercy noticed that the woman who had stood up for her was still in her office too. Mercy couldn't help but look in on the beautiful banker with her shining blond hair and expensive clothes.

'You've got it so easy,' Mercy thought to herself. 'Probably always have had.'

Mercy had no doubt that woman had been born with a silver spoon in her mouth. The right school and the right university had been her birthright. She probably lived in the kind of glossy apartment Mercy could only ever hope to clean. She was exactly the kind of woman Ed Taylor would end up with.

The woman looked up and saw Mercy looking in. Mercy turned away quickly, almost missing Juliet's flutter-fingered 'hello'.

Chapter Twenty-Four

𝄞

NOLAN was finding it very hard to sleep. It wasn't like him at all. Ordinarily, Nolan O'Connor did not have trouble sleeping. Even his mother had commented that he slept the sleep of the innocent, no matter what he had been getting up to. Now Nolan was waking at four in the morning, every morning, like clockwork. And the first thing that came to his mind each time was Cosima Esposito. What was it about that damn woman? Sure, he had fallen in love with her the moment he met her at a benefit in New York. He could remember it so clearly – the drama of her long dark hair and the red dress that showcased her boobs as though they were a pair of sugar-dusted doughnuts. And they had had a very passionate courtship. But he had been married to her since then. No matter how sexy she looked, he knew for certain that she could be a monumental pain in the arse. She could be jealous and selfish and utterly irrational to boot. He had felt enormously relieved when the divorce came through. And the past five years had been fantastic. He'd enjoyed all the fun he'd had as a single man prior to meeting Cosima, with the added bonus that he was richer and more famous now and the quality of the totty was commensurately higher.

Why was she on his mind so much? Was this what was called 'unfinished business'?

The following day, Cosima looked as beautiful as ever when she arrived for rehearsal. She had been taking care not to get burnt out on this tour. While some of the younger cast members hit the hottest nightspots in town every evening, Cosima would have a quiet dinner and an early night with Andrew. The result was that she glowed with health and vitality. Nolan could hardly stand it. He had to bury himself between those breasts again.

'So,' said Cosima, as she surreptitiously pinged her elastic band. 'How did it work out with the PR girl?'

'I excused myself and had room service,' said Nolan.

'Why?' asked Cosima. 'Did you forget to pack your Viagra?'

'It's our first full performance tonight. I want to make sure I'm at my best,' Nolan said primly.

Karl said he was very pleased to hear it.

But disaster was about to strike.

Nolan and Cosima may have been on fine form but Donald Law, who was to play the evil Baron Scarpia, suddenly found himself put out of action by a sore throat caught by snogging a twenty-something accountancy student who liked to dress in leather at the weekends. The rest of the cast weren't made privy to the circumstances of Donald's getting ill, of course, but they all had to deal with the consequences. When Karl heard the news, he was beside himself with anxiety. Donald's understudy, Damiano Banfi, had flown back to New York that very morning, having heard that his elderly mother had been taken into hospital. The poor chap's mother was dying, Karl could hardly expect him to fly back.

But it left the company without a decent baritone. And the role of Scarpia was no three-line piece.

After a fruitless morning spent calling every baritone within three hours' flying time of London, Karl called the principal members of his company together to tell them what had happened. The choices as he saw them were that they would have to cancel the first performance altogether or they could quickly work up something else so that the crowd wouldn't be entirely disappointed. Perhaps Nolan and Cosima could do an evening of their best love duets?

'But people have paid to see *Tosca*,' said Cosima. 'They don't want to see our greatest hits.'

'I can do it,' said Nolan.

Karl and Cosima looked at him in confusion. 'Do what?'

'I can sing Scarpia.'

'But you're a tenor,' Karl and Cosima pointed out in unison.

'With incredible range,' Nolan reminded them. He was in fact quoting directly from a review in the *New York Times*.

Karl looked sceptical. Cosima announced, 'It can't be done.'

'Placido did it,' Nolan pointed out.

'Er, yeah,' said Cosima. 'You're talking about Placido *Domingo*. One of the best singers of his generation. One of the best tenors ever.'

Nolan nodded. He considered himself to be the best of his own crop of tenors at the very least.

'I suppose . . .' said Karl hesitantly. 'I suppose it wouldn't do any harm to hear Nolan sing a few of Scarpia's songs.'

'It's a waste of time,' said Cosima. 'He won't be able to do it.'

'Give me a chance,' said Nolan.

The rehearsal accompanist was called back in to work. He sat down at his piano every bit as sceptical as Karl and Cosima. Andrew Fleetwood also joined them. He had been expecting to have some time alone with Cosima that morning, so felt he had every right to be at this impromptu rehearsal if that was keeping her from him.

Nolan sang a few scales, taking it deeper than usual. Cosima affected an expression that suggested the sound of them was hurting her ears. And then, with a nod to the pianist, Nolan launched into Scarpia's second act entrance.

'*Tosca e un buon falco!* . . . *Certo a quest'ora* . . .' Tosca is a good falcon . . .

Cosima, who had been lolling in her chair, sat upright and narrowed her eyes suspiciously. Andrew Fleetwood frowned hard in concentration as he listened for the slightest mistake. There was none. Nolan hit every note.

'You know what this reminds me of,' said Bill the pianist as he came to the end of the music and gave Nolan a round of applause. 'It reminds me of that moment in Britain's Got Talent when that hairy woman opened her mouth and sang "I Dreamed a Dream."'

Karl certainly thought he was dreaming. Nolan wasn't the best baritone he had ever heard, but he was far from being the worst. If he could keep it up, it might just work.

'I had no idea you could do that,' said Karl. 'You're a dark horse.'

Nolan shrugged but he looked towards Cosima as if hoping she would confirm it.

'Will you let me try it tonight?' he asked.

Karl looked at Cosima. The rest of the company would go along with whatever he said. His word as musical director was their command. Only Cosima had to be convinced. And if she could be convinced, it would certainly save him a headache. The show could go on. He knew that some people would be disappointed to see a performance without Donald Law and with a well-known *tenor* in the deeper baritone role, but he was equally certain that the majority of the audience would have no idea that anything was awry. They would be pleased to see Nolan if he was singing a medley of Peter Andre's greatest hits. If Karl stepped out onstage before the performance and begged their indulgence for a slightly different evening at the opera than they had anticipated, he was sure that he would get it.

'This is ridiculous,' said Cosima. 'If you're seriously intending to let Nolan sing a role he's barely prepared for, who'll play Mario?'

The problem was not that easily solved. Nolan's understudy, Antony, had also recently been laid low with strep throat and, while he was singing well enough to play Spoletta, Karl knew that he would make a disappointing lead, even if he managed to get through all three acts without needing a lie down.

It was Andrew who came up with the solution. He couldn't keep the excitement from his eyes as he considered the impact of his suggestion.

'I can sing Mario,' he said. 'You all know I've played the

role several times. Though the costume won't fit me too well,' he pointed out, reminding everyone that Nolan was a bit of a porker compared to Andrew, who had recently lost eleven pounds on Atkins.

'This is crazy, said Cosima.

'I think it's worth a shot,' said Karl.

Nolan and Andrew agreed.

'Nice work, O'Connor,' said Andrew. 'I look forward to singing alongside you.'

They shook hands on the plan. Bill the pianist wondered if he was the only one who was reminded of the moment two boxers touch gloves before they pound each other's heads in.

Andrew's sudden elevation from cast member's boyfriend to cast member required some extra practice, of course. Andrew was thrilled to be able to play Mario if only for one night. Subconsciously, he wanted to show that arrogant cock Nolan that he was his equal as a singer, and his better as Cosima Esposito's lover.

But it didn't go exactly as planned. At least not in rehearsal. Cosima, who had quickly become used to singing with Nolan again, was surprisingly impatient as Andrew tried to catch up to the part on an unfamiliar stage. Of course, he had watched numerous dress rehearsals and actual performances, but that was different from being up there on the stage. The set looked quite different when you were right in the middle of it.

Cosima sighed quite audibly when Andrew asked if they could go through their first song together for a fifth time. And matters were made worse when Andrew saw Nolan, just offstage, give a little smirk at his ex-wife's obvious annoyance.

'Will you please ask the other cast members to stay out of sight unless they are about to enter a scene,' Andrew complained to Karl.

Cosima had to give Nolan 'the look'.

Things got better during the afternoon. Andrew finally got the blocking right. All that was left was to make a few tweaks to Nolan's costume so that it would fit him more snugly. The wardrobe mistress appeared with a mouthful of pins and started to adjust the back of Nolan's trousers.

'Your waist is smaller,' she observed. 'But your shoulders are wider. You look like you're going to burst out of that shirt.'

Andrew looked across at Nolan. He'd scored a point at last. Nolan pretended not to notice. Cosima stayed clear of them both. She told Karl that she just needed a few moments of peace to gather herself for the night ahead. What she really wanted was to be away from her ex and her boyfriend and their silly schoolboy posturing.

The news that Andrew Fleetwood would be replacing Nolan and that Nolan would be playing Scarpia was duly typed onto a flyer to be inserted into the programmes. Notices were tacked onto the doors of the opera house, so that anyone who really objected to the change of cast could ask for a refund. No one did. To any regular opera goer, the chance to see Andrew Fleetwood sing was just as inter-esting as seeing old-timer Donald Law. To see Nolan tackle a baritone role was a real coup. And so the first night of the tour went ahead as planned and they opened to another full house.

'The gods are with us,' said Karl.

It certainly seemed that way for a while. At the end of Act

One, Andrew told Cosima he was very pleased with how the performance was going. The audience, who had been informed that he had stepped in at the last minute, gave him a very healthy round of applause as soon as he opened his mouth. He fancied that it was a bigger, better and longer round of applause than Nolan had received for his first big solo as Scarpia.

However, it was all to kick off in Act Two, during the scene in which Scarpia has Cavaradossi dragged in to his lair for questioning. Andrew had spent the entire first interval psyching himself up to play this moment where, under torture, he would deny any knowledge of his fugitive friend, thus putting his own life at terrible risk. It was an important moment in the opera; a moment of dramatic intensity. Would Cavaradossi bend to Scarpia's will? Of course, almost everyone in the audience knew that he wouldn't (it said so in the programme), but Andrew wanted them to believe that, for the first time in the history of Puccini's *Tosca*, the outcome might be in doubt. He wanted to sing in such a way that the audience believed he was in genuine pain and danger. He wanted to give them proper drama. And he did. He sang as though each note dragged another vital organ from his body. He twisted as his captors held him in their iron grasp, with his face as every bit as contorted as his body. To act so bodily and still get every note out with such clarity was quite a feat. Andrew knew that everyone in the theatre would understand and appreciate his efforts.

But then, as Andrew sang '*Non lo so*' (I don't know) for the second time, Nolan rolled his eyes and winked at the audience, as if to say 'What a drama queen!' And Andrew caught the end of Nolan's little piece of pantomime. Why else had half the left side of the auditorium had to stifle a giggle? Jesus, that man. Andrew could not believe that Nolan would have been such a prick! To make light of his big moment like that. It was completely out of order.

Andrew would not let Nolan's silly little prank undo him. He finished the scene with the blaze of real hatred in his eyes. The audience, knowing nothing of the professional and personal rivalry between the two men, were merely impressed by the realism that the two men brought to the onstage relationship between Cavaradossi and his nemesis. Most of the people in the wings assumed they were simply seeing an outstanding performance. No one backstage had caught Nolan's wink or knew anything of Andrew's blood rage. No one except Cosima, that is. She saw it all.

'The bastard,' she hissed under her breath.

The scene played on. Cosima, as Tosca, was brought in to learn her lover's fate and be offered a chance to save herself by grassing him up. Cosima loved the second act. She especially loved her costume, an empire-line dress that glittered with more sequins than a whole line up at the Crazy Horse. On her head she wore a spectacular tiara. Around her neck hung an enormous diamante crucifix, shooting out shards of light that appeared to be coming straight from her heart as the gigantic jewel nestled in her cleavage. Cosima always felt at her most beautiful as she joined this scene in Act Two. That night, however, she entered with a look of thunder on her face that was thoroughly at odds with the beauty of her dress and general appearance.

Tosca too was questioned by Scarpia and defended her lover for as long as she was able. But the sound of Cavaradossi being tortured offstage (Andrew was still angry as a bull stung on the backside by a hornet and bellowed in an especially tormented way), soon made Tosca crumble and admit the whereabouts of the fugitive, her lover's friend. After that, Cavaradossi's fate was sealed. He would be executed.

For the previous two weeks, the former husband and wife had been playing lovers. The relationship between Scarpia and Tosca was altogether closer to what Cosima had felt for Nolan the past five years. When it came to the moment where Tosca stabs Scarpia in the heart, Cosima did look positively murderous. Nolan rolled on the floor, hamming it up something rotten as Cosima tried to finish her song.

And at the very end of the scene, when Tosca has to reach into her dead tormentor's pocket to retrieve the papers that will ensure a safe passage for her and her lover from Rome, Nolan played his masterstroke.

'E avanti a lui tremora tutta Roma,' Cosima half-whispered the last line of the act. 'Before him the whole of Rome trembled.' It was beautifully done. But as she leaned over him, and gently, almost tenderly, laid her crucifix upon Nolan's bleeding chest, he gave one final, extremely dramatic, shudder, sending her shrieking into the air like a terrified cat.

Cosima's composure was completely shattered. Instead of creeping slowly from Scarpia's room, as was called for by the score, she high-tailed it out of there, barely managing not to shout, 'Nolan O'Connor, you total shit!' before the curtain came down.

Nolan almost bust Donald Law's costume, he was laughing so hard as he came backstage to find that while most of the cast were doubled over in laughter with him, Cosima and Andrew were ready to commit murder for real. Karl was also unimpressed.

'It's really not on, Nolan. Really not at all. You can't play Scarpia for laughs.'

'What did I do wrong?' Nolan asked, all faux innocence. 'I was just trying to inject some verisimilitude. Everyone knows that corpses often give a final shudder as the air escapes from their lungs.'

'Oh!' Cosima turned around in a great swishing of skirts and flounced away from him.

'It's one thing to monkey with another guy's moment,' said Andrew. 'But if you're out to make a laughing stock of Cosima too, then you're going to have me to answer to.'

'Oh, lighten up,' said Nolan. 'It was wrong, sure, but the audience enjoyed it. I was starting to get the feeling that my big lines would be drowned out by the snores if I didn't liven things up.'

That was too much for Andrew. He took a swing at Nolan. Nolan was momentarily surprised and looked as though he might fall over, but he quickly recovered himself and took a swing back far more effectively. Andrew hit the deck.

'Nolan! Andrew! Stop it!' Cosima was back on the scene and shrieking at the top of her well-insured lungs.

Andrew struggled back to his feet and swung for Nolan again, connecting only with the belly of his costume that was padded for the stab scene. Nolan didn't feel a thing. Andrew did feel quite a bit, however, when Nolan's fist connected with his head.

'Somebody stop them!' Cosima was yelling. 'Somebody pull them apart!'

She tried to throw herself into the middle of the action, but was swiftly pulled back out again by the costume mistress who feared for the expensive train of Cosima's dress. It was studded with ten thousand real Swarovski crystals! Karl attempted to calm things down but the two tenors took about as much notice of him as they usually did (which is to say, not much at all) and carried on punching and kicking and tearing each other's extremely costly costumes. Now the wardrobe mistress was almost as hysterical as Cosima.

'Stop them! Stop them! Oh my God. Not that jacket!'

Who knows what would have happened had the bell to announce that the interval was drawing to a close not sounded. Actually, it didn't stop Nolan, who had already died onstage and had no more singing to do. He was very happy to keep on fighting. But Andrew was a performer to the very nuclei of his cells and it was he who held his hand up.

'Enough,' he said. 'Enough. I've got to go back out there. The audience expects—'

'Pussy,' said Nolan, under his breath but clearly audible to Andrew who went for one last punch.

'Stop!' the little lad who was to sing the 'Shepherd's Lament' at the beginning of the next act eventually called a halt. 'My mum and dad are out there watching.'

The words of a child brought the two men to their senses. At least, temporarily.

'Don't think this is over, O'Connor,' said Andrew, as he allowed one of the make-up artists to dab real blood from his lip. At least his character was meant to look tortured and beaten, she reminded him by way of consolation.

Cosima's character might also be excused for looking a little ragged, but she wanted to look ragged in a very specific glamorous way and so her make-up had to be touched-up too. She passed Nolan as she hurried to her dressing room. He knew he had to make amends.

'You are an asshole,' she hissed. 'I've got a good mind to walk out on the tour because of this.'

'Cosima, I'm sorry,' said Nolan. 'I did some stupid things out there. Childish and selfish things . . . But I am sorry.'

'If I thought for one moment that your apology was anywhere near sincere . . .'

'It is. Look . . .'

Nolan plucked a rose from one of the many bouquets that had spilled out of Cosima's room and now lined the corridor. He handed it to her with a flourish. Cosima took the rose, pulled its pretty head off and handed Nolan the stalk.

And so, once again, Cosima and Nolan were not on speaking terms and the planned first night party had three very notable absentees.

In his hotel room, Nolan asked himself why he had behaved like such a fool. He wanted to have some proper excuse next time Cosima deigned to speak to him. The only thing he could think of to tell her was that he had been nervous about giving his first public performance as a baritone. By trying to lighten the moment, he was trying to make sure that no one could take him seriously because if he had given the performance his all and failed, the disappointment would have been unthinkable. If, however, he knew he hadn't given it his all, then the critics couldn't hurt him. He could always kid himself that at some point in the future he would ace the part because he knew he had kept something in reserve. He had sabotaged himself in self-protection. Was that what he had done with his marriage too?

Chapter Twenty-Five

FLORENCE was very glad to be leaving London. She had not had what you would call a 'restful' couple of nights. The hotel was a madhouse. If she thought it had looked grim when she arrived there during the day, then that was nothing compared with how it was when the residents returned at six in the evening. Residents? More like *Resident Evil*. The group perpetually hanging around on the wall outside the hotel, since you couldn't smoke indoors, looked like extras from Michael Jackson's 'Thriller' video. Zombies the lot of them. As Florence scuttled past them, she couldn't help thinking they were eyeing her up, wondering which of her limbs they would gnaw on first.

When she returned from her first afternoon of enforced sightseeing, there was a different person on reception, a big bald-headed guy, who looked every bit as confused as the woman on the desk earlier when Florence said she had already checked in.

'Were you referred by the council?' he asked as his colleague had done before.

'No,' said Florence. 'I was referred by a travel agent I will not be using again.'

Opening her case, Florence had the feeling that someone else had already been inside it. The neatly packed contents had definitely shifted. Best-case scenario was that one of the policemen had been through her underwear. She didn't want to think of any of the other residents touching her stuff. She might get scabies. For that reason, she stripped the bed. If anything harboured nasty bugs it was that blanket. Unfortunately, the bare mattress was not a comforting sight. It was covered in indescribable stains.

Florence brought out the spare towels she had not expected to use until Italy. Heavens, she thought. If London is this bad what on earth will Rome be like? She used the towels as bedclothes for a twenty-minute nap. But she couldn't sleep. She just lay there itching. The only thing to do was go to the opera house early.

The scraggy group of ghouls who had measured her up on the way into the hotel, gawped as though they had just seen an alien when Florence stepped out in her finery. She pulled her shawl tightly over her cleavage, but still they whistled.

'You look mighty fine,' said one of them.

Never one to forget her manners, no matter what the circumstances, Florence thanked the man. He rewarded her with a grin that showed all his gold teeth.

'I'm Emmanuel,' he told her, holding out his hand. 'I'm guessing that you're new in town. Let me tell you, if there's ever anything that you need, Emmanuel can get it for you.'

'Thank you,' said Florence again. The only thing she needed was for him to release her hand. As soon as she was out of sight, she dived into her handbag for her little bottle of hand sanitiser and rubbed it right up to her elbows.

So, the hotel was awful. Florence would later discover, thanks to Kasia the receptionist who felt very sorry for her and allowed her to stay in her room while the other guests were kicked out at nine the next day, that it was in fact a bail hostel. From time to time they also accommodated people who were visiting relatives at Holloway, the nearby women's prison.

'You shouldn't have ended up here,' she said. 'There are a lot of bad people around. The police are always in this place looking for drugs and guns. They were looking for a gun this afternoon.'

'Why do you work here?' Florence asked her.

'I don't have much choice. My English isn't very good. I can only get cleaning jobs otherwise.'

'But to have to put your life at risk every day! To have to deal with people carrying guns!'

'There are many more people carrying guns in your country,' Kasia pointed out.

Florence nodded. It was food for thought.

The only consolation London had brought was that Florence had seen Nolan sing a baritone role. What heaven! It made her admire him even more. She knew of only one singer who had managed the transition so successfully. That one moment of opera history was enough to make the hell of London quite worthwhile. Florence couldn't wait to get to an Internet café to email Nolan and tell him how proud she had been of him on his first night.

As Florence boarded the Eurostar, she wondered whether Nolan and the rest of his company were on the same train. If they were, they would undoubtedly be travelling in one of the first-class carriages. Florence, with her budget, was firmly in economy. But she was looking forward to Paris enormously. Things could only get better.

Florence was wrong about Nolan and his crew. They were travelling in a decidedly economy-class way too: on a coach through the Chunnel. Only Cosima escaped the misery of the M25 and, at the other end, the Périphérique. She had left London City Airport in a private jet, courtesy of Domaine Randon, taking Andrew Fleetwood with her. She had some promotional duties to discharge according to her contract with Martin et Fils. While Nolan and the others ate plastic tasting sandwiches in a roadside service station, Cosima attended a glittering lunch party to launch Martin et Fils' new collection, called in a nod to Cosima's talents, 'La Bohème'. Though there was nothing particularly Bohemian in that sense about the pieces Cosima modelled. You wouldn't get much change from a million if you wanted the necklace and the earrings.

But Cosima understood that the ridiculously expensive pieces, hand-crafted and so precious that she had to be shadowed by a bodyguard even when she went to the loo, were not what it was all about. The photographs of this launch and the glossy advertising campaign would boost the sales of Martin et Fils' less expensive lines too. And Mathieu Randon had recently told Cosima that in the autumn they were planning to launch a perfume in time for the Christmas market. Cosima was invited down to Grasse, where the perfume was being developed, to choose between the last two phials. Duncan was already negotiating her contract to be the face of the scent, which would also be called 'La Bohème'.

So, Cosima was all set to enjoy a very luxurious time. Which was enhanced by the thought that Nolan was somewhere on a bus.

Chapter Twenty-Six

MATHIEU Randon's chateau near Épernay was a sight to be seen. The enormous white house with four fairy-tale turrets, was set well back from the road. It took ten minutes to drive the length of the driveway with its corridor of tall, stately trees. Peacocks strutted around the perfectly manicured gardens that had once been the playground of a comtesse who was a close friend of Marie Antoinette.

Randon himself was there to greet Cosima and Andrew when they arrived in a Domaine Randon limousine. Cosima was deeply flattered by such personal attention. Randon was a fascinating man who had always attracted plenty of gossip. He came from a wealthy Champagne family. As a young man, he had dated actresses and models. He'd been quite a catch, with his enormous luxury goods empire behind him. He had never married. Always the playboy. Until, that is, he was sent into a coma when a falling wine barrel hit him on the head during an earthquake at the

Domaine's California winery. Apparently, he had emerged from the eighteen-month coma quite a different man. He turned to God. At one point, he even talked about giving up business in favour of building a monastery on the side of a mountain in Italy. That plan, however, had fallen by the by. On the site of the proposed monastery was a chi-chi spa resort. Randon was back in the boardroom. He was one hundred per cent himself again.

'Thank God,' said his long-suffering assistant Bellette, when she recounted the tale to Cosima.

Cosima was also glad to be dealing with the old-style flirtatious Randon. She very much enjoyed the frisson of sexual tension when he kissed her lightly on the ear.

'Yeah right,' said Andrew, when Cosima told him. 'He was kissing your earring.' He indicated the enormous sparklers. 'Don't they belong to him?'

Cosima shrugged Andrew's comments off as jealousy.

Andrew had mostly recovered from his spat with Nolan but all was not quite as it had been. Before he punched her ex-husband, Andrew had been the most mild-mannered, laid-back guy Cosima had ever met. But something had changed after the fight. Perhaps it had given Andrew an extra shot of testosterone. He certainly seemed to be puffed up, somehow. As he squired Cosima about the Martin et Fils event, he was unusually proprietorial, sticking to her like a shadow. At times it had been just a little embarrassing. It reminded her of a dinner party long ago when a friend had commented that Cosima's rather hopeless boyfriend of the time was 'marking his mount' by acting in the same way. The words came back to Cosima now and their intimations of animal husbandry made her feel a little queasy.

The truth was, Cosima couldn't help thinking that if the fight had been allowed to get to its natural conclusion, the result would not have gone in Andrew's favour, though that was not what he seemed to believe as he strutted around the jewellery launch. Cosima felt guilty even thinking otherwise. Andrew was her boyfriend and Nolan had started the incident. Of course she should be loyal to Andrew and agree that he would have been the victor. She didn't have to say it out loud. But she couldn't even say it inside her head. And the more Andrew strutted, the less Cosima admired him. If only he had left it at swinging one punch. A token gesture at defending her honour. That would have been enough. In continuing the fight to the point at which everyone could see that Nolan had the superior strength and then, despite having had the fight broken up by a child, acting like he was the victor, Andrew had rather spoiled the effect.

Now, whenever she looked at Andrew's split lip, Cosima couldn't help thinking of Nolan. So strong and wiry. A fighter and . . . oh God, she mustn't say it, not even to herself. A lover.

Cosima and Andrew were sharing a hotel room, of course. When the Martin et Fils event was over, they headed back to Paris and their suite at the Ritz for a rest. Once the bellboy who had brought up their luggage had been sent away with a tip, Andrew backed Cosima up against the bed and leaned over her so that she had no choice but to sit down on it. He was already unbuttoning his shirt.

'I feel incredibly horny,' he told her.

Horny? Ugh.

Cosima didn't feel horny at all. The very word 'horny'

from Andrew's lips made her want to wrap herself in a grey blanket and get out her rosary.

'Later,' she said. 'I'm exhausted.'

She climbed under the covers with her clothes still on. Andrew disappeared for a shower. By the time he came back, Cosima was feigning a very deep sleep.

Chapter Twenty-Seven

JULIET waited anxiously for her weekend date with Christopher to arrive. Her heart could not help but leap when she saw his Aston Martin pull up to the kerb opposite her building, though she knew that it had to be for the last time. Perhaps he realised that this was to be their last meeting too. Perhaps he had arranged this meeting for the specific purpose of telling her the bad news she already knew and explaining what it meant for their relationship. The end. It had to be the end.

That evening would be the first time that Juliet had been alone with Christopher since the night she discovered his wife was pregnant again. It was clear as soon as she opened the door to him that he was as anxious about this meeting as she was. After a week without seeing each other, they often experienced a moment of awkwardness before they relaxed into their role as lovers rather than colleagues again. But still he kissed her as though nothing had changed. Then he went straight to the kitchen to open a bottle of wine in a parody of comfortable domesticity.

'What are you cooking?' Christopher asked.

'Nothing. I thought we might get a takeaway,' said Juliet. What she had really thought was that she would tell Christopher that she knew about Caroline right away and that he would leave immediately and that she would not feel like eating once he had gone.

'OK.' In the sitting room, Christopher threw himself down onto the sofa and patted the empty seat beside him. Juliet remained standing.

'Come on, Jools. I haven't seen you for ages.'

'I don't want to sit next to you.'

'Whatever is the matter?'

'It's over,' said Juliet simply.

'What do you mean? I don't get it. Why? What's changed? What have I done?'

Juliet winced. He really didn't seem to know she knew about the pregnancy and he obviously wasn't in a hurry to confess. In that moment, she disliked him intensely. What a worm.

'I know about the baby,' Juliet said quietly. 'Caroline told me at the opera benefit.'

'What?'

'You mean she didn't tell you first?' Juliet snorted.

'No. I mean, of course, but ... How did she tell you? Why?'

'She felt the need to explain why she wasn't touching the free champagne. I don't suppose she thought the news was supposed to be confidential until you could work out how to tell your mistress. When were you going to tell me, Chris?'

'I . . . I . . .' he stuttered.

'She's having a baby in six months. You must have known when we were in Milan on my birthday.'

'Actually, she told me just after we came back. I didn't tell you sooner as I was trying to work a few things out first. I didn't think there was any point upsetting you until I knew exactly what I was going to do.'

'What can you do?'

'I'm going to tell her I'm leaving her,' said Christopher.

'You can't,' Juliet said evenly. 'She's having your baby.'

'I wouldn't be the first man in the world to leave a pregnant woman. I'd make sure she's cared for financially. That's all she wants from me anyway. God knows she never stops telling me I'm useless. So long as she has access to my cash and a nanny twenty-four-seven, she'll be fine.'

'I can't ask you to do that, Christopher. And I don't want you to.'

'But I want to! I would do anything for you. I don't want this to break us up.'

Juliet shook her head. 'How can we get through this?'

'But we're meant to be together, you and I. You're the only good thing in my life. Having you has been the only thing that's enabled me to stay in my stupid, empty marriage anyway.'

'That and the sex,' Juliet pointed out. 'It's pathetic. Christopher, I can't carry on like this. I don't want to. Now, if it's all right with you, I think you had better go.'

'No.' Christopher refused to leave Juliet's side. He stood up and grasped both her hands. Then he cupped her face and turned it towards him, forcing her to look at him. 'We've got to talk this through.'

'I can't do this anymore,' Juliet repeated. 'God knows,

I shouldn't have got involved in the first place. But this is ridiculous, Chris. If you were ever going to leave Caroline, you would have done it within the first six months of this stupid affair. All that stuff about staying until the children were old enough to understand. They'll *never* understand. Not if you wait until they are parents themselves before you tell Caroline you don't love her anymore. And that's another thing I find hard to believe. Haven't had sex in eight years? Do you expect me to believe that this new baby is the result of a one-night stand with your own wife?'

Christopher started to nod.

'Juliet, I . . . I don't know what I'll do without you. You round out my life.'

Juliet gave a sad little snort. 'I don't want to be the person who makes it possible for you to stay in your marriage by offering you the kind of simple company and adoration you claim you don't get at home, only with no strings attached. Well, I want strings. I want to be someone's everything. I deserve that.'

'You *are* my everything.'

'I want to be acknowledged in public. I want to be in a relationship where I can wake up with the man I love every morning. I don't want to have to spend Christmas and birthdays on my own. Maybe I want to have a family too.'

'I'll divorce her. I'll call her right now and tell her everything. While you're sitting here. If that's what you want.'

'You can't afford it,' said Juliet. 'Three children? The court will give her everything and leave you rotting in some corporate let flat. I know you wouldn't be able to live with that. You'd hate it and you'd blame me. Just face it, Christopher. It was nice while it lasted. We should have ended it before it began.'

Christopher seemed not to hear her. 'I love you and I am going to make this right. I can afford to get a divorce. I've worked it out. I can pay her off no problem. I've been offered the chance to do a deal that could net some serious money.'

'Really?' Juliet paused. 'Have you been offered another job?'

'Not exactly. No. But—'

'Then what are you talking about?'

'I can't tell you right now but I promise I am doing everything I can to make sure that I can walk away from Caroline and be with you. I've got a plan.'

'So have I. And it no longer involves you.'

'Juliet.'

Christopher made another grab for her, pulled her tight against him and forced his mouth against hers. It took a monumental effort for her to pull away from his embrace but she did it.

'You have to go,' she said. 'If you ever loved me then at least start treating me with some respect now.'

'You cannot do this to me,' Christopher was angry now. 'You can't desert me like this.'

Juliet tried to physically push Christopher towards the door. When he did not budge, she pummelled his chest with her fists.

'You have ruined everything,' she said. 'We were never going to be together and you knew it. You knew it all along. I never want to see you again.'

'Juliet!'

Christopher might have stayed to fight but right then his mobile phone began to ring.

'Shit.'

And ring and ring.

'Answer it, for God's sake,' said Juliet.

Of course it was her. Caroline.

'What?' A frown came over Christopher's face as he listened to his wife garbling excitedly. 'Is he OK? Where are you now? I'll be right there as soon as I can.'

He cut off the call.

'I've got to–' he began apologetically.

'To go. I know. Your family needs you.'

'My son fell off a quad bike. They think he's broken his arm.'

'Then go to him,' said Juliet, opening her front door. 'But please, don't even think about coming back to me.'

Christopher cursed the gods as he headed back downstairs to his car. Why did this have to happen now? He wrenched the driver's door of the Aston open with a violence and carelessness he had never before used on his beloved automobile. He threw it into gear and stamped down on the accelerator. Just as he was leaving Juliet's street he saw in his rear-view mirror a familiar figure getting out of the car that had been parked behind him. He was carrying flowers. What was *he* doing here? Much as he wanted to know more, Christopher did not have time to find out.

Chapter Twenty-Eight

𝄞

*I*NSIDE her apartment, Juliet collapsed onto the sofa and began to cry ferociously. The emergency call had been perfect really: a timely reminder, if Juliet needed one, of why she had to let Christopher go. They had no future. He had a wife, two sons and another baby on the way. They would always come first for him. Still it seemed so very unfair to have to say goodbye to this man she had genuinely loved, and when the doorbell rang again, her deceitful heart gave another little skip. She wanted it to be him but he should be on the road to Shropshire, to his parents-in-laws' house and his injured son. She prepared herself to tell him so.

'Is this a good time?' The screen of the intercom was filled with flowers. It wasn't Christopher. It was David.

'It's not a good time,' he concluded when Juliet didn't answer at once. 'You did say you were going to be working this weekend. I'll go away again. I'll just leave these here.

They were giving them away in Waitrose and I thought they'd cheer up your miserable bare flat.'

'Thanks a lot,' said Juliet.

'Ah! You're alive. I'm sticking the flowers in the porch. You better come down and get them before they get nicked.'

Juliet wiped the fresh tears from her cheeks with her sleeve.

'You can come up,' she said.

'You've been crying,' David observed when Juliet let him in.

'No shit, Sherlock,' said Juliet.

'Want to tell me about it?'

'Nothing to tell.' Juliet deftly moved the two glasses of wine that Christopher had poured to the kitchen sink. She didn't want David to know he wasn't her first visitor that evening. 'I guess it must be the time of the month.'

'Fine,' said David. 'I won't press you for details. Shall I go?'

'No.'

Contrary to her expectations, Juliet did not want to be on her own that evening. 'I was thinking of getting a takeaway. I can get enough for two. And we can finish this bottle.'

'Good idea,' said David. 'Terrible thing to be drinking alone.'

'I shouldn't have surprised you like I did but I wanted to apologise,' said David, as he cleared away the empty Chinese food cartons from their takeaway and Juliet put the flowers in the vase. They had polished off the best part of a second bottle of wine and Juliet had been very happy to have company.

'What do you need to apologise for?' she asked.

'For kissing you the other night. You must have been

mortified. Anyway, the flowers were to say sorry. Lilies aren't too romantic, I hope.'

'They're beautiful. But you don't have to apologise. I liked it. It was . . .

'Just like you remembered?' said David tentatively. 'It was for me.'

'Yes.'

'But I guess we're just meant to be like ships that pass in the night, you and I. Sharing one kiss every decade.'

'I suppose so. Though I don't suppose you'll be quite so keen once another ten years have passed.'

David stood up to help Juliet carry the now heavy vase from the kitchen sink to the table.

'Pity,' said Juliet.

'I agree,' said David

He held her gaze for a second too long. He put the vase down.

'Do we really have to wait another ten years?'

Juliet felt the flame flickering in her spine again, but it could be different this time. Why shouldn't they kiss? Christopher was no longer part of her life. The loyalty she ought never to have given him was just a memory. Perhaps this was what she needed. Someone to push Christopher out of his place in her heart. Now it was Juliet who initiated the kiss. She stepped towards David and kissed him hard, putting all the energy of her anger towards Christopher into this new passion. If she had surprised David, he wasn't fazed for long. He kissed back just as hungrily, his earlier apologies forgotten too.

Forgetting the flowers, wine and washing up, they moved from the kitchen to the bedroom. As they stepped into the room, David picked Juliet off her feet and laid her gently on the bed. He lay down beside her and traced the contours of her face, running his fingertip down over her nose to her lips. She planted a kiss on his fingertips. They kissed again. Juliet's heart was racing. She arched her back and pressed her body against his. Suddenly they seemed to be wearing too many clothes.

Again it was Juliet who moved things forward now. David's eyes registered delighted surprise as she tackled the buttons on his shirt. As he stood up to take off his trousers, Juliet pulled her simple summer dress off over her head and threw it to the floor. The fabric was so light that for just a moment it was borne upwards like a streamer let out in celebration. She smiled to see David's naked chest covered with a masculine layer of hair that she didn't remember from their encounter all those years ago. She wondered briefly how much she had changed too but David did not seem to be in any way disappointed by her more womanly figure. Falling back onto the bed, he gathered her into his arms again. His warm hands roamed her skin. He nuzzled her hair and neck, greedily breathing in the scent of her. As her mouth brushed across her ear, Juliet gave a shiver. The sensation was almost unbearable and yet so exquisite at the same time. She groaned in near ecstasy as David traced the contours of her earlobe with his tongue.

At the same time, David's hands continued to explore Juliet's body. He cupped his left hand around her right breast. Her nipple stiffened so that it showed clearly through the fine fabric of her bra. Juliet moved to make it easy for him to undo the clasp and thus slip her bra off. David bowed his head to meet that nipple with his mouth.

After so many years of wondering what it would be like to be with David, Juliet was relieved that the reality was so different. She had imagined that their coming together would be awkward, clumsy even, but they were no longer just out of university. Whomsoever had had the great good fortune to love David since Juliet had seen him last had taught him well. David was the lover that all women dreamed of, taking as much care to ensure her pleasure as he did his own. Now he was helping her out of her knickers. His hands carefully moved her legs apart. His fingers moved to the smooth silken tuft of her pubic hair. Juliet couldn't help gasping as she felt him make contact with her clitoris, sending more shivers of arousal up and down her spine like sparks.

Juliet moaned as she pushed her body against his. She felt the muscles of her pussy contract around his fingers in a pulsing rhythm that quickly gathered speed and intensity. His mouth was back on hers, his tongue flickering inside her mouth, smothering the cries she wanted to make. Cries of surprise and excitement.

Having spent so much time in her head in recent weeks, Juliet was astonished to feel so very physical again. Her blood raced throughout her, amplifying the waves of sensation that started where David's hands and tongue touched her. She felt as though she was being made love to by a thousand men. Her nipples, her lips, her clitoris. David was everywhere, like a conductor bringing an orchestra to a fabulous, simultaneous crescendo.

'Oh, please!' she cried as her orgasm cascaded through her body. 'David! Please! Oh God!'

David carried out, wringing every possible note of ecstasy out of her, leaving her panting on the pillows. Panting and laughing, as though she could believe for just a moment that Christopher had never been part of her life at all.

*   *   *

Temptation

'Are you going to tell me who made you cry?' David asked, as they lay side by side in the darkness.

'I'd rather not,' said Juliet. 'But thank you for putting a smile back on my face.'

'Any time,' said David. 'Starting right now, if you like.'

Chapter Twenty-Nine

Damn Nolan O'Connor. Cosima had been happy with her life before this tour. Sure, she had money worries. Every time the mailman came she expected another terrifying demand from the IRS. But apart from that, her life had been coming together most successfully. She and Andrew had been getting on famously before he flew to join her in London, hadn't they? She had been delighted to be with someone so kind and generous who understood her profession, someone who would never cheat on her. It was hard to find that kind of man.

But Nolan O'Connor had spoiled it all, without even trying. His stupid stunt in London should have diminished him in Cosima's eyes. It should have made it easier to hate him. After all, he had not only upstaged Andrew, he had tried to upstage Cosima too. But the subsequent fight had made Andrew the loser in the situation. He was the one who looked like an idiot now. And who had been acting like an idiot ever since.

Take that afternoon. Donald Law claimed that he was still too unwell to join the company in France. He had stayed behind in London. 'Exposing himself to even more germs, I've no doubt,' said Karl, secretly disgruntled that Donald had never fancied him. Anyway, naturally Andrew offered his services again and naturally Nolan was only too pleased to reprise Scarpia, which he actually considered to be the more interesting role. As the company rehearsed on yet another new stage, Nolan asked Andrew if he wanted to play the torture scene 'exactly like we did in London'. He even gave a wink as he said it. But it was Andrew's response that made Cosima cringe.

'Anytime you want to pick up where we left off with that fight, O'Connor, I'm ready. I'll even let you have the first punch.'

Nooooooo. Screaming inside, Cosima balled her hands into fists. Couldn't Andrew see what an idiot he was being? His advantage over Nolan was that he didn't have to use his fists to get his point across.

And then, having delivered his ridiculous challenge, Andrew crossed the stage and threw his arm around Cosima's shoulders as though she were some dim little opera WAG. She shrugged his arm off again. She hated him right then.

'Paris needs you,' she texted Donald Law. 'I need you. Will you hurry the fuck up and get better?'

Florence was greatly relieved to discover that her hotel in Paris was not a repeat of the fleapit in London. It was a little way out of the centre of things for sure, but it was well appointed, clean and the other clientele did not look as though they might be carrying firearms. Moreover, there was no question that she would be allowed to stay in her room all day if she felt like it. Exhausted from her time in London, she gratefully slept all the way through her first afternoon in France.

She felt fresh and well rested when she set out for the Paris Opéra later that evening. The seat she had obtained for this performance was an especially good one. Dead centre and just five rows back from the front. If Nolan was going to see her in the audience at any stage of the tour, then in all likelihood tonight would be that night, so Florence made an effort to look her very best. She even stopped off at a beauty counter in Galeries Lafayette and managed, with her rudimentary French, to persuade the assistant to give her a free makeover. Florence didn't ordinarily wear very much make-up at all, but there was something about the women in the French capital, with their effortless chic, that made her want to raise her game.

Nolan was as spectacular as ever in the role of Scarpia. Florence was thrilled that her hero was turning out to be so versatile. It gave her even greater scope for fantasy when she thought about the songs he would sing for her and her alone. The only downside was that singing Scarpia rather than Cavaradossi meant that Nolan was on the stage for only the first two acts, whereas that bitch Esposito still got to appear in all three. Never mind. If Florence closed her eyes, she could imagine that Nolan was still up there. Andrew Fleetwood had a similar voice. And, of course, there would be a curtain call.

That night's was a very special curtain call. Florence was sure that Nolan had seen her. He had looked right in her direction while Esposito and Fleetwood were taking their bows. He had looked in her direction and smiled. And she had thrown a flower onstage. A red rose. He must have noticed that.

But once the curtain had fallen for the last time the audience were slow to get out of the auditorium and by the time Florence located what she thought was the stage door, the cast and orchestra were long gone. As Florence waited in vain, Nolan was already tucking in to steak frites at a bistro near the Palais Royal.

Florence returned to her hotel in something of a funk but then she had a thought. Perhaps she should take a chance and straight out ask Nolan to meet her before or after a show. After all, there couldn't be many opera fans who were making the effort to follow the entire tour.

She logged on from the hotel's computer and, after some struggle with the strange layout of the French keyboard, sent this email via Nolan's site.

> I was so happy when you gave me that special smile tonight. It meant a great deal to me to spare that little moment with you. I will be on every single leg of the tour. I know you're probably busy with rehearsals and promotion and all, but it would be nice if you could carve out some you and me time. Here is a list of my hotels . . .

'You and me time.' When Nolan's manager Karen, who occasionally logged into Nolan's fan mail when he was away on tour, read Florence's words, they made her shudder. Her assistant Laetitia agreed. Nolan must have been encouraging the poor little sap again. Well, Karen was going to put an end to that. She had Laetitia reply to Florence's email curtly, with a response that would do for all the weirdoes who sent him love notes.

> Nolan O'Connor will not be answering his emails while on tour in Europe. Please direct any urgent correspondence to his manager Karen Royle . . .

Hopefully Florence Carter would get the message.

Chapter Thirty

MERCY'S unhappiness about Ed was soon eclipsed by other worries. Francis seemed to have developed a serious attitude over the past few months. It was hard to relate the man he was becoming with the small boy who once had begged his big sister to stay in his room until he was safely asleep after being terrified by his first reading of *The Gruffalo*.

'Francis,' said Mercy. 'You need to show our mother more respect.'

Francis kissed his teeth. 'I don't need no one telling me what to do.'

'And you won't have to have anyone telling you what to do once you've left home, but while you're living here – under our mother's roof – acting like a man involves being kinder to Mum. You have no idea how upset she gets when you walk out to see your friends just as she's putting your food on the table.'

'She never said nothing about it to me.'

'Do you mean to say that you need to be told the way you've been acting is ignorant? We were raised better than that.'

'Why should I listen to a word you say,' Francis hissed. 'What do you know? You're nothing but a cleaner. A charwoman. Cleaning up after people who do real jobs. If you had any respect for yourself you wouldn't be doing that.'

'Having respect for myself includes earning a living instead of signing on,' Mercy spat back. 'And if this is the only work available to me right now, I'm going to take it. I don't want any handouts.'

Mercy's relationship with her brother was worsening by the day. Having adored him from the moment he was born – she had been desperate for a sibling – lately she found herself actually starting to dislike him. She had expected that things would be a little rocky once Francis became a teenager, but she had not expected him to change so dramatically and so suddenly too. Some of the things he said to her and to their mother made her wonder if the Francis she knew and loved had been abducted by aliens and replaced by something that looked and sounded like him but didn't have a scrap of his heart. She couldn't remember the last time he had tossed a kind word in her direction.

'Mum,' Mercy said. 'Do you think you ought to have a word with Francis about school? About how important it is? The way he's acting, he thinks he's going to magically walk into some great job.'

'He's a teenager,' said Melody again. 'His whole body is awash with hormones. Give it a couple of months and he'll be himself again. I don't want to alienate him right now.'

It was no use. Mercy knew that every time Melody wanted to chastise her son, she would see the face of sweet Xavier Hale and remember what had become of him. That was what would happen if she got heavy on Francis. He would feel forced out of the home and God only knew what might become of him then.

Mercy knew, however, that it was just as easy for a boy to get into trouble while he still slept under his mother's roof.

That was another odd thing. Francis had recently quit his part-time job at Alpha Sports and yet the loss of income did not seem to have had any effect on his spending power. If anything, he was suddenly dressing in more conspicuously expensive clothes. He was wearing the kind of trainers that he claimed he had been unable to afford even when he worked in a sports shop and got a hefty discount. When Mercy tried to ask him, without flagging up her suspicions, where he got the cash from, Francis told her that he was spending his savings. She could tell from the sneer to his smile that he thought she believed him.

But there was only one real way for a kid like Francis to be earning so much money. He must be selling drugs. Mercy knew that Francis had smoked drugs before. She'd decided against telling their mother, since it was something that all the kids in the neighbourhood seemed to go through. But *selling* drugs. That was something else. The cliché of the old-style laid-back hippy dealer as seen in *Withnail and I* was not the kind of dealer you met in this part of London. There was no such thing as an independent drug dealer for a start. Even Mercy knew that. The teenage dealers, such as Francis aspired to be, were nothing but underworld Avon ladies, working for much bigger fish who would never get their hands dirty by going door to door with their goods. But if the teens didn't meet their targets the consequences were far worse than missing out on the latest perfume samples.

Mercy wished there was something she could say that would make her brother realise the idiocy of his career path and the potential for terrible danger. But she knew that he wasn't open to hearing her now. He had been very clear that he thought she was a loser. And perhaps she was. Since that night at the Anglo-Italian reception, she had certainly been acting like one. Why should the opinion of one woman who didn't know her at all have set her back so far?

That night, for the first time in a long while, Mercy opened the Royal College of Music's website and browsed through the courses. How she envied the students who were pictured at the top of each page. They had made it. Could she?

It seemed to Mercy that the best way to discover if she ever had a chance of making it as a singer was to get herself some singing lessons. Her school music teacher, Mr Heywood, had always been very encouraging but singing wasn't really his thing. He played the guitar and the piano and drums. The voice wasn't his area of expertise.

Mercy found a singing coach on the Internet. There was one in Brixton. Mercy carefully copied down the phone number onto a Post-it note and stuck it inside her purse. Every time she got her purse out, to buy milk or top up her Oyster card, the number was there to remind her of the first step towards her ambition.

It was quite some time before she got round to taking that first step. Still, the woman who answered the phone sounded friendly enough. Private lessons were ruinously expensive but the teacher said that she would be very happy to accept Mercy on the next small group course. That would cost considerably less but still worked out at two hundred pounds for ten weeks.

'Thank you,' said Mercy. 'I'll have to think about it.'

She didn't think about it for long. Two hundred pounds was a lot of money but Mercy knew girls who would spend that much on a pair of shoes. In comparison, it seemed like a small amount to spend on starting to bring such a big dream into reality. Mercy called back the singing teacher and said she wanted that last place on the group course.

She was reminded of the line at the beginning of *Fame*. 'Right here's where you start paying ... In sweat.' Wasn't that the line? Sweat would have been easier than two hundred pounds. Blood likewise. But Mercy knew she would find the money somehow.

Chapter Thirty-One

𝄞

THAT Friday, the touring company had a day of leisure in Paris. Andrew suggested that he and Cosima might take a day to see the sights, but she told him that she needed to do some shopping, knowing that he wouldn't be especially keen to join her for that. What she really needed was a day to herself. Some space to think.

So, while she wandered up the rue du Faubourg, dipping in and out of the designer shops and gathering a few bags on the way, her mind wasn't really in it. She stopped for lunch in a small café and spent most of the hour just staring into space, hoping for inspiration. A solution.

It had been a terrible mistake to agree to have Andrew on the tour. Sure, it was wonderful for the audiences that he had been able to step in and sing Cavaradossi when Donald Law fell ill and Nolan took over as Scarpia, but now the shine had worn off and Cosima was faced with the prospect of having to do the rest of the tour singing Tosca to

Andrew's Cavaradossi. And somehow, playing at being the passionate lover of a lover she no longer felt passionate about was far worse than singing the same part opposite the ex-husband she claimed to hate. It was ridiculous.

Cosima's phone vibrated to let her know she had a text. It was from Donald Law. She had texted him earlier to see how he was getting on. In fact, she had been texting him several times a day, in the hope that it might speed his recovery.

'Feeling much better, sweetheart,' he wrote now. 'Will be joining you all in Paris tomorrow!'

'Onstage too?' Cosima texted hopefully.

'You betcha,' was Donald's reply.

'Oh, thank goodness,' Cosima exhaled with relief. She texted Donald her fondest love.

Finally, she knew what she had to do and, at last, she would be able to do it.

'Andrew,' said Cosima, after she told him that Donald was coming back. 'I'm afraid this isn't working for me.'

'What?' Andrew looked up from his paper. 'What isn't working? This room?'

Cosima shook her head.

'This . . .' she waved her arms around.

'You mean you're not enjoying having me on the tour?' Andrew translated.

Cosima didn't exactly nod but her expression gave her away.

'Darling,' said Andrew. 'That's OK. I know what it's like to have someone tag along with you like they're on holiday while you're actually working. I understand. If you feel as though my presence here is more a source of stress than support to you, then I'll happily take a couple of days off. I can visit my cousin in the south of France. I'll take the train. I've always wanted to take the train to the Côte d'Azur. I can rejoin you in Italy. I'm sure you can still overnight from Nice to Milan.'

'Andrew,' Cosima interrupted him. 'I'm not talking about a couple of days.'

Andrew refolded his newspaper and set it down on the table beside his chair.

'Go on.'

'I mean, this whole thing isn't working for me.' She threw her arms out in a gesture of near despair. 'This. You being here on the tour. You. Me. Our relationship.'

Andrew looked surprised. It struck Cosima that perhaps he hadn't been aware that the atmosphere between them had become increasingly strained.

'I thought that I could make it happen. I thought when I met you that I was ready to get involved in something new.'

'But you don't feel you're ready?'

Cosima nodded.

'Is this about Nolan?'

'God, no,' Cosima lied. 'Of course it's not about Nolan. He and I ... we're ... you know, Andrew. Nolan and I are long finished. I promise. There isn't even a breath of love between us anymore. But that doesn't stop me from feeling ... I don't know. Maybe I'm just not cut out for a relationship at all. It all went wrong with Nolan. Every relationship I had before I met Nolan went wrong too. Why on earth should I have had a better chance with you?'

Andrew got up from his seat and wrapped his arms around her. He made soothing sounds and stroked her hair as though she were an overwrought toddler. For a moment or two, Cosima settled into his embrace. But not for long. Soon she was disentangling herself again.

'Cosi,' said Andrew.

'Please don't call me that.' Nolan was the only person she had ever let call her Cosi.

'Cosima, then. Sweetheart. Please don't do anything rash. You know how much I care for you. I love you. I want to make this work. Everyone gets the colly-wobbles when they feel they're moving towards a deeper commitment. And I do feel as though we're moving towards a deeper commitment every day. Don't you?'

Cosima nodded vaguely, but she didn't agree with Andrew at all. When she had realised that she and Nolan were moving towards a deeper commitment, she had been over the moon. She could think of nothing she wanted more. Even the word 'commitment' coming from Andrew, made her feel anxious and trapped.

'I'll go away for a few days,' Andrew continued. 'Give you some time to think about this properly.'

'I have thought about this properly!' Cosima exclaimed. 'Do you think I would have told you I don't want to be with you without thinking about it properly? Andrew, I'm not an idiot. I know my own mind. I have thought about nothing else since this tour began and I'm decided. I don't want to be with you any more. I can't do it.'

Andrew sat down heavily on the bed and threw his hands into the air.

'Women!' he exhaled loudly. It did nothing to help his case.

The news spread around the company like wildfire. One of the girls saw Andrew leaving the hotel with his bags.

She asked him when he would be rejoining the tour and he told her that he wouldn't. He and Cosima were no longer together. Less than an hour later, Nolan knew what had happened. Though he managed to look unconcerned as he heard the tale in the hotel spa, inside his heart was leaping. Cosima had got rid of that Muppet! The way was clear for him at last. Though of course he would have to proceed slowly, as was confirmed when, later that evening he knocked on Cosima's door to ask if she was OK and she shouted, 'I didn't do this because of you, you know!'

Nolan backed away. Though, of course, the fact that she had been so quick to claim that she hadn't broken up with Andrew because of Nolan told him everything he needed and wanted to know. She was in love with him for sure. It was simply a matter of time.

Florence Carter had spent her last day in Paris trying to track Nolan down. She had put on her walking shoes and visited every luxury hotel in Paris, trying to persuade the receptionists to reveal Nolan's whereabouts by claiming she had an urgent message from him. By the time she did track him down, asking for the second time at the Ritz, and finding the desk manned by an inexperienced girl who didn't know that she wasn't supposed to reveal her guests' identities, Nolan was already on his way elsewhere.

Foiled again, Florence took a slow walk to the Eiffel Tower. She joined the queues waiting to take the lift up to the viewing platform. It was not the sort of journey one really wanted to make on one's own. If Florence hadn't felt a little bit lonely before she boarded the lift, then her fellow passengers did nothing to make her feel any less so. The lift seemed to be full of people travelling in twos.

One day, Florence told herself. I will come back here with the man that I love.

Meanwhile, the man that Florence loved was at the back of a coach travelling towards the Alps, surreptitiously flirting with one of the girls from the orchestra while the woman he loved sat at the front of the coach, gazing out into the passing countryside, wondering if she was absolutely mad to have let a catch like Andrew Fleetwood slip through her hands.

Chapter Thirty-Two

𝄞

Since their last evening together, when Juliet broke off their affair despite Christopher's claim that he was working to bring home a fortune that would solve everything, the ex-lovers had remained in an uneasy truce. There was to be no escape. They hadn't seen each other privately again but there was no getting around the fact they had to work together.

For Juliet, it was close to purgatory. It seemed that never an hour went by without some reminder that Christopher was married and expecting another addition to his family. Meetings were interrupted by phone calls from the doctor's surgery. Lucy, Christopher's PA, who had been nicknamed (very privately) the Rottweiler because of her ability to stop anyone from interrupting a meeting, was nonetheless unable to refuse Caroline when she insisted that she had to speak to her husband.

'I don't care if he is with an important client. I am calling from the doctor's surgery.' And Lucy, fearing that she might be obstructing the passage of very important news, would have to get up and go into the meeting room, which had no phones, to fetch Christopher out. He would leave white-faced and return with a frown. It seemed that Caroline was never calling with news that needed to be acted upon immediately. He was furious that she dragged him out of a meeting with one of Evgeny Belanov's associates to tell him that her weight and blood pressure were absolutely within the normal range for the stage of the pregnancy.

'Could that news not have waited half an hour?' Christopher asked Juliet.

Juliet refused to comment. She was torn between hating Caroline for having kept Christopher from her and having a natural sympathy for a woman carrying a child. Of course Caroline wanted Christopher to know that everything was fine with the baby. It was *their* baby, after all.

At the same time, it seemed to Juliet that she was suddenly surrounded by happy family units. A run of terrible British summers had been broken at last. The sun was out and so were the young parents with their pushchairs. Young mothers smiled at Juliet as if to say, 'this could be you', leaving her feeling worse than ever that, thanks to having wasted so much time with Christopher, she might never be the woman pushing the pram.

Perhaps it was because she was lonely – David was away on business and so their fledgling relationship had yet to take flight – that Juliet surprised herself by agreeing to see Christopher one more time. He promised he had something to tell her that would convince her that within a matter of weeks, he would be able to cut loose from his family respon-sibilities. They arranged to meet after work in a bar where they had conducted much of their affair. But the final blow came before they had a chance to meet: Caroline emailed Juliet a picture of her baby scan.

She did not need to write anything in the body of the email. The grainy picture said it all. It said that Christopher and Caroline were, to her mind, still very much together. And it said that Caroline knew that Juliet had more than a passing interest in the welfare and status of Christopher's family.

If Juliet had ever believed that Christopher could sort this mess out, leaving him free to be with her, she could no longer believe it now.

'Perhaps she just thought you'd be interested,' said Christopher when Juliet told him what had happened over a drink in a bar near the office.

'Christopher,' Juliet sighed. 'She knows we had an affair.'

'But . . . she would have said something.'

'She has. That email was warning me off. And, you know what, it worked. I'm sticking by what I told you the other night. I cannot do this anymore.'

Christopher's face crumpled. 'You can't leave me. I'm doing my best to make things right.'

But it was too late. As Christopher started to cry, Juliet felt something in her heart shift quite irrevocably. She had seen Christopher cry before – when his brother was sent to prison – but this time she felt no urge to throw her arms around him and try to make it better. Instead, she saw him as his wife must see him. He was a pathetic little man who was used to having things exactly as he liked them. He had a wife, he had a lovely family, and he had a loving mistress. Now that perfect set-up was starting to crumble, Christopher was turning on the tears. Through embarrassingly loud sobs he pleaded mitigation. He had never been properly loved until he met Juliet. His parents had been cold. Was he going to be punished for the rest of his life? Nothing was ever his fault.

Juliet put a hand on his shoulder and gave him a dismissive sort of squeeze.

'I'm going home now. I'll see you in the office tomorrow morning.'

By the time she reached the tube station, Juliet was crying too. But she had done the right thing. She knew that. And there was to be no going back.

Christopher did not go home that evening. He returned to the office. David Sullivan had given him some very complicated instructions on setting the key-logging programme into action and he needed to have some time at his desk without anyone else around. Though Juliet had washed her hands of him, that didn't mean that Christopher could back out of the scheme. James Dean had no intention of allowing him to do that. On his last visit to see Nat in prison, Christopher had been reminded of the things at stake. Nat told him that one of Dean's enemies, inside on a murder charge, had recently been carried out of the prison in a box.

'They said it was suicide,' Nat whispered. 'But everyone knows differently here.'

Whether it was true or not, Nat had aged dramatically since James Dean came into the brothers' lives. He had started to smoke the cigarettes that Christopher brought in for him. He got through three in the space of that visit. When Christopher flinched at the sight of a Range Rover coming down the road towards him outside Anglo-Italian's offices, he knew that Dean's mission to control the brothers by fear was all but complete.

Christopher was surprised to find that Lucy was still at her desk. He had forgotten that she had asked to work late so that she could take a long weekend to go to a friend's wedding. Christopher was embarrassed to be caught red-eyed.

'Did Chelsea lose?' Lucy joked.

'Allergies,' said Christopher. 'There's a lot of pollen about at the moment.'

'I've got some antihistamines in my desk,' said Lucy.

Of course she did. Lucy was wonderfully efficient. The very model of an 'office wife' that most businessmen (and women) hoped to find in their PA.

Lucy returned with the tablets and a glass of water.

'Thank you,' said Christopher.

'My pleasure,' said Lucy. Then she added with a wink, 'Your wish is my command.'

Christopher watched Lucy wiggle back to her desk. If only all the women in his life were so eager to make things easy for him. Caroline certainly wasn't. And now Juliet had good reason to hate him too. Would she act on it? Christopher began to wonder how he could make sure she didn't.

Chapter Thirty-Three

Mercy had shocked herself by arranging her first professional singing lesson. Perhaps it was for the best that she didn't have much time to think about it and in doing so start to get nervous, though it would have been nice to have a little more time to practice. She wondered about her fellow pupils. How good would they be? Would she match up to them in any way?

Her dreams were starting to come alive again. There was no doubt in Mercy's mind that a professional singing teacher would know how to make the best of her. She withdrew the money she would need for the lessons the day before the course was due to start, planning to pay for all her lessons in one go, despite having been told she could pay in instalments; Mercy wanted to make sure that nothing kept her from her ambition. Having handed over the full amount would act as a useful spur. If she paid by piecemeal then she would miss classes as something more pressing would come up. It always did.

With the money in her hand, Mercy headed home to help her mother make lunch.

But Mercy got home to discover her mother in something of a state. Melody had her handbag open on the kitchen table. Everything she ordinarily kept in it was laid out on the oilcloth. Her ancient tube of Lancôme lipstick. Her Oyster Card. Her house keys. The little folding photo frame in which she kept two pictures: Mercy and Francis as babies, almost identical except that she was in pink and he in blue. And there was her wallet. Melody picked the wallet up and started looking through it again.

'I don't get it,' she said. 'I swear I took two hundred pounds out of the bank this afternoon.'

'Two hundred pounds?' Mercy echoed. It was unlike her mother to take out any more than fifty at a time for fear that she might lose the cash on her way back to the house. 'What did you take out two hundred pounds for?'

Melody indicated the ancient fridge freezer in the corner of the kitchen. Its judder and shudder had provided a bass-line to the sounds of Campbell family life for years. The noise of its elderly motor reverberated around the whole house when it was particularly stressed out, especially just after Melody had filled it with shopping, as she had done only that morning. But now it was silent. The motor had finally given up. Which explained the urgency of replacing the thing. One of the young lads who lived next door was an electrician. He told Melody he didn't think he would be able to find parts for such an old machine and that she was better off buying a new one.

'But I have to do it quickly,' she said. 'So the food inside doesn't thaw.'

Mercy had her hand on the refrigerator's door handle.

'Don't open it,' her mother pleaded. 'There's steak in there for your brother. It will be ruined.'

Steak for her brother, thought Mercy. Of course.

'I was going to buy a new fridge from the man by the market. He said he could deliver this afternoon if I chose one he had in stock. But by the time I got to the shop to pay him, my money had gone.'

'You think someone took the money out of your bag while you were walking there?'

Melody shook her head. 'I would have noticed if someone came near my bag. I know I would. And besides, wouldn't they have taken the whole purse?'

That much was true.

'I don't understand it. I must have left it at the cashpoint, it's the only explanation.'

It was a pretty implausible explanation to Mercy.

'Did you come home after you went to the bank?' Mercy asked.

'Yes, I came here to get my umbrella. You don't think someone broke into the kitchen while I was upstairs?'

Mercy didn't think that at all. It didn't take a detective to work out what had really gone on. The thief didn't need to break into their house. He lived there.

'Have you asked Francis?' Mercy suggested.

'He was upstairs in his bedroom listening to music. He wouldn't have heard anyone come in.' Melody completely missed the point of Mercy's question. 'Oh,' Melody took a gulp of air. 'The thought that a thief came into my house.'

'Don't think about it, Mum.' Because it never happened.

Melody sat down at the kitchen table and cried after a phone call to the bank revealed, of course, that no community-minded citizen had found two hundred pounds left at the cashpoint and handed in it. She looked at the old refrigerator with wild eyes, imagining the food she had bought that morning for the whole week already beginning to thaw and be ruined. That food represented even more money she couldn't afford to lose.

Mercy couldn't stand it. She dug into her own purse.

'Here, Mum. I can give you the money.'

Mercy held out ten twenty-pound notes to her mother.

A dozen different emotions passed over Melody's face. Astonishment, gratitude, suspicion. Mercy reacted to the suspicion. Did Melody really think Mercy had taken this money from her purse and was now trying to give it back?

'I took the money out of my savings for some singing lessons,' she said. 'I'm supposed to be starting tomorrow morning. But I can wait for a few more weeks. Unlike the steak,' Mercy added.

The thought of the steak going to waste jolted Melody into action.

'Thank you, my darling.' Melody pressed a perfumed kiss onto Mercy's cheek. 'Thank you. You don't know how grateful I am. Thank goodness you're here to look after your silly old mother. How I could have left that money at the cashpoint . . . I'll call in at the bank again on my way back from the freezer store. Perhaps some kind soul will have handed my money in by then.'

'Perhaps they will,' said Mercy.

Of course, no one had handed in any money. And so Mercy was two hundred pounds short of her singing course. She did not look forward to calling the singing coach to let her know that she would not be attending her first official lesson.

'Nine o'clock in the morning too early for you, is it?' she asked.

Mercy smarted at the idea that anyone could think she was lazy.

'I just don't have the money right now,' said Mercy. 'It was silly of me to pretend that I could afford it.'

'If you want something badly enough,' said the teacher. 'You'll find the money.'

Francis Campbell wanted a great many things badly enough to do whatever it took to get the money. Mercy's instinct had been right. Francis had taken the money from his mother's purse, but he fully intended to get the cash back to her, with interest. He had hoped to be able to do it before she even noticed the money was gone. Francis needed the two hundred quid as seed capital to buy stock for his first little foray into retail.

Chapter Thirty-Four

𝒯ʜᴇ touring company reached Rome minus Andrew Fleetwood but otherwise in good shape. In true diva style, Cosima had announced that she wanted to be alone as the company left Paris, but as soon as they crossed the Italian border, she seemed to perk up. By the time the company principals checked into the Hotel Eden on the Via Ludovisi with its view over the whole of the Eternal City, Cosima seemed to have forgotten all about Andrew Fleetwood. Though he hadn't forgotten about her, if the number of texts he was sending to her hourly were anything to go by. After the first twenty, she simply deleted them unread and hoped that he might soon start to feel as relieved to be uncoupled as she did.

Besides, Cosima could not fail to be uplifted by the company's arrival in Italy. Cosima loved to be in Italy. Especially Rome. It wasn't just that it was a beautiful city. For Cosima Rome had special, familial resonance. Her paternal grandparents had been born within a few streets of each other in the nearby port of Civitavecchia. They'd sailed to New York separately but met and fell in love when Cosima's grandfather overheard her grandmother complaining loudly, in her Roman accent, about the state of American tomatoes. Now just the sound of spoken Italian made Cosima feel at home. When she ate Italian food, she was in heaven.

Meanwhile, Cosima's truce with Nolan was still holding up. During rehearsals, they sat next to each other and didn't rush to opposite sides of the room whenever there was a break in proceedings. Karl was stunned when they said they would both join him for lunch. So far on the tour he had not persuaded them to eat at the same table. But now they were delightful company. Karl noted that in Nolan's presence, Cosima suddenly seemed to glitter in a way that could not be replicated by draping her in all the jewels that Martin et Fils had to offer.

After a wonderful rehearsal at the opera house, the company had an evening at leisure. Once everyone else had cleared off, Nolan dared to ask Cosima if she might care to join him for supper and to his delighted surprise, she agreed.

'Where are we going?' she asked in the cab back to the hotel.

Nolan stalled for time by saying that he was waiting for a confirmation from one of Rome's most chi-chi spots. Then, the second Cosima went to her room to change, he raced to the concierge and began a scramble to find somewhere. Anywhere. It was high season and the city's restaurants were packed. But the concierge at the Eden was a miracle worker and came back fifteen minutes later with a confirmed reservation at Ludovisi's, an old-school restaurant in the Trastevere, popular with the very smartest Romans. Nolan could have kissed him. He knew Cosima would be impressed.

Cosima looked simply ravishing when she met Nolan in the lobby later that night. With her long dark hair piled on top her head in a messily elegant bun and wearing a dark green dress that made the most of her shoulders and décolletage, she could have given a young Sophia Loren a run for her money. Nolan was even more delighted when, defeated by city's cobblestones in her high heels, Cosima threaded her arm through his for balance on the walk from the taxi to the restaurant. It was the first time Cosima had touched Nolan outside their performances of *Tosca*, since the divorce came through. The feel of her soft warm hand on his arm made Nolan's skin prickle and tickle with anticipation. The smell of her familiar perfume took him hurtling back through the years to the last time they had walked in the Trastevere. Had twelve years really passed since then?

It was set to be a wonderful night. The weather was balmy. Not too humid or hot. The maître d' of the restaurant, who was a big fan of the opera, had arranged, even at such short notice, for the lovers to have an excellent table on the terrace: a table where they could see and be seen. What was the point in having a goddess like Cosima Esposito at your restaurant if the whole world couldn't know about it?

Cosima and Nolan accepted a complementary aperitivo and posed for a quick photograph with the owner of the house in return. They dined extravagantly. Five courses. A bottle and a half of wine. Limoncello. Cosima had always loved Limoncello. And now Nolan recalled the first time he had seen her drink the vile yellow stuff.

'Do you remember the first time we came to Rome?' he asked. 'Together?'

Cosima allowed herself a small smile. Of course she did. Nolan didn't need to know that she had thought of little else on this leg of the tour. Cosima had been waiting for him to mention it first.

It was almost exactly twelve years since Cosima and Nolan took that romantic trip together. At the time, Cosima was understudying the part of Liu in *Turandot* at the Royal Opera House and Nolan was in *Don Giovanni* in Vienna. They hadn't seen each other in almost a month. Rome seemed like a good place for the long-distance lovers to meet up. A wonderful place. Cosima spent a small fortune on special underwear for the trip.

They had stayed in a charming little apartment by the art school on the Via Margutta that belonged to the friend of a friend. Nolan told Cosima that it was the actual apartment where Gregory Peck entertained Audrey Hepburn in *Roman Holiday*, which was one of Cosima's favourite films. It wasn't the apartment, of course. The rooms were pokey but they didn't care. Back then, their whole world was contained within their embracing arms.

They spent afternoons walking around the narrow streets and ancient monuments holding hands, oblivious to the drizzle that marred the whole weekend. Nothing could dampen their happiness. They had each other.

Nolan proposed to Cosima beside the Colosseum. He had planned to make his proposal by the Trevi Fountain but there were so many people crowding the monument,

Cosima had started to get anxious about pickpockets after two small boys jostled her and they had given up and gone for a coffee instead. After that they jumped into a horse-drawn carriage and jumped off again onto a cobbled-street. Cosima nearly lost a heel to a gap between the cobbles. She had looked set to explode with fury but Nolan's proposal had stopped her in her tracks.

'Cosima Esposito, stop whining. I want you to be my wife!'

'Oh my goodness,' she had pressed her hand to her heart.

To help her decide, Nolan sang a piece from *La Bohème*. It brought the whole street to a standstill. Soon a crowd had gathered around them, snapping pictures. A few people who had an inkling of how special Nolan's voice really was (who perhaps even recognised him) recorded snatches of the singing on their video cameras.

By this point, Cosima was in floods of tears. She nodded her 'yes' and Nolan swept her into his arms for a passionate kiss that drew a round of applause from their fellow tourists.

They headed back to the apartment, tripping over their own feet as they walked with their arms wrapped tightly around one another and their lips locked together. In the lift up to the apartment, Cosima stripped off Nolan's shirt. He struggled to find the zipper on her dress, so that, laughing at his fumbling, she had to show him where it was.

They tumbled out of the lift half naked, to the shock of the elderly woman who lived on the same floor. Nolan tipped an imaginary hat to her but she would ignore them when they crossed paths for the remainder of their time in Rome.

The newly engaged lovers didn't care. Cosima was already inside the apartment. She snaked out an arm and pulled

Nolan in after her. She let her dress drop to the floor. She kicked off her silly shoes. Nolan, minus his trousers, followed her to the bed.

Cosima threw herself down on the mattress. Nolan hesitated for a moment, taking in this front row view of his new fiancée in all her glory. Cosima made the most of it too, posing herself to best effect on the white linen. Her thick dark hair fanned out across the pillow. She licked her lips, luscious and full with excitement. Nolan let his gaze travel down over her body. She was wearing expensive-looking red silk lingerie that he hadn't seen before, the perfect wrapping for such a delicious present.

'Come on then.'

Cosima beckoned Nolan forward with a finger. He leaned over her. As soon as he was close enough, she reached up and circled his neck with her arms, pulling him down upon her. Her eyes were laughing as he rolled onto the bed beside her and they tumbled over and over until she was on top.

Nolan's hands roved all over her body, tracing the smooth luxurious lines that filled his waking thoughts and his dreams.

'I have to have you inside me,' said Cosima, as she wriggled out of the little red slip and sat back down astride Nolan's strong thighs.

His penis stood up proudly between them, harder than Cosima had ever seen it before. The clear signal of Nolan's desire made her own desire feel even more urgent. She wrapped her fingers around him.

With her free hand, Cosima took off her bra and released her fabulous full breasts from the crimson silk that had been holding them so prettily. Nolan was delighted by the sight of his two old friends. He reached up to touch them. Cosima giggled as his fingers brushed her nipples, making them pucker and harden.

By now, Nolan was set to beg Cosima to let him thrust into her, fearing that he would come in a second whether she was ready for him or not. She moved so that his penis was directly beneath her and sank down about him with a grateful sigh.

When Cosima put her mind to it, there was nothing Nolan could do to stop her racing him to his climax. Nolan roared her name as he came deep inside her that night. When she finally stopped shaking with her own orgasm, she fell upon him, laughing softly into his neck.

'Now don't you think that was a virtuoso performance . . .'

When he had recovered from being taken so spectacularly, Nolan made love to Cosima again in such a way that she had no doubt that he was serious about his feelings for her. She told him that he was the only man who could make her body sing as well as her voice. She couldn't wait to vow to be his for the rest of her life.

They got married at City Hall in New York. It was a small ceremony. They wanted to get married as quickly as they could, and the municipal office was all that was really available to them at such short notice. The reception too, was somewhat less extravagant than Cosima might have dreamed of as a girl: just a meal for twenty at their favourite local Italian restaurant. The restaurant owner sprang for the bill, telling the bride that over the years she had been coming to his trattoria, he had come to consider her one of the family. Cosima, who had lost her father as a very young girl, was moved to tears again. People were so very kind.

So, their wedding had been modest, but that didn't mean it was any less wonderful than a grand church ceremony with all the trimmings. And Cosima and Nolan agreed as they fell into bed that night (their own bed in their own apartment. A honeymoon would have to wait until they could afford it) that they had never been happier.

'It's been the best day of my life,' said Cosima.

'There will be better to come,' Nolan promised.

Oh, if only it had turned out like that, Cosima thought to herself as she and Nolan sat opposite each other on the terrace of Ludovisi's restaurant now. She looked down at their hands, which had somehow become entwined on the pure white tablecloth, and shook her head sadly.

'So many memories,' she said. 'So many *sad* memories.'

'Some of them must be happy,' Nolan tried.

Of course there were happy memories too but Cosima hadn't dared think too much about the good times since the day their divorce came through. It was easier not to, since thinking about the parts of their relationship that had worked could only make the pain of losing it worse.

It wasn't just about the great sex. The truth was that Nolan O'Connor was the only man who had ever truly made her heart sing. No one had made her laugh so hard or sigh so loudly (with desire and frustration). Ever since their divorce, Cosima had tried to convince herself that she should want nothing to do with such an immature, selfish little prick of a man, but the alternative had turned out to be worse. Men like Andrew Fleetwood were as reliable and faithful as the proverbial old slippers. But it turned out that Cosima was a woman who needed the crippling beauty of a pair of exotic high heels to truly feel alive. When you've loved like that, when you've experienced a passion that makes you see the point in living, you can't go back. And if the chance ever comes to have that love again then, of course, you can't help thinking you should take it, even if the pleasure comes with a whole other world of pain.

Cosima untangled her fingers from Nolan's and picked up her glass. She knocked back the last half inch of Limoncello in one.

'We should go,' she said, thinking that it was best to end this conversation right now, before it got even more sentimental. Nolan obliged. He called for the check but the maître d' told the two stars that he would be honoured if the restaurant could foot their bill.

'It is just so wonderful to see you back together again,' he said. 'I saw you perform *Tosca* at La Scala.'

'Don't mention La Scala,' Nolan joked.

'Oh, La Scala,' Cosima sighed. It was clear by now that she was more than a little bit drunk.

Nolan suggested that they take a scenic route back to the hotel. As they neared the Colosseum, each knew for certain what was going through the other's mind. The conversation dwindled to silence while the tension between them rose. But it was a different kind of tension now, more like the nervous anticipation that had gripped them both before their very first kiss.

'Oh Nolan!' Just as Nolan was making his mind up that he would sweep Cosima into his arms, she saved him the bother and leaped into them, pressing her lips against his with gratifying urgency.

Chapter Thirty-Six

𝄞

By the ancient walls of the Colosseum, Cosima and Nolan kissed like the young lovers they once were, tongues entwined, their hands roaming freely. It wasn't long before Nolan had his hand up the back of Cosima's blouse. They were so absorbed in one another, that they barely registered the sound of a woman's anguished scream.

'Get a room,' said a passing British tourist to the amusement of his friends.

'Shall we?' Nolan whispered naughtily.

Cosima nodded. 'I thought you'd never ask.'

They went back to Cosima's suite at the Hotel Eden. Nolan was momentarily disgruntled to discover that Cosima's room was so much better than his, but the sight of his former wife in her lacy black underwear soon took his mind off the accommodation.

'Come here,' he pulled her close to him, burying his face in her glorious chestnut hair, just breathing in the scent that he had missed so much.

'Oh, how I've longed for your body,' he sighed as his fingers made an inventory of every bare inch of her soft, olive skin. He sat down on the edge of the bed and she stood between his legs. Cosima was every bit as wonderful as he remembered. She arched her back so that the cleavage Nolan had lusted after for so long was suddenly very much in his face. Nolan moaned with ecstasy as she released the catch on her bra and his hands cupped her perfect breasts, while his lips sought out her nipples. Cosima gasped as he massaged her nipples to arousal with his tongue.

The reunion of their two bodies was every bit as fabulous as Nolan and Cosima had dared to imagine it might be. There had been no awkwardness. They came back together as though they had been apart for five minutes instead of five years.

'Was it as good as you remember?' Cosima asked.

'Better,' Nolan replied.

'It just feels right, somehow,' said Cosima, almost to herself.

'Like coming home,' Nolan agreed, as he wrapped his arms around her and drifted into sleep.

Florence Carter could not believe what she was seeing. As she wandered through the Trastevere, she had given up expecting to see her love, but there he was, sitting on the terrace of a restaurant. At first, he appeared to be alone. But Florence soon noticed that there were two half-finished glasses of wine on the table. And so she couldn't just barge in there and announce herself.

She had braced herself for Nolan's companion to be a woman. She had prayed that it wouldn't be. But when she saw that he was with Cosima Esposito! As Cosima sashayed back to her seat at the table, Florence's blood began to sing in her ears. What was he doing with that bitch? After all the pain Cosima had put him through. Surely he wasn't trying to butter the fat cow up. Was he doing it deliberately to upset Florence for a transgression she didn't understand?

Florence considered her options and decided that she had none. She could stay and watch Nolan and Cosima eat their dinner, or she could go back to her hotel. As the tears started to run down her cheeks, she realised that she had to get away. The last thing she wanted was for Nolan to glance up and see her there. But at the same time, she *couldn't* walk away. She was in love with Nolan. She wanted to know what he looked like when he was eating. She wanted to know what he was having. She wanted to know where he planned to go when he was finished. And whether he would go there alone.

So she had followed them on their romantic walk.

Florence stood outside the Hotel Eden for almost two hours before she admitted to herself that Nolan was not going to come back out again that night. She went back to her own far more modest hotel and woke the manager, begging him to allow her to use the hotel's 'business centre' (really just a PC in a cupboard).

Her clear distress prompted the manager to be kind.

'I have to write to someone urgently,' she said.
'Has there been a death?' the hotel manager asked.
'Something very like a death,' said Florence.

Nolan O'Connor, I don't know if I can even bear to look at you ever again . . .

Chapter Thirty-Seven

$\oint$

JULIET received the email asking her to see the head of human resources as she walked from the tube station into work. Though the email was brief and said nothing much, to Juliet it said everything. She had been copied in on many similar emails during the panicky early months of the previous year, when the credit crunch was turning the entire financial world upside-down and Anglo-Italian shed almost a third of its staff. Since then, the company had managed to get itself back on a fairly even keel. There hadn't been any redundancies for a while and none had been hinted at. All the same, Juliet had a feeling that HR would not want to talk with her about whether she was happy with her working environment or thought she needed a more ergonomically correct typing chair. And she was right, though only to a certain extent. She was not about to be offered redundancy.

'Miss Hunter.'

The formal manner in which Helena Roberts, the HR

officer, who knew her by her first name, called her in had Juliet immediately on guard. As she stepped into the office, Juliet noticed right away that Martin Ford, an employment lawyer, was there too. He was someone Juliet knew well enough to exchange pleasantries with, but that afternoon he did even not look up from the file on the desk in front of him. Martin opened the file and began the meeting, still without looking up.

'Miss Hunter, you've been called in here this morning because we've been made aware of several emails sent from your account that seem to suggest insider dealing.'

'What?' This was not what Juliet had been expecting, not at all.

'It has been decided that you will be suspended from your position pending a full investigation.'

'Do you want to tell me exactly what I'm supposed to have done?'

Martin continued. 'We have print-outs here of the email exchanges in question, between you and a Mr. Adeki in Nigeria regarding the imminent sale of part of Evgeny Belanov's business. You knew about that.'

'About the sale, yes, but . . .'

'These emails contain confidential information that could be used by Mr. Adeki to his advantage. You understand what that means?'

'Of course, but . . .'

'Your trading account has already been suspended,' said Martin.

'This is ridiculous,' Juliet protested. 'These emails weren't sent by me. I haven't even heard of this Mr. Adeki. What is going on here?'

Helena intervened. 'We know this is stressful,' she said.

'And if someone else has been using your email account then we will get to the bottom of it. But you can't remain here in the Anglo-Italian offices while an investigation is underway. Now, I understand that you may have personal effects in your office that you need to collect. I'll have someone escort you to the sixteenth floor so you can sort that out right now.'

'This is crazy,' said Juliet. She got up, ready to give Martin and Helena a piece of her mind, but two security guards had appeared behind her as though summoned by a wizard from thin air. They stepped forward the moment her bum left the seat, making it quite clear that any display of emotion would not be tolerated.

'Fine,' said Juliet. 'I will be talking to a lawyer.'

Juliet felt all eyes upon her as she walked the corridor back to the office she had worked in for the past five years. It was clear that someone had already been through every folder, every drawer of her desk. They'd even emptied and badly refilled the make-up bag she kept in the bottom drawer so that she could go straight from the office to dinner. They'd probably been looking for a memory stick hidden beneath the lipstick and mascara. Her computer screen and the hard drive were gone, leaving behind a clear square in the dust that Juliet hadn't noticed before. Michaela, her PA, followed Juliet and the security guards into her office.

'What's happening?' Juliet asked her.

'I honestly don't know,' said Michaela. 'I don't know what's going on at all.'

Her anxious expression made Juliet certain that Michaela was telling the truth.

'Could you get me a cardboard box?' Juliet asked, bowing to the inevitable.

Michaela obliged and soon Juliet had packed what few truly personal possessions she kept at the office away. As she did so, one of the IT bods appeared to take her company laptop, her BlackBerry and the little electronic toggle she used to get updated access codes while on the move. She managed to prevent herself from crying by comforting Michaela who had not done so well at hiding her distress.

'Don't worry,' said Juliet. 'I'll be back.'

She was confident that within hours she would be reinstated with grovelling apologies from the idiots in HR.

Juliet didn't feel quite so confident as she was escorted from the building after surrendering her Anglo-Italian pass. An investigation may have been pending, but the security guys acted as though she had been caught bang to rights. Guilty until proven innocent.

Juliet went straight from the Anglo-Italian office to the offices of Mountford Madden, the law firm, where she met with Derek Foster, the employment lawyer who had negotiated her contract five years before. He was only too keen to represent her in her current predicament and began making calls right away.

As she learned more about this mysterious client in Nigeria, she had supposedly been feeding privileged information, Juliet became more and more certain that someone was setting her up.

Who that someone was seemed fairly obvious to Juliet. She called Christopher from the lobby of Mountford Madden. He didn't take her call. She left him six messages, asking him to be in touch with her at once. He didn't respond.

Juliet knew exactly what had happened. After Caroline

sent the scan and Juliet reacted by telling Christopher that reconciliation was impossible, Christopher had panicked. He had assumed that her loyalty to him would not last beyond the end of their affair and that now they had broken up, she would make life difficult for him. And so he had engineered this investigation. And made sure that she was told of the charges against her while he was not around to face her anger. His cowardice made Juliet want to weep.

'Rest assured that we will get you reinstated as quickly as possible,' said Derek Foster. 'I'm sure we'll get to the bottom of this before too long.'

Leaving her lawyer's office, Juliet was desperate to hear a friendly voice. She couldn't call David. He was in the States that week, attending some big IT conference. It was only four in the morning in California. She didn't want to wake him up and so she had to content herself with writing an email that David would receive when he got out of bed. Perhaps he would have some insight as to what she should do next.

The way she saw it, Christopher was the only person at Anglo-Italian who had any reason to want her out of the way. All she had to do was prove it.

Chapter Thirty-Eight

𝄞

Unlike Juliet, James Dean had plenty of business contacts in Lagos. Just five years earlier, he couldn't have found Nigeria on a map, but now he was in touch with his new Nigerian associates on a daily basis. Nigeria still led the world when it came to the so-called 'Advance Fee Fraud' or 419 Scam – in which punters were encouraged to part with their bank details in order to help a 'government official' move funds for the enticement of a nice big fee. Of course, there was no money and no fee. Those idiots who responded to the scammers' call would have their accounts emptied out. Simple as that.

After so many *Daily Mail* and BBC *Watchdog* exposes, Dean wouldn't have believed that the badly written email or fax telling the recipient that they would receive an enormous payment for helping to clear some funds for a stranger would ever work again. But it did. Every day, greedy, stupid people opened their emails and thought it would be a great idea to send a stranger all the information he or she needed to clean the sucker out. The schemes netted thousands every day with virtually no effort on the scammers' part at all. Dean had got himself a slice of it by helping a very prominent Nigerian gangster escape justice in the UK. The scam had given him a taste for white-collar crime. Now Dean thanked God for stupidity and greed. They kept his wife in Dolce and Gabbana.

Dolce and Gabbana. Versace. Cavalli. There was nothing that Tara Dean couldn't have. She had married very well. James Dean considered himself to have made a great success of his life. He was the youngest of four, raised in a two-bedroom flat on a council estate by a single mum. He shared a bed with a brother until he was six and a half. These days he sent his 'dear old mum' ten grand a week and the council flat had long since been upgraded for a mansion near Chelmsford.

For Dean, the last five years had been all about expansion. Many of the old-school British gangsters had seen their turf invaded by gangs from Eastern Europe, the 'Stans or Somalia. Unable to compete with rivals who had been hardened by real deprivation and even war, rather than simply having grown up without colour TV, some of the East End old-timers just hung up their boots and retired to the Costa Del Sol. But James Dean wasn't ready to retire. And where his former colleagues saw the end, he saw opportunity. Like any foresighted entrepreneur, he set about equipping himself with the staff he needed to negotiate with these new players in the game. He started to employ translators, which shocked the newcomers who tried to intimidate him into coming to the table instead. Dean played up the advantage of his local knowledge. In particular, he knew that all the new boys would be interested in Dean's long-standing relationships within the British police and the judicial system.

Evgeny Belanov was particularly impressed by Dean's connections with officers at every port and airport in the United Kingdom. Dean occasionally filled a whole flight from Jamaica with drugs mules, sure in the knowledge that the customs officers would all be on their tea break when his team touched down. Belanov could use that free passage of goods. And so Dean's most valuable business partnership so far had been forged, with Dean flying to the French Riviera to shake hands on the association on the deck of Belanov's huge yacht, as though they were the CEOs of two extremely respectable businesses.

Indeed to the outside world, James Dean was starting to look quite respectable. You couldn't get as rich as he had done without attracting attention and the best way to divert some of that attention was to make genuine investments. He started by buying up businesses that ran largely on a cash basis like dry-cleaning firms. He'd bought into some building firms during the property boom and finally he bought a second division football team. He was especially pleased with that (though three years later, he sold the football club just as quickly as he had bought it, after his star player made a pass at his wife. Sold for relative peanuts, the club soon went downhill and the star player never kicked a ball again, after a nasty car accident).

Had James Dean risen so quickly and spectacularly in legitimate business, he would have had a knighthood.

Chapter Thirty-Nine

'WHAT you looking at? You looking at me?'

Francis Campbell pulled shapes in front of his bedroom mirror. He was like any other teenage boy, practising his hard-man stare, except that the prop he was using as he acted out his fantasies next to a wardrobe covered in Chelsea FC posters was a very real Smith and Wesson. Francis pointed the gun at his own reflection and made as if to pull the trigger.

'Bang,' he said. 'You are lookin' at a killah.'

'Francis! Francis!' His mother called up the stairs. 'Your dinner is on the table.'

'Be right down, Mum.'

Francis stopped posing. Carefully, with the reverence due a weapon that could cause so much harm, Francis secreted the gun in a locked box beneath his bed, covering it with a layer of porn magazines. He knew that if his mother bothered to open the box, she would not look beneath those mags because she wouldn't want to touch them, lest the filth rub off on her.

Then Francis headed downstairs, looking every inch the innocent boy that his mother still believed he was. Mercy was there too, in her overalls, ready to leave for her night shift as a cleaner. Mercy looked at her brother, throwing his arms around their mother and thanking her profusely, with scepticism. Francis looked at his sister with pity.

'What are you doing tonight?' Melody asked her favourite boy.

'I'm going to see some of the boys,' he said. 'Probably watch a DVD.'

'That is nice,' said Melody. 'You know, you are more than welcome to invite your friends round here. We have a DVD player too.'

'I know, Mum. But I don't want to put you to any trouble.'

'It's no trouble to me. I want you to feel like you can have your friends over.'

'So you can keep an eye on me?' Francis said with a wink. 'I'm all right, Mum. You wouldn't want my friends over. They might mess up your nice tidy front room.'

Melody beamed and looked over to Mercy as if to say, 'Look how thoughtful your brother is.'

Mercy left the house just a few moments after her brother. The same Range Rover that Mercy had seen the previous week was there at the top of the street. She saw Francis climb into the back seat. She paused, watching for a moment. The other guy in the back of the car appeared to cuff her brother around the head and not in a playful way. Mercy immediately felt as protective as she had done when Francis was a small boy but by the time she got to the end of the street, the Range Rover with her brother inside it was long gone.

Mercy brooded on what she had seen for the rest of the night.

Francis wasn't worried about what he was getting himself into. He wasn't going to end up like Xavier Hale. What Xavier's mother, and his own, neglected to mention about Xavier now that he was dead was that the boy had always been a class one idiot. He was two years above Francis at school and Francis had heard people laughing about Xavier's stupidity. It wasn't just academic stupidity. He was, as his teachers like to write in their end of term reports, an 'easily led' sort of boy. That is how he ended up in the wrong crowd in and out of school. And that is how he ended up taking drugs for the first time.

Xavier Hale was the worst kind of dealer. Far too often he sampled his own goods. It got to the stage where he wasn't selling anything at all, just keeping it for himself. He'd go on three-day binges. And since he wasn't selling anything, he didn't have the money to pay back his own suppliers. That was why he had been killed.

Francis was not that stupid. Apart from a little grass, he had never touched drugs in his life. He would sell Class As but he would never, ever take them himself. He had seen the way they made people act. At best, a few lines of coke would make you talk crap for a couple of hours. At worst, they would steal away your life.

In a funny way, Francis had paid attention to the message he heard at his struggling school. Francis's form teacher encouraged his students to look for inspiration in those who had already succeeded. 'Look for people who have already made it to the place you want to go,' he told them. 'Call that person up. Make a contact. Ask for help. Get yourself a *mentor*.'

Mentor. Francis liked that word. And that was what he had looked for. But Francis didn't rush to the library to pick up a self-congratulatory biography by the likes of Sir Richard Branson or Lord Alan Sugar. He picked up an anonymously penned book about the real-life gangster families who were running Britain's booming shadow economy. And he was especially taken by the story of one poor Essex boy made rich, if not good. Francis decided to model himself on James Dean.

So when he heard one of the older guys in the barber shop running off at the mouth about having met Dean, his new hero, Francis took a careful mental note. All he had to do was find a way to get close to him. Francis determined that he would offer himself as an apprentice to the most successful man in the game.

It hadn't taken long to make the right connections. Within a week, Francis found himself in front of one of Dean's foot soldiers in an anonymous-looking house on Herne Hill Road. Francis had agreed that he would find two hundred quid in cash as a deposit for drugs that had a street value of a grand. If he could sell the drugs in the space of the weekend, he was in. He should consider this his probation.

'No sweat,' said Francis. He already had buyers marked for a third of the total. Greg, his former manager at Alpha Sports was a middle-class white kid who liked to think he was cool. He'd never bought drugs before. Though he'd always liked the idea, he'd been too frightened of the dealers who hung around outside the tube station, believing that they would just as likely stab him as hand over a wrap of coke. So when Francis said that he could get coke for Greg and all of his friends, he took the chance. Francis had worked for him. He wouldn't screw him over.

It was a win-win situation. Francis told the clueless Greg that the going rate for an ounce of coke was twice what it actually was, which meant that Francis had a built-in margin for error. He only had to sell half the coke to cover his essential costs. Dean's lackey need never know.

But if Francis had thought that all he had to do to ingratiate himself to James Dean was be a good salesman, he was mistaken. Good salesmen were easy to find. As long as people had disposable income there was a market for drugs. In fact, when the economy was bad, there was an even greater market for drugs. People need to be cheered up, Dean explained as though he were plugging the latest feel-good film.

For Francis to prove himself truly useful, he had to be prepared to go further. That was where the gun came in.

While Dean had managed to evade justice for quite some time, he knew that the day might come when one of his bent coppers suddenly straightened out. For that reason, Dean wanted to minimise his risk. Carrying a firearm was a fast track to hard time inside. If someone Francis's age were caught with a gun, however, it would be altogether less serious. And thus Francis had been chosen to be one of Dean's gun-holders, ready to rush to his boss's side with a firearm whenever one should be required. And equally ready to hide the gun when it's work was done.

Chapter Forty

𝒮INCE their surprising reunion in Rome, Cosima and Nolan had been a proper pair of lovebirds again. Some of the less respectful members of the company made gagging motions when they saw the two principals walking hand in hand. In many ways, Cosima and Nolan had been so much more interesting when they were fighting! Everyone had enjoyed the barbs they hurled at each other. They wanted, if they were honest, to see Cosima reprise Miss Piggy. Seeing the off-on lovers locking tongues instead of horns was not so great.

Still, Karl had news to liven things up for everybody. 'We've had a request for an impromptu gig,' he said. 'In St Petersburg. I don't see why we shouldn't since we're going to be there anyway. It's a private concert for Evgeny Belanov.'

'The oligarch?' Cosima asked.

'The very same. Apparently he's a big fan of Cosima's.'

'Oh, my goodness,' said Cosima. 'Yes!'

Cosima didn't need to consider the offer for a second. She was extremely flattered at the thought that the oligarch had asked her to sing. Belanov had sent her roses about a year previously. She knew he was a fan. The chance to sing at his private residence was not one she wanted to miss. She immediately began to wonder if she could persuade Mathieu Randon to lend her some jewels for the occasion. It should be easy to convince Randon of the sense in it. Belanov's friends would be great customers for Martin et Fils. And of course, Cosima wanted to look the part.

The rest of the chorus was similarly delighted. The girls buzzed with the idea of it, each of them hoping they might find an oligarch of their own at Belanov's glittering party: someone who could take them away from the drudgery of life on tour. It really wasn't half so glamorous as it sounded. The lowliest members of the chorus and the orchestra were staying in far more modest hotels than the principals. Sometimes they even had to share rooms. They were not about to complain about doing an extra gig if it meant, as Karl explained, that their accommodation in St Petersburg would be significantly upgraded. That was even before he mentioned the fee, which would double the take-home pay of some of the cast members.

Only Nolan objected on the grounds that he would be tired from all the travelling. He was quickly shouted down. He could do it, they told him. It wasn't as though they were going to perform a whole opera. This was a massive opportunity for the less well-paid members of the company.

'Please tell Mr Belanov that we would be delighted to accept.' Cosima had the last word.

*   *   *

So, Cosima was delighted with the way that life was working out. But Florence Carter had not got over seeing the love of her life reunited with his bitch of an ex. Was he screwing Cosima again just to upset her? She couldn't eat. She couldn't sleep. She hadn't changed her clothes in three days. The receptionist at the hotel in Verona had actually wrinkled her nose as Florence stood in front of the desk.

On the train to Verona, Florence had considered heading back to the States early. Once in Verona, she emailed her travel agent to ask if he could fix an early flight outta there. His reply was disappointing. He had booked Florence's transatlantic flights from London on a non-refundable basis, he explained, in order to keep her costs low, exactly as she'd requested. She couldn't change the date or time on her ticket either. He could easily find her a new ticket, however. There was availability. But it was high season, he explained. Florence was looking at having to spend thousands of dollars, even for an economy seat. She just didn't have that money. Every penny of her redundancy package had been 'invested' in this bank-breaking attempt to make a connection with Nolan O'Connor.

The only option was to push on with the rest of the tour, travelling on trains she had already paid for, staying in her non-refundable rooms. She was stuck in Europe for as long as Nolan was. Though she didn't have to watch the opera. In Verona, she considered staying in her hotel room in protest, rather than attending the sell-out performance of *Tosca* in the arena – the Roman amphitheatre – to show Nolan she was turning her back on him but with just half an hour to go, she hurried through the town to her seat.

The people on either side of her edged away just a little when Florence sat down in a billow of skirts and body odour.

In the end, Florence was glad that she had made the effort. She was convinced this time that Nolan had seen her. And as the cast took their curtain call, he had winked at her! She saw it!

'Oh, Nolan.' She pressed her hand to her heart and then gestured with open arms towards him, as though she were releasing a dove of peace in his direction. When she saw his smile, she could forgive him anything.

So as usual, when the performance ended, Florence rushed to find the performers' exit. But the amphitheatre at Verona was so huge and so full of people that night, that she had no chance of even getting outside the ancient monument before Nolan and the rest of the cast were on their executive coach and on their way to Venice, which was the next stop on the tour.

Florence was disappointed, of course, but the connection she felt with Nolan that night had given her quite a boost. She wandered back to her hotel, discovering to her delight that her route took her past the balcony that was held to be the very same balcony where star-crossed lovers Romeo and Juliet played out their tragic affair. Over the years, tourists had come to view Juliet's balcony as a shrine for lovers with Juliet as its saint and there were hundreds, if not thousands, of entreaties for love scribbled on paper and left as offerings for the tragic girl.

Florence wrote her own little wish onto a piece of paper. No prizes for guessing what it was. And after that she had to content herself with writing an email.

Dear Nolan,

You may have noticed that you haven't heard from me for a couple of days. That is because I have been very angry with you. I have used up nearly all my life savings to come with you on this tour and I have to say that you don't seem to be very grateful. There have been numerous opportunities when you could have taken a little time to see me. In Rome, for example, when you had a rest day. You knew where I was staying and yet you chose instead to spend time with the woman you supposedly can't stand! Oh yes, Nolan. I saw you. I saw you both. Outside that cosy little trattoria. Holding hands across the table. How do you think I felt when I saw that!

I was so furious I could have walked over there and spat in your dinner. And then to see you kiss her! God knows what you could have caught from that hussy. Didn't you learn your lesson the first time around? Luckily for you, I am a very forgiving woman. So when I saw you wink and wave at me tonight, I decided to give you another chance. But I can't keep on giving you more chances, Nolan O'Connor. At some point soon, you are going to have to prove to me that you deserve my faith in you. If I don't hear from you before the tour gets to St Petersburg, then trust me, there will be consequences.

Karen logged on to Nolan's website the next morning with a mixture of dread and guilty excitement. Her assistant Laetitia sat beside her, bouncing up and down in her chair at the thought of what they might find.

'Has she written? Has she written?' Laetitia asked.

'Hang on,' Karen scrolled down through the mailbox. Nolan got an inordinate amount of spam about penis

enlargement. And for one disappointing moment, Karen thought there was nothing from Florence after all, but ...
'Here it is!'

Laetitia clapped her hands together with glee. Karen prepared to read the email out loud.

'Do the accent,' said Laetitia.

'I will not,' said Karen. 'It's bad enough that this poor woman thinks she is writing to Nolan and Nolan alone.'

'Spoilsport.'

Karen read out the rest of the email then sat back in her chair and frowned at the computer screen.

'"Trust me, there will be consequences" ... You know what,' said Karen. 'This really isn't funny anymore.'

'You're right,' said Laetitia. 'It's frickin' hilarious.'

'Seriously,' Karen frowned at her young PA. 'We shouldn't be laughing at this woman. We should be telling her to go get some help. I'm starting to get anxious. She has never even spoken to Nolan face to face and yet she's sent him Cartier cufflinks and now she's spending her life savings following him around Europe on this silly little tour. She's already stalking him. What if she does something stupid?'

'How stupid?'

'Like kills herself. Or ...' Karen took a deep breath. 'Tries to do something to Nolan.'

Laetitia looked suitably horrified. 'Like when that mad fan stabbed Monica Seles?'

'Ended her career,' Karen nodded gravely. 'I mean, a death would be a great thing for Nolan's recording sales in the first instance but then ... I intend to retire on the back of Nolan O'Connor's earnings. He is my best client and now that he's revealed himself to be a competent baritone as well as a world-class tenor, if he takes care of his voice and doesn't get screwed to death by a pair of blond twins, he could be singing into his eighties. I am going to call Nolan now and tell him to be on his guard. And then I am going to call some lawyers and see if anything can be done to keep Florence Carter from going within a hundred feet of him.'

'There are no actual threats to Nolan in her emails,' Laetitia pointed out.

'But surely any fool can see this woman is madder than a box of frogs.'

Nolan listened to Karen's concerns but in reality he was oblivious to the agony he had inflicted on Florence Carter. He was thoroughly wrapped up in his reignited love for Cosima. They drifted around Verona like newly-weds. When they paused in front of Juliet's balcony and admired the bronze statue of the unfortunate girl they wished for something very different than Nolan's hopelessly obsessed fan had written on her piece of paper.

Chapter Forty-One

𝄞

*T*HAT week, the nights were hot in every sense of the word. Europe was in the grip of a heatwave, but Nolan and Cosima's new love for each other was enough to set the sheets on fire in a snowstorm.

In Venice, La Serenissima, the lovers stayed at the Hotel Cipriani. During those hours when they did not have to perform or be in rehearsal, they lay on the ocean-wide bed, listening to the sound of the water outside the window. From time to time they took a vaporetto to a tiny restaurant off the tourist track, but every moment they spent outside the bedroom, was full of anticipation and longing. The Cipriani boatman turned a blind eye when Nolan and Cosima couldn't keep their hands off each other long enough to get back behind closed doors.

On their last night in Venice, they dined in the cosy glamour of Harry's Bar. As the taxi-boat navigated the dark choppy waters of the canal back to the hotel, Nolan and

Cosima were already lip-locked. Cosima snaked her fingers between the buttons on Nolan's shirt, feeling his warm skin, already slightly moist with the heat. At the hotel, Nolan couldn't wait for the Cipriani staff to help Cosima on shore. He jumped onto the jetty and hauled her out of the boat himself, then carried her back to their suite.

Safely inside, Cosima stripped Nolan of his shirt and fondled his chest hair while he unzipped his trousers. Cosima was wearing a wrap dress, very easy to get out of. Nolan took hold of one of the ties and Cosima twirled herself naked, like Cleopatra freeing herself from the carpet. Cosima was ready to rip off her lingerie too, but Nolan had her pause for a moment, so that he could admire her.

'I don't know what I did to deserve you coming back into my life,' he said, as Cosima turned this way and that to give him the benefit of her pneumatic embonpoint. 'But thank you, God. C'mere.'

Cosima leaped into Nolan's arms, so that he staggered back and collapsed onto the bed. Growling theatrically, Nolan rolled Cosima over so that he was looking down into her face. He stroked her cheeks. Cosima adopted a luxuriant pose, with her alabaster arms stretched over her head. She practically purred as Nolan nuzzled her cleavage. Wrapping her legs around him, she caressed his calves with her perfectly pedicured toes.

Dragging himself away from Cosima's breasts for just a moment, Nolan slid down and off the bed so that he was kneeling on the floor with Cosima's feet resting lightly on his shoulders. He pressed a kiss onto each instep and another on each ankle. He followed a path of kisses back up her legs to the edge of her dove grey silk knickers. Cosima giggled as he traced the edge of the elastic with his tongue. He edged the panties down and touched his lips to her aching clitoris but she reached down towards him and encouraged him to lie on top of her again, face to face so that she could kiss him once more, tasting herself on his lips. With her underwear out of the way, she opened her legs around him and placed her hands on his buttocks, urging his pelvis towards hers.

Cosima groaned appreciatively as Nolan edged his way inside her. His penis was harder than she had ever felt it before. He wanted her as much as she wanted him. That confirmation made Cosima's own arousal grow more urgent in response. Inside her body, Cosima could feel Nolan's penis as though it had become part of her. She could feel the pulse of the blood flow as he drove into her.

Nolan's breathing grew more laboured and louder. Each time he powered down into Cosima's warm and welcoming pussy, she pushed her hips upwards to meet him. He tucked his hands beneath her buttocks, lifting her and bringing her closer still.

Cosima threw back her head, exposing her long white throat. All the sensation in her body was centred on the point where Nolan entered her. All she could hear was the rush of blood through her veins and the sound of their breathing.

The excitement finally overtook them. They couldn't wait. The build-up to this climax had started the moment they stepped out of the hotel to go to dinner. It had gathered pace as they gazed at each other across a table in Harry's Bar. Cosima had been ready to come the moment Nolan closed the bedroom door behind them. Now Nolan held his breath as he rode her harder. Going incredibly deep inside her. Right to her core. Cosima closed her eyes and cried out.

Nolan sighed her name as he came inside her. When she

finished shuddering with her own climax, Cosima pulled him to her one more time, covering his dear face with kisses and tears of happiness.

Cosima had forgotten how good it could be to make love in such a way that every part of you was involved. Not just your body but also your mind. Your soul. It wasn't just about a tangle of limbs and an exchange of body fluids. Sex with Nolan – her soulmate – was simply transcendant. When she observed as much to him, he agreed wholeheartedly.

'Making love with you is like making love for the first time, every time,' he said.

'What?' asked Cosima, propping herself up against the pillows. 'You mean I'm clumsy and don't know what I'm doing?' she teased.

'No, my love.' Nolan pulled himself up so that he could kiss her. 'You are a silly goose.'

Cosima sank back down beneath him, perfectly reassured.

'I am the luckiest woman in the world.' A pause. 'Don't you think you're the luckiest man?'

'I know I am.'

Chapter Forty-Two

MERCY noticed the empty desk on the sixteenth floor at once. There was no trace at all of the blonde who had stuck up for her all those weeks ago, except for a pot plant on the windowsill which looked rather worse for wear. Mercy picked the plant up and dumped it without ceremony into the bin section of her trolley.

She wondered briefly what had happened to the woman. Did she jump or was she pushed? But Mercy didn't dwell on it for long. All she wanted to do was get back home so that she could make sure her brother hadn't come to any harm.

Though in theory he was still supposed to be at school, studying for his GCSEs, these days Francis was out every night. He left the house almost as soon as he had eaten whatever his clueless mother put on the table and he wasn't back until the early hours. Once, when Mercy got up early to catch an extra cleaning shift, she passed Francis on his way in.

'You've got to be at school in two hours,' she told him.

Francis merely kissed his teeth at her.

The truth was that, even in her wildest dreams, Mercy had no idea of the scale of her brother's endeavour.

What kid would still think about going to school when he could easily make five hundred a week in profit on drug deals? What possible apprenticeship could earn Francis that kind of money or keep his interest in the same way? Francis was not some idiot who was going to be happy working as an assistant to some dumbshit plumber or plasterer. Dealing required the best of Francis's skills. He was a born negotiator. A salesman.

The expansion of Francis's empire was impressively fast. And as a reward for all the revenue he brought to James Dean, Francis found himself invited to watch Chelsea play West Ham from Dean's private box. Francis kept the fact that he wasn't especially interested in football to himself. Instead, just like a banker getting ready to meet an important client, he swotted up on everything he would need to know to make small talk.

That afternoon at the football match was interesting. Dean's associates had brought along a gaggle of beautiful women who all clucked over and petted Francis as though he were some kind of trained monkey. It was frustrating to say the least. He wanted to get a proper conversation with his hero, instead he kept getting sent for another bottle of champagne as though he were the hired help.

His mood was improved somewhat when one of the girlfriends took him into the private bathroom and gave him an enthusiastic blow job – what fifteen-year-old boy wouldn't have appreciated that – but it plummeted again when he heard the girl talking to another, older woman, who described Francis as 'employee of the month'.

'Fucking hell,' said the girl who had taken Francis into the bathroom. 'I only gave him a blow job because I thought he was a footballer.'

'You daft cow,' said her friend. 'He's just some kid.'

Just some kid ... The insult made Francis all the more determined to bring himself to Dean's proper attention. A couple more glasses of champagne later, he felt bolder and he finally pushed to the front of the crowd that surrounded Dean. When he got there, Francis knew he had just one chance to impress. Unlike the grown men who crowded around Dean like groupies, Francis was not going to bow and scrape. He addressed James Dean man to man.

'You know I'm good,' he said. 'Now I want you to show some real faith in me.'

Two days later, Francis took delivery of ten thousand pounds worth of cocaine.

Three days later, a real disaster struck.

Mercy had the feeling that something terrible had happened even before she got to the house. A group of women were clustered around the front gate. In the middle was Melody, sobbing as her friends comforted her.

'It's a good job you're here,' said Melody's best friend Chiara. 'Your mother won't go back inside the house on her own.'

'What's happened?'

'Somebody burgled you,' Chiara explained.

Melody had returned home from her supermarket trip to find the back door hanging off its hinges.

'I don't understand it,' said Melody. 'It's not as though we have anything to steal.'

And indeed, it seemed as though the burglars had thought the same but only once they had caused several hundred pounds worth of damage by getting themselves inside.

The police arrived within half an hour of being called, by which time Melody had worked out that nothing had been taken. It was odd. The television was cheap but surely it would have fetched enough cash to buy a bump of crack. Likewise, the burglars had left the DVD player. They'd left the CD player in Mercy's room. They'd left her one real gold necklace. They'd left the microwave. They'd even left the jar full of cash on the top shelf in the larder.

'They might have been disturbed,' the police officer explained. 'Maybe while they were deciding what to take, someone came to the door.'

The police dusted for fingerprints but Chiara warned Melody that she needn't hope for any kind of resolution to the matter.

'Nothing was taken. The police aren't going to waste time looking for a burglar who didn't take nothing, even if he did break down your door.'

'I hope you can claim for the door on your insurance,' said the girl who had dusted for prints.

'We don't have insurance,' said Melody.

And so the door was replaced with a plain wooden board, nailed at the corners. It would keep the draught out but little else.

Looking into her son's room as she toured the house with the police, Melody had not noticed anything out of the ordinary. Francis had always been a messy child. The pile of clothes on the floor was not unusual. Nor, Melody assured the police, was it odd that the entire contents of Francis's bookshelves had been pulled off and dumped on the floor.

'He does that,' she said. 'When he's looking for something, he gets frustrated and he doesn't put things back. If I've told him once–'

'OK,' said the WPC. 'We'll take your word for it.'

But when Francis opened the door onto his bedroom, he immediately saw a different picture. The untidy pile of clothes may have been his doing, but not the jumble of books and CDs on the floor. Not this time. And Francis noticed at once that a corner of the locked box he kept under his bed was peeping out from beneath the valance. Someone had been in his room. And, with his heart sinking he realised that they had been in that locked box. Finding it empty – Francis wasn't such an idiot that he would leave a gun and ten grand's worth of coke in such an obvious place – they had lifted the board upon which the box lay and found his secret stash beneath.

Fuck. The gun was safe, since Francis had it with him, but the one thing that the burglars had taken was the one thing Francis couldn't admit he'd ever had, let alone lost. He sat down heavily on the bed just as his mother appeared at the door with a cup of tea.

'I'm starting to feel a little better,' she said, as she sat down beside him. 'The council says they'll replace the door tomorrow, only with much better locks this time, so we don't have to worry about coming home to such a sight again. And nothing was taken, so,' Melody patted her son's hand, 'in a funny way, we're actually better off than we were this morning. We're going to have a lovely new door.

It will look better than the old one and we'll all be much safer.'

Francis looked at his mum with unseeing eyes. 'Yeah, Mum,' he murmured. 'That sounds great.'

His nightmare was just beginning.

Chapter forty-four

JULIET didn't have time to wait for the investigation into the alleged insider trading to take its course, which was what David sensibly suggested she do when he responded to the news that she had been suspended from her job. He said he appreciated that she was shocked but she really had no option but to remain calm and wait for more information.

'If you say you're completely innocent of what they're accusing you of, you know that I believe you,' he told her. 'And before too long an investigation will prove it to be true.'

'But if the emails were sent in my name from my terminal, how on earth will they be convinced it wasn't me?' Juliet asked.

David told her not to worry about it. But how could Juliet not worry when her career was at stake? If she was dismissed from Anglo-Italian for an offence she hadn't committed, she would never work in banking again.

'Maybe you could say you were sleep-emailing,' David said in a further fruitless attempt to placate her.

'I did not send those emails. You're making light of this,' said Juliet.

'I don't mean to. I'm trying to cheer you up.'

Juliet decided it was time to end the phone call before it took a turn for the worse. She didn't want to add falling out with David to her list of woes.

'I'm sorry that I'm not there in person to help you through this,' he said.

David had been called away to do some business in the States the day after they first made love. His absence had made the whole episode between them seem more and more like a dream.

'I'll be with you as soon as I can,' he promised her now. 'We'll get through this together.'

Juliet thanked him for his promise but remained quite unconvinced that David could do any more than she could on her own. At least not in the conventional way.

She needed to get back into the Anglo-Italian building quickly. Even if she couldn't get a look at her hard drive, she felt sure that some trace of Christopher's involvement with all this would be in his computer but how could she gain access to it again?

When escorted from the building, she had been relieved of her security pass, though she was told that a photograph of her would remain on the system and she should not attempt to re-enter the building at any cost. Juliet had always suspected that security at the Anglo-Italian building wasn't that tight, but even the thickest of the guards would recognise her if she tried to walk in the front door again so quickly. She could claim to have left something behind but she knew that they would just have someone in her office look for said item so that they could bring it down to reception with no need for her to pass the toughened glass barrier.

In any case, Juliet really needed some time *alone* with Christopher's files. And that meant getting into the office after everyone else had gone home.

Juliet spent the next couple of hours trying to work out an answer to her problem. She went online to the Anglo-Italian website. There was no point trying to log in to her email but she found it useful to look at a picture of the company's building while she waited for inspiration to strike. There must be a weak point. There must.

There were other companies in the building. Perhaps she could claim to be going to a meeting in one of those firms. That would get her as far as the lifts. But she would have another problem when she got to the sixteenth floor upon which Anglo-Italian reception was situated. You couldn't get to the offices proper without going past another reception desk, unless you had a special lift pass that enabled you to activate the lift buttons to the upper floors. And, of course, Juliet no longer had one of those.

The ground floor of the building contained several shops. There were a couple of places selling coffee, a shirt shop, a store specialising in cufflinks and a dry-cleaner. If Juliet could get behind the counter in any one of those places, then perhaps she would be able to access the emergency stair well. A sixteen-floor walk would be worth it. Yes. That was an idea. But which shop?

Juliet grabbed her coat and set off for the City. She had never really looked at the ground floor shops properly before. She only used one of them: the dry-cleaner. Fortunately, she had an excuse to go there. She'd dropped off a pile of shirts three days earlier.

'Hello, Juliet,' Harry the dry-cleaner made a point of addressing all his customers by name and normally Juliet appreciated the thoughtfulness. That day, however, it was an irritation. If he called her by name, he would be far more likely to remember that she had been in.

As Harry searched through his racks for Juliet's shirts, Juliet peered into the darkness behind the counter. How far back did the store go? And was there a door at the back of it? There must be.

'What are you doing back here?' Harry asked.

'I've . . . er . . . I was just wondering if you had a toilet.'

Harry indicated a tiny door.

'There's one in there but it isn't really meant for customers. I'd be embarrassed. Your own office is right next door, yes?'

'Well, yes, but . . .' Do I have to spell it out for him? Juliet wondered. She pulled a face that suggested urgency and Harry relented.

He wasn't kidding. Considering the dry-cleaner's stock in trade was providing people with pristine laundry, it really didn't do to look too closely at how he did it. The staff bathroom was tiny and cluttered with bottles of chemicals and a pile of toilet rolls that suggested a recent visit to the wholesaler. A bare bulb hung from the ceiling and the room had no window. No way into the secret heart of Anglo-Italian here.

Juliet left the dry-cleaner with three perfectly ironed shirts but she was no closer to getting back to Christopher's desk than she had ever been. Undaunted, she found herself a tucked away corner in Starbucks and hoped that inspiration might come with an espresso.

It did.

At about quarter to five, the rush hour began. Just a trickle at first but soon a great flood of office workers was heading for the entrance to the tube station and the long escalators that would take them down into the tunnels. The thought of those escalators made Juliet think of a television documentary she had once seen about salmon heading back to the place they had been born to spawn. How amazing it had been to see the fish throwing themselves upstream. Juliet could never understand why they didn't stay down-stream and mate and spawn there. It would have taken so much less effort. But it seemed nature had a bigger plan. Survival of the fittest.

Her coffee finished, Juliet headed for the tube station herself. It was halfway down the escalator that the image of the salmon came back to her. There was a stationary staircase between two of the down escalators. A surpris-ingly large number of people were too impatient to take the moving staircase and were jogging down the static one, but a single person, one human salmon, was struggling up through the middle of them. Because not everyone was heading home right then. There was a small but signifi-cant band of people who were just arriving to begin their working day. The cleaners.

'Yes!'

Juliet had done enough overtime to know exactly what time the cleaning team clocked off. At half past ten, she was waiting outside the back entrance to the Anglo-Italian building. At ten thirty-seven, her wait was rewarded.

'Hey,' she called out of the shadows when Mercy Campbell appeared.

Chapter Forty-Five

'Who the—'

Mercy did not expect to find anyone waiting for her that evening and so, when she heard her name called from the darkness, her first instinct was that it must be some kind of trap. Seeing her brother's new associates in the Range Rover that time had made her wary of everyone, even those people who purported to be your friends. Just because someone knew your name, didn't mean you had to stop and talk.

'Hey!'

But this woman seemed determined. Mercy broke into a run to escape her but the woman was faster and she soon caught up. She grabbed Mercy by the arm. Mercy swung around, arms flailing, aiming her handbag at the woman's head.

'Calm down!' the woman shouted. 'I don't mean you any harm. Please. I just want to talk to you.'

'Who are you?'

The woman removed the hood from her head, revealing her bright blond hair.

Mercy squinted in recognition.

'I know you, don't I?' she said.

'Sort of,' said the woman. 'I used to work in there.' Juliet jerked her thumb backwards to the Anglo-Italian building. 'Sixteenth floor. The one you clean, right?'

Mercy nodded. She recognised the woman now.

'You've got the office at the far end of the corridor,' she said.

'Had the office...' Juliet corrected her. 'I got fired yesterday afternoon.'

'Oh,' said Mercy. 'I'm sorry to hear that.'

'Look,' said Juliet. 'It isn't such a great idea for me to be seen hanging around here. Do you think we could go somewhere and talk? Perhaps I could buy you a drink?'

Mercy couldn't begin to imagine what the woman wanted with her, but she agreed all the same. After all, at the opera house, while Ed stood there like a lemon, this woman had in a small way, fought for Mercy's honour. She owed her at least a drink's worth of listening time.

'Where can we go?' Mercy asked.

'There's a nice wine bar about five minutes away. It's discreet. I should know. I used to go there for exactly that reason.'

Juliet chose the bar where she and Christopher had conducted much of their affair and where she had definitively ended their relationship just a week earlier. Now she was sitting in the same bar, at the same table, with one of the office cleaners. How far had she fallen? How much should she say?

'I love this music,' said Mercy, as Juliet brought a glass of red for herself and a Diet Coke for Mercy to their table. 'It's from *La Bohème*.'

'You like opera?'

'Love it,' said Mercy. 'I used to want to be an opera singer.'

'Really?' Juliet was ashamed to admit, even if it was only to herself, that she would not have been more surprised if Mercy had announced that she was training to be an astronaut.

'Yeah. But it's an expensive business, singing lessons.'

'Couldn't you get a scholarship?' Juliet asked.

'What's one of those?' said Mercy.

That was the end of the small talk. Juliet had to tell Mercy what she wanted. She had decided while waiting for Mercy to finish her shift that it was best to keep the story simple. She wouldn't tell Mercy that she had been having an affair. She would simply say that she thought one of her colleagues had stitched her up and exaggerate the risk to everyone else.

'There's no reason why you should believe me,' said Juliet. 'Except that I hope you can tell that I'm a decent person and I wouldn't be asking you to help me if I didn't genuinely think that something bad is going on. Something that has the potential to cost a lot of jobs. It's already cost me mine.'

'I'm sorry.'

'All I need is a little bit more information. I'm pretty certain that the main reason why I got fired is because someone in that building thought I knew more than I should. There are some very sharp practices at Anglo-Italian, Mercy. What I need is someone on the inside who can help me gather the evidence I need to go to the police. You get in there every day. You could go into the system for me.'

'I can't do that,' said Mercy. 'I wouldn't know how to get into the computers.'

'You don't need to know. I'd tell you everything. Exactly which machine you need to look at. The passwords. It would be really easy. All you would have to do is slip a disc into the hard drive and transfer a few things onto it. I'd pay you very well.'

Mercy bit her lip. She could certainly use the money. And she guessed that Juliet knew that, because she quickly came back with a figure.

'Two hundred pounds,' said Juliet.

'Two hundred?'

'Three?'

Juliet clearly thought that Mercy thought she was low-balling her. If only she knew. It would take Mercy the best part of a month to earn that kind of cash.

'I promise that it would be incredibly low risk to you. I know exactly where the info I need can be found. If you follow my instructions to the letter, then what I'm asking will take you five minutes. No more than that. You just have to make sure you're not seen.'

Mercy felt a peculiar prickle creep up her spine. It was true that Juliet seemed like a nice enough woman. The memory of that night at the opera certainly counted in her favour. As did the fact that she hadn't mentioned it in order to help guilt Mercy into taking part in her scheme. But Mercy was aware that only a fool would get involved with something illegal on the strength of one cheap drink in a wine bar. Because this had to be illegal, right? Juliet was asking her to steal data. If Mercy got caught, she had a feeling that it would not be a simple matter of handing back the disc and losing her job. If Juliet was right that this was information that could bring down a bank, then her former colleagues were not going to take the theft lightly. Mercy had heard that Anglo-Italian had pressed charges against a former cleaner who stole a laptop from a store cupboard. Mercy hated her job. She didn't particularly give a toss if she lost it but she did not want to get a criminal record in the process. She couldn't get involved. In any case, it was quite possible that Juliet was a fantasist.

'I'm sorry,' Mercy said, mentally putting the money – a singing courses' worth – back in the box.

'Five hundred?' said Juliet.

'It's not the money,' said Mercy. 'Though God knows I could use it. I'm sure you understand that I would be a fool to do something illegal for someone I've only just met.'

'You're my only hope,' said Juliet. She began to get tearful. 'I need to know who stitched me up and there's no way I'm getting back into that building myself.'

Mercy hated to see another woman cry but she could not be drawn in. 'There is one possibility,' she said.

One of the girls on Mercy's cleaning team had just disappeared. No one knew for sure what had happened. On Monday night, Victoria was there as usual, larger than life and twice as loud. On Tuesday, she simply didn't turn up. Hazel was used to losing staff, but the last person she had expected to lose was Victoria. She hadn't given Hazel any reason to believe that she was unhappy at work. On the contrary, Victoria seemed to love working at Anglo-Italian. She told Mercy that she loved all the girls who reminded her friends back in Zimbabwe. And now she was gone. On Thursday, one of the other girls had called by the flat Victoria shared with some relatives. She wasn't there. No one was there. But the door was boarded up and nailed shut. Hazel concluded that Victoria must have fallen foul of the immigration services, grassed up by the elderly neighbour whose middle-aged son was a BNP councillor.

Hazel was sad to lose one of her best employees. Mercy was sad to lose a friend. But she was also irritated to have to pick up Victoria's work for no extra money while the team was one short.

'You could do it,' she suggested to Juliet.

'What? You're telling me I should apply for a cleaning job?' Juliet said, before she realised that she had just handed Mercy an insult. Ironic, given that she had stood up for her when Caroline did the same. 'I mean, not that I think it's beneath me, but ... I'm sorry. I didn't mean to suggest ...'

'I understand,' said Mercy. 'I wasn't suggesting that you take Victoria's place because you need the money. You obviously don't.'

'Not yet anyway,' said Juliet ruefully.

'But if you really want to get back into the building and get the information you need to nail the man who stitched you up, then it strikes me that taking a job as a cleaner is the perfect way to do it.'

Juliet agreed with Mercy's logic. 'It's a nice idea,' she said. 'But Anglo-Italian just suspended me as a banker, there's no way they'll have me back as a cleaner. I'm banned from that building. There was no messing around. I was given ten minutes to collect my belongings in a cardboard box before I was escorted from the building by two security guards. They'll never employ me again.'

'But Anglo-Italian won't be employing you,' said Mercy. 'The contract cleaning company will. And I have to say, my boss at City Clean Stars isn't all that bothered about taking references. Most of the women I work with aren't even supposed to be in the country, let alone working in a high-security environment like a bank. All you need to do is convince Hazel you know how to use a mop, then you can get into the building and do whatever it is you need to do. I'll just pretend I don't know you.'

'Mercy,' Juliet grinned. 'I do believe you may be a genius!'

Mercy shrugged.

'Look, all I can do for you is tell you there's a vacancy and tell you who to call about it.'

'That's all I need. Thank you. I can get a job as a cleaner. I'll ace the interview.'

Mercy looked at Juliet with her neat pink shirt tucked into her jeans and her tiny pearl earrings. Hazel would hate her on sight.

'A word of advice,' Mercy said. 'If Hazel says she wants to meet you for an interview, you can't turn up looking like this. You've got to look, well, you've got to look more like you need the job. Do you know what I'm saying? Your hair. Your make-up. Those earrings. They're all wrong.'

Juliet's self-consciously touched her hair.

'I mean, they're not *wrong*. They're very nice. They're just ...'

'Not the right look for a job as a cleaner. I get it.'

Mercy nodded. 'You've got the idea.'

'I'll fix it,' said Juliet. 'I'll do whatever it takes.'

'I hope it works out,' said Mercy. 'It sounds like you could use a bit of luck.'

The very next day, Juliet put the plan into action. She called the number for City Clean Stars that Mercy had given her first thing and got herself an interview at five. Hazel was very keen to find someone to replace Victoria before the increased workload lost her any further staff. It had happened before. The loss of one particularly well-loved staff member could cause an exodus. That was the last thing Hazel needed.

Juliet dressed for the interview very carefully. She left her 'interview suit', the Paul Smith number she had worn for her final round interview at Anglo-Italian, in the wardrobe and instead pulled out the jeans she had relegated to painting gear. They were covered in streaks of Farrow and Ball paint. Juliet regarded the painting trousers critically. Surely even someone going for a job as a cleaner would make sure her jeans were clean? But Juliet didn't have much choice. All her other jeans were designer numbers: James, Seven, Sass and Bide. And Mercy had warned her that Hazel would sniff any hint of money out.

So Juliet topped off her tattiest jeans with a ratty old shirt and a pair of trainers. She didn't bother with make-up and scraped her hair back into a high ponytail. A Croydon facelift. As a final touch, she decanted her wallet and mobile phone from her favourite Marc Jacobs tote into a Waitrose 'Bag For Life' plastic carrier. She would have to hope that the Waitrose carrier wouldn't count against her too. There was no time to look for a more downmarket 'label'.

It seemed like a lot of effort to make, but as soon as she got to the interview, Juliet was glad she had gone the extra mile. She understood at once what Mercy had meant about her boss sniffing out any hint of inauthenticity. The moment Juliet walked into the room, she felt Hazel scan her, taking in every aspect of the way she looked from her dull hairdo to her battered trainers. But Hazel didn't bat an eyelid at Juliet's scruffy appearance. Nor did she seem bothered by the fact that Juliet didn't have a CV.

'Have you worked as a cleaner before?' she asked.

Juliet nodded. And it was true. She had worked as a cleaner at a hotel once. For a fortnight. Until she was asked to clear up a puddle of vomit and walked on the spot. It hadn't mattered then. She was a student. There were other temporary jobs to be had. She spent the rest of the summer helping out at a local joinery firm, typing invoices and filing receipts.

'Well, you'll probably find this easier,' said Hazel. 'You're less likely to be fishing johnnies that won't flush out of the bogs. Not to say that never happens. But you know what I mean. No tips though, in office work.'

Were there tips in hotel work? Juliet had never found anything left behind in the rooms at the Travelodge but condom wrappers and cigarette butts and, once, a pair of soiled underpants.

'When can you start?' Hazel asked.

Was that it? Did she have the job?

'Whenever you want,' Juliet told her.

'Good. I've lost three girls this week. One to immigration and two to bloody laziness. They all think they're up to it but the hours finish them off. None of them want to work Friday nights, the young ones. You'll work Friday nights though?'

Juliet nodded. What else did she have to do?

'Good. You'll need to fill this form out. Name and address. And your bank details. If you've got an account, that is.'

She pushed the piece of paper across the table. 'You can read, can't you?' Hazel asked.

'Just about,' said Juliet.

'Good. Leave the form on the front desk as you leave and I'll see you at the goods entrance to Anglo-Italian tomorrow night. Send the next girl in.'

Juliet made to shake Hazel's hand but withdrew quickly when she realised that was the last thing Hazel expected from the people she interviewed. Or wanted, in all probability. Juliet shuffled to the door, instead, taking care to keep her low-key demeanour in place. She nodded to the next girl, who was sitting on a stacking chair, staring into space despite the magazines on the table in front of her.

'You're on,' Juliet told her. The other girl stood up and, slack-jawed and dead-eyed, made her way into Hazel's room.

Juliet waited until she was outside the building before she allowed the smile to creep over her face. She couldn't quite believe it had been so easy. That night she would walk through the goods entrance of Anglo-Italian. She was in.

Chapter Forty-Six

𝄞

$\mathscr{F}$RANCIS put off revealing that the coke had been stolen for as long as he possibly could but he couldn't keep pretending that everything was fine for long. Dean's men wanted their money. Francis had promised that they would see a return on their investment within days. He was going to have to disappoint them. He could only hope that they would be charitable about it. Francis figured that dealers must get done over all the time.

But not to the tune of ten grand.

Francis felt sick to his stomach as he climbed into the back of the Range Rover that Friday evening. He felt even worse when, an hour and a half later, he found himself in front of the main man.

'It was stolen,' said Francis.

'A likely story,' said Dean. 'How many times do you think I've heard that particular line? What am I supposed to do with that information, Francis? Do I ring up my insurance broker and ask if I can put in a claim? Yes, sir. Ten thousand pounds' worth of cocaine. What did it look like? Well, it's white, it's powdery ... You're a fuckwit, Francis. What are you?'

'A fuckwit,' Francis repeated dutifully.

Francis wasn't sure that he was going to be able to hold onto the contents of his bowels for much longer. So far, he had managed to escape any blows. And Dean had seemed reasonably relaxed, though he claimed not to believe Francis's story. Still, Francis felt certain that it was a matter of time before he came to serious harm. He couldn't rely on the fact that he was just a kid to save him. After all, hadn't he been the one who'd insisted that he knew what he was doing and could be trusted as well as any grown man?

'Now, Francis,' said Dean. 'I like you. You've got some guts. I liked your style at the football. You were brave enough to stick your neck out. And you've been brave enough to come here today and tell me what I'm starting to think might actually be the truth. You remind me of myself when I was your age. But ten grand is ten grand. And now, dear boy, you owe me.'

Francis nodded.

Dean pounded his left fist into his right palm as though he was warming it up. Here comes the crunch, thought Francis. He winced in anticipation.

'You've got a week to get me my money back. I don't care how you do it. I've got every faith that you'll come up with some big plan. But if you don't get me my money back, then you'll owe me even more in interest. And then we'll have to start talking about proper reparations. I might have to get you to do a few difficult jobs for me. Do you understand?

'I understand,' Francis nodded. Relief rushed through his body. He knew he was a long way from being out of trouble but for now he wasn't lying on the floor with his blood pouring out into the gutter and that felt good. He was going to make it out of this meeting alive and that, as far as negotiations with Dean went, was a far better result than he could have hoped for.

'Now you better head off and start thinking about how you're going to pay me back,' said Dean. 'Run along.' He waved Francis in the direction of the front door. The man who had been standing by that door throughout the conversation now opened it to usher Francis out.

'But I . . . we're miles out of London,' Francis dared to observe.

'What? You need a lift?' asked Dean. 'No chance.'

'But . . .'

'You're a young man,' said Dean. 'You can use the exercise.'

The first sign that Francis happened across told him that he was twenty miles outside the M25. With no money for a train and his mobile phone confiscated, Francis was in for a very long walk home.

Chapter Forty-Seven

𝄞

Just a fortnight back together and already it was starting to feel like old times for Nolan and Cosima. The problems had started (well, restarted) in Venice, when Cosima accused Nolan of flirting with the hotel receptionist as they were checking out, and got much worse in Vienna when Nolan and Cosima went off on their own for dinner. The conversation began simply enough. Cosima and Nolan were still filling each other in on the comings and goings in their respective extended families over the past five years. There was a great deal to catch up on.

'I just knew he was gay!' Cosima exclaimed at news of Nolan's cousin Gerry who had gone into the priesthood and left it again to migrate to San Francisco and become a personal trainer.

'Triplets!' laughed Nolan, when he heard about Cosima's friend Katrina. 'How is she coping with that? She could barely take care of herself.'

The catch-up made for plenty of laughs. Nolan found he was surprisingly interested to hear about the people he had been glad to see the back of five years ago. But eventually, as was inevitable, they ran out of gossip about the people they had in common and were left with only themselves to talk about. Cosima, who had sunk the best part of a bottle of wine, grew sentimental.

'I thought about you every day,' she admitted to her former husband. 'God knows I didn't want to. But I did.'

'And I you,' said Nolan.

'What we have is a real once-in-a-lifetime love,' said Cosima.

'*Twice* in a lifetime,' said Nolan, referring to the fact that they were trying again.

'I couldn't even look at another man after you and I broke up. Not for ages. Andrew was the first. It took me four and a half years to even go on a date. I thought I was over you but . . . look how that turned out.'

'Poor Andrew,' Nolan nodded. Inside he was thinking 'sucker'.

'Every time a man expressed an interest in me, I would straight away compare him with you. And I would always find him wanting. They were never quite as funny as you. Or as handsome. Or as good a singer.'

Nolan grinned. 'So, you're admitting it at last. I am the better tenor.'

'I suppose you are,' said Cosima. 'Though Andrew is a very close second.'

Nolan gave a comedy roar at that news.

'OK! OK! He's nowhere near you,' Cosima admitted. 'When I had to watch him singing, it would take everything I had not to cover my ears. It was hell to have to sing opposite him in London. Sheer hell.'

Nolan was loving every minute of this.

'My greatest fear was that he would suggest he and I collaborated on some project and I would have to tell him how I really rated his talents.'

Nolan squeezed her hand. 'No need to worry about that now.'

'Oh, Nolan. Why did we let it go on for so long? I thought about picking up the phone and calling you a thousand times. Why couldn't we just have swallowed our pride a little sooner? I can't bear to think how much time we've missed, being apart.'

'It's all right, my darling. We're not going to waste a single moment now.'

Cosima gave him a watery smile as she struggled to contain tears. 'Good. I never want to be apart from you again.'

But then came the million-dollar question.

'Tell me,' she said. 'Because I think it's important for us to be honest with each other. You know exactly what's been going on in my love life for the last five years. There's just one thing I need to know from you. I don't want or need to know the names of every girl who crossed your path. There's only one that I have to know about.'

Nolan stiffened.

'Nolan, did you ever have a thing with Judy Shephard?'

'A thing?'

'You know what I mean.'

'With Judy Shephard?'

'Yes. Judy. I know she always had a soft spot for you. Did you ever return the compliment?'

Cosima made it sound light-hearted, but Nolan's brain was already on red alert. He knew that Cosima was obsessed with her fellow soprano, Judith Shephard. The two women had hated each other on sight when they met for the first time in rehearsal for *La Bohème* at an opera festival in Sussex. Casting them opposite each other as Mimi and Musetta, was like putting two Siberian tigresses in the same cage. They were both beautiful, intelligent and talented. They were both used to getting their own way. Judy dubbed Cosima 'Miss Piggy' for her frequent outbursts. Cosima dubbed Judy 'The strumpet who sings like a trumpet'. It didn't help to foster good relations between the women that Judy was especially popular with the boys on account of her ability to finish a yard of ale in record time as much as her ability to hit the high Cs. She had been Miss Northampton Yard of Ale for three years running.

Nolan did not want to engage with Cosima on the subject of Judy Shephard. He tried to attract a waiter's attention on the pretence of needing more water.

'Come on, Nolan,' Cosima persisted. 'You can tell me. I promise I won't mind. It's just that I need to know. It's important that we don't have any secrets from one another. We're making a fresh start, you and me. That means wiping the slate clean. Think of this dinner as an amnesty. Whatever you tell me now, we'll put behind us. But if you lie to me this evening and I find out later that you and Judy got it on while we were apart, then I will feel totally humiliated. She and I might have to work together again. All the trust will be gone.'

Shit, thought Nolan. Cosima was not going to let this go. The waiter responded to his gestures at last. While the waited fiddled about with the glasses, Nolan considered his options. And while he was considering his options, he couldn't help but picture Judy Shephard, who had once taken him to a nudist beach, where he spent the entire day face down on the sand out of embarrassing necessity while Judy drove all the straight men within half a mile crazy with the dangerous curves that had graced the September page of a charity calendar. Judy was a wonderful woman. A smile was never far from her generous mouth.

The waiter left. Cosima leaned forward with an expression of polite interest on her face as she waited for Nolan's answer. You might have thought she had merely asked him whether he wanted to split a dessert. She looked happy enough. Perhaps the amnesty she spoke of was for real.

'Well,' he began. 'There was one time. It was while I was in London doing *The Marriage of Figaro*. Judy had to fly to Spain in a hurry to see her mother who'd been taken ill on a cruise that was docking in Barcelona. She couldn't take her three boxers, of course, so she asked me to look after them. When she came back from Spain, she brought three bottles of Rioja – one for each dog – to thank me for helping her out. We sank them all that Sunday afternoon and ended up in–'

Nolan didn't get to finish the sentence.

'You asshole.'

'But you said–'

'You complete and total asshole!'

Cosima let out a great sob that drew the attention of the entire restaurant.

'Cosi,' Nolan tried to calm her. 'It was just that one time. It meant nothing.'

'*Nothing*!' Cosi shrieked. 'You threw away my love for you by sleeping with that tramp!'

'You said this was an amnesty.'

'That was when I thought you'd tell me "no". Oh, Nolan! You've broken my heart!'

Cosima lifted the whole table and tipped it into his lap, before stalking off out of the restaurant, her long hair flying behind her like a flag. The entire restaurant was agog at the spectacle: a real treat that would be talked about long after the two opera stars' official Vienna performance was forgotten.

It took Nolan a while to get out from under the restaurant table. By the time he had managed that and smoothed the ruffled feathers of the maître d', who had never seen such behaviour, this not being Paris or Rome, Cosima was long gone. When Nolan got back to the hotel, he discovered that Cosima had already moved him out of their room. His bags were in the corridor. She had thrown most of his clothes out willy nilly, so that all the world could see what kind of underpants he favoured.

'Cosi,' he knocked on the door. 'Let me in. We need to talk about this.'

But the lady was not for talking. The only sound Nolan heard from inside the room was that of the deadlock being activated. With a heavy heart, Nolan trudged down to the lobby, where the receptionist told him (with no small delight, Nolan decided) that there was not a single spare room in the house. The entire hotel was rammed full of opera fans on package deals, it seemed.

And so Nolan found himself spending the night in some grotty little place by the main train station, ruing the stupidity that had made him think honesty could possibly be the best policy where Cosima was concerned.

Compared to some of the hotels she had been staying in as she followed Nolan across Europe, Florence thought that the station hotel in Vienna was not bad at all. The bed was clean. There were no stray public hairs in the shower. And breakfast was included. That was a real boon to Florence who had gone severely over budget as the dollar had plummeted against the euro since she flew out of New York.

It was while Florence was walking through the lobby of the hotel to the breakfast room that she caught sight of Nolan O'Connor. He was at the reception desk. But the sight of the object of her affections in the lobby of such a modest little hotel was so incongruous to Florence, and it was so early in the morning, that she didn't even stop to look twice. She was in the breakfast room and being led to a table before the reality of the situation struck her. Nolan O'Connor was at her hotel. Not bothering to explain to the restaurant manager, Florence ran back to the lobby.

Nolan was already gone.

'That man!' Florence said to the receptionist. 'That man! It was Nolan O'Connor, right? The opera singer? What was he doing here? Was he looking for me?'

The receptionist found it impossible to follow Florence's quick fire questions.

'Who was he? That man? Did he leave a message?'

Nolan must have come looking for her, Florence concluded. She had written to tell him that she would be at this hotel. He must have come to find her at last. And she had missed him because while the receptionist was calling to tell her she had a visitor, Florence was already out of her room and walking down eight floors to the breakfast room. Florence had missed Nolan by seconds.

The receptionist, trying to make some sense of Florence's

excitement, pushed the reservations book towards her and pointed at a name. 'O'Connor.'

'Oh praise the lord!' said Florence. It was him. 'What is this? Was he in the hotel the whole night? And you didn't come and find me?'

The girl on the desk merely shrugged.

'He came to see me and nobody let me know?' Florence could not believe her misfortune. Stupid, stuck-up Viennese cow. 'Why didn't anybody tell me?'

Florence scrolled down the page in the book for her own name but couldn't find it. Against the number of her room was written the name of Florence's travel agent.

'Aaaaaaghhhh,' she wailed. No wonder they couldn't find her. 'Which way did he go?'

The receptionist pointed westwards. Florence ran out onto the street, but Nolan was long gone by now. There was no sign of him on the pavement. He was probably in a taxi. Perhaps, thought Florence, he thought that she had deliberately misled him about the hotels she would be staying in. She had to get a message to him as quickly as possible to let him know that it was the fault of the incompetent hotel staff that she had been unable to track him down. She sent an email right away.

Later that day, Florence called her parents and told them the news.

'Well, dear,' said her mother. 'We're glad to hear you sounding so much happier. We were very concerned when you called from Verona. But, tell me, sweetie, are you making sure to take your tablets every night?'

'Mother,' said Florence. 'Nolan O'Connor came looking for me. This was not a hallucination.'

*   *   *

When Nolan got back to the grand hotel to join the rest of the cast after his night in exile, Cosima affected not to know him.

Business as usual, thought Karl the director.

'Cosi,' Nolan tried one more time. 'This is ridiculous. Judy meant nothing to me. I was lonely. We got drunk. But in any case . . . We were on a—'

'Don't you dare say "we were on a break",' said Cosima. 'I can't believe I ever thought it was a good idea to give you a second chance. Now the minute I get back to New York I will have to get myself tested since I don't suppose for one moment you had the sense to have safe sex with that tart.'

Nolan slunk back to the safety of the chorus, who were always pleased to see him, though this time he steered clear of the prettier ones. He had no doubt he would still be under surveillance. Being dumped didn't mean being entirely off the hook, alas.

That lunchtime, the company left Vienna for St Petersburg. The only high spot of the day for Nolan was when Antony, who was playing Spoletta, asked him if it was true that he'd slept with the legendary Judy Shephard *and* her sister. Nolan had no idea how the story came to be so embellished, but he enjoyed Antony's obvious envy and was happy when the younger man offered his knuckles for a 'fist bump', which Nolan understood was quite the sign of approval.

Once in St Petersburg, Nolan and Cosima were back to having separate rooms. Nolan was fine with that. He could use a rest from the ice-cold looks she was giving him. And no longer was it just Cosima who was dishing out the death stares. Her little coven had obviously heard the tale and now Nolan was on the receiving end of hate in triplicate. Nolan couldn't wait to have a few hours on his own.

But at half past seven the cast reconvened in the lobby of this latest hotel and Nolan was the consummate professional as he escorted Cosima into the limo for the drive to Evgeny Belanov's summer palace.

Chapter Forty-Eight

JAMES Dean had become quite the regular in St Petersburg over the past year and he was very pleased to get an invitation to Belanov's opera evening, though he hated the terrible wailing himself and would far rather have spent the night listening to Bruce Springsteen. Still, an invitation from Belanov was one you didn't refuse, especially if you wanted to get ahead. So Dean told Belanov that he was delighted to accept. Tara, his wife, was delighted too. Dean would have gone by himself and let Belanov find him some fit young Russian concubine for the night, like last time, but it was Dean's eighth wedding anniversary that weekend and he knew there would be hell to pay if he didn't take Tara with him on the three-day trip.

Tara Dean needed no excuse to buy yet another new pair of Louboutins, but she knew she needed to make a special effort for the trip to Russia. She had seen how the Russian women dressed even for a simple lunch in London and she was determined not to be outdone. She paid a small fortune for a gold sheath dress from Versace and about the same on a series of mesotherapy sessions to help her shrink into it. She bought shoes from Louboutin, of course: a pair of python platforms (also dyed gold) that cost more than her first car. Then there had been the requisite spa day at the Berkeley Hotel in preparation. She'd had a facial, a massage, a body scrub, a mani-pedi. A quick shot of Botox. A spray tan. And then an afternoon at John Frieda to touch up her dark brown roots so well that no one but her mother would know she wasn't a natural blonde. Dean himself hadn't guessed for the first three years they were together because, of course, she had nothing 'down there' to give the game away. She'd been having Hollywoods since she turned sixteen. It was an important touch when it came to attracting the kind of guy she had hoped to snare as a husband.

The end result was pampered perfection, as if the breath of God had made a Bratz doll flesh. But it was Dean who put the finishing touch to the look with his anniversary present: a pair of yellow diamond earrings, each stone the size of a quail's egg.

'Precious for my precious,' he said. He said that every time he bought her jewels.

'Oh, treacle! They're beautiful!' Tara Dean was the only person on earth who could get away with calling her gangster husband 'treacle'.

'I know you want to look special for me.'

'Of course I do, my little honey-puff.'

But Tara Dean was especially looking forward to showing those Russian tarts that Essex girls could out-bling the best of them.

*　　*　　*

Of course the Deans stayed at the very best hotel in town. Belanov had offered to put them up in his summerhouse, but though Dean and Belanov were supposedly the best of friends, Dean felt somewhat safer in the hotel. Wherever he travelled, Belanov had an armed security detail that made the US presence in the Gulf look like Dad's Army. Dean didn't want to get on the wrong of Belanov on his own turf. Or get caught up in the crossfire if some other oligarch chose that weekend to take a pot shot at him. And so he and Tara, and his right-hand man Tony stayed at the Grand Hotel Europe. They accepted Belanov's offer of a chauffeur however.

The weekend was organised with impressive precision. Just an hour after his arrival in St Petersburg, Dean and Tony were collected in a limo to be driven to a business meeting with representatives of Belanov's interests from all over the world. Dean tried hard not to be impressed by anything, but he couldn't help but be a little awed as he was led into the cavernous meeting room in the basement of Belanov's own home. The multi-cultural audience gave the place the feel of a Bond movie crowd scene. Baddies only.

Meanwhile, the gangster WAGs (and they were all women. No 'civil partners' for the men Belanov associated with, at least, not in public) were also collected from the hotel for some compulsory afternoon activity. For the ladies, Belanov's highly professional team had organised a cultural excursion to the museum at the Hermitage, which would be closed to the public for the duration. Belanov's extremely sophisticated fourth wife Nadezdha would be joining them and she had personally ensured that they would be shown around by one of Russia's foremost art experts.

A woman from America, who had had some great work

done on her face, Tara noted, gushed with delight at the thought of it.

'This is just wonderful. I have been begging Harry to take me to the Hermitage for years!'

Tara was shrewd enough not to say out loud that she would rather have spent the afternoon shopping. She was eager to see if it was true that the likes of Dior and Versace carried blingier, brighter, more expensive stock for the Russian market. Instead, she resigned herself to an afternoon spent looking at art, which was something she hadn't done since she had been forced to as part of a general studies course at school.

Unfortunately, her choice of shoes for the visit to the Hermitage was not a great success. The nude patent Louboutin courts looked simple enough. The almond toe was almost foot shaped. But the day that Tara went to buy them, the shop did not have her size. She had taken a pair a half size smaller than usual in the hope that they would stretch and, of course, they hadn't stretched anywhere near enough. The pinching did not make it any easier for Tara to be enthusiastic about art.

The only interesting thing about the afternoon was that she got to see Belanov's wife up close. Nadezdha Belanov had become quite the feature in the gossip columns in the UK. She was often pictured sharing confidences with Gwyneth Paltrow in the front row of the Paris fashion shows. She was close friends with Angelina Jolie too. They had bonded after Nadezdha donated some money from the Belanov Foundation to one of Angelina's projects in Africa. Of course, Tara secretly hoped that some of Nadezdha's stardust would rub off on her.

But Tara didn't get a chance to start schmoozing

Nadezdha Belanov that afternoon. There were too many women in the group. Half of them had brought translators too, which swelled the numbers until they looked more like a coach group than an exclusive private party numbering the wives and girlfriends of some of the wealthiest men in the world. And in any case the American woman with the good face job had soon muscled right in on the hostess, sharing observations about the art works that Tara, who had zero interest in anything but clothes and shoes, couldn't hope to match. She would have to ask Nadezdha about her dress later on that night. Nadezdha was bound to be wearing something fabulous and all women liked to be complimented on what they wore.

Thankfully, there was just a little time left after the Hermitage tour for the female guests to whizz around the shops. In the space of the afternoon, Tara had come to the conclusion that the outfit she had brought with her from London would not be special enough for the event ahead. So the Versace she had liked so much was relegated to the bottom of the suitcase while Tara found herself a full length Cavalli number instead. It was a floor-length white silk halter neck with gold trim. It would show off her tan to perfection. And, in a rare moment of economy, Tara was pleased to note that she would not need to buy new shoes to go with it. The Louboutins would match perfectly. When James came back from his meeting, he nodded approvingly. He was one of those rare men who noticed what women wore and he wanted his wife to look her very best.

'Yes,' he said. 'I think long is right for tonight. It's going to be seriously glamorous. You're still wearing the earrings, though?'

'Of course,' said Tara. 'Those yellow diamonds would look good with anything.'

But they looked especially good when Tara was wearing nothing else at all. Carefully taking off her dress so that it wouldn't get crumpled, Tara let her husband take another good look at his investment. It wasn't long before his eyes drifted down from those vulgar rocks to Tara's impressive man-made embonpoint. Her breast job was the best thing he'd ever bought for her. The 34Es sat very well with Tara's natural assets: her slim waist and narrow hips. Her long legs the colour of a Caramac bar (Dean had been mad for those sweets as a child). Her feet . . . well, her feet did not look so good after years spent crammed into ridiculously high-heeled shoes, but the Louboutins concealed her bunions passably well and, in any case, Dean liked making love to Tara best when she had her shoes on.

Dean threw his wife down onto the bed. Then, while she lay spread-eagled, gazing up at him with huge, unblinking eyes, he started to undress himself. He pulled his belt out of its loops so quickly that it made the sound of a whip cracking in the air. Tara recoiled just a little.

'Oh Dean,' she said when he was fully naked and his small but perfectly formed penis was half erect. 'I'll do anything you want.' She rolled over.

'You better,' said her husband, as the leather belt snapped lightly against Tara's bottom.

At quarter to eight, a veritable fleet of limos arrived at the hotel to take Belanov's guests to the opera house. The hotel staff flew into frenzy, opening doors and escorting everybody to their cars. Looking around the lobby as she and James waited to be attended to, Tara was comfortably assured that she was the best-looking of the non-Russian wives. Some of them were positively dowdy. It was different story at the other end. Belanov and his wife were at the door, greeting their guests in person.

Nadezdha Belanov glittered from head to toe. Her silver dress was overlaid with a cobweb of crystals (or perhaps real diamonds) that reflected so much light she appeared to be surrounded by a bright white aura that emanated straight from her heart. On her head was a tiara that Tara would later discover had belonged to one of the Romanov girls, who perished with their royal parents at the start of the Russian Revolution.

'I hope you will enjoy the evening,' said Nadezdha as she shook Tara's hand.

Tara trotted out the compliment she had been preparing since returning from the Hermitage. Nadezdha said 'thank you' but there was no warmth in her eyes. No connection at all in fact. No recognition that they had spent the whole afternoon together. Tara's fantasy of dining with Trudy and Sting (more of the Belanovs' friends) slipped a little further away.

Chapter Forty-Nine

𝄞

*L*IKE Tara Dean, Cosima had been very concerned that her dress for the evening should be glamorous enough for the company.

Karl had explained to Belanov that it would be impossible for them to stage a full version of *Tosca* in his summer palace. The ballroom might well be able to accommodate seven hundred but there was none of the equipment needed to move the enormous sets. Instead, the company would give a straightforward recital. That meant that Cosima couldn't possibly wear her second act costume from *Tosca*.

'It will look amateurish,' she said. 'We don't want them to think that we've come from a dress rehearsal.'

And so, Karl's assistant was set to work contacting Mathieu Randon to find out if he would be kind enough to lend Cosima jewels for the evening.

As luck would have it, Mathieu Randon was a great

friend of Evgeny Belanov. Belanov had recently bought a small vineyard in Burgundy on Randon's recommendation. Since coming into his money, Belanov had been a valuable customer for pretty much all the Domaine Randon Group's luxury brands. All Belanov's wives (except the first, who still wore the Swatch he had given her for her twenty-first birthday as she shuffled around her studio apartment in Moscow) were decked out in Martin et Fils jewels. Randon had even named a specific cut of diamond after Nadezdha, so of course he had been invited to Belanov's summer party.

'In fact,' he told Cosima. 'It was I who suggested to him that he ask you to sing. I told him that you would be heading in his direction this summer.'

'Thank you,' said Cosima.

This was an incredible piece of luck. As was the fact that Randon was the kind of man who understood that jewels as fine as those made by Martin et Fils would be let down by an unremarkable dress. Randon had one of the staff at Estrella, the most exclusive of Domaine Randon's women's fashion lines, send Cosima photographs of a range of couture dresses that had yet to make their catwalk debut. Cosima was thrilled to see that one of the scanned photographs, of a dark blue velvet dress with a deep sweetheart neckline made for *serious* jewellery was annotated 'Angelina?' That could only refer to La Jolie. Perhaps this dress was set to grace the red carpet at the Oscars. Cosima liked to think she shared the same colouring as Angelina Jolie, if nothing else, so she couldn't resist asking for that dress to be brought to Russia. She also chose a pale cream silk number, which was somewhat more summery and therefore perhaps more appropriate for the time of year.

In the event, when the dresses arrived, on Mathieu Randon's private jet, no less, Cosima found that she liked the cream silk number so much better. Like her costumes for Tosca, it had a flattering empire line that showcased her knockout décolletage.

When she telephoned Randon to thank him for having had the dresses and a seamstress to take up the hems delivered to her hotel, and told him of her eventual choice, he murmured his approval.

'I can imagine how well the colour looks against your complexion,' he said. 'And the diamonds too. I can think of no better setting for my jewels than your bare skin.'

Cosima felt a shiver of delight travel down her spine at the compliment. She wished that Nolan might have heard it. He needed to know that he wasn't the only powerful man who found her attractive. Powerful? Huh. Nolan was a minnow compared to the likes of Randon and Belanov. He was a mere hired entertainer. A court jester. As was she, the thought came to her later ...

But in the dress and the diamonds, with her glossy dark hair piled high on her head and held there by a band that glittered with yet more carats, Cosima might have passed for a duchess in any company. She felt confident that she would not look like the poor relation at the party after the performance.

Neither would Nolan. Cosima had to grudgingly admit that he looked his very best in a suit by Trianon, another loan from Domaine Randon. He was still wearing those Cartier cufflinks though. And finally, Cosima couldn't hold back from asking him just as they were about to take the stage.

'Those cufflinks are Cartier. Who on earth gave you Cartier cufflinks?'

'Perhaps I have a secret admirer,' said Nolan.

Cosima's eyes flashed hate.

However, Cosima managed to channel that hate into something very special for the performance. The ballroom in which the concert was to be held hadn't been built for the purpose but the acoustics weren't all that bad.

The company sang extracts from *Tosca*, of course. Then Nolan and Cosima sang Mimi and Rodolfo's first duet from *La Bohème*. The audience seemed appreciative. Cosima had guessed that the friends of such a wealthy man would be a cultured bunch. She noticed only a little shuffling in the middle of the room and that was soon forgotten when she finished singing the Queen of the Night's aria from *The Magic Flute* and the audience leaped to their feet as a man to applaud.

'Thank you,' Cosima blew kisses in happy gratitude. 'Thank you,' she mouthed again with her eyes firmly fixed on Mathieu Randon, who had led the standing ovation. That did not go unnoticed by Nolan.

Chapter Fifty

Needless to say, Tara Dean wasn't a big fan of opera. The outfits of the female singers and their jewels went some way to distracting her from the boring warbling but she couldn't follow the songs at all, even though the libretti were helpfully provided in English for Belanov's guests.

The party afterwards also proved to be quite boring. Once Tara had checked out what her other Russian rivals were wearing, she was left standing on the edge of one of Dean's business conversations. She was frustrated that she couldn't start a conversation of her own because nobody seemed to speak proper English except that tart of a translator who was getting much too cosy with James for her liking, laughing and touching his arm whenever she wanted to make a point. Tara might as well not have been there.

So, she was relieved when Belanov brought the Irish tenor, Nolan O'Connor, into their fold and delighted when

Nolan seemed to be interested in talking to her. Tara had Irish relatives and they soon found common ground, talking about the best golf courses in the west of Ireland. Thank God, thought Tara, he doesn't want to talk about opera.

'Do you play golf?' Nolan asked.

It was a boring subject, but less boring than Puccini. And it wasn't long before they moved onto the best bars in Dublin and the best pints of Guinness they'd ever tasted. When Nolan told a rather blue story about an old girlfriend called Judy Shephard who could drink a pint in under fifteen seconds, Tara decided that she was beginning to have fun.

However after half an hour, Tara noticed that Dean had disappeared. She was pissed off that he hadn't told her he was going, and doubly pissed off when she noticed that the translator had disappeared too. Most women would have assumed that their husbands were conducting business, but Tara knew her husband better. He had taken that translator to one of the sumptuously appointed bedrooms upstairs. He was shagging her. Tara could feel it in her bones. And so she redoubled her flirtation with Nolan. Every time a waiter passed by, she took a glass of champagne, knocked it back and grabbed another one. Tara Dean could hold her drink, but it wasn't long before she was swaying. She swayed in Nolan's direction. He, still on duty and practically sober, reached out to steady her. Tara wrapped her arms around his neck, laughing. From the other side of the room, Cosima saw it all.

As did Dean's henchman, Tony.

'I need to go to the toilet,' Tara slurred into Nolan's ear.

'You'd better hurry along then,' said Nolan, pleased that he might have a chance to get shot of her. Though she had stayed on the opposite side of the room all evening, Cosima was bound to have noticed that Tara had suddenly got tactile.

'I'll fall over if you don't come with me,' she said.

'All right then,' said Nolan. 'I'll walk you as far as the door.'

'Will you help me pull my knickers down?' Tara asked him, within earshot of several Russians who spoke rather better English than they pretended.

'I'm sure you don't need any help with that,' said Nolan but, gentleman that he was, he decided he had better take her to the bathroom quickly, if only to make sure she didn't pass out on the marble floor on her way.

Thus pretty much the entire party saw Nolan escort Mrs James Dean from the room. That was all they needed to know. They didn't see what happened once Nolan and Tara were out in the corridor. They didn't see her push him against a wall and attempt to wrap her legs around his waist. They didn't seem him peel her off, decline the offer to 'suck her tits' and try to persuade her to go into the bathroom alone.

God knows, back in the day, Nolan would have shagged Tara Dean in a heartbeat. She was an attractive woman. She had the kind of looks that promised a very good time. Nolan had nothing against fake boobs. But something had changed in him over the past few weeks and that night in particular he did not want to live down to Cosima's expectations of him, even if they were 'on a break'.

So, Nolan handed over the care of Tara Dean to the babushka attending the ladies' room. He slipped the old woman a banknote to make sure she would do the job properly, though he hadn't got used to the currency and wasn't sure whether he was giving her the equivalent of ten quid or a hundred. Then instead of going straight back into the party, Nolan went out into the beautiful garden of Belanov's home to enjoy the white night. Within seconds he had forgotten Tara Dean and was thinking of Cosima once more.

Chapter Fifty-One

𝄞

JULIET had convinced Hazel that she was just an ordinary woman down on her luck, looking for any employment she could find, but she would take no chances that evening. She spent the afternoon at the hairdresser getting her blond hair dyed a dull shade of brown.

'Are you sure?' asked the hairdresser. 'Your hair is such a lovely colour.'

Juliet managed to convince her that she just wanted a wash in wash out colour for a fancy dress party.

'What are you going as?' the hairdresser asked her.

'The host's worst nightmare,' Juliet smiled to herself.

She completed the disguise with a pair of glasses with plain lenses. The thick frames did nothing for her. They were the kind of glasses that didn't cause anyone to make passes, which was fine by Juliet. If anyone looked at her at all, she wanted them to look away again just as quickly. She didn't need anyone to find her attractive. She wanted to be forget-table. Just another girl in blue from City Clean Stars.

The disguise worked. Even Mercy, who knew that Juliet was going to be there, looked straight through her.

'Wow. You look different.'

'Can't take any chances,' said Juliet. 'One of my former colleagues might be working late.'

Juliet was assigned to work alongside Mercy, which was exactly what she had hoped for.

'You'll have to pull your weight,' Mercy warned her, as she stepped aside to let Juliet take the trolley.

In the goods lift up to the sixteenth floor, Juliet held her breath. This far, it had been easy, but what if she betrayed herself when she saw a familiar face? She resolved once out of the lift, to keep her eyes firmly on the floor.

For the first five minutes, Juliet kept her head down as she worked out who was still around. Her PA Michaela wasn't there, though Juliet was pleased to see that her collection of gonks was still on her desk, suggesting that she hadn't been suspended just because Juliet was. Anneli, who had always prided herself on knowing everything about everyone, was just turning off her PC and putting on her coat. She looked in Juliet's direction but her gaze went straight through her. Mercy was right. To the people with 'proper jobs' at Anglo-Italian, the cleaners may as well have been ghosts.

Still, Juliet kept to the other end of the corridor, until she was certain that Anneli had gone.

After that, the coast was clear. When she thought about it later, Juliet would realise that she had not been in any danger of meeting Christopher or any of the other guys she had so recently worked with that night. England was playing

Italy. No red-blooded Anglo-Italian employee would miss that match.

There was no point in waiting to try to break into Christopher's computer. Juliet was well aware that the clock was ticking on her plan. Every second was a second closer to Christopher having done the gangster's bidding and cleaned away the evidence afterwards.

Mercy was only too glad to let Juliet have Christopher's room as part of her 'beat'. 'He's a slob,' Mercy explained. 'His desk is always covered in coffee cups.'

Including, Juliet could not help but notice, the mug she had bought for him on a brief trip away to Iceland.

It was the work of mere seconds to get into Christopher's files. Christopher had always been sloppy about security. He kept the toggle that would give him a variable access code in the unlocked top drawer of his desk. Though the IT department continually sent out memos asking people to change their passwords frequently and not to choose words that were too obvious, Christopher Wilde had not changed his password in five years.

Juliet held her breath again as she typed in the letters and they were represented on screen by little stars. S.P.A.D.A.R.I. It was Italian for swordsman and the name of the hotel in Milan where he and Juliet had first made love.

She was straight in.

Juliet wasn't entirely sure what she was looking for, so she started with Christopher's most recent emails. She plugged her name into the search function. Nothing came up except a couple of emails she had sent herself before she was put under investigation. She tried her initials. That threw up nothing either. There was nothing to suggest that Christopher knew anything about Juliet's dismissal in his email files, but that wasn't conclusive.

Once Juliet had looked in the obvious places, she searched the deeper reaches of Christopher's hard drive. She found the file where he stashed his own personal banking correspondence. She searched through that, cutting down the task by looking only at those files that had come into existence since when she estimated to be the date that Caroline became pregnant. There was nothing obvious. But after half an hour when she thought she would go cross-eyed, trying to speed-read dates and names, she hit paydirt. She found a file, within another file, which was named 'Juliet'.

She clicked on the tiny icon and the pc began to whirr into action. But this file was not what Juliet had expected. A password prompt appeared. Juliet entered the only password she had ever known Christopher to use: SPADARI, but for once it didn't work. Juliet entered the names of Christopher's sons. The make of his car. His wife's name. Nothing happened.

'Shit,' she muttered to herself. This file was titled with her name and password protected with a password that she couldn't guess. It had to be about her. She fished a memory stick out of her overall pocket and was just about to copy the file onto it when she heard Mercy exclaim in surprise.

'Hazel! I wish you wouldn't creep up on me like that.'

Mercy surprise had given Juliet the warning she needed. She quickly abandoned the download and closed down Christopher's PC. By the time Hazel came to look in on her, Juliet was dusting Christopher's prized golf trophies.

'Don't bother with those,' said Hazel. 'The bloke in this office is right arrogant twat.'

'Is he?' asked Juliet as she struggled to keep the smile off her face.

Chapter Fifty-Two

'You look a little preoccupied,' said Mathieu Randon when he caught up with Cosima by one of the windows overlooking the endless gardens that surrounded Belanov's summer palace.

'Oh.' Cosima had been surprised. She put her hand to her throat as though to protect the diamonds. When she saw that it was Randon who had joined her, she relaxed and let her hand drop back to her side. Randon took her by the shoulders and kissed her on both cheeks.

'Your performance was absolutely wonderful,' he told her. 'Transporting, in fact. It made me wish I could lock you up in a bird cage and put you in a corner of my house so that you would always sing only for me.'

'Really?' That was quite something.

'Yes,' said Randon, looking deep into her eyes. Cosima felt that familiar shiver of excitement again. He truly was a very attractive man. Though he must be in his late fifties, everything about him – the way he walked, the the way he smiled – betokened a much younger man. One in his prime. Something animal inside Cosima reacted to him no matter how hard she tried to be cool in his presence.

'So,' Randon continued. 'Are you going to tell me what was making you look so sad?'

She could hardly tell him that she was looking sad because she was wondering what the hell had happened to Nolan O'Connor. One minute he was talking to that blonde piece. The next . . . She had jumped to the same conclusion as everybody else. It made her look like such a fool. But Randon wouldn't want to hear it and she didn't want him to think she wasn't available at least to flirt. So, instead, she said, 'I was thinking about having to give back these diamonds.'

Randon gave a hearty laugh.

Cosima recalled having been told that the necklace she was wearing would retail at half a million. Ordinarily that would have meant being shadowed by a bodyguard the whole time she was wearing it, but that evening Randon had announced that he was more than happy for Cosima not to have her own security detail. Belanov's palace was a fortress. No one would try anything on.

'That necklace does look especially beautiful on you,' said Randon. 'As if it were made for you, in fact. We'll have to come to some sort of arrangement.'

Cosima put her hand to her throat again. But this time it was because part of her had imagined Randon sinking his teeth deep into her neck.

'Another concert perhaps,' Randon continued. 'A very private one.'

Cosima felt her cheeks colour. Randon's expression left

her in no doubt that what he had in mind was not another demonstration of her peerless talents as a soprano.

'I have admired you for a very long time,' he said. 'Nothing would make me happier than to be able to give you a fraction of the pleasure that you have given to me over the years. Both with your voice and, more recently, with your wonderful company.'

Was he about to proposition her?

'I'd like you to join me on my yacht next weekend. The *Grand Cru* will be moored just off Portofino. I'm sure you know the place. There is excellent shopping there I understand.'

'Next weekend I will be singing at Covent Garden,' Cosima told him.

'Only if you want to. I will make sure that nobody misses you. I'm sure your understudy will be delighted to take the stage and the opera house knows they can rely on a very generous donation from Domaine Randon to make up for any inconvenience.'

Cosima looked back into the room. There was still no sign of Nolan or that blond bitch. She put her hand to the diamonds around her neck again. The jewels that she was wearing right then would more than cover the money she owed the IRS. But even if Randon wasn't serious when he suggested that he would be willing to part with them for the pleasure of her company, there seemed to be very little downside to spending a weekend on a yacht with a billionaire. This latest break-up with Nolan, and the way he was behaving, sneaking off with that vile drunken woman right under her husband's nose, had left Cosima feeling that she wanted to desecrate the memory of their love in some way, to prove that it meant just as little to her as it did to him.

Allowing Mathieu Randon to seduce her would be the perfect way to do that.

'Shall we take a turn around the garden?' Randon suggested.

Cosima accepted his arm.

Nolan had been watching the swans on Belanov's artificial lake for almost an hour. As he sat on a marble bench, imported at great cost from Italy, he hadn't noticed the time passing at all. He was mesmerised by the graceful creatures as they glided silently on the silvered water, in time with one another with the fold of their virgin white wings and the incline of their necks perfectly matched in a way that even the best ballet dancers failed to achieve after hours of practice.

Was it really true, Nolan wondered, that these creatures mated for life? Regardless of whether it was a fact, the thought of such a lifelong bond made the appearance of the swans that night seem significant somehow. Nolan couldn't help but see the two birds as symbolic of his relationship with Cosima. Was this a message from some higher being, telling him to try again with that frustrating woman?

Nolan decided that it was. It was ridiculous that Cosima would be willing to throw away their enduring love for one another because he had not been celibate while they were divorced. That they had come back together was a miracle. They had to make it work. Nolan resolved to go back into the party and ask Cosima to leave with him right then. Even if they did not sleep for a week, they were going to talk all their differences through, properly this time. Nolan was certain that if only Cosima shut up for long enough, he could convince her that they had something worth saving. He would tell her everything. He'd reveal at last how vulnerable loving her had made him feel. They could have a wonderful future together if only she would let go of perceived misdemeanours long since past.

Nolan got to his feet. As he was standing, the birds on the water took flight. It was all the encouragement he needed to believe that his plan had celestial blessing. The swans were flying back towards the house, towards Cosima, the beautiful, frustrating, wonderful love of his life. And there she was, stepping out onto the veranda. On the arm of Mathieu Randon.

The swans flew over the top of Belanov's palace and out of sight. Cosima did not see Nolan but Nolan saw Cosima only too well as she smiled up at Mathieu Randon and Randon leaned towards her and cupped her face in his huge, and doubtless well-manicured, hands. Nolan knew that he was about to kiss her.

'So much for lifelong love,' Nolan muttered. Without going back through the ballroom, he walked round the house to the driveway and asked one of Belanov's henchmen to get him a cab.

Chapter Fifty-Three

𝄞

JAMES Dean was not a happy man. As soon as Tara and Nolan left the party, Dean's number one goon Tony went to find his boss and tell him what was going on. The gangster had immediately broken off his 'business meeting' with the translator, who was teaching him the Russian for 'fuck', and raged through the corridors of Belanov's palace in search of his faithless wife. He threw open the door of every bedroom, disturbing quite a few clandestine trysts but not Nolan and Tara. He didn't think to look in the ladies' room. So, he found nothing. But as far as Dean was concerned, Nolan and Tara's continued absence was conclusive proof of their guilt.

And when eventually Tara resurfaced, she was unable to put her husband's mind at rest. Though she was pretty certain – secretly slightly insulted – that Nolan had simply escorted her to the bathroom, she couldn't remember for sure what had happened. And her husband's rage frightened her so much that she dare not admit she had been flirting with Nolan because she was jealous of the translator. Instead, she kept silent and let Dean fill in the gaps and soon the story started to look like this. Nolan O'Connor had been flirting with Tara, surreptitiously filling her glass in the hope of getting her drunk enough to persuade her to sleep with him.

Tara had no idea how long she had been in the Ladies and the babushka on the door had no idea that her corroboration of Nolan's innocence could be so important. Not that anyone thought to ask her.

'I'll fucking kill him,' James Dean raged.

'Not a good idea,' said Tony who had the misfortune to be in the same room when Tara reappeared.

'Are you telling me to calm down?'

'Not in so many words.'

'Good. Because no one fucking tells me to calm down,' said Dean. 'I want that woman,' he pointed at Tara, 'On a flight back to London before I fucking kill her too.'

Dean's translator whispered an urgent instruction to the PA who had been assigned to Dean for the duration. Tara shivered and cried. She wasn't about to disobey her husband's wishes. She had yet to admit to him that she had no idea what had happened to the priceless earrings he had given her for her birthday (the toilet attendant had considered them part of her tip and was planning to give them to her granddaughter. She had no idea they were worth more than she could earn in a decade).

Though just an hour later, James Dean seemed to be feeling more sanguine and had rejoined the party and the buxom translator to boot, no one who knew him had any doubt that this was not the end of the story.

*　　*　　*

While James Dean bayed for his blood, Nolan was totally unaware that he was in such hot water. As far as Nolan was concerned, he himself was the man most grievously wronged at Belanov's summer ball. He could not believe that Cosima had thrown their love away for a man like Mathieu Randon. The man's reputation made Nolan's look squeaky clean. How was it possible that Cosima could rail on Nolan for being a sexually incontinent bastard, then let that monster Randon stroke her face while she purred like an alley cat on heat? Randon's private life had been all over the tabloids. He'd bedded everyone who was anyone. What made Cosima think Randon's obviously insatiable lust was forgivable while Nolan was cast aside for admitting he hadn't been a monk, when he was officially single?

Money. It was the obvious explanation. The only explanation. And it made Nolan feel a whole lot worse. When he and Cosima first got together they had been happy to share a studio flat in the filthiest building in Manhattan. Had Cosima's head been turned while she was modelling for Randon's jewellery company? It all started to make sense. The row in Vienna had come right after Cosima heard they would be performing at Belanov's summer party. Right after she found out that Randon would be in attendance. Suddenly it seemed quite likely that Cosima had deliberately manufactured the break up in order to make sure that she was free to submit to Randon's advances.

Nolan gave his pillow a hearty thump. To think he had been ready to lay down his life for her.

Oh the perfidious woman, to choose money over love!

As Nolan was beating seven colours out of his pillow and calling it Mathieu Randon, Cosima was getting similarly physical with the soft furnishings in her own room. God, she had never felt so humiliated! Randon had planned to try it on in the garden, of course. She knew that. But as he leered over her, Cosima had seen a pair of swans flying overhead and it was almost as though she heard Nolan's name in the whisper of their wings.

'They mate for life, swans,' Cosima had told Randon.

And Randon had just laughed at her and replied, 'That's because they don't live very long.'

Having followed his colourful private life in the gossip columns over the years, Cosima saw in that response that Randon was not approaching his seduction of her with anything like the sincerity her vanity had led her to imagine. She found herself wondering what Nolan would have said in the same situation and knew that it would have been something fabulously lyrical and romantic. Suddenly, thinking better of allowing Randon to have his way, Cosima looked back towards the ballroom, hoping to catch sight of Nolan without that silly blonde. Meanwhile, Randon took hold of her face and started to pull her towards him quite roughly. He squeezed her cheeks so hard that her mouth puckered up like that of a grouper fish. Cosima was shocked and turned off by how physically careless he was being with her. She shook herself free of his grip.

'I'd like to go back inside,' she said.

Randon tried to catch her again. Cosima darted away from his hands.

'Mr Randon,' Cosima said firmly. 'I think we ought to keep this professional.'

She was shocked again to see something like anger flare in his dark eyes, but after gathering himself, he agreed with her.

'You're right,' he said evenly. 'In which case, you had better take those diamonds off before you lose them.'

He called for a guard and had the man help Cosima remove the necklace and her earrings there and then.

'Do you want me to take the dress off too?' she snarled at Randon.

'If you'd agreed to that, you might have kept the jewels,' Randon retorted.

She was in no mood to stay on at the party after that exchange. She couldn't bear to walk back through the ballroom with her décolletage now so glaringly unadorned and so she unknowingly followed Nolan's path around the side of the house to the driveway.

'I'm a big fan of your singing, Miss Esposito.'

The kind words of the valet who ordered a car for her did nothing to make her feel better. All she wanted was to get back to the hotel and take a long hot bath. Mathieu Randon had treated her like a slut. Meanwhile, Nolan was spending the night with a real one. Standing outside the party that thousands of women all over the world would have killed to be able to attend, Cosima just wanted to be back home. She wanted to sink into the red velvet sofa in her cosy apartment and nurse a cup of hot chocolate like Nolan used to make for her whenever she was feeling low. Suddenly, Cosima felt small and lonely and a very long way from New York.

But the following day, Cosima came out of her corner fighting. Finding Nolan in the breakfast room of the hotel, she confronted him about the blonde.

'What? That dozy tart? She could barely stand up,' Nolan told his ex. 'I helped her to the ladies' room, that's all. I didn't want anything to do with her but she insisted that I helped her out. I gave the attendant some roubles to take care of her. And then I left her to it.'

'And went where?'

'Out into the garden. Which is where I saw *you* kissing Mathieu Randon.' Nolan mimicked Randon's accent as he snarled the Frenchman's name.

'I was not kissing Mathieu Randon,' Cosima exclaimed.

'Well you were doing a good impression of two people kissing. Not that it's any of my business in any case. You and I have broken up, remember?'

Cosima pouted. 'I was not kissing that man.'

'Whatever you say. But I *really* did not fuck that stupid Essex girl.'

Cosima wanted to believe Nolan. She really did. But she simply couldn't. She had noticed Tara Dean very early in the evening and at once registered that the blonde from Essex was everything she would never be. Tara Dean was slim and toned. She had the figure of a supermodel. Her face was a model's too. She'd probably worked as one.

Cosima couldn't help but be envious. She knew that she herself was fit and she had the kind of body that one needed to support an excellent voice, but, like all women, Cosima was bombarded daily by an image of perfection that very few would ever achieve. She wasn't immune to the pressures exerted by advertising and the fashion mags. Even now that she appeared in fashion mags herself, as the face of Martin et Fils, she wasn't convinced that she had the kind of beauty that made others take notice. Somehow, knowing that her photos had been airbrushed did not make Cosima believe that every other advertising image had been subjected to the same treatment. She assumed instead that she made for especially poor raw material. She would never be tall enough, slim enough, good enough. Of course Nolan would prefer a woman like Tara Dean to her. Any man would, she was sure.

'But she's exactly the kind of woman you want,' Cosima stated baldly.

'Don't be stupid,' said Nolan.

'No. She is. I know it. Whenever I catch you looking at a woman, it's somebody like that. Someone tall and blond and—'

'Orange-skinned and married to a psychopathic bouncer. For Christ's sake!'

'You like that sort of look,' Cosima continued. 'How could you ever really have loved someone who looks like me?'

'I don't know how to convince you,' said Nolan. 'And the truth is, I don't know if I can be bothered to try anymore. This is hard work, Cosi. You and me. It always was and it looks like it always will be. We called it a day five years ago and that's how we should have left it. We should never have tried to start this up again. I'm sorry.'

Cosima opened her mouth to protest, but Nolan finished his coffee, picked up the newspaper he had only been pretending to read, and left.

Chapter Fifty-Four

𝄞

𝐹LORENCE Carter found Russia intimidating and frightening. Though the Berlin wall had long since come down and the once mighty Soviet Union was now just a collection of small, warring 'Stans, Florence couldn't help feeling that at any moment she might be snatched from the street and thrown into jail for the simple crime of being from the Land of the Free. For that reason, she stayed inside her hotel for the whole of her time in Russia, venturing out only to see Nolan sing.

And it was a lacklustre performance. She had come all the way to Russia to see the kind of performance she could have expected from any amateur chorus in New Jersey but she had to be there. She still didn't know if Nolan knew she had seen him at her hotel in Vienna.

When she got to the stage door, as usual, she had missed Nolan by a long time. He had climbed into the limo to take him back to the hotel before Florence was able to get out of the auditorium. However, that evening, Florence did catch some of the cast as they exited. Though she wasn't interested in getting their autographs, she was able to glean something far better. Information about her beloved.

The singers who played Scarpia and Spoletta respectively lingered on the pavement as they waited for a car.

'Bloody hopeless performance tonight,' said Donald Law.

'You're telling me,' said Antony. 'I just wanted to put my head in my hands when he started "Lucevan E Stelle" with a bum note.'

Florence bristled slightly to hear Nolan's colleagues berating his performance, though she knew it was fair comment.

'What's wrong with him today?' Antony asked.

'It's all about Cosima,' Donald sighed. 'Apparently, he caught her making out in the bushes with that French bloke – Random, is it? – at Belanov's after-show party. He's devastated.'

'I thought they broke up in Vienna.'

'Vienna, Venice, Venezuela,' said Donald. 'Those two have got together and broken up in every town you care to mention, but right now they are off again and this time Nolan seems to think it's for ever.'

Florence couldn't help herself. She sprang out of her place in the shadows.

'Did you say that Nolan O'Connor has broken up with Cosima Esposito?'

Donald and Antony both took an astonished jump backwards as Florence leaped into the middle of their conversation. The two men looked at each other for a clue what to do about the dishevelled-looking creature who'd just addressed them. Her eyes were glittering with the dangerous gleam of fanaticism that both men recognised. Anyone who makes a living by performance can expect to meet at least one passionate loony in the course of his career. A primeval sort of fear froze both men.

'Is it true?'

Fortunately, at that moment, the car arrived. Before the chauffeur could get out to open the doors for them, Donald had wrenched the passenger door open and he and Antony tumbled inside, leaving Florence alone on the pavement once more.

'Who was that?' Donald asked.

'You mean, what was that?' said Antony. 'Nolan has a very unfortunate line in fans. Do you think we ought to tell him.'

'He's depressed enough as it is,' said Donald. 'But yeah, we ought to tell him to be on the lookout for a crazy lady.'

Walking back to her hotel that evening, Florence no longer felt that St Petersburg was a scary place. She hugged this new piece of information about Nolan's relationship status to her heart. All her hopes flourished again. He had tried to find her in Vienna. Now she had confirmation that Cosima was off the scene. It was just a matter of time.

Act Three

Chapter Fifty-Five

WHEN Mercy got home from work that evening, it was to find a note on the kitchen table from her mother, saying that she had gone to the accident and emergency unit. She'd tried to phone but Mercy's mobile battery must have died. She didn't get the call.

Without even stopping for the glass of water she had been thinking about all the way home on the sweltering tube, Mercy turned on her heel, pulled her jacket back on and headed out to the hospital. Her mind was racing. Who had been hurt or taken ill? Was it her mother? Unlikely, since Melody had had time to make the note in her elegant, tidy handwriting. Please God, don't let it be Mum, Mercy prayed.

Getting into the waiting room, Mercy found her mother at once. Melody was pacing the bleak tiled floor, wringing a handkerchief between her hands.

'Your brother is in there,' she said, nodding down the

corridor towards a cubicle around which the curtains had been drawn.

'What happened?' Mercy asked. 'Is it serious?'

'The doctor says he'll be OK. It's just a couple of stitches. But . . . oh, Mercy. Someone attacked your brother with a knife! Who would have done such a thing? Why would they pick on our Francis? He's always been such a kind boy. He always keeps himself out of trouble.'

Mercy winced at her mother's pain. Melody had no idea who her son was any more. To Mercy, Francis ending up in the emergency unit like this was inevitable. And perhaps it was a good thing. While she was glad that his brush with knife crime had not been fatal, she hoped that it had been frightening enough to make him reconsider the type of people he had started to call his friends.

'You're hurting me!' came Francis's voice from the other end of the corridor.

Melody picked up her skirts and ran on down there but the nurse confirmed that Francis didn't want anyone to be in there with him. He was keeping up the hard man act even now.

Eventually, the doctor emerged from the curtained cubicle and Melody and Mercy were allowed inside. 'He's going to be OK,' said Dr Brown, who was young and petite and didn't look as though she would be up to handling the gore she had to see on the average Friday night in A & E. 'You just need to make sure he keeps the wound clean. Make an appointment with your GP to have the stitches taken out in a few days.'

'Will his hand be one hundred per cent when the stitches are taken out?' Melody asked.

'He should have pretty much full use of it again, yes. He

was very lucky. A few millimetres in the wrong direction and he might have severed a major artery or lost a finger.'

Melody wailed.

The doctor laid her hand on Melody's arm. 'But he didn't. It's going to be OK. Of course, since it's a knife wound, I'm going to have to report the incident to the police.'

Francis, wild-eyed, assured her there was no need.

'It's not my choice,' said the doctor. 'I've got to.'

When the policemen arrived, Francis was not in the mood to be helpful. When he was questioned about the incident that had landed him in hospital, he claimed that he had not been attacked in the street at all. He said that he had been at home in his mother's kitchen, making himself a cheese sandwich.

'I wasn't being careful,' he said. 'The knife slipped. That's all.'

It was clear that the police did not believe him, but no matter how many different ways they phrased the questions, Francis's answers were always the same. He had slipped and cut his hand while making a cheese sandwich. It was cheddar cheese. What more did they need to know?

'You think you're making a fool out of me,' the policeman said in a low warning voice. 'But trust me, Francis. We're going to be keeping an eye on you.'

'What?' Francis shot back. 'Every time I'm making dinner?'

They took Francis home later that night. And for the first time in a while he stayed in the whole of the next day and ate the food his mother had made him as soon as it was put on the table. Melody fussed around him endlessly, periodically raising her hands to the ceiling and thanking God for having taken such good care of her son.

'You told the police who did it?' she asked several times. 'I want to see justice being done.'

'Relax,' said Francis, as he allowed his mother to lift his feet onto a footstool. 'They're gonna get theirs.'

At ten o'clock Melody went upstairs to bed, leaving her children alone.

'You think you've been pretty clever,' Mercy hissed at her brother. 'But next time you might not be so lucky. What was it about, Francis? Did someone stiff you on a drug deal?'

Francis ignored her. He just carried on watching television.

'Do you want to die?' she asked him. 'Because that's what you're setting yourself up for. You're dealing with the kind of people who wouldn't think twice about killing you.'

'It's a dog eat dog world,' Francis acknowledged. 'But trust me, sista. I ain't no poodle. The man who did this to me is going to get slotted.'

'And you think that will sort things out? You're going to knife him back?'

'I ain't gonna get my hands dirty. I got people to do that for me now.'

Mercy looked at her brother in a mixture of incomprehension and despair. What was he talking about?

'My man will take care of it.'

At midnight, a car sounded its horn outside the house. Francis rose to his feet and shrugged on his jacket, an action made far more difficult than usual than by the bandaging around his hand.

'You're going out again? Tonight?'

'What do I want to stay in with you for?'

'But ...' Mercy looked towards his hand. 'Don't do anything stupid,' she begged him. 'Remember what it says in the Bible about revenge. These people will get theirs, Francis. But you don't have to be the one to give it to them.'

'What? You telling me I should wait for the Lord? Oh Lord!' he threw his hands up in the air, parodying all the believers at the church they had attended since childhood. In that moment, Mercy hated him. Her loving little brother had become a strutting, arrogant cock.

'I don't want to talk to you anymore,' said Mercy.

'Good. Because I don't want to hear anything you've got to say.'

Mercy looked out of the window. She saw her brother climbing, with some difficulty, into the back seat of a black Range Rover. She didn't get much of a look at the guy in the driver's seat, but she saw something that had surprised her. She had thought that her brother would have fallen in with the local yardies. Men who had known him since childhood. But the guy in the driver's seat of the Range Rover was white.

Francis seemed to be getting off lightly. Being given a week to find ten grand had seemed like a gift compared to the beating he had been expecting. But what Francis didn't understand at that point was that Dean wasn't the only nutter he needed to worry about. The men who had turned over his mother's house and robbed Francis of his stock were not content with their windfall. By rising to prominence in the dealing scene so quickly, Francis had attracted a lot of attention in the underworld and attention in the underworld is usually unwanted. There were people out there who felt that Francis had muscled in on their territory and they wanted their back-rent in blood. More than ever, he needed the protection Dean could offer him.

Dean's henchman laughed when he saw Francis's heavily bandaged hand.

'You hurt yourself opening a pickle jar?' he asked.

'Yeah,' said Francis.

'So, how's the fund-raising going? A sweet little thing like you could go door to door to all your mother's friends with a sponsorship form. That's probably the best way.'

'I'll get the money,' he said.

'There'll be a lot more blood if you don't.'

Chapter Fifty-Six

𝄞

JULIET was sure she was close to making a breakthrough. Over the course of the week, she had downloaded onto a memory stick half a dozen files that she believed would prove to be linked to her dismissal. She was still a little worried that the method she had used to gather the evidence would count against her, but she tried not to think about that.

Having made copies of all the files within 'Juliet', Juliet checked Christopher's email again to be sure that he'd written nothing incriminating since she last looked. She found nothing by searching for her name, but then the heading of an email sent the previous week caught her eye. She had completely overlooked the email before, having concentrated on searching for references to herself. The heading was 'About last night . . .' It had been sent by Christopher's PA, Lucy.

Thank you for last night. I can't believe that what
happened between us actually happened! I do hope you
won't think badly of me.

I can't really remember what happened

... came Christopher's reply.

You'll have to show me all over again. Four Seasons at
Canary Wharf? Tonight?

Juliet leaned heavily on the desk as nausea washed over her.
Was Christopher screwing Lucy?

There was only one thing that would make Juliet feel better.
She picked the raciest exchange between Christopher and
his personal assistant and clicked forward. Into the address
window, she typed the email address for Christopher's wife
and before she had time to think better of it, the private
correspondence between Christopher and Lucy Wallis was
winging its way across cyber-space to crash like a meteor
into the cosy world of Caroline Wilde.

Back from Russia and still in a bear of a mood, James Dean
was getting impatient. He had David Sullivan call Wilde
out to Essex for a meeting to discuss progress of the AI
project. Christopher had not been quite as productive as
anyone hoped.

'Look,' he said. 'A lot of what you're asking me to do is
very difficult.'

'On the contrary, it's very simple,' said Dean.

'You think so? I don't think you really understand quite

how much security there is at Anglo-Italian. I can't just randomly go into people's offices and ask if I can slip a disc into their computer. There are people around all the time. I'm collecting the information you need as quickly as I can.'

'I did warn you that we might need more than one contact at Anglo-Italian to get everything done quickly,' David interrupted. 'The longer it takes, the higher the risk we'll be discovered.'

Dean thumped his fist on the table. 'I don't want to have to write this off. I've invested a lot of money in the pair of you.'

Christopher snorted.

'What does that mean?' Dean reacted to the snort.

'Well, I haven't seen any of this big investment, have I? You've had me doing all this shit. Risking my job. Risking arrest and prison, for what? How do I know that you'll hold up your end of the bargain?'

'But you have been getting something for all your hard work,' said Dean, his eyes glittering like a sewer rat's.

'What? Tell me exactly what I have been getting?'

'Your brother is still alive, isn't he? Not a hair on his head has been touched since you joined forces with me. My protection is a very valuable thing when you're languishing at Her Majesty's Pleasure.'

'For fuck's sake,' Christopher exploded.

'Are you getting mad at me, Christopher?' Dean asked. 'You must know that's not a very good idea. Here, this will keep you going for a while.'

Dean reached into his wallet and pulled out ten crisp fifties. He handed them to Christopher, who handed them straight back.

'I don't want your cash. I want to be out of this.'

'Now, you know that quitting isn't an option.'

Before he could continue on that theme, Dean had to take a call. Alone with David for the first time since they'd met in that service station car park, Christopher took the opportunity to ask if he had seen him in Juliet's part of town.

'Quite possibly,' said David. 'My mother lives in that neck of the woods. She's not been well.'

That explained the flowers he had been carrying. Christopher waited a beat and then he asked, 'Was it you who took the photographs of Juliet? Perhaps when you were visiting your mother?'

'Juliet?' David said the name as though it were unfamiliar to him, despite the fact that it was the name of the project.

'The blackmail photos,' said Christopher for unnecessary clarity.

'Oh. Those.' David shook his head. 'Nothing to do with me. They were taken before I signed up to this project.'

'OK,' said Christopher sounding unconvinced.

'Seriously,' said David. 'I never saw your girlfriend until Dean showed me the one of her doing the down-facing dog while we were having a beer one night.

'Great.' Christopher winced at the thought of that photograph in particular. He hoped that Juliet would never find out she had been photographed while practising yoga in the nude in the privacy of her own bedroom.

'What's he got on you?' he asked David now.

'Nothing,' said David. 'Nothing at all.'

David Sullivan often wondered how many of Dean's associates actually liked the man. There were plenty who seemed friendly enough towards him. And David had heard stories of startling generosity. Dean's closest associate, Tony, told the story of his niece, who had been diagnosed with leukaemia at the age of seven. Dean had paid for her to be taken to a clinic in the United States, where a new treatment for the disease was being pioneered. He had paid for all her treatment, and for her family to be put up in first-class accommodation the year that she had to stay there. When Caitlin was given the all clear, Dean paid for her and all of her classmates from the UK to go on an all-expenses paid trip to Disneyland to celebrate.

David murmured his agreement that Dean was a great and bounteous man whose kindness knew no limits but he couldn't help but think that the altruism was very carefully calculated. Having seen Dean's generosity to his niece and her family, how could Tony ever betray his boss? Dean must have know he had bought Tony's loyalty for life.

David had been observing James Dean very closely. It was Dean's unpredictability that was his real strength, he decided. Everyone who associated with him walked on eggshells, never sure if they were up for a stick or a carrot.

Right then, as Christopher Wilde was leaving in a fury, Dean wrapped his arm around David's shoulder.

'I like you,' he said. 'I think you're a lot like me. You're self-contained. No one can tell what you're thinking. Except for someone else who is thinking the exact same thing.' Dean tapped the side of his nose with a finger, and then laughed.

David found it faintly amusing that Dean thought they had anything in common beyond this ridiculous account-sweeping scam. To David, Dean's observation proved that in some ways he was dangerously stupid. Like his name-sake, Dean lived his life as though he were in front of a camera, imagining the camera angles as he delivered a pretty speech.

Dean thought he had David all worked out. They'd talked about their childhoods a couple of times, when Dean was deep in whisky and thought. Dean had teased David about the softness of his upbringing. A nice middle-class family in the Home Counties. Private education. Music lessons. By contrast, Dean's upbringing had been a war zone: a council estate, a mother who shoplifted to feed her children, numerous 'uncles' passing through. But then David revealed the details of his parents' divorce and the new stepfather who beat him black and blue.

'Until I was big enough to hit him back,' said David. 'He never raised a finger to me again after that.'

It was his stepfather's violence that had led David to take up martial arts. He'd demonstrated his skill on Tony the first time the three men met, bringing him to his knees though Tony had six inches and fifty per cent more body weight to throw around.

Dean approved of David's thoroughly rounded set of skills. 'If I'd had different chances in life, I would have ended up like you,' he said. 'I would have gone to university. Got myself a nice job.' He looked a little wistful. 'But I got lucky instead. How many of the guys you were at university with can say they drive a Bugatti Veyron?'

'Not many,' David admitted.

'Never mind. You'll be able to get a very nice car when all this is finished. What you going to do with your money, David? Buy yourself a place in Spain? Pick up a couple of birds?'

'Yeah, probably.' Though David already knew that he wouldn't see a penny for his part.

Dean relied on instinct to choose the people he worked with. But David knew for certain that instinct wasn't enough. Especially not now. It wouldn't have taken much for Dean to find out David's real story. Not if he'd wanted to. But he hadn't bothered. He was too focused on the big flashing pound signs. Whenever Dean thought about serious money, it was as though he was entranced, which made it very easy for he wrong kind of person to infiltrate his empire. And as far as James Dean was concerned, David Sullivan was the worst kind of wrong.

Chapter Fifty-Seven

𝄞

*H*AVING just discovered that the man who had turned her life upside down had been as faithless to her as he was to his wife, Juliet was all the more keen to have her revenge on him quickly. As soon as her shift was over and she could retrieve her mobile phone from her locker, she called David. If anyone could interpret the data she had found, it would be him. David took her call but told her he wouldn't be able to get to her until much later that evening. He had returned from New York the day before but had been working out of town. In fact, he was still trying to wrap up a meeting. As soon as he was able, he would be in his car and on his way to her.

'Thank you,' said Juliet. 'It's really important.'

'You bet,' said David, seeming to misunderstand the nature of Juliet's urgency. 'I have been longing to see you all week. I'll call you when I leave this place.'

* * *

While she had to wait for David, Juliet was not in the mood to be alone. She couldn't face going back to her empty flat, which seemed to her to be a constant reminder of what she had missed out on by setting her sights on Christopher Wilde. The bare walls. The lack of any family photographs. She had almost certainly thrown away her chance at ever having the family life she craved for five years with a married man. The thought of being in that flat right then filled her with something approaching depression.

So Juliet asked Mercy if she would like to have a drink after work.

'All right,' said Mercy. 'I'll have a quick one.'

Juliet didn't tell Mercy what she had discovered about her former lover. Instead, when she tried to explain why she didn't want to rush home she said, 'I just feel as though something has shifted. I need to get used to it.'

'You mean with regard to finding out about your dismissal?'

'Sort of,' said Juliet.

Mercy didn't push for more details. But Juliet and Mercy had developed something of a friendship over the brief time that they had been working together and now it was Mercy's turn to tell Juliet more about her life. Juliet asked about her passion for music. Mercy told Juliet how thrilled she had been to get Ed's invitation to the Anglo-Italian opera night.

'That's where I first saw you,' she said. 'You stood up for me that evening. You were talking to some other woman. Tall with blond hair and a sour-looking face. I think she was married to Ed's boss.'

Definitely Caroline, thought Juliet. Sour-looking was just about the perfect description.

'Anyway, we were standing quite close by and she was talking pretty loudly so I couldn't help overhearing when she told you and the rest of the women standing there that Ed had turned up with a cleaning lady. Not even a pretty one at that, which must mean that Ed's gay or likes a bit of rough. I don't know what made me feel worse.'

Strangely, Juliet felt embarrassed, though she knew that the shame shouldn't be hers. 'I didn't realise you heard that. I'm sorry.'

'You don't need to be sorry. When she said that she thought Ed was dating beneath him, you stood up for me. You said it didn't matter what I did. Ed had the sense to know that I was a decent person and who cared if I cleaned toilets for a living. At least I wasn't living off him. I wanted to say thank you for that. You could have laughed along with her.'

'I didn't think what she said was funny.'

'You're right. And you said that to her face. I thought that deserved some respect.'

'You deserved more respect. Sadly, people like Caroline Wilde like to think that anything outside their narrow little life is beneath them.'

'You were having an affair with her husband,' Mercy observed.

'Yeah,' Juliet smiled sadly. 'Made it even easier for me to hate her. How did you guess?'

'Well, if all this,' she indicated Juliet's City Clean Stars overall, which was half-hanging out of her bag. 'Was to do with your dismissal alone, wouldn't you have been better off letting a lawyer deal with it?'

'Good point,' Juliet admitted.

'Anyway, I wasn't so bothered by what that woman said,'

Mercy continued. 'What bothered me was that Ed didn't do anything about it. We were just a few feet away. I heard every word and I knew that he did too. And yet he didn't say anything on my behalf. He let me stand there and be humiliated and tried to pretend that it hadn't happened.'

'Is that why you told him you couldn't see him again?'

Mercy nodded. 'I told him I already had a boyfriend.'

'And do you?'

'Sadly not. But I couldn't go out with Ed again after that. Knowing that the kind of people he mixes with every day think I'm beneath him. And knowing that he must think it too on some level, if he didn't tell that woman where to shove her stupid opinions.'

'I think it's possible,' said Juliet carefully, 'that Ed thought he was sparing you further humiliation by not getting into a fight. You saw what happened when I called her on her gossip. She didn't care at all. Ed may have expected the same outcome. And he may have been worried that Christopher would take exception to Ed standing up to his pregnant wife. Everyone has been worried for their jobs these past few years.'

'But . . .'

'I know,' said Juliet. 'It doesn't excuse Ed's behaviour. I'm just trying to explain it. I know that he liked you very much.'

'Really?'

'Yes. I remember, before the opera night, how excited he was to have met someone he thought really shared his interests. He's not had a lot of girlfriends that I know of. There's always some pretty girl hanging around his desk but none of them hold his attention for very long. He was incredibly happy to have found you.'

Mercy sighed. 'And I was pretty pleased to have met

him too. But I can't help thinking it was all just a novelty for him. Look at us. We couldn't have come from more different backgrounds. He went to the same school as Prince William. I went to a school with a knife-detecting arch in the playground.'

'And why would that bother Ed? Sounds to me like maybe you're not so free from prejudice yourself.'

Mercy laughed. 'Yeah. Maybe you're right. But it doesn't matter now, does it? I'm sure he's moved on.'

'I don't think so. You should see if he wants to go for a drink or something.'

'Seriously?'

'I think he'd be delighted.'

'Yeah. Whatever. So, have you got everything you needed?'

'Almost,' said Juliet. 'I'm starting to build up a pretty clear picture of why I was stitched up. I just have to get the facts straight and then I'll be taking them to the police.'

'Good for you.' Mercy and Juliet chinked glasses.

Chapter Fifty-Eight

𝄞

*L*ATER that night, while Mercy sat in her bedroom, delightedly catching up with Ed's news over the phone, Francis was on the other side of the wall, taking a rather less amiable call. Of course he had failed to find the ten grand he owed James Dean. Not that he hadn't done his very best to come up with the cash. He'd tried everything. But three burglaries had netted him just five hundred quid. As the deadline drew nearer, he started getting truly desperate. He considered a Rolex robbery and headed up to Notting Hill for the purpose, but when it came down to it, he couldn't bring himself to tackle some innocent punter on his way home from the office, so instead he had hung around until the early hours and stolen a car: a vintage Bentley.

'What the fuck am I supposed to do with that?' asked Dean's sidekick Tony when Francis called him to say what he'd scored. 'A fucking baby blue Bentley. For God's sake, put it back before anyone notices it's missing. Then get your fucking arse over here. It's time we worked out a proper repayment plan.'

The next call Tony took was from his boss.

'That unfinished business from last weekend. I want it attended to now.'

Tony just shook his head when Francis arrived at their appointed meeting place.

'You're a muppet,' he said. 'What are you?'

'A muppet,' Francis answered dutifully.

'You lost the coke, you've made a lot of enemies,' he nodded at Francis's still-bandaged hand. 'And you still owe Mr Dean ten thousand pounds. You, my boy, are in big trouble.'

Here was the deal. Francis's debts would be written off and his problems with the local, lesser gangsters sorted out by Dean's foot-soldiers if, first of all, he carried out a small favour for the ultimate boss.

'A hit?'

Tony nodded.

'You want me to take someone out?'

Tony simply nodded again.

'You mean like kill someone?'

'That's what a hit usually means,' said Tony.

'I'll do it,' said Francis. 'Who do you want me to take out?'

Tony was surprised. He had expected the kid to bottle it. He had seen so many young lads like him before. All very hard until it came to the real dirty work. Tony was certain that when he described the situation, the kid would turn chicken. After all, Tony had put an end to plenty of lives in his time and he wouldn't want to take this job on. A public face in a public place. He had struggled not to laugh out loud when James Dean announced what he wanted.

'No one makes a monkey out of me,' Dean said. 'And no one disrespects my missus.'

Tony thought that was laughable too. As far as he was concerned, Tara Dean was a slapper. Always had been. Always would be. He had no doubt that in a couple of years, the boss would put her out to grass in any case. Trade her in for a younger model and start the process of making his perfect woman (boob job, hair extensions, nails like fucking talons) again.

The kid should have seen that it was a hopeless situation. He should have known that he could walk away. If he kept his head down, Dean would soon forget about the squirt, as would the local men he had offended. But the lad still wanted to prove he was a hard man. Humiliation and hormones were a dangerous combination. Francis said again, 'I'll do it.'

'All right,' said Tony.

'But I ain't doing it just to clear my debt to Dean. This is serious. You're going to have to tell the Big Guy I need something on top.'

Tony snorted.

'I know why you want me to do it. You're thinking I'm just a kid. They won't lock me up for long. But if I'm going to do any time at all, I want to be doing it for a hundred grand a year. Cause you and I both know that I ain't going to be getting on no management training scheme when I get out of this one.'

The kid was a psycho. Deano should be here to see this, Tony thought. He'd probably give the boy a proper job. Personally, Tony was starting to find the lad creepy.

From time to time, Tony wished for a quiet life. Sure, he enjoyed the big house he lived in and the great car he drove, but there were definitely moments when he thought wistfully of his former life as an employee of the Royal Mail. Set hours and no need to sleep with a baseball bat under his bed (he would have preferred sleeping with a gun under his pillow but his wife expressly forbade that in case he had a bad dream and accidentally blew her head off).

Life as James Dean's most valued sidekick was starting to take its toll. The trappings of a wealthy lifestyle were definitely tarnished when Tony remembered the faces of the people he had fucked over to get his six-bed detached house with indoor swimming pool. He told his wife that he would give it all up tomorrow and she agreed but they both knew that it was no simple matter of tendering his resignation. He had signed his contract with James Dean in blood. Francis Campbell was about to do the same.

Chapter Fifty-Nine

DAVID finally arrived at Juliet's flat at two in the morning.

'I drove as fast as I could,' he said. As he stepped over the threshold, he held out his arms to her. Juliet stepped into them and they started to kiss.

'What happened to your hair?' he asked.

'I thought I'd have a change.'

'Hmmm. A brunette. It's like having a new girlfriend.'

'Am I your girlfriend?' Juliet asked in surprise.

'I hope so,' said David. As he kissed her neck, his hands crept inside her dressing gown. He rubbed his thumbs over her nipples, encouraging them to harden into excited little points. Juliet felt her body respond to David's kiss eagerly. It had been well over a week since they were last together and there was so much to explore but Juliet was too preoccupied to make love right then.

'Not yet,' she said. 'I've got something to show you first.'

'OK,' said David. 'If you must.'

'I must,' said Juliet. She unravelled herself from his embrace and led him into the kitchen where her laptop was open on the table. She had loaded the files she had copied from Christopher's computer onto her machine and put in the password. She'd cracked it sooner than she thought. It was Trinity. A reference to her bracelet and the ring he'd bought his wife. Thank goodness Christopher had a limited imagination.

'I found this on Christopher Wilde's PC.'

'What is it? Pictures of him wearing ladies' clothing?'

'No. It's much more incriminating than that, if I'm right.'

'How did you get it?'

'Since you've been in the States, I got back into the Anglo-Italian building by taking a job as a cleaner. That's why I had my hair dyed brown,' Juliet added.

'You're kidding.' David looked suitably amused. 'Very clever.'

'So, I easily got access to his machine, because the stupid man hasn't changed any of his passwords, and while I was going through his hard drive, I found file called "Juliet" that I couldn't get into at first. Of course I downloaded it because I thought it might pertain to me. But I don't think it does. I think it's something much more interesting. David, look at this. This is a key-logging programme, isn't it? For capturing people's passwords.'

David looked at the garble of code on the screen. If anyone should recognise this programme, he should.

'I think you're right,' he said.

'Then why has Christopher got it?'

'Maybe someone planted it on his machine.'

'Or maybe he was going to plant it on someone else's machine. Like mine. There's all this other stuff too. Look.'

She had David examine the other files hidden within 'Juliet.'

'Do you know what I think this looks like? I think that Christopher is trying to plant some kind of account sweeping programme. Like that one they were planning to use at that Japanese bank. Do you remember that?'

Of course David did. He worked in IT security.

'It all makes sense. He's running a key-logging programme to get the passwords he needs to set it up. How far do you think he's got?' Juliet asked.

'I can't tell,' said David quietly.

'This must have been what he was talking about when he said he'd found a way to get enough money to fund his divorce. No wonder he wanted me out of the way. It all makes sense now.'

'I don't see the connection,' said David. 'Why would he want to get rid of you? From what you've told me you've worked really well together for the past five years.'

Juliet knew she couldn't keep her secret any longer. The story wouldn't make sense to anyone else without this crucial detail.

'We were having an affair.' The words came out like a sigh. 'We've been having an affair almost since I started at Anglo-Italian. I know it was wrong but I honestly believed for all that time that he would eventually leave his wife, until a few weeks ago, when she announced that she's pregnant again. Of course I broke up with Christopher and now he wants me out of the way in case I rumble him. And he's done it in such a way that will distract attention from what he's up to. Everyone will be busy investigating my pathetic bit of alleged insider dealing while he's busy planting key-logging software on the bank's entire system. First thing tomorrow, I'm going to the police.'

'I wouldn't do that if I were you,' said David.

'Why not?'

'For one thing, I just don't think it sounds that plausible. I mean, what does Christopher know about IT systems? I can't help thinking that you'll be making life difficult for yourself if you go to the police with nothing but these files to go on, not to mention that you've obtained them in an incredibly dodgy way. You could be getting yourself involved in all sorts of agony. Endless investigations. And your relationship with Christopher would certainly mean that if anything really were awry, you would be under some serious scrutiny too. Trust me, the police will make any FSA investigation into those emails sent from your account seem like a quick dental check-up compared to an anal probe. I can't help thinking that your best bet is to tell the arsehole Wilde that you know he's had you edged out and then lean on him for some serious references when you're cleared. You're brilliant at what you do. There will be another job out there for you. You should just concentrate on moving your career someplace else and leaving Christopher Wilde behind you. It's always worked for me. If someone breaks my heart, they don't get a second chance.'

'I'm not going to give him a second chance to break my heart.'

'But you're proposing going down a road that could keep him at the forefront of your life for a very long time. Isn't it better to cut your losses? Negotiate a fuck off settlement, and then look for a job that will really fulfil you. The best revenge is living well,' he added.

'David,' said Juliet. 'Do you really think this is just about getting revenge? That the only reason I want to bring Christopher Wilde to some sort of justice is because he wouldn't leave his wife for me? This isn't just about being a woman scorned, for fuck's sake.'

David held his hands up.

'I can't believe you would think that of me. This could be about a major fraud. I'm under investigation, for God's sake, and I don't really know what for. It's about me getting the high jump to make sure it stayed covered up. And it's about the possibility of a great many people that I have a lot of respect for finding themselves in the same position if I don't take the initiative.'

'I think you should stay out of it, Juliet,' David insisted. 'If it is such a big fraud, then the chances are we're not just talking about a couple of geeks with a computer. Who knows who Christopher is involved with? Losing your job could be the least of your worries.'

'What? Are you telling me that I'm about to uncover some huge mafia plot and wake up to find a horse's head on the pillow beside me?'

'I know a bit more about this sort of thing than you do,' said David. 'IT is my area, remember? It's not just teenage hackers who try to get into your bank account these days. For every legitimate banking operation there is a shadow operation employing people with the same, if not higher, levels of skills to infiltrate that operation and siphon off the money.' David took Juliet's hand across the table. 'And I don't want to see you fall foul of those people. They're the kind of people who would not think anything of ending your life if you started to pose any kind of threat to their livelihood. They terminate people like you every day.'

'"Terminate!" Oh, for God's sake, David. You've been reading too many conspiracy theories.'

'If you insist on getting involved, then I can't support you.'

'I'm not asking for your support.'

'But I want to support you,' said David. 'You do understand that, don't you? I want to be the person you turn to and I want to be the person who takes care of you.'

Juliet shook her head. 'You just want me to let this go?'

'I do. Because I don't want you to get in over your head. Especially not when in all likelihood, you'll come out looking like a fool. I think you've already acted like a fool. You've effectively broken into Anglo-Italian. You've committed theft in taking copies of those files. Why? Because you're obsessed with a man who treated you like a whore.'

'That's what this is really about, isn't it? The David I remember cared about this kind of thing. You would have been just as concerned about the possibility of fraud as I am. You're angry because I told you about Christopher.'

'You're right I'm angry,' said David. 'I just don't understand what you were doing with that man. Of all the men out there you could have been involved with, you set your sights on somebody else's husband. I didn't have you down as the kind of woman who would do that. I thought you had higher standards.'

'Do you think I wanted my life to work out like that? I fell in love.'

'You wouldn't know what love was if it bit you on the face,' said David.

'What's that supposed to mean? You don't know what you're talking about. Christopher and I were in love.'

'And you're obviously still not over him. In which case, I don't know what I'm doing here. I love you, Juliet, but I'm not going to be made to look a fool. Don't mess with this stuff,' he said, waving his hand over the laptop. 'You'd be far better off spending your time asking yourself what makes you value yourself so little that you'd throw yourself away on a married man who has been as dishonest to you as he has to his wife.'

'Fine,' Juliet didn't try to stop David leaving. 'And don't come back. Like I need someone as judgemental as you in my life. Fuck off.' She slammed the door after him.

After David had gone, Juliet went back to the files she had lifted from Christopher. She was frustrated by the way things had gone with David. She had been relying on him to tell her exactly what she had found, but the way he had reacted told her that she had uncovered something interesting. The police would have people with David's skills, she was sure. All she had to do was present them with her hunch.

It was only much later, waking at 5 a.m., that Juliet really thought about what David had said again. His reaction made much more sense when she thought about some of the conversations she and David had shared as students. She knew that his parents had divorced as a result of his father's infidelity but it was his mother's subsequent remarriage that had really screwed his life up. David had had a terrible relationship with his stepfather. But did he really think that the blame could be laid at the foot of the woman who had enticed his real father out of an unhappy marriage? Juliet felt that he was casting her in the same role. Or perhaps it was straightforward jealousy, now that he and Juliet had taken their friendship a step further? Had he really just said that he loved her?

Juliet decided that she would give David some space. He would come round, she was sure. It had been a mistake to tell him about Christopher so suddenly and so late at night when he was tired and almost certainly reacted more dramatically than usual as a result. That was it. But regardless of what David thought of her motives, Juliet was not going to let Christopher get away with it.

Chapter Sixty

THE final week of the opera tour was awkward to say the least. After St Petersburg, the company played a penultimate date in Helsinki. Cosima and Nolan did not exchange a word except onstage. The strained atmosphere between them seemed to poison the atmosphere surrounding the entire company. Fights broke out over such petty things as who had used the last Earl Grey teabag in the kitchenette at the back of a tour bus. One of the cellists quit and flew back to London early, vowing to retrain as an accountant.

Florence kept up with the company every step of the way, though her trip of a lifetime had become more of an endurance test. She was tired and bedraggled, getting hardly any sleep as she waited up night after night, checking her email and her phone for any news from Nolan.

Luckily Nolan was only aware of one of the women who were after his guts.

* * *

Nolan's manager, Karen, had sent Florence what she hoped would be a final email. After hearing through Nolan, Antony and Donald's account of the woman who had accosted them in St Petersburg, Karen did not want to take any chances. She passed the information on Florence's whereabouts to the police. Unfortunately, they said there was little they could do given that Florence had not actually committed a crime under their jurisdiction. Karen felt better for having handed the information over, however, and though her lawyer told her that he didn't think Florence's correspondence had reached a level of harassment that would make a restraining order easy to obtain, Karen wrote to tell her that measures to put such an order in place were underway. Furthermore, she added, such measures were being taken at Mr O'Connor's personal request.

> He no longer wishes you to contact him. He has found your persistence to be creepy and annoying.

Karen pressed 'send' and hoped that would be the end of it.

Picking up that email in an Internet café at the airport, Florence could not help but wail out loud. Her fellow customers in the café were momentarily distracted from their own online endeavours to see what was going on. Florence's cry was so anguished that, like the hotel manager in Rome a couple of weeks before, they would have been forgiven for thinking she'd just had news of a death.

Florence reread the email in the hope that the joke would become obvious. But this was no joke. Nolan found her persistence 'to be creepy and annoying'. How could he say that, after all the loyalty she had given him over the years? She had supported him with her encouraging letters and thoughtful gifts from the very beginning. She had been an ardent admirer of Nolan's talent at a time when many of the critics doubted his ability to move into the top league of performers in which he found himself now. She had offered him a shoulder to cry on during his divorce from Cosima. And lately, she had offered her love and companionship again, while he endured a six-week long tour in his ex-wife's company.

Florence would have given anything for Nolan. She had given up her car and her house and her friends in order to follow him around the world. That wasn't creepy and annoying persistence. That was devotion.

Florence drafted a response to Karen, full of invective and hate. What did Karen know about Nolan's feelings? Had she not read that last email, the one that Nolan sent Florence when the tour was in rehearsal in London? Nolan had been grateful for Florence's encouragement then. He had written to her personally. And didn't Karen know that Nolan had turned up at Florence's hotel in Vienna? Karen was obviously poisoning Nolan against her because she was in love with him too. The stupid old bag.

Florence managed to send her email just as her flight was called. The flight back to the United Kingdom would give her plenty to time to get her thoughts straight. Or brood on the matter to a dangerous degree, depending on your perspective. It also gave Karen time to write one more dangerously mendacious email reply.

You are deluded. Mr O'Connor most certainly did not seek you out in Vienna and upon hearing such nonsense, he has asked me to pass on your correspondence to the police at once.

Chapter Sixty-One

THE tour was set to end as it had begun, back at the Royal Opera House in London. The company were very glad to get back to Heathrow. For most of them, London was home and as soon as they got to the airport, they skittered off back to their flats and terraced houses to check mail and veg out in front of the television for a while. To most people, the thought of a European tour with an opera company sounded incredibly glamorous. Everyone who had taken part in such a tour knew otherwise.

'I feel like I've been on one of those OAPs' bus tours,' said Donald Law. 'And I have no desire to go on one again.'

In London, Cosima checked in to Claridge's. She had insisted upon Claridge's for the last two nights of the tour. She wanted to be pampered and could rely upon the staff at her favourite hotel for that. A reservation at Gordon Ramsay's in-house restaurant for Cosima and her manager Duncan who had flown in specially was swiftly organised.

Cosima poured her heart out to Duncan. She felt she could rely on him for a valuable insight into the mind of a man.

'I can't identify with Nolan,' said Duncan. 'I've never met anyone so frightening heterosexual in my life. But, if I were a straight man, I can tell you that I would be thrilled to have you on my arm. There isn't another woman in the world I would rather spend time with.'

'He said it was too much like hard work,' said Cosima. 'Being with me. Do you think I'm too much like hard work?' she asked her manager.

'Of course not,' said Duncan, all tact. Though in truth, Cosima was one of his most demanding clients. There were few other singers for whom he would miss a weekend on Fire Island with an officer from the NYPD. But he knew that if he didn't show up for at least two nights of the tour, Cosima would threaten to move agencies again. She needed so much reassurance. Perhaps it was because she had lost her father at such an early age. Sometimes she reminded Duncan of the rescue cats he had adopted from the cats' home. Their early experiences of abuse made it impossible for them to believe than anyone might really simply want to care for them now. They cowered from every caress, or far worse, came out scratching.

Oh Cosima, thought Duncan, as they parted in the lobby (Duncan was staying at the Metropolitan. If he brought someone back to his room that night, he did not want the entire opera world to know). Cosima, Cosima. Always standing in the way of her own happiness. When Duncan heard that Cosima and Nolan had got back together, he had been pleased for them both. To break up with him over something he had done while they were apart was insane. If only she could see how much Nolan had to put up with. And how much he would have put up with, just to be with her. Still, Duncan couldn't blame him for having given up at last.

With Duncan out on the pull, Cosima settled into the ocean-wide bed in her Claridge's suite. Who could fail to have a restful night in such a beautiful hotel? Cosima, that's who. She picked up the ridiculous 'pillow menu' and ordered a whole bunch of different types in the hope that one of them might hold the key to a good night's sleep. Still no luck. Even with her bed piled high with cushions, Cosima was no nearer to nodding off.

Two nights from now she and Nolan would sing together for the last time on this tour. Possibly for the last time ever. Though she had been counting the days since the disaster that was St Petersburg, subconsciously, she had been dreading the passing of each day like a child who knows that at the end of the summer holiday is another term of double maths.

If Cosima and Nolan parted company at the end of this tour without resolving this latest set of issues between them, there was a possibility that they would never be resolved. They might never see each other again. It wasn't as though they had friends in common. Their friends and acquaintances had split into definite factions after the divorce. Cosima was on the point of losing him forever.

A very long way from Claridge's, Florence's heart sank as she realised that her London accommodation was the same hotel where she had started out. The Far From Majestic on the Caledonian Road.

'You're back,' said Kasia in astonishment. 'You said we'd never see you again.'

'I ran out of money,' said Florence.

'What a stroke of good fortune for me,' said Emmanuel, who was still lurking in the lobby.

Kasia shot him a look that said 'leave the girl alone'. Emmanuel went back to picking at his nails with a penknife.

'I'm afraid the deal is the same,' said Kasia. 'No bathroom. Single bed.'

'It doesn't matter. I just want to lie down,' said Florence. 'I'm going back to the States tomorrow and I don't care if I never see London again.'

'Haven't you enjoyed your trip?' Kasia asked her.

'It's been terrible,' said Florence.

'Oh?' Kasia leaned forward on her desk. 'Want to talk about it?'

Florence shook her head. How could anyone understand?

'Suit yourself,' said Kasia handing over a room key and a brown towel that had seen better days. Much better days.

Florence unpacked her suitcase and sat down on the bed. A great deal had changed since she was last in that room. She had sunk so low that she didn't even spread her own towel on the bed before she sat down on it. And eventually she laid her head on the pillow without bothering to freak out about bed bugs and other cooties.

Six weeks earlier, she had been full of excitement. The tour of Europe had held so much promise. Nolan had said that he would look out for her at every show and she felt sure that seeing so much devotion on her part, he would soon come to invite her to step over the line from fan to friend, which would inevitably lead towards her becoming his lover and muse. But that didn't happen. Now she could no longer pretend that Nolan O'Connor cared about her at all. Perhaps he had started to, but then Cosima Esposito got in the way. And then his manager had poisoned him against her to the extent where he was threatening to call the police. Now Florence was left with nothing. She had spent everything she had to take this trip. She was going back to New Jersey to live with her parents, sleeping in the single bed she had used as a child. She had no car. She had no job. She had no friends. And now she had no hope.

What was the point of carrying on? Florence could not live with this feeling of emptiness. Most of the time she felt so awful she couldn't even cry. She needed something to take her mind off it. But what? She didn't drink. She had been raised in a dry household and saw no need to change that when she grew up and left home. Right then, however, she decided she needed vodka. Kasia would know where to find it. Perhaps she would even share a drink with her. Perhaps she really would be willing to listen to Florence's tale.

The thought of talking to Kasia gave Florence a little lift but by the time she got downstairs, Kasia had already clocked off and been replaced by the big guy with no hair. Florence didn't want to share a drink with him. But Emmanuel was more than happy to escort Florence to the nearest pub and help her spend the last of her sterling.

'I've got a problem,' Florence told him over her third vodka tonic. Three more than she'd had in half a decade.

'Ain't nothing I can't fix for you,' said Emmanuel.

Chapter Sixty-Two

𝄞

CHRISTOPHER had not been having a great day. Dean was getting impatient about the implementation of David Sullivan's scheme. Sure, Sullivan shared the brunt of Dean's anger too but that wasn't much comfort to Christopher. All he wanted was a quiet life. How had it become so ridiculously complicated?

As he drove back from Dean's house in Kent – slowly as he could, he was in no hurry to see Caroline – Christopher battled with the urge to call Juliet. If only he could take the junction of the M25 that would lead him to her home. If only she would be there with open arms and a welcoming smile. But she wouldn't. He had let her down so badly.

Lucy was the other option. Christopher knew that if he called her she would drop what she was doing right away, even though it was already past ten o'clock. But Christopher didn't like going to her shared flat in Clapham with its depressing seventies kitchen that seemed to be a gathering place for every spotty youth in the area. He didn't know what he had been thinking, taking Lucy to bed that night at the conference. And it was sheer madness to have let things continue since. He would have to let her know that it was over as soon as he could.

In fact, he decided, there was no time like the present. He pulled off the motorway and into a service station. He grabbed himself a cup of coffee and called Lucy's landline from a quiet corner of the depressingly filthy canteen.

'Oh, hiya!' she sounded pleased to hear from him. 'What are you up to? Do you want to come over?'

To the hovel she shared with three antipodeans, thought Christopher. No thanks.

'I'm not calling to ask if I can see you,' he said.

'Oh.' Even that one syllable seemed to betray Lucy's disappointment and anxiety over what might come next.

'Look,' said Christopher. 'What happened at the conference. And since then. We both know that it shouldn't have happened at all. I should have had more self-restraint. And more respect. For you.'

'What are you saying?' Lucy cut to the chase.

'I'm saying that we can't continue to have a romantic relationship. You know that I'm a married man with a third child on the way. You deserve someone better than me. And it's important to me to end this right now so that we can salvage our working relationship. I don't want to jeopardise that.'

'And have to get rid of me. Like you did Juliet.'

'I don't know what you're talking about,' said Christopher.

'Sure you don't. Look,' she said. 'It doesn't matter to me. You're right. I do deserve someone better. You're too old for me for a start. And I don't want to lose my job.'

'Your job was never in danger,' said Christopher, horri-fied that she thought he might have something to do with the current investigation into Juliet, though of course he did. It was David Sullivan who had suggested the means for making sure Juliet was out of the way with the fake emails that pointed to insider dealing. It had seemed like a good thing at the time. 'The last thing you want at this stage of our project is for a spurned woman to be logging your every movement,' David had explained.

'Like I said,' Lucy continued. 'It doesn't matter. I'm not going to say anything so we can carry on just like before, right?'

'Right,' said Christopher.

He ended the call. He was relieved that he'd at least got rid of one complication but Lucy's tone had been profoundly depressing. He was too old for her. He was just forty-five. Was that what she considered old?

He certainly felt old as he continued his drive home.

It was half eleven before he turned his Aston Martin into the street where he lived. He had hoped that Caroline would already have gone to bed by the time he got there. No such luck. As usual every light in the house was on. The boys were almost certainly on their computers, playing violent games with their friends online. Christopher knew of one kid who had been taken to California on holiday that summer but seemed to be spending the entire time indoors, playing war games with Christopher's youngest via the Net.

Anyway, Caroline was still up but she was not in the mood for games, though her laptop was on the coffee table and open to her emails. Christopher could tell the moment he entered the room that he was for it in some shape or form. What could have happened today, in his absence, that caused her to greet him with a face like thunder and the words, 'You utter, utter bastard.'

Lucy must have sent the emails. So much for her 'so what' attitude on the phone. She had clearly not been so cool about the break-up of her fledging romance as she pretended. Christopher could only shake his head in despair as Caroline showed him the emails that had been forwarded to her address. There weren't many, but they were all incriminating.

'You went to bed with her the night I had those contractions!' Caroline spat at him. 'You bastard. I might have lost our baby and you were screwing your bloody PA.'

'She's a fantasist,' Christopher tried. 'I've never seen these emails before. She must have made them up for one reason or other.'

'They're sent from your email address.'

'She has access to my emails,' said Christopher. 'Of course she does. She's my PA.'

But Caroline wasn't buying the story that Lucy had an enormous, unrequited crush on her husband and had crafted the emails herself as some kind of twisted prank.

'You must think I'm some kind of idiot. If anyone had the unrequited crush, it was you. I remember the way you looked at her on the night of the opera benefit. Your tongue was practically rolling on the floor. You couldn't resist it, could you? I dare say she only got her tits out for a dirty old man like you because she was hoping for a promotion. You're an utter shit and I can't believe I didn't divorce you years ago!'

*   *   *

Christopher spent the night in the guest bedroom. Through the thin wall, he could hear Caroline on the phone until the early hours, ranting and raving with the odd waver towards a tone that sounded suspiciously like glee to her sister Jane, who was holidaying in the Hamptons with her far more successful husband. Christopher knew that Jane's husband was an absolute dog, but he had a private jet and that seemed to go some way to making up for it. Jane knew which side of her bread was buttered. At breakfast, Caroline was talking divorce lawyers. Christopher had given up protesting his innocence.

'For god's sake,' he said instead. 'It was a one-off. You won't let me anywhere near you because of the baby and . . .'

'What? So you're saying it's my fault now? Because I'm pregnant with your child?'

Is it my child? Christopher wanted to ask. Is it really?

Christopher took his black mood to work. He couldn't believe Lucy's front. She was already in the office and sitting at her desk as though butter wouldn't melt in her mouth.

'What the fuck do you think you were doing?' Christopher stormed at her. 'You nasty little bitch. I told you I was sorry that anything happened between us and I was ready to make up for it, but you had to go and send those emails. My wife is pregnant. Do you have any idea what your selfish little move has done to her?'

'What are you talking about?' Lucy leaned away from him.

'Don't come the innocent with me. Emails from my email address. Emails you had sent to me. Forwarded to my wife.'

Lucy was horrified. 'I really don't know what you're

talking about. I haven't sent any emails to anyone. Why would I do that?'

'Because you're an immature little cow.'

'Now hang on.'

'You were worried about losing your job before, you better be bloody worried now.'

Christopher's shouting had brought the other secretaries to see what was going on. Anneli decided to take a stand and marched straight into Christopher's office, placing herself bodily between him and Lucy.

'Just back off,' she shouted at Christopher.

'This is none of your bloody business,' Christopher replied.

'It bloody well is,' said Anneli. 'You're abusing one of my staff. What the hell is going on?' She looked at Lucy.

'He's gone mad,' she said. 'He just came in and started shouting at me.'

Christopher knew that there was no way he could clear his name without revealing their brief affair.

'She,' he pointed a shaking hand at her. 'Forwarded some private emails to my wife. Emails which implied that I had an extra-marital affair.'

Anneli's mouth twitched. Christopher understood then that she wasn't surprised by the revelation.

'I didn't send the emails,' said Lucy. 'I swear. Why would I do that?'

'This is a serious matter,' said Anneli. 'And it will have to be investigated.'

'Oh Christ,' said Christopher under his breath.

'We can get IT to find out exactly when and where those emails were sent from,' said Anneli. 'That seems to me to be the best way to start getting to the bottom of it.'

'For God's sake,' said Christopher. 'There's no need. I know where they came from.'

'I didn't send them!' Lucy insisted again. She turned on the waterworks now. And Christopher was doomed.

'I can't have you abusing my staff,' Anneli told him. Christopher could tell that she was enjoying this. She had been waiting for her chance to square up to him, ever since he had given her a lukewarm appraisal that she believed had halved her bonus in one of the bank's best years.

'Fine,' said Christopher. His reputation in the office was already shot to pieces. If he was going down, then he was going to take that little bitch Lucy with him. 'Find out where the emails were sent from. I'm pretty sure you'll find they were sent from this stupid girl's own machine.'

Anneli wrapped her arm around Lucy's shoulders. Tears were pouring down Lucy's face now. Her nose was running. She looked a complete state and so very young, Christopher could hardly believe he had found her attractive. He should have known she was too immature for infidelity.

'I didn't do it,' she said one more time.

'There, there,' said Anneli. 'Don't you worry. We're going to prove that for you. In the meantime, certain other people would be well-advised to try to cool off.'

Chapter Sixty-Three

𝄞

$\mathcal{M}$ERCY had given up on her brother. She had resigned herself to the fact that nothing she could say was going to make him reconsider the life he seemed to be drifting into. He had no respect for her anymore.

But when she discovered that her prized recording of Cosima Esposito singing Tosca was no longer on her bookshelf, she was ready to tackle him all over again. Forget jewellery or money. That CD was her most valuable possession. She loved the opera. She loved the singer. She could have replaced the CD. But the one that Francis had obviously taken was the one that she had been given at school, when she won the school music prize. The only prize she had ever won, her only real achievement in life so far.

'How much did you get for it?' she barged into Francis's room. He was lying on his bed, smoking a joint, and holding it out of the window between puffs. He was a hard man now. But not so hard that he would flout his mother's no smoking rule. Mercy was faintly amused to see him sit up so abruptly, as though in fear of being caught by their mum.

'What you talking about?' he snapped back when he recovered his composure.

'You know,' said Mercy. 'What kind of man are you? First you steal from your mother's purse. And now you steal from your sister. And you steal the one thing that meant anything to me at all. How much did you get for it, Francis? How much did you really think you could get for an opera CD? Were you that desperate? Two pounds? Three pounds? For something that was *priceless* to me.'

A slow smile spread across Francis's face. Mercy was enraged at the sight of it. But before she could hit him, her little brother reached for the remote control on his beside table and hit 'play'.

'You mean this CD?' he said, as the strains of Nolan O'Connor singing 'E Lucevan le Stelle' filled the air.

'You've been listening to it?' Mercy could not have been more surprised if she had discovered that her brother was considering the priesthood.

'What's so funny about that?'

'But . . . you're always telling me you hate it.'

'That was when I was a kid,' he said. As though he wasn't still nine months off turning sixteen. 'I decided it was time for me to get some culture.'

Mercy sat down on the end of her little brother's bed and stared at him in wonder. 'Are you serious?'

'I am,' he said, taking another big drag on his spliff. He offered the soggy roll-up to Mercy, who shook her head.

'Bad for my voice,' she pointed out.

'This is the one you've always wanted to sing, yes? The one where the guy gets shot in the end.'

'Yes,' Mercy nodded. '*Tosca*.'

'Why does he get shot?' Francis asked. 'When does it happen? Tell me the story.'

Mercy pulled a face that asked, 'Are you for real?'

'I want to know everything about it.'

So Mercy told him everything about it. And they listened to the opera all the way through.

'Mario Cavaradossi is painting a fresco in a church when he discovers that a political prisoner is hiding in the crypt. He helps the prisoner to escape, but in doing so, arouses the suspicions of his jealous lover Floria Tosca who thinks he is hiding another woman. Scarpia, who is searching for the fugitive, uses Tosca's jealousy to find Cavaradossi's secret out ...'

Mercy wasn't sure how much of the story went in. At times, Francis seemed to be drifting into a drug-induced doze. But he perked up towards the end, when she told him how Cavaradossi faces the firing squad, for what Tosca naively believes will be a mock execution ahead of their escape by sea, as promised by Scarpia in return for her submission to his desire.

'She tells him to fall down as soon as the soldiers fire. And stay down until they have gone. But Scarpia has double-crossed her, of course, and the soldiers never had instructions to spare the painter. They shoot for real and he falls down dead, with Tosca thinking that he must be a brilliant actor because his fall was so realistic.'

'And he stays down until the curtain comes down?' asked Francis.

'Well, yes,' said Mercy. 'Because he's really dead. And when Tosca realises what has happened, and hears Scarpia's guards closing in on her, she decides there's no point living any longer. She runs to the top of the castle walls and throws herself to her own death.'

'That's sad,' said Francis.

'Yes. It's pretty tragic.'

'Yeah,' said Francis.

'But I could listen to Cosima Esposito and Nolan O'Connor sing about anything. They could sing a shopping list and I would want to hear it.'

Francis nodded vaguely.

'You know they're going to be doing *Tosca* here in London this week. As part of a European tour.'

'I heard that,' said Francis.

'You did?'

Mercy's little brother was full of surprises tonight.

'I would give my right arm to see it,' she said.

'I'll see what I can do,' said Francis.

Mercy gave her brother a playful punch in the arm.

'Yeah, right. I really enjoyed sitting here with you,' she said. 'Listening to my favourite opera. It meant a lot to me.' Mercy reached out and stroked his cheek. 'You're a good guy, Francis. You should start playing the piano again. If you put your mind to it, you could achieve so much more than I ever could. You could get your GCSE and stay on at school and do your A-levels and go to music college.'

'Don't get carried away,' said Francis. 'I only said I liked a couple of CDs. You got your own dreams, sister. You got to pursue them for yourself. I can't be living my life for you.'

'You're right,' Mercy nodded. 'What was it you wanted to be again? Ah yes,' she reminded him of his own dreams as a five-year-old. 'You wanted to be a dustman.'

'Out in the sunshine all day,' Francis mused.

'In England?'

'I'll be a dustman in Jamaica,' he replied.

Francis stood up and kissed her little brother on the fore-head. She felt so full of love for him again. And so relieved that the kind, funny young man she once knew had not really disappeared. Sure, he was obviously mixed up in some heavy and dangerous business, but Mercy was reassured by this glimpse at the old Francis. He would get bored of his unsavoury friends soon enough. Or they would get bored of him. And then she would have her brother back. And Melody would have her beloved son. There was still time to steer Francis back to the good life.

Back in her bedroom, Mercy ruminated on the one very true thing her brother had said to her that evening. She had her dreams and she had to pursue them for herself.

Having reconnected with Ed had infused her life with a sense of optimism that had been missing for quite some time. Following that first conversation when she called up to explain that there was no boyfriend, they had met for coffee as soon as they could. The subject of Mercy's singing had come up again, of course. Ed suggested to her that he ask his aunt whether she might take Mercy on as a pupil.

'I'll take you to meet her at my parents' house,' he suggested.

An invitation to meet the parents. They had only just started talking again. Of course, it didn't necessarily mean anything. Perhaps Ed was the kind of guy who took girls home all the time. Friends. They hadn't even kissed. Not at that point, anyway. But when they had finished their coffee, Ed had walked her to the tube station and before they headed off in their separate directions – her to south London and him to his fabulous executive flat in the Wharf

– he had kissed her. Perhaps his intention was merely to kiss her on the cheek, but if that was the case, he missed, and caught her instead on the side of the mouth. Mercy instinctively turned into the kiss, and without saying anything, she and Ed were soon engaged in a full-on snog, of the kind Mercy had been hoping for since the first day she met him.

Fifteen minutes later, they were still in each other's arms at the top of the escalator. It was Mercy who broke away, embarrassed by the jeers of a group of lads passing on their way to the pub. Ed was red-faced too and he stammered as he asked Mercy, 'Will you go out with me?'

Mercy laughed. She hadn't been asked that question since primary school, but she could see that Ed was serious. Perhaps he wasn't as sophisticated as she thought.

'I would love to,' she said.

Chapter Sixty-Four

$\mathscr{B}$ACK inside the Anglo-Italian building, the IT department were delighted to be involved in a scandal. By the following day, they had discovered, to everyone's surprise, that the emails had been sent from Christopher's own PC.

'Why would I send them myself?' Christopher sighed. 'Lucy can access my email from her computer.'

But the emails had been sent at ten, moments before Christopher had called her and found her at home. Indeed, Lucy had left the building four hours earlier. Anneli remembered seeing her leave.

'You can check the CCTV cameras if you want,' said Lucy. 'I didn't come back in until this morning.'

Christopher didn't need to check the CCTV cameras. He knew that he hadn't called Lucy to break off their tryst until after ten o'clock, which meant she had no motive when emails began their journey to Caroline's laptop.

It was a mystery but one that he was determined he would solve.

Who else had access to Christopher's emails? Plenty of people could have got to his PC, but, as the girl swore on her mother's life, no one but Lucy knew Christopher's password.

There were some very clever people in the IT department, but did any of them really hate Christopher so much that they would try to jeopardise his marriage? Did any of them even know about his personal life?

It struck Christopher that perhaps this was something to do with James Dean. Had the sicko got David Sullivan to hack into Christopher's account? Christopher could see why Dean would want to be able to monitor his correspondence, but this was an act of such petty malice. And as far as Christopher knew, he had been doing everything Dean required of him to the letter. A stunt like this was more likely to make Christopher mutinous than malleable.

Christopher decided it wasn't Dean. Had Dean wanted Caroline to know about his infidelities, he had the photographic evidence, after all. 'And a picture paints a thousand words,' was one of Dean's favourite sayings whenever he was dangling Christopher over the proverbial barrel.

Christopher spent the day studying the faces of his colleagues. Maybe one of them had been leaning over Lucy's shoulder when she typed his password in one day. He made a mental list of the people who might hold a grudge. It quickly reached double figures. A badly handled round of redundancies had left those who kept their jobs anxious and disgruntled. None of the staff had been especially pleased with their bonuses that year and no amount of assurance that it was merely a reflection of the market conditions would convince some of them that they hadn't been personally slighted by the disappointment of their unmet expectations. Christopher knew that his trips to head office in Milan were seen by others to be a jolly he didn't deserve.

'Jesus,' Christopher hissed under his breath as he realised the true extent of hatred for him within his own department. Sometimes he wondered whether he had any friends at all. His brother had got him into a god-awful mess. His wife and children hated him. Even the family dog bared its teeth at him on occasion.

Christopher had not stayed late in the office for a long while. He had junior staff to do the grunt work. As he explained to them, the best contribution he could make to the success of the bank was in the schmoozing of old and new clients. He had occasionally used the analogy of himself as the great hunter, dragging home the woolly mammoth so that the rest of the tribe could eat and make themselves some shoes. Just because he was absent from the office for long periods of time, did not mean he wasn't doing anything.

But that night, for the first time in a couple of months, Christopher was in the office when the cleaning team arrived. He looked up for just a second when one of the women started up a vacuum cleaner in the corridor. Just a second. But it was long enough.

'Shit.' Juliet hadn't counted on this. She had been working as a cleaner for almost two weeks and not once had she encountered her ex-boss and lover. She had counted on him sticking to his usual habits, which included leaving the office by six o'clock come hell or high water or global financial meltdown. She'd taken it for granted that she could get access to his PC unhindered.

And then he looked at her.

He won't recognise me, Juliet told herself. Her hair was still brown. She was wearing the thick-rimmed glasses. The unflattering overalls added at least ten pounds to her carefully honed figure. Surely, he wouldn't guess that this nondescript cleaner was Juliet.

All the same, she couldn't take a chance. In her pocket was the memory stick she had been using to download all the information she needed. Just that evening, she had been planning to download just a couple more files from Christopher's PC. Now she had a better understanding of what she was looking for, she wanted to be sure she had every scrap of evidence she could find. If she was caught, then she could say that desperation had driven her to take a cleaning job. But if she were caught with the memory stick in her pocket, then it would be obvious that she wasn't only interested in getting minimum wage.

The memory stick had to go. Abandoning her vacuum cleaner and her trolley, Juliet made a beeline for the men's room. There was a large sign outside the door, warning anyone who cared to use it that a woman was working inside. Mercy. Juliet rushed in.

'Is anyone in here?' she asked her colleague.

'No. I put the notice up before I—'

'Good.' Juliet raced straight by Mercy and into one of the cubicles. Quick as she could, she climbed onto the loo seat and popped the memory stick on top of the cistern, which was placed high on the wall in faux Victorian style. It only occurred to her afterwards that she should have checked that the cistern did not have an open top first. Thankfully, she was lucky. The cistern had a lid to it and her hard work did not end up in danger of being flushed away.

'What are you doing?' Mercy called through the door.

'I was caught short,' Juliet lied. She couldn't tell Mercy what she had really done. The fewer people who knew where the memory stick was hidden, the better. The last thing she wanted was for Mercy to glance in the direction of its hiding place if she were questioned in this very room. And there was a distinct chance of that. Juliet had a feeling that the net was closing in with great rapidity.

And she was right. The abrupt way in which Juliet had turned off her vacuum cleaner and raced off down the corridor, leaving her equipment behind her, had caught Christopher's attention. And as he briefly wondered what had caused the cleaner's sudden exit, another thought popped into his mind. How much that woman's profile had reminded him of . . .

'Juliet!'

Christopher pushed his chair away from his desk and was on his feet in seconds. It was her. It had to be. She had not expected to see him and that was why she had left the scene with such speed. But what was she doing here? By the time he was out in the corridor and trying to guess where Juliet would have fled to, he was beginning to form an idea.

Juliet. Of course it was she who had forwarded those emails to his wife. She must have guessed what his passwords were. He had a suspicion that she had always known but he hadn't thought to change them after she was pushed from the company. Of course she had come back because she knew he had been involved in her suspension and she intended to have Christopher's head. How ironic that she had chosen to try to sink him in the way he had got rid of her.

Juliet was standing by the basins when Christopher caught up with her. She was with another cleaner. The black girl that Ed Taylor had a thing about once upon a time. Juliet didn't try to pretend she was someone else. She took her glasses off and looked Christopher straight in the eye.

'I didn't know you wore glasses,' he joked. 'What are you doing here?'

'I needed a job.'

'I thought you'd been suspended on full pay.'

'You know how much I hate being idle,' said Juliet.

'Indeed. The devil makes work for idle hands,' said Christopher. 'Nice work, Juliet, sending those emails. Caroline will divorce me, of course. Which is what you always wanted.'

'It doesn't make a difference to me anymore.'

'I didn't think you were the vindictive type.'

'Ditto. You threw the first missile, Christopher. By setting me up to lose my job by exactly the same method.'

'You've got no proof of that.'

Juliet looked at the floor.

'Still, you got your own back. Now I suggest you leave. This situation could compromise the investigation into your job.'

'I'll go,' said Juliet.

But she wasn't about to be allowed to walk out alone. As he had left his office in pursuit of his former lover, Christopher had instructed one of the few remaining juniors on the floor that they should call security. Security duly arrived: two guards, who towered over Juliet, Mercy and Christopher.

'What's the problem?' one of them asked.

'I believe that this woman,' Christopher pointed at Juliet.

'*This woman!*' how her heart stung.

'This woman,' Christopher continued, 'is a former employee of Anglo-Italian who was barred from the premises as one of the conditions of her redundancy. I don't know how she managed to get back in the building as a cleaner, but she definitely should not be here and I'd like you to escort her off the premises now.'

Juliet didn't protest. Mercy reached out a hand as if to give her comfort, but Juliet shook her head.

'She didn't know anything about it,' said Juliet as she passed Christopher on her way out of the men's room and out of the Anglo-Italian building under escort for the second time in a month.

Christopher decided that it was best that the rest of the company thought the email incident was the beginning and end of it. But he himself was not quite convinced. For an hour after Juliet was evicted from the building, Christopher pored over every email he had on his desktop, trying to work out what Juliet might have been looking for and what she might have found. He could find nothing obvious. Apart from the correspondence Juliet had already sent to Caroline, his emails were a record of what he considered to be a set of wholly innocent transactions. He could find nothing that incriminated him at all. He had taken great care to ensure that all his compromising communications with James Dean's people were done in the utmost secrecy. Those emails between him and Dean's office that remained on the Anglo-Italian system were no different from those between Christopher and any other major private banking client. There was nothing suspicious. If Juliet had read any of this then she must have come away disappointed.

Christopher didn't stop to think that Juliet might have been looking for something other than emails. After searching every note he'd ever written, he started to come to the conclusion that perhaps Juliet really had gone to such extraordinary lengths with the sole purpose of making trouble at the Wilde family home. He didn't have to tell Dean what had happened, did he?

Chapter Sixty-Five

♪

MERCY could only stand by and watch as the security guards marched Juliet from the building that evening. She had warned Juliet that was what she would do. She could not afford to risk her job. But she had a feeling that would not be the last she heard from her new friend. And she was right.

Juliet was waiting for Mercy outside the Anglo-Italian building in the same shadowy spot she had chosen for their first meeting.

'You're late,' said Juliet.

'Lots to do because we were short-handed. Are you OK?' Mercy asked. 'Did they call the police?'

'No,' said Juliet. 'That would have been too embarrassing for Christopher Wilde. He doesn't want to advertise his affair.'

'Then that's good,' said Mercy. 'Hazel is furious but you got away with it.'

'It's not the end of it though.'

'What do you mean?'

'Because I had a feeling I might get rumbled, I hid a memory stick on top of one of the cisterns in the loos on the sixteenth floor. In the Gents. Third cubicle as you walk in. You've got to get it for me.'

'What?'

'Go back in. Pretend you've forgotten something.'

It was a small thing to ask for but Juliet offered Mercy two hundred pounds for her pains. That immediately alerted Mercy to the importance of the damn thing. But it was easy to achieve. Mercy was pretty sure that Anglo-Italian would not have fitted CCTV cameras in the Gents since Juliet was discovered. It was illegal – wasn't it? – to have a CCTV camera directed into a toilet cubicle. It must be. All Mercy had to do was get that memory stick without being caught. It would take seconds.

'Two hundred pounds,' Juliet repeated more insistently.

Singing lessons. New shoes. A gift for her mother. Mercy nodded.

'Wait here.'

Back inside the building, she placed her 'cleaning in progress' sign right across the door of the Gents. It should do the trick. She had been interrupted only once in her entire time at Anglo-Italian, by a banker who had eaten bad oysters at lunch. She went into the cubicle and started to feel about on top of the cistern.

This time she was interrupted by Hazel.

'What are you doing?' she caught Mercy balancing on a toilet seat. 'I thought you went home. You don't have to dust the top of the cistern. They don't pay for it and our insurance won't cover you falling in.'

At which point, Mercy did exactly that. She got her foot stuck in the toilet. Hazel helped her out.

'Come on,' she said, as Mercy took off her damp shoe. 'What was it you were looking for?'

'Nothing,' said Mercy. The truth was there was nothing to find. Either Juliet had got the cubicles mixed up, or someone else had got there first.

Hazel narrowed her eyes. 'Is there any chance you were looking for this?'

Hazel put her hand into her pocket. When she unfurled her palm the memory stick was nestling in the middle of it.

'Great place to hide things, top of the cistern. You wouldn't believe what I've found up there in my time here. Money, cigarettes, drugs. When your friend Juliet was marched out of the building, I had a feeling it was something more than some looney woman wanting to get close to her ex. What's on this memory stick, Mercy? What did she tell you? It must be worth a lot of money if she's asked you to risk your job getting it for her.'

'Have I risked my job?' Mercy asked in a small voice.

'If this contains Anglo-Italian data you have.'

Hazel turned the memory stick over in her hand. 'Such a little thing, innit? They say that one of these sticks contains more memory than all the computers they used to launch the moon landings.'

Mercy had not felt quite so uncomfortable in a while. She was damp and now hot as well, as she waited for Hazel to tell her what she was going to do.

'Where are you supposed to drop this off?' Hazel asked.

'She's waiting for me outside,' Mercy whispered.

'In that case, we mustn't keep her waiting. Come on.'

*　　*　　*

Juliet glanced at her watch. Mercy had been gone for quarter of an hour. It shouldn't have taken her that long to find the stick. With every second that passed, Juliet grew more anxious. When she saw Mercy exiting the building with Hazel and clocked the grim look on Mercy's face, Juliet was sure she was in trouble.

The three women went into the wine bar where Juliet had been romanced by Christopher and where she had tried to persuade Mercy to help her bring him down. Juliet bought three drinks. Hazel was unequivocal about the fact that it was Juliet's round. Once the wine was on the table, Hazel asked, 'Now what's this all about?'

Juliet told Hazel the whole story. There was no point keeping any secrets. She would be going to the police in any case.

'So, you're saying that this could bring the bank down, the information you've got on here.'

Juliet nodded. 'It's the evidence I need to get the police involved.'

'Must be worth quite a bit. To you and to Anglo-Italian,' Hazel mused. 'How do I know that you're not the crooked one here?'

'You don't,' Juliet admitted. 'You just have to take my word for it.'

'Make it worth my while.'

Juliet handed over two hundred pounds. That seemed to be enough to convince Hazel that she had no further questions. She handed Mercy a twenty then folded the rest of the notes into a neat little roll and tucked them into her handbag.

'I wish you all the luck in the world,' Hazel said to Juliet. 'Sounds like you're going to need it.'

With Hazel gone, Juliet and Mercy were left alone again. Mercy tried to hand the twenty back to her former colleague.

'I messed up,' she said. 'I'm really sorry.'

'No need to worry about it,' Juliet told her. 'I got exactly what I needed. And I would have paid twice what she asked for.' Juliet counted another two hundred out of the roll in her handbag. 'I promised you this. I know you need the money for singing lessons and, trust me, this information is worth far more than four hundred to me. Mercy, I hope everything works out for you. In life. In love. In everything.'

'And I you.'

The girls hugged each other briefly.

'Good luck,' they wished each other.

Juliet called David that night. He took her call for the first time since they argued about her affair with Christopher Wilde. He seemed happy to hear from her though it was quickly obvious that she wasn't calling to make small talk.

'I think I've got all the evidence I need to prove that Christopher is intending to set an account-sweeping programme in place but I really want you to take a look at it. Will you do that for me? For old friendship's sake?'

David said that he would. He would be with her as soon as possible, which, alas, would not be until the following evening. Juliet was happy enough with that. She needed David to tell her exactly what she had to make her conversation with the fraud squad more convincing.

'Eight o'clock?' she suggested. 'My place.'

Chapter Sixty-Six

THE following evening, with an hour to go before David arrived, Juliet headed out to the off-licence for a bottle of champagne, certain that David would confirm she had something worth celebrating. She walked to and from the shop, the way she always did.

Juliet liked to think of herself as a streetwise sort of girl. In the fifteen years she had spent in London, she had managed to keep out of trouble. She made sure that she kept an eye on her safety at all times. She had a sixth sense for the kind of person one shouldn't sit next to in a tube carriage. She never travelled home alone if she'd had more than a couple of drinks. It disturbed her greatly to see other women drunkenly dozing on the shoulder of a complete stranger on the tube ride home. How could they have so little regard for their own well-being as to put themselves in such a vulnerable position? Once she was out of the tube, Juliet always walked home via the brightest, busiest streets.

She never wore an iPod, since that might prevent her from hearing someone approaching her from behind. She would cross the road if she saw a gang of kids loitering on a corner. She was always alert to possible problems.

And yet she did not notice that someone was following her home that evening.

She thought that she was home free when she put her key in the front door of her building. But the moment she pushed the door open, she realised much too late that someone else had his hand on the door and was shoving it with such force that she fell to her knees in the hallway.

'What the fuck?' she shouted, scrabbling to her feet and expected a fight for her handbag.

'Just get up and go upstairs,' said the man, whose face was covered by a balaclava. He was already taking her by the elbow and pulling her upright.

'Hel–' She didn't get the word out before he clamped his hand over her mouth.

'Just keep quiet,' he whispered in her ear. 'I'm not going to hurt you. I promise I'm not going to hurt you. But you just have to do as you're told. We're going into your flat and you're going to hand over everything you've found at Anglo-Italian.'

Tense as a deer pinned to the floor by a pack of dogs, Juliet strained to recognise that voice. Because she did recognise it, didn't she?

Chapter Sixty-Seven

🎼

$\mathcal{S}$INCE their evening listening to opera together, Mercy had felt reassured that her brother would soon be back in the heart of the family. As she got ready to go out to work, she heard music blasting from Francis's room. But it wasn't the usual rap. It was *Tosca* again. And that gave Mercy even more confidence that Francis was on the mend.

She knocked at his door with the intention of wishing him a good evening as she headed out but above the music, Francis couldn't hear a thing. And so Mercy surprised him. She surprised him just as he was tucking a gun into his belt and hiding it beneath the flap of the jacket he only ever wore to church.

'Francis!'

He whirled around to face her, simultaneously pulling the gun from his belt and pointing it straight at her face.

'Fuck!' he exclaimed when he saw that it was his sister. 'What the fuck?'

'What the–? You tell *me* what the fuck. You've got a gun!'

'Of course I've got a gun,' said Francis, bringing it down from Mercy's nose.

'What do you need a gun for?'

'A man's got to protect himself.'

'Francis, you're not a man. You're a fifteen-year-old kid.'

Mercy knew at once that she had said the wrong thing. Her brother's eyes flashed with anger. But she also knew that she had to take a stand over this. She had to try and persuade him that he was making a big mistake. She had to get that gun out of his hands.

'Are you crazy? You cannot take that out of the house. If you get caught with that gun, you'll go to prison. Francis, it's a mandatory prison sentence.'

'Not for someone my age.'

'You think a young offenders' institute will look better on your CV? Jesus,' said Mercy. 'As though that's the biggest problem anyway. Francis, have you gone mad? You know what they say about knives. If you carry a knife, you're more likely to get hurt by a knife. If you carry a gun–'

'No one messes with you,' said Francis, with a slight smirk.

Mercy didn't laugh.

'Where did you get it? Who gave it to you? Are you holding it for someone else? You must be. Why don't you take it back to them and tell them to risk their own jail sentence?'

'Because I need it for my work.'

'What? Can you even hear what you're saying? Francis, I am not letting you leave the house with that gun. I want you to put it back in that metal box and leave it there until the police come to fetch it. If you give it up, they won't ask any more questions, I'm sure. But this is the only way. Because you aren't leaving that room with a pistol.'

'You really think you can stop me?'

'You'll have to come through me. What are you going to do, little brother? Blow my head off?'

'Mercy, just get out of the way. Just pretend you didn't see nothing and go back to listening to your stupid opera.'

'I'm not moving until that gun goes back in the box and you tell me just who it belongs to.'

Mercy got out her mobile and began to dial 999, but before she could plug in the last digit, her phone was flying across the room to smash against the wall. She never would have believed that her beloved younger brother would raise so much as a finger to her but Francis had hit the thing right out of her hand. And he wasn't stopping there. Having got rid of the phone, Francis brought his fist holding the gun, up beneath Mercy's chin, knocking her to the floor and into unconsciousness with just one blow.

As he saw his sister laid out on the carpet, Francis felt a pang of guilt. Having checked that she was still breathing, he took a pillow from his bed and put it beneath her head. Then he covered her with his duvet. She would be fine, he told himself. Bruised and angry for sure, but ultimately fine. And later, when all this was over, he would be able to make some serious amends.

But for now, he had work to do.

'Sorry, sis,' he kissed her on the forehead and left, quietly closing the bedroom door behind him.

Chapter Sixty-Eight

MEANWHILE, at Covent Garden the audience was beginning to arrive. The lobby of the opera house buzzed with excitement about the evening ahead. People had sold their grandmothers to get tickets for that evening's performance. There were no returns, yet a queue a hundred long still waited hopefully on the off chance that someone with a ticket might meet a terrible accident on their way across the piazza.

Behind the scenes, the singers began to warm up. Cosima made her way to the costume department to be helped into her Act One costume. Though Cosima's own hair was fabulously lush and beautiful, she still required a wig for the part. Mostly because the empire-style do the part required would have taken hours to fix each day. This way, it only took half an hour to do Cosima's hair instead of the two it would have taken to set and curl it.

'Bloody itchy thing,' she complained.

'Last time you'll have to wear it for a while,' the wardrobe mistress reminded her.

Karl was making his rounds.

'How's the crowd?' Cosima asked him.

'Full house.'

'I'll give it my best,' she sighed.

In his dressing room, Nolan was equally low-key about the performance ahead. Karl could barely raise a smile. Still, the first act went without a hitch. Cosima injected a levity and playfulness into Tosca's appearance that Karl would not have expected given her downbeat mood in the changing room, and she kept the lightness even when Nolan sang 'Mia jalousa', which he managed, to his credit, to sing with equal playfulness and not in an especially pointed way. Donald Law's performance of Scarpia was exemplary. Mostly because the young buck who had given him the throat infection was going to be in the audience and he desperately wanted to impress him. Indeed, the final song of the act, sent shivers up everyone's spine.

The choreography of the crowd entering the church while Scarpia sings of using Tosca to lay a trap for her lover was flawless. Karl in particular loved the part where four flag-bearers entered and dipped their standards before the cross. Their timing was perfect. It was a small detail but it tickled him and he knew from drifting around the Paul Hamlyn Hall during the interval that many other people appreciated it too. Opera did have a very special magic to it. The same small scene in a movie would have had to be shot a thousand times to achieve such perfection.

Karl donned a disguise to walk around the restaurants during the interval. It was simple – he had the girl in wardrobe stick a moustache beneath his aquiline nose – but very effective. He walked past several of his close personal friends without attracting attention. Thank goodness they were raving about his work at the time.

'He is one of the greatest of his generation,' said Michael.

'He is *the* greatest,' said Sandeep.

Karl glowed. Though perhaps Sandeep's enthusiasm could be discounted since the poor boy had had a hopeless crush on Karl for years. Fortunately Karl had moved on before the men revealed that they had in fact been talking about somebody else.

After that inadvertent little ego boost, Karl continued on his way, stopping at the bar to buy a glass of champagne. Two women were talking about how much they fancied Nolan O'Connor. A third woman, short and dumpy and looking a little greasy, glared at their frivolity. She looked so fierce that Karl felt compelled to move a little further down the bar, which is where he found himself standing next to a strikingly good-looking young boy, who was nursing a whisky on ice. Very good-looking, and very young. He must be eighteen, since the barman had served him a drink, thought Karl naively. Though he could have passed for younger. Karl couldn't take his eyes off the young man. He had such a wonderful profile. There was a hint of the young Jamie Foxx about him. In his imagination, he was already casting him in his next production. Karl wondered if the boy was a singer or a dancer. It wasn't often you saw such wonderful young men at Covent Garden. If they were there they were inevitably escorting a grandmother or, more often, studying the arts.

The bell for the end of the interval rang. The young boy necked his whisky. Karl saw the opportunity to make small talk.

'There's no need to make yourself ill,' he said. 'It will take at least ten minutes for this lot of coffin-dodgers to get back to their seats.'

The young boy looked at him.

'What are you saying?'

'I was just saying there was no need to neck your drink like that. Can I get you another one?'

'I ain't no batty boy if that's what you're saying,' the young man responded.

'Gosh. No. Heavens. No. Of course,' Karl spluttered.

But the young man slammed his glass down on the bar and was gone, leaving a big tear in the fabric of Karl's so far wonderful evening as he went.

Karl slunk backstage to make sure there had been no great calamities in his absence. There was an end-of-term feeling about the company. Those who did not have to sing again were already kicking off the party, swigging champagne and planning late-night revels at those London clubs which best suited their particular persuasions. In contrast, Nolan and Cosima were both as dour as the last two final-year students to finish their exams. Karl tried to chivvy them both up by telling them how their Act One performances had gone down. He even embellished a little.

'Better than La Scala,' he told Cosima.

'Thanks,' she said flatly. Then she went back to scowling at her reflection in the mirror as another, even more elaborate wig was arranged on her head, complete with the tiara that never usually failed to make her smile.

In the grand tier box she had all to herself, Florence Carter played agitatedly with the beads on her favourite necklace.

From time to time, she checked the contents of her handbag. She felt the weight of that bag on her knee. She knew that no one had been near it since she arrived at the opera house and breezed through the security check, and yet she couldn't believe that everything was still as she had packed it. As the orchestra struck up and second act began, she put her hand inside the bag and checked one more time. She shivered ever so slightly as her fingers brushed cold steel.

Chapter Sixty-Nine

TERRIFIED though she was to have been accosted on the steps of her own building, Juliet was determined not to give in. As her attacker tried to wrestle her into her flat, she made a grab for his balaclava. It came off easily, revealing what she'd already guessed. It was someone she knew. David.

'David, what are you doing?' She pushed him away with as much force as she could muster. David slumped, winded, against the doorframe. Now that she knew who had been following her, Juliet lost all fear. 'Is this some kind of a joke?' she asked him, swinging her bag at his stomach and winding him again. She rubbed at her wrist, grazed from where she'd landed on the rough-bristled doormat. 'I asked you, is this some kind of fucking joke?'

David caught his breath. 'I'm afraid it's not.' He stepped towards her again, his shoulders squared, reminding her that he was so much bigger. 'I had hoped you wouldn't have to know it was me.'

'What were you thinking? I invited you here. You don't have to break in.'

'I'm going to need everything you downloaded from Christopher's machine.'

'I was going to show you.'

'I need to take it away with me.'

'Fuck off. Why do you want it?'

'For your own protection.'

'You're not going to try to convince me I'm in mortal danger again. What is it? I'm at risk of losing my life through interfering with this scam and incurring the wrath of a nameless, faceless crime lord.'

David grabbed the top of Juliet's arm and marched her further into the flat.

'He has a name. And a face. And he's my boss. I've been working for a man called James Dean.'

'The actor?'

'As far as I'm aware, the only time he's been on the screen is when appearing on *Crimewatch*. He's an old-fashioned Essex gangster and he's the man who commissioned the account-sweeping programme that Christopher was going to install at Anglo-Italian. It was my masterpiece.'

'No,' Juliet shook her head. 'You told me you'd been working in the States.'

'Crime's been just as successful at globalisation as McDonalds. Now I need you to give me everything you've found and we'll say no more about it.'

'This isn't a Famous Five story, David. You'll need to be more convincing than that.' But it seemed he was in deadly earnest. While Juliet was still trying to take in this sudden change in her friend's demeanour and remember where she'd left her laptop, David had pushed past her into the sitting room and was already picking the machine up. As Juliet watched in horror, he walked to the window she'd so carelessly left ajar and threw the laptop out onto the pavement below.

'What the–?'

'I need the rest,' he said. 'I know you've made copies.'

'And you're not having them.'

'Don't make me hurt you,' said David.

'I would have thought your conscience would prevent you from hurting me. The David I knew ten years ago wasn't given to using violence to get what he wanted.'

Now Juliet was slowly backing into her kitchen. David followed at a little distance. It wasn't much, but it was enough of a distance to enable Juliet to slam the kitchen door shut between them. And quick as a flash she pushed the table against it, jamming it shut while David pushed from the other side. It wouldn't hold for long, but it gave her enough time to make her getaway.

There was no back door to Juliet's flat, but the kitchen window led onto a fire escape. With the memory stick in the back pocket of her jeans, Juliet climbed out of the window and on to the rickety iron ladder. She had never tried the ladder before. It had occurred to her several times since she moved into the flat that she ought to have investigated her exit strategy in case of an emergency. But she had expected that if an emergency came, she would have at least a little time to take things carefully. Now she was shimmying down that ladder as though the devil himself were behind her. She heard David force the kitchen door open with a crash.

'Juliet!'

She was still twenty feet from the ground when David leaned out of the kitchen window.

'There's no point running. You won't get very far.'

Juliet suddenly realised that she had run out of ladder. The damn thing got nowhere near the floor but took her to a neighbour's roof terrace. And every window that led from the terrace was barred. There was no way forward but a sheer drop to concrete twenty feet beneath. She'd end up as smashed as her laptop on the street in front of the house. It wasn't like it was in the movies.

David was already climbing down the ladder towards her.

'Keep away from me.' Juliet reached for something, anything, with which to defend herself. She picked up a flowerpot. The tomato plant that had been growing within it had long since died. She brandished the pot at David and as he got closer she hurled it at him, but he ducked out of the way and the pot smashed harmlessly behind him.

She picked up another.

'Stop with the missiles,' said David. 'You know you're a terrible shot.'

He was advancing upon her fearlessly.

'I just need you to hand over everything you've got to me.'

'I've already called the police,' Juliet told him.

'I'm sure you have,' David agreed. 'But trust me, this isn't a story they're going to believe or understand. You're in way over your head with this stuff, Juliet. James Dean is not a man who takes very kindly to anyone who interferes in his business. Do you really think you're going to stand opposite him in a court of law and get away with it? He knows where you live. He knows where your family lives. And he's a man who bears grudges. Is it worth risking your life to see Christopher Wilde go down?'

'It's not about Christopher anymore,' said Juliet. 'The

programme you were planning to activate at Anglo-Italian would have robbed thousands of hard-working people. There's nothing James Dean can threaten me with that will make me give you what I've found.' She backed up to the edge of the terrace and glanced behind her. The sheer drop was no shorter. The sudden perception of depth made her wobble.

'Get back from there.'

She stumbled. David reached for Juliet's wrist. She didn't know if his intention was to hurt her, but as she tried to pull away, he tightened his grip so that her skin was dragged until it burned.

'Juliet, listen to me. You have no idea. James Dean has had members of his own family shot for giving him socks at Christmas. One of his ex-girlfriends got a dozen red roses and a face full of acid on Valentine's Day. I dread to think what he might line up for you.'

'The police will protect me.'

'Ever heard the term "bent copper"? You can't do this on your own. You and I, standing here – this isn't a scene from some film. You're not going to jump the last twenty feet to the floor, land with a somersault, brush yourself off and keep running. You'll break your back. And even if you don't break your back, you're not going to stand up in court, denounce one of Britain's biggest gangsters and see him banged up for life. He got off a murder charge once, despite having carved his initials in his dying victim's chest. He will get off any charge you care to make against him and then he will make your life hell.'

'Maybe my life couldn't get much worse,' said Juliet.

'Brave words, but stupid. Give it up, Juliet. You can't do this alone.'

Suddenly, Juliet broke free of David's grip. She made a run for the edge of the terrace. Twenty feet down, but if she swung over the bar and hung on, that would slow her descent a little. Halve the drop. But in reality, she had no chance of pulling the *Charlie's Angels*-style feat off. She realised her mistake the second she took off and found herself dangling from her fingers, too terrified to let go. Too tired to hang on.

'Shit,' David leaned over the barrier and grabbed her by the wrist. 'You do have a death wish after all.'

'Get me up,' she begged him. 'Don't let me drop down there.'

David hauled with every bit of strength he had. But while Juliet lay panting on the floor, David had no time to comfort her. Instead, he whipped the memory stick out of her pocket and crushed it beneath his foot.

'David!' Juliet stretched out her hand to rescue the information she had worked so hard to get but it was too late. It was destroyed. And then David picked what remained of the stick up and tossed it out into the gardens that backed on to Juliet's building. It was gone.

'Now, for God's sake, let's go inside,' he said. 'You and I need to talk.'

Chapter Seventy

THE truth of David's involvement with the account-sweeping heist was more complicated than Juliet could have imagined. As she nursed a cup of tea, the whole episode began to seem surreal. She still had faint marks around her wrists from when he'd dragged her back to safety. And now they were drinking tea. It was a very British sort of affair. Which was apt, considering David's next revelation.

'I haven't been entirely honest with you,' he said. 'I don't work for James Dean. I work for MI6.'

MI6. The government intelligence agency. Juliet couldn't help sniggering.

'You expect me to believe that?' she asked.

David nodded.

'You work for MI6? Like James Bond.'

'Not quite like James Bond. But yes, I do. Since going to South America. They approached me when we were at college, but I thought they were kidding. Five years later they approached me again. For Queen and Country,' he half laughed. 'And for the past year I've been following James Dean. He has a great many interesting international connections. You could call him the Richard Branson of the underworld. We're not especially interested in him. He spends everything he raises on cars and shoes for the missus, as far as I can tell. But some of the people he has connections with are funding far shadier enterprises than Harvey Nicks or Christian Louboutin. He's been working with members of a crime cartel that has links to al-Qaeda.'

'You're kidding.'

'I don't think he really understands. He just takes his cut. He doesn't ask what's going to happen to the rest of it. But working for Dean put me in a great position to get access to these people. They all wanted in on my big banking scam. I was even flown to Russia to meet Belanov.'

'So you knew that Christopher was involved all along.'

'I did.'

'Did you know that I was having an affair with him?'

David nodded. 'I'm afraid so. Dean needed to get some dirt on Christopher to persuade him to help us out. His brother . . .'

'Nat?'

'That's the name. His brother Nat had already spilled the beans about Christopher's bit of fluff. Dean got some photos . . .'

'Oh god. Of me?'

David nodded. 'To prove to Christopher that he was in serious shit.'

Juliet closed her eyes as though she could imagine exactly what the photos had revealed. 'And that's why you tracked me down after all this time. Pretended you just happened to find me on Facebook. Just so you could get more information.'

'That's not true,' said David. 'I didn't need any information from you. But I did want to keep an eye on you. Because I was concerned for your safety.'

Juliet snorted.

'Trust me,' said David. 'There was nothing you could have told me that I didn't already know.'

'So you say. But if you're telling the truth. If you have as much dirt on this Dean guy as you say you do, how come he isn't already in prison?'

'James Dean is far more valuable to us out of prison than in it. For some reason, all the scum in the world are attracted to that man like iron filings to a magnet. Getting close to Dean is like having access to a Rolodex labelled "bad guys". That's why he keeps on slipping through the net. He thinks it's because of his way with bent coppers. We know it's because we keep having him thrown back to attract the bigger sharks.'

Juliet shook her head. 'Why should I believe you?'

'Because you've known me for half my life?' David suggested. 'And because I meant it when I told you that you mean more to me than any other woman in the world.'

Juliet was oddly stung that he didn't say he loved her again. She searched his face. David looked away but not before she thought she saw what she was looking for. He stroked a tentative finger over the red marks on her right wrist. He did mean what he said.

'But whether you do believe me or not, it really doesn't matter. What matters to me is that I no longer have to worry about you. You've got nothing to take to the police now. Dean has no reason to come after you anymore. You're safe.'

'I could still go to the police and tell them what's going on.'

'Trust me. It wouldn't result in an arrest. Not of James Dean at least. Just keep your head down, Juliet. Start looking for a new job. Build your life back up again.'

'What will happen to Christopher?' Juliet asked.

'I'm sure he'll get his comeuppance one day,' said David.

Minutes later, David was gone, leaving Juliet with no souvenir of the meeting but a red welt around each of her wrists where he had dragged her back onto the terrace. She had promised herself that she would go to the police as soon as he left, but in his absence, she felt less sure that there was any point. What she did instead was check her flat from top to bottom for any evidence that what David had said was true. Had she been under surveillance? She found nothing. At least nothing that she would have recognised as some kind of bugging device. When she'd finished her sweep, she stood at each of her windows in turn and looked out to see from where someone might have kept watch on her comings and goings. But this was a London street. When it came to places for a photographer to get a good view of Juliet's flat, there were simply too many to count.

She wondered what David had seen.

As the last of the sunlight disappeared, Juliet called him. She would ask to see him and get him to go through everything he had told her one more time. He owed her that. But David did not pick up her call. In fact, an automated voice announced that the number she had dialled was no longer in use. As suddenly as he had come back into her life, David Stevenson had disappeared.

Chapter Seventy-One

In the wings of the opera house, Cosima Esposito prepared to make her entrance.

Onstage, Nolan launched into 'E Lucevan Le Stelle', undoubtedly one of, if not the, most emotionally charged moments in the opera. As she heard her former lover sing of Cavaradossi's undying love for Tosca, Cosima could not help but be moved.

'Oh! Dolci baci, o languide carezze.'

In that moment, Cosima remembered every one of the kisses they had shared. But *'Svanì per sempre il sogno mio d'amore,'* he sang on. *'A dream of love vanished for ever.'* When he sang those words, Cosima could not stifle any longer the sob that had risen in her throat.

'E non ho amato mai tanto la vita!' Nolan's voice broke on the last note. Whether he had done it deliberately, or not, he broke Cosima's heart with that note all over again. Antony, who was playing Spoletta, had to pinch her to bring her back to the real world before she missed her entrance.

As she followed Antony up the stairs, stumbling as she went, Cosima wasn't sure she would be able to sing a single note without crying and she didn't. But it didn't matter. There was not a dry eye in the house as she crooned, '*Gli occhi ti chiuderò con mille baci e mille ti dirò nomi d'amore.*' '*I shall close your eyes with a thousand kisses and call you a thousand loving names.*' And Cosima regretted all the far from loving names that she had called Nolan over the years.

But then the guards came on.

'*Tieni a mente: al primo colpo, giù . . .*' '*Remember to fall at the first shot!*' Tosca told Cavaradossi. Fall down and stay down until I tell you to move. Cosima sang those words so sweetly. She clung to Nolan as she told him of her plan. They shared a final kiss.

The lovers were parted and Nolan was led to the stake. As the guards lashed him to the wood, his whole body still seemed to strain towards Cosima. She in turn stretched out her arms to him. She had to be held back. After all, the score called for her to play a woman pretending to believe that her beloved would be dead in a matter of moments.

The music reached a crescendo. The guards took their marks and drew aim on their prisoner's heart. To the side of the stage, Cosima covered her mouth as if to stifle a cry. The shots rang out. Blood exploded from Nolan's chest to cover his pure white shirt like a blossoming of funeral flowers. His knees buckled – more realistically than he had ever managed before, Donald Law noted from the wings. Nolan slumped at the base of the stake. The guards marched off and Cosima waited seconds before she raced on to sing her final aria.

'*Presto, su! Mario,*' she sang. '*Mario! Su! Presto! Andiamo!*' The score called for Nolan, in his part, to remain on the floor, of course. So it took a few moments before Cosima noticed that there was anything different about the way he was playing the scene that night. But when she did . . .

'Aaaaaaaggggggghhhhhhh!'

Cosima's scream rent the opera house. The audience jumped as one before leaning forwards in their seats again. Cosima Esposito was one amazing soprano. But . . . .

'Oh my God! Somebody help me.'

She wasn't singing anymore. This wasn't part of the score.

'Help! Help me!'

Cosima got to her feet. Her hands were bright red. The front of her dress was crimson with gore.

'Somebody help me!' she shouted to the wings. 'Somebody. Somebody . . .'

She fell back to her knees and pressed both her hands to her lover's heart. Cautiously, a stagehand stepped out into the lights.

'Cosima?' he half whispered. 'Cosima, is everything OK?'

'Just call a fucking ambulance,' she screamed. 'He's been shot. He's really been shot. Somebody fucking shot Nolan!'

Chapter Seventy-Two

𝒯HE shooting threw the opera house into chaos. It took a moment for the audience to register what Cosima was the first to discover, but as soon the punters realised that Nolan O'Connor had been shot for real, panic quickly followed.

Where had the shot come from? Was the shooter among the soldiers onstage? Or backstage? Or had Nolan been shot from the stalls? The entire audience was on its feet and pressing towards the exits. Women and grown men screamed. Gentlemen in dinner suits trampled old ladies in their haste to get out of the auditorium. There were some significant casualties as a result of the stampede.

Meanwhile, Francis Campbell sat on his hands in a grand tier box, looking every inch the teenage boy he really was. The gun his sister had begged him to get rid of lay on the floor between his feet. He closed his eyes tightly but the horror he had just witnessed played out over and over in his mind. The crescendo of the music. The guards taking aim.

The shots. The blood. Nolan O'Connor's slightly stunned expression as his knees buckled and he crumbled to the floor. All the colour draining from his face as the blood pumped from his body onto the boards. God, there was so much blood.

The man was dead. He had to be. Francis had seen some shit in his short life but he had never seen someone bleed like that and survive. A direct hit to the chest. It was what Francis had come to see and yet he could not believe it had actually happened. Five minutes earlier, the gun had been inside Francis's bag and he had been wrestling with his conscience. He had been studying the face of the man on the stage for too long. He'd found himself enjoying the performance and made the fatal mistake of beginning to like the man he had been sent to assassinate.

That's when Francis told himself he didn't have to go through with the hit. Dean couldn't get that angry. Francis was just a kid. Then Francis reminded himself that Dean could get angrier than anyone imagined and it wasn't only Francis who would suffer if Dean were pissed off. He knew where Francis lived, of course. That meant he knew where Melody and Mercy lived too. Dean had people everywhere. Francis couldn't bear the thought of what would happen to the only two people who meant anything at all to him if he bottled out of his mission now.

And so the third act of *Tosca* played on. Cosima Esposito was back on the stage. Her hair wild. Her dress dishevelled. She clung to her onstage lover and told him of her plan for escape. She showed him the bloodstained papers that would give them free passage to the port at Civitavecchia and a new life beyond. She sang sweetly of the plans she had for life after she and Cavaradossi escaped the Castel Sant'Angelo.

'*Senti effluvi di rose? Non ti par che le cose aspettan tutte innamorate il sole . . .*' '*Don't you feel that everything is in love, waiting for the sunlight?*' All he had to do was pretend to die. He just had to fall to the ground. She told him how to look convincing. And then the soldiers returned.

Francis felt the weight of the gun in his hand. He had listened to Mercy's CD of the opera a thousand times that week. He knew the exact moment when the soldiers onstage would fire their guns and Cavaradossi would die. Just five bars away now. Four bars. Five beats. The end of a life.

Francis had raised the gun but weakly, so weakly. He couldn't do it. He wouldn't do it.

But he must have done it. Though Francis thought he remembered dropping the gun to the floor without pulling the trigger, the man on the stage lay still and silent in a pool of blood that shone as black as oil in false moonlight on the fake castle. And the woman who played Tosca was screaming. Not pretending to scream but screaming for real and bringing half the theatre running towards her while the rest started running away.

'He's been shot! He's been shot!'

Francis slumped in his chair with his head in his hands and started to weep for his mother, for his sister and for himself.

Chapter Seventy-Three

𝄞

BUT the shot that almost killed Nolan O'Connor had not been fired from the Grand Tier box where Francis Campbell was curled up on the floor like a foetus. As the crowds whirled around the lobby of the opera house, unsure whether they should try to retrieve their coats before they fled, a small group of people were determined to talk to the police.

Had Francis taken a shot at Nolan from where he was sitting, he would have hit the tenor in the back but Nolan had been hit from the front. And from high above the stage. A group of people from the left-hand side of the theatre reported seeing someone stand up in a balcony box.

'There was a woman on her own in that box,' said one of the witnesses. 'I noticed her precisely because she was alone. And with tonight's tickets being so sought after! It seemed incredible to me that one woman would have had a box to herself when she could have sold the other tickets for a fortune!'

'What did she look like?' the police officer asked.

'Kind of wild,' said one witness.

'A little crazy,' another agreed.

'I saw her in the bar during the interval,' said a third audience member. 'I have to say she smelled somewhat unwashed.'

Florence Carter was easily tracked down. The tickets for the balcony box had been bought in her name. Back when she had planned her trip, she had blown the budget on a box to herself with the vague thought that she might have friends to take with her by then to help make this last evening of the tour extra special. Perhaps, she'd daydreamed, they might even be people that Nolan had introduced her to. No such luck.

Though Florence had fled the theatre with great speed and efficiency, she had not gone very far. She confessed instantly. She told the police, when they caught up with her, that the moment she left the auditorium she was overcome with remorse. Some part of her had woken up to the reality of what she had just done and, realising that Nolan might be dead, she wanted only to throw herself into the Thames and join him in the afterworld. She settled for going back to her hotel on the Caledonian Road and throwing herself onto her bed for a hearty sob. That was where the officers found her, thanks to the travel itinerary she had emailed to Nolan's website.

They felt some sympathy for the poor girl. She was a mousy little thing who looked much too small and timid to have caused so much trouble. There was no defiance in her as she listened to her rights. She didn't want to phone anyone who might be able to help her. She wanted only to know about Nolan.

'He's not dead,' an officer at the station confirmed. 'His costume was padded with bags of fake blood for the scene with the firing squad. It slowed the bullet down. He should make a full recovery.'

'Oh, thank goodness!' exclaimed Florence.

'But we still have to arrest you for attempted murder.'

Florence didn't protest. She knew they had no choice. She admitted she'd got the gun she attempted to kill Nolan with from Emmanuel, the no-mark who hung around the hotel's reception day after day. But even as the cuffs went on, Florence was suddenly blissful. Nolan was still alive and where there's life . . . at least now she had proved that she was absolutely serious about him.

Nolan may not have been dead but he felt bloody awful. As at all large venues, there were paramedics on hand at the theatre and they were onstage within seconds of the realisation that one of the shots had not come courtesy of the department of special effects. They attended to Nolan in front of at least fifty anxious fans, since to move him backstage before they knew where the bullet had hit him might have been fatal. Once they had established that it was safe to move him, he was taken to the hospital. Cosima insisted on accompanying him.

'I am his next of kin,' she said. It was almost true.

Of course, she didn't have time to change out of her costume, and at three in the morning, she was still dressed as Tosca, though her wig, with its ringlets, sat on a chair in the corner of Nolan's hospital room like a small, well-cared for dog. Cosima took a seat by Nolan's bedside. She held his hand. He was groggy. The surgeon had insisted on a general anaesthetic before he started digging around in Nolan's chest.

'Ooooow,' Nolan groaned as he tried to sit up. Cosima pressed him back into the pillows.

'You're not to try to move,' she said. 'Not yet. Just lie back down and go to sleep.'

'What happened?' Nolan asked.

'You were shot.'

'Did one of the prop guns go off?'

'It was your number one fan,' Cosima told him. 'Miss Florence Carter. They've already taken her into custody.'

'Jeez,' Nolan exhaled painfully. 'What did she want to shoot me for?'

'I can't possibly imagine,' said Cosima, with a wry smile.

'What are you doing here?' Nolan asked.

'How on earth could I not be here? I may not be talking to you, Nolan O'Connor, but it turns out that I still care.'

'You do?'

'I do. When I thought you might have been killed . . .' Cosima's face went white with anguish. 'There was so much blood.' She showed him the dried dark patch on the front of her dress. 'Though having said that, half of this is probably the fake blood that was hidden in your shirt in any case.' She lifted the material of her skirt to her nose and took a sniff.

'Cosi,' Nolan grimaced.

'Hmmm. Smells disgusting. But can you imagine how much we could make if we put this dress on eBay?' Cosima joked.

Nolan sank back into the pillows and closed his eyes. His face softened a little and Cosima thought he must be going back to sleep. She smoothed his hair away from his brow and whispered 'I love you'.

Nolan's eyes flicked open.

'Oh, hello,' said Cosima. 'I thought you'd drifted off.'

Nolan shook his head.

'Did you mean what you just said?' he asked.

'What? About putting my dress on eBay? Not really . . .'

'I'm not talking about that.'

'Then what?'

'Did you mean what you said just a minute ago, when you thought I was asleep. When you told me that you loved me?'

Cosima blushed.

'You heard that?'

'I haven't lost my hearing. Did you mean it?'

'Every word,' said Cosima as tears began to make her eyes glitter.

'I still feel the same way,' said Nolan. 'I love you too. When I thought I was dying, it was your face that I wanted to see. I could hear only your voice. Cosima Esposito, you are the love of my life.'

'And you mine, Nolan O'Connor.'

'Then what are we waiting for? Let's promise never to be apart again. Let's get married.'

'Are you asking me to marry you?' Cosima's voice rose in excitement.

'Yes,' Nolan struggled to pull himself upright again. 'Yes. I want nothing more in the world than for you to be my wife. Cosima . . .' he began his proposal.

'Hang on,' she said. 'Not while I'm sitting here in a hairnet.' She grabbed the wig and put it back on. 'That's better.'

Nolan smiled at his silly ex-wife and her indefatigable vanity.

'Cosima Esposito,' he continued. 'Will you marry me?'

Cosima tried to hesitate but she could not keep the grin from her face. 'Yes,' she said. 'Yes, yes, yes!'

She threw herself onto her ex-husband and new fiancé, dislodging a drip in the process and setting off an alarm that brought the entire nursing staff running. As the doctor fitted the drip back into Nolan's arm, he warned him against indulging in too much passion before he was able.

'If you are not careful right now, making love could kill you,' the doctor warned.

'I can't think of a better way to go,' said Nolan.

Chapter Seventy-Four

O_F course, with the police swarming all over the opera house, Francis Campbell had no hope of getting out of the opera house without his gun being discovered and as a result he was in big trouble. Though even as he was being led from the building in handcuffs, when he heard that he hadn't fired the shot that hit Nolan O'Connor, he felt as though he had been given a second chance.

Melody Campbell could not believe that her beloved son had been found with a gun. Francis was questioned about his motives, of course. But he never admitted the real reason for his taking the firearm to Covent Garden. He said that he had taken the gun into the opera house for a dare. To prove that you could get a firearm past the security there. It was clear that the police didn't believe him, but the alternative explanation, which was that there had been two obsessive nutters out to kill Nolan O'Connor that night, seemed even more implausible.

Still, Francis could not escape a short spell inside. It would have been shorter still, but he refused to say who had armed him in the first place. That turned out to be a smart move.

A few days after his release (early for good behaviour), Francis found himself being followed down the street by the familiar Range Rover.

Tony leaned out of the passenger window. 'Mr Dean says you don't owe him anything anymore, so long as you keep your head down and your mouth shut. You don't know us and we don't know you.'

Francis nodded tightly. 'Right.'

When the car was out of sight, Francis lifted his eyes to heaven and offered up a small prayer of thanks. From now on, things would be different.

Francis went back to college and completed his GCSEs. But he wasn't the only one who returned to his studies with renewed determination and enthusiasm.

Though she might have been forgiven for never talking to her brother again, Mercy had come to forgive him for laying her out cold that terrible night. She took longer to forgive him for having wasted a box when Cosima Esposito was performing at Covent Garden. But he had done his time and he had learned his lesson. Meanwhile, Mercy's life had seen a great many changes too.

Ed was now a firm fixture in her life. Mercy loved to have someone with whom to share conversations about music. And whenever Ed had a spare ticket for something, which was often, it had Mercy's name on it. They were inseparable, whenever Mercy's cleaning job allowed.

'You don't really want to be a cleaner for ever?' Ed said one afternoon.

'Of course I don't,' said Mercy irritably. 'I want to go to the Royal College of Music. But I only have the qualifications to clean toilets. You know that.'

'How many GCSEs have you really got?' asked Ed. She'd told him before and was frustrated that he didn't seem to believe her. Obviously no one left his school without a qualification to their name.

'I've only got a music GCSE. That won't get me anywhere.'

'But what do you need? You could sit your exams again now. Nothing is impossible, Mercy.'

'But it'll take years. I'll be almost thirty by the time I've got all the qualifications they ask for.'

'One day you'll be thirty regardless of whether you do the qualifications or not. So really, what possible reason do you have not to do them?'

'The cost.'

'I'll help you,' said Ed.

'I can't take your money.'

'Think of it as sponsorship. Look, I have every faith that you'll make it if you try. If I lay out a bit of cash now, you'll feel obliged to sing at all my birthday parties for the rest of your life. I have no doubt that eventually your services as a singer will be far outside what I can afford and I'll have got myself a bargain.'

Mercy could only laugh at that. But Ed was serious. From the day he first suggested that he could help, he badgered her all day every day with texts and phone calls, asking if she'd called such and such a college about re-sitting her English literature GCSE. Or whether she had set up any singing lessons with the tutor recommended by his aunt.

*   *   *

After that, Mercy had every incentive to work. No longer was it just her ambition she was working for. Ed's involvement, via the generous cheque he had written to cover Mercy's singing lessons and the tuition she needed to get the GCSEs she had missed out on so that she could quickly progress to A-levels, meant that she had his happiness to consider too. She could not fail.

Ed certainly wanted to keep a close eye on his investment and now they were an item. Ed was invited to Melody's house in Streatham. And Mercy was invited to Ed's family home in Norfolk.

'It's a flippin' stately home,' Mercy said in a text she sent to Francis. Talk about intimidating. But Ed's parents were warm and welcoming and the subject of opera gave Mercy an opportunity to shine and be her most brilliant, passionate best.

'My parents loved you,' Ed assured her on the drive back to London. Mercy could not have wished for any better news.

But there was better news.

'I love you too,' said Ed.

With Ed's support, Mercy felt she could do anything.

Chapter Seventy-Five

𝄞

ℋᴇʀ Majesty's Prison Service took receipt of one more notable new offender during the year after Nolan was shot at Covent Garden.

Caroline Wilde was especially disappointed with the way her husband was arrested. She had decided to forgive Christopher for his indiscretion with Lucy – her sister Jane had made the very good point that she could use his infidelities as a way of squeezing him for the things she really wanted in life – and let him return to the marital bed. But then the police arrived right in the middle of a catered lunch party for sixteen of Caroline's most important and influential friends and enemies. The lunch party was supposed to be a chance to show off. Instead, having sixteen guests in the house when the police turned up meant that there was no chance whatsoever of keeping Christopher's arrest quiet until lawyers had sorted out what could only be a bloody awful mistake. No matter what happened now, Caroline would never be able to hold her head up at the tennis club again. It was the final straw.

The police allowed Christopher to collect together a few belongings. A sweater. Some clean underwear. Caroline followed him upstairs, under police escort, and set about berating him with such ferocity, she was lucky she didn't end up on a domestic violence charge.

'You have ruined my life!' she told him in no uncertain terms. 'I could have married anyone. Anyone at all. But I chose you. And what have you given me in return for all my years of support and devotion? Humiliation, that's what. Nothing but humiliation. I don't care if I never see you again. If you ever manage to get out of jail, then you will be hearing from my divorce lawyer.'

Christopher Wilde was almost relieved when the officers helped him into the patrol car and took him away from all that. From Caroline and her constant carping. From the teenage children who only bothered to acknowledge his part in the family when they wanted to borrow some money. From the dull old house in a part of London he hated with its country kitchen covered in bloody Cath Kidston oilcloth and the scatter cushions everywhere. Was that what he had worked so hard for all these years? Even the family dog – that hideous, dribbly pug Caroline had insisted upon for her fortieth birthday – seemed to hate him. Prison would be a bloody holiday from all that crap.

There was nothing about his life he would miss. Nothing that he hadn't already lost. As he leaned his head against the cool window, he thought about Juliet.

* * *

Christopher didn't need his lawyer to tell him that he was in deep trouble. Once the charges had been made, his biggest fear was that he would find himself in a cell with one of James Dean's associates. Christopher didn't finger Dean, of course. There was no point. Best to take the fall and hope that when he got out, Dean might be kind enough to slip him a few quid for his loyalty.

Prison was not like Eton. The HMPS didn't take into account whether other family members had been before when they were allocating prison space. In fact, they actively discouraged placing siblings together, but overcrowding meant that for a few months at least, Christopher and Nat were reunited on the wrong side of the bars.

'Sometimes,' said Christopher to his brother as they played yet another game of dominos, 'I think that this is what you had in mind all along.'

Chapter Seventy-Six

𝄞

JULIET, who had quit Anglo-Italian despite being exonerated by the investigation into the alleged insider trading, heard about Christopher's arrest through Mercy, who, of course, heard of the scandal through Ed.

'You were right,' said Mercy. 'There was an account sweeping scam.'

'Who discovered it?' asked Juliet, since she knew that she had not gone to the police. Her last encounter with David had left her too shaken for that.

'You're not going to believe this,' said Mercy. 'Hazel blew the whistle in the hope of a reward. She said she'd overheard a conversation about it. An investigation was made and she turned out to be right.'

'Did she get a reward?'

'Enough to quit cleaning.'

Juliet felt little satisfaction when she heard about Christopher's arrest. Though he had made carpaccio of her heart, she believed that underneath it all Christopher Wilde was a good person, whose fall from grace was due to the fact that he always chose the easiest path rather than the right one.

A year later, Juliet opened the Cartier box one more time. She held the beautiful bracelet in the palm of her hand and remembered the day in Milan when she thought she had found true love. Once, just the thought of that bracelet would have sent arrows of pain through her heart. Now when she looked at it, she felt only a dull ache of sadness. But she didn't want to keep it anymore.

Later that same afternoon she put the bracelet on eBay with the intention of donating all the proceeds to Great Ormond Street hospital. The winning bidder told her via email that he had bought it as an anniversary present for his wife of forty years. Juliet was satisfied that it had gone to a good home and the hospital was pleased with the money raised.

It wasn't just Juliet's affair that was fast drifting into memory. The hideous crash that first turned the financial world and then the whole world upside down was beginning to fade from people's consciousness. New enterprises had sprung up in the wake of the banks' downfall, like dandelions pushing through concrete, and after a period when Juliet thought she would never see the inside of an office again, the head-hunters were calling once more. She was taken out to lunch and dinner at least four times a week as the recruiters tried to persuade her to take various roles that would net them a huge commission. None of the jobs especially interested Juliet and she continued to take the odd consultancy contract while she waited for something more exciting. About six months later, she received a call from a head-hunter asking her to interview for a government position. Juliet wasn't keen but the head-hunter insisted. 'At least meet them,' he begged. Juliet conceded and a meeting was duly arranged.

The following day Juliet presented herself at an anonymous-looking building in Vauxhall. She was kept waiting for so long that she had made up her mind to leave when she was called inside a plain-doored office.

'David,' said Juliet when she saw the man inside the office. 'David Stevenson. I thought I'd never see you again.'

'Do you think I would have let that happen?'

Juliet shook her head. 'But what are you doing here?'

'I work here. Welcome to MI6.'

'So, what's this about? I was told this was a job interview.'

'It is. Of sorts.'

'Are you going to offer me a job?'

'I think you'd make a very good secret agent.'

'Would I get to drive an Aston Martin?'

'Almost certainly not.'

'In that case, no,' said Juliet. 'In any case, no. I don't feel the need to risk my life for Queen and Country. I'll just pay my taxes instead.'

'Don't you want to think about it?'

'No,' said Juliet simply. 'I've already thought about it. I've thought about it a lot since that night you pulled me over the balcony. If you were telling the truth, would I be able to do the same thing? Would I be able to put my personal life on hold and pretend to be someone else? Could I lie for a living?'

'I don't exactly see it like that,' said David.

'Did you nail your Mr Dean?'

'As I said, he's much more useful to us on the outside. I do believe he's up for an MBE.'

Juliet shook her head. 'And Christopher is in prison. What a crazy world.'

'Mad indeed,' David had to agree. 'So I can't persuade you?'

'No.'

David nodded. 'That's a pity. But the good thing is, if you and I aren't going to be colleagues, I can ask you to have dinner with me again. I assume you're still auditioning for the first Mr Hunter.'

'I don't know about that,' smiled Juliet. 'But I would always be happy to have dinner with an old friend.'

Epilogue

Ten years later.

Mᴇʀᴄʏ Campbell's time at the Royal College of Music had been a revelation. Never had she expected to work so hard or to find hard work quite so enjoyable. It was a good job she developed the habit, however, since the hard work only continued after graduation. Thankfully Ed was there for every step of the journey.

Now Mercy's hard work was about to pay off in a big way. Judy Shephard the soprano had tripped over one of her dogs and badly sprained her ankle just four days before she was meant to sing Liu in *Turandot* at Covent Garden. Mercy was drafted in as her replacement.

As she opened her mouth to sing her first line, Mercy felt her heart swell with a happiness she had never imagined possible.

Out there in the audience were all the people who had

ever meant anything to her in her life. There was her mother and her brother. Her husband Ed and her six-year-old daughter Floria, who had been given special dispensation to stay up long enough to see the first act. Mercy had even managed to track down her old music teacher, John Heywood, who was so stunned to hear that one of his former pupils was being tipped for an Ivor Novello award rather than an ASBO that at first he assumed the invitation must be a joke.

Singing opposite Mercy as The Prince was Nolan O'Connor. It was Covent Garden's greatest coup. Since his brush with death on the same stage all those years earlier, Nolan's fame had exploded. He was now a household name. A face familiar even to people who thought Puccini was a type of pasta. Being asked to sing at the opening ceremony of the Rugby World Cup had augmented his fame. The subsequent single stayed at the top of the charts for a month and became the drinking song of choice for inebriated young men everywhere.

Mercy's Covent Garden debut was a triumph. Having spent three nights unable to sleep in anticipation, she was astonished at how natural it felt to take the stage in a leading role. It was as though she had been singing Liu her entire life. The critics would agree. And so would Nolan's wife, who was in the audience.

'Darling, you were wonderful,' said Cosima Esposito-O'Connor. 'I will have to look to my laurels.'

Now, faced with her heroine of over fifteen years, Mercy did lose her voice.

'That's it,' said Ed, as they climbed into the taxi for the ride home. 'The fat lady has finally sung.'

'Are you calling me fat?' Mercy asked in mock outrage. She gave her husband a playful punch.

'I love every inch of you,' Ed told her. 'I always will.'

Mercy was happy with that.

Tosca

GIACOMO Puccini's opera, *Tosca*, with its Italian libretto by Luigi Illica and Giuseppe Giacosa was premiered in Rome in 1900. It is based on Victorien Sardou's play *La Tosca* and tells the story of Floria Tosca, a passionate singer, prone to fits of unreasonable jealousy, and her lover, the painter Mario Cavaradossi.

Act One

The story begins in the church of Sant'Andrea della Valle, where escaped political prisoner Cesare Angelotti is hiding in the Attavanti family chapel. An elderly sacristan shuffles in to pray the Angelus. Meanwhile, Mario Cavaradossi is at work on a painting of Mary Magdalene that he has unwittingly based on the Marchesa Attavanti, who often prays in the church. He compares the blond Magdalene with a minature of his dark-haired lover, Floria Tosca. When the disapproving sacristan leaves, Angelotti emerges to be recognised by his old friend Mario. Mario shares his food then hurries Angelotti back into hiding as he hears Tosca calling outside.

Suspicious Tosca questions Mario as to whether he has company. Recognising the Marchesa in Mario's painting, Tosca explodes with jealousy, but Mario manages to reassure her that the painting has her eyes. With Tosca gone, Angelotti re-emerges, but a cannon signals that his escape from prison has been discovered. Mario takes Angelotti to hide in the well at his villa. The sacristan returns with the choirboys to sing the Te Deum. They are silenced by the entrance of Baron Scarpia, chief of the secret police, in search of Angelotti.

When Tosca returns to find Mario, Scarpia shows her a fan with the Marchesa's crest and suggests it proves Mario is unfaithful. Tosca vows revenge and Scarpia schemes to have her help him find Angelotti.

Act Two

At the Farnese Palace, Scarpia anticipates the pleasure of bending Tosca to his will. Having failed to find Angelotti, the spy Spoletta brings in Mario, who is interrogated while Tosca is heard singing at a royal gala downstairs. She enters just as her lover is being taken to be tortured. Unnerved by the sound of Mario's screams, she reveals Angelotti's hiding place. Mario is carried in; realising what has happened, he turns on Tosca, but the officer Sciarrone rushes in to announce that Napoleon has won the Battle of Marengo, a defeat for Scarpia's side. Mario shouts his defiance of tyranny and is dragged to prison. Scarpia suggests that

Tosca gives herself to him in exchange for her lover's life. Tosca, forced to give in to Scarpia's wishes or see Mario killed, agrees to Scarpia's proposition. The baron pretends to order a mock execution for the prisoner, after which he is to be freed. As soon as Scarpia has written a safe-conduct for the lovers Tosca grabs a knife from the table and kills him. Tearing the document from Scarpia's dead hands and placing candles at his head and a crucifix on his chest, she slips out of the room.

Act Three

As dawn is breaking, a shepherd boy sings. At the Castel Sant'Angelo, Mario awaits his execution. In despair, he writes a farewell note to Tosca. Suddenly Tosca runs in with news of the fake execution and their pass to safety. The lovers rejoice for their future. As a firing squad appears, Tosca advises Mario on how to fake his death convincingly. The soldiers fire and leave. Tosca urges Mario to get up, but when he fails to stir, she discovers Scarpia's treachery. The execution was real. As Spoletta rushes in to arrest Tosca for Scarpia's murder, she curses Scarpia, then leaps to her death from the walls of the prison.

Acknowledgements

With thanks to Bill, Jacky and Steve Sillery for a wonderful few days spent plotting this book in Abruzzo. To my sister Kate and brother-in-law Lee for letting me have the run of their house while finishing this first draft (and apologies for letting the dog have the run of the house while I was at it). Thanks to Mum and Dad for looking after me so well in the run-up to my deadline. Thanks to Mark Carroll for being so patient when I brought the edits on holiday. Thanks to Carolyn Mays and Francesca Best at Hodder and copy-editor Justine Taylor for three very useful sets of notes. Finally, thanks to Judy Shephard, to whom this book is dedicated, who made a very generous donation to the British Red Cross in return for the chance to be featured in these pages. I hope I've done you justice!

Read on for a taste of Olivia Darling's glamorously sexy novel ...

Priceless

Love, honour, betrayal.
What would it take to make you risk your
reputation, your livelihood or even your life?

On London's glittering art scene there's only one thing worth more
than a Leonardo da Vinci and that's revenge.

When native New Yorker CARRIE is asked to set up a new auction
house in London, she seizes the opportunity to settle an old score.

In rival auction house Ludbrook's, LIZZY is sleeping with her boss.
Which could be her best career move. Or her worst.

And out in the sticks, divorced and desperate to secure a better
future for her child, SERENA is about to embark on a daring artistic
enterprise that could spell disaster for them all.

Out now in paperback.

HODDER

Prologue

*I*N a small village on the south-east Mediterranean coast of Italy, in a room with windows that opened out right on to the sea, an artist was painting a portrait of a young girl. The girl was positioned at a table by the open window with a fig in her hand. The sunlight fell on her hair, turning it from plain yellow to a sheet of glittering gold. Her face was smooth and flawless, pink-cheeked and red-lipped without any need for artifice. Her expression was as sweet and calm as an angel's as she looked out on to the waves. Her name was Maria and she was modelling for a portrait of her namesake, the Virgin Mary herself, captured in a moment of quiet reflection before the annunciation.

But the thoughts that were running through the mind of the lovely Maria were more than a little at odds with the subject of the painting. Maria was thinking about the man behind the canvas, Giancarlo Ricasoli, the artist who was recording this moment for posterity. They hadn't spoken much; he had told her he preferred to work in silence. But she had heard quite a bit about him and what she knew of his reputation made her shy.

'How much longer will I have to sit like this?' she chanced to disturb him as she saw her father's boat come into the harbour.

'Are you uncomfortable?' Ricasoli asked.

'No,' she said. 'But I will have to go to mass. It isn't long now.'

'Ah, church,' said the artist. 'Of course.'

Maria had heard that Giancarlo Ricasoli didn't go to mass. Apparently the priest had given him a special dispensation on the grounds that he'd already spent as much time in the church as an ordinary member of the flock might spend there in a lifetime while he was painting the fresco on the ceiling. Having promised that he would provide a beautiful Madonna and Child for the priest's private residence as soon as he had finished this annunciation for which Maria now posed, Ricasoli had been assured that no more would be said about the matter. At least not officially.

Maria wished she had a talent that could allow her to be excused another hour in that dark old church. But dodging mass was the least of it. She'd heard other things about the artist too. She'd heard that in Florence he had been responsible for the ruination of not one but *five* young women. All had been models for his interpretation of the meeting of Christ and Mary Magdalene. All of them were virgins when they were first summoned to his studio and fallen women by the time they left.

And so Maria was horrified when it was first suggested that she sit for this painting of the Virgin Mary before the Annunciation, as were her parents. They too knew of the artist's reputation. Wasn't it true that five angry fathers had chased Ricasoli out of Florence? But then the artist told Maria's father how much he would be willing to pay for the privilege of painting his daughter. It was more than her father could hope to make in a year. And the priest had vouched for the artist, saying that he was a changed man since he'd come to their little village by the sea. 'I believe he is a good and proper man at heart,' the priest said, after beating Ricasoli at cards. So it was agreed that Maria would sit for the painting that was destined for the walls of a church near Naples. Her aunt Stefania, her father's sister, would chaperone.

Right then, however, Maria's aunt was doing a pretty bad job. Ricasoli had offered the older woman a glass of wine with their simple lunch and she had taken it. And another. Now Stefania was snoring lightly on a couch at the other end of the studio, in a most undignified position, shoes off, bare legs akimbo and her skirts hiked up to her thighs.

'I should make a sketch,' Ricasoli joked. 'I need someone posed like that for my depiction of the fallen in purgatory.'

'Don't you dare,' said Maria. 'She would be so upset.'

'Ah, sweet Maria,' Ricasoli sighed. 'Always thinking of other people. I hope that I can capture your good pure heart in this painting of mine.'

The way he said 'good pure heart' made Maria wonder if Ricasoli really thought such a thing was an asset.

While he dabbed away at something on the canvas; a crooked line or a smudge of colour gone awry, Maria regarded him closely, grabbing the chance to stare as closely as he had stared at her.

He was handsome. And he had a sophistication rarely seen in the local men folk of her little fishing town. When he wasn't dressed in his artist's smock, grubbily colourful where he'd wiped his brushes clean, he was adorned in the finest silks. He wore the latest fashions from Florence and Rome. Maria had often spied on him from her bedroom window, which had a good view of the road down to the harbour where he took his evening promenade. Of course, it hadn't occurred to her that was how he had first noticed her with her shining blonde hair and chosen her for his innocent Mary.

What was it like to be ruined? Maria wondered. How did it happen? As Ricasoli turned his back to her while he mixed some more pigment, Maria regarded the artist again. He was a surprisingly big man. He had a way of carrying himself that made him seem lithe and slim, but as he bent over the pot of ground lapis with which he was to paint her robes she could see that his shoulders were wide and strong. His buttocks, in their tight buckskin trousers, were square and powerful. Utterly masculine. Maria had a sudden flashing vision of what they might look like naked. Pumping. She had seen two people making love once, in a field behind the village. The woman's small heels pressed into the man's buttocks as he thrust into her. Suddenly Maria found herself imagining her own feet against the artist's flesh.

He had finished mixing his paints. On the couch, her aunt was still fast asleep.

'Are you ready to continue?' he asked.

Maria nodded as she gave one last stretch to get the blood back into her limbs. Ricasoli's eyes travelled the length of her body as she did so and Maria luxuriated in his look for as long as it took her to remember that such vanity was almost certainly a sin. She sat back down at the table and picked up the fig she had held in her hand for the last three days. The fruit was warm and sticky; its ripe skin was stretched tight and ready to burst. Maria assumed the position as closely as she remembered it.

'Not quite,' said Ricasoli. He stepped up onto the podium on which the table had been placed to make the best of the light coming through the window and the shadows and shards of brilliance it cast upon Maria's face. 'A little more to your left,' he told her. Maria shifted in her seat. 'No. Too far. Wait. You were here. More like this.'

Very gently, he took her chin in his hand and tilted her face towards him. But when he had her where he thought she should be, he did not immediately take his hand away. Maria looked at him with huge unblinking eyes. He had never before laid a hand on her to help her into her pose. Ordinarily, her aunt Stefania would be standing right beside him, ensuring that such a thing didn't happen. From the back of the studio, the sleeping chaperone let out an enormous snort.

Maria and the artist jumped apart. Was that snore enough to have woken her up? It seemed not.

'You moved,' Ricasoli said to Maria. 'Now I will have to put you into position all over again.' Once more he took her chin in his hand and tilted her face towards the light. But this time he did not stop when she was in the perfect position for the painting. He kept on tilting her face until they were almost nose-to-nose. She let out a small gasp of surprise as he said, 'I'm going to do it.'

'Do what?' she asked in a squeak.

'This.'

He kissed her.

Maria had never been kissed by a man before. Not like that. She had wondered if she ever would be and, if she was, whether she would be good at it. It turned out that her older sister was right. It came to her as though she had always been kissing. Maria let herself fall into the tender trap.

The artist's lips were so warm and gentle. As he kissed her, his fingers explored her long, fine neck, her bare shoulders, her soft décolletage. Never touched before.

Maria felt a blush rise on her skin. Her heart beat faster. Her head and stomach felt light. As Ricasoli continued to touch her, she realised she wanted to throw her clothes off and feel his hands on every part of her. She trembled as she felt her body begin to unfurl for love. At the same time she squeezed the fig so hard it split open in her palm.

On the couch in the corner, her aunt slept on. Ricasoli held out his hand and invited Maria to step behind the screen where she changed out of her own clothes and into the Virgin's robes each morning.

'What if she wakes up?'

'We'll say you were washing your hands,' said Ricasoli, as he sucked fig juice from her forefinger.

'I'm going to be ruined,' thought Maria.

And it was wonderful.

Chapter One

$\mathcal{I}$T was the moment he sucked whipped cream from her fingers that Lizzy Duffy realised her relationship with her boss had changed irrevocably. Subsequently, losing her virginity to him was either the best – or the worst – career move she could possibly have made. As she lay on her back in Nat Wilde's bed, worrying at a cuticle and examining a cobweb in the corner of his bedroom ceiling, Lizzy decided that it was probably her worst move. And staying the night had compounded it. She remembered something she'd read in some magazine: don't act clingy after the first time you have sex. It was clingy, wasn't it, staying the night in the hope of a reassuring cuddle? Nat had fallen asleep right after he'd come. Lizzy knew she should have got straight up and caught a taxi home right then to prove she wasn't bothered. Beside her, Nat slumbered on, seemingly unmoved by the same dilemma.

What on earth had possessed her? Fact was, Lizzy knew exactly what had possessed her. Nat Wilde had possessed her the moment she first laid eyes on him at her interview for a position in the Old Masters and Nineteenth-Century department at Ludbrook's, the auction house on New Bond Street. Fresh from her master's degree in art history at the Courtauld, Lizzy had prepared a pretty speech about her passion for nineteenth-century British watercolourists. But she didn't have an opportunity to deliver it. Nat Wilde was running late. He breezed into the Ludbrook's office fifteen minutes after the interview had been due to start. He was slightly inebriated, having lunched with his best friend Harry Brown, head of Ludbrook's' department of fine wines, at their gentleman's club on St. James's. Nat picked Lizzy's CV up from the desk and seemed unable to focus on it. Then he looked at her, focused very well on the hem of her skirt, and said, 'You've got the right degree, you're pass-ably pretty and you wear short skirts. You're hired.'

The right thing at that moment would have been for Lizzy to take offence but before she could open her mouth to protest at such a superficial and sexist dismissal of her proper talents, Nat Wilde smiled at her. And it was the kind of smile that made her feel he had been joking about her being 'passably pretty'. That was an understatement, of course. He found her far more attractive than that. Lizzy couldn't help but smile back. She was smitten.

'Your first assignment,' said Nat. 'Tell me about this little painting right here.'

Her heart still fluttering like a hummingbird with the hiccups, Lizzy followed Nat Wilde across the room. Balanced on a shelf was a small watercolour of a farmer bringing cows in from the field at the end of the day.

'Artist?'

'Easy,' Lizzy trotted out the name.

'Real?'

Lizzy peered closely. 'I think so. The only way to know is to see the signature. But he wouldn't have signed a piece this small on the front. You'd need to turn it over and . . .'

'Already done that,' said Nat. 'Put a reserve on it of ten to twelve grand. What do you think?'

'I think that's just about right,' said Lizzy. 'How about you?'

'I think you and I are going to work together very well.'

And they did.

Never before had Lizzy found getting up for work to be such a pleasure. She was thrilled to be working with the art that she loved surrounded by fellow enthusiasts. She had long been determined to have a great career in an auction house but now she had an added incentive to sparkle. Each morning she veritably sprang out of bed at the sound of her alarm. She spent at least an hour getting ready, blow-drying her fine blonde hair into something resembling a do. And oh how her efforts were rewarded. Nat Wilde could make her day with a wink and the winks were plentiful. Nat and Lizzy had flirted like crazy for the past six months. And now here she was. In his bed.

That afternoon's sale at Ludbrook's had been a barnstormer. Lot after lot bust through the ceiling prices Nat had predicted. And finally, Nat achieved a price of seven figures for an early nineteenth-century oil. It went to a Russian collector. All the good papers would cover the news.

After such a successful day, Nat announced that the entire team deserved a treat. He utilised his direct line to the maitre d' at The Ivy and booked a table for eight o'clock.

'Sit here,' said Nat to Lizzy, patting the seat beside him. 'You're my right-hand girl and I want you on my right hand.'

Lizzy settled into the seat, catching the envious glances from the other girls in her department – Olivia and Sarah Jane – as they found themselves at the other end of the table, between the two bespectacled boys, Marcus and James.

'Champagne!' Nat announced. He ordered a bottle of Champagne Arsenault's Clos De Larmes, which Lizzy understood was the good stuff. It certainly went down easily. They polished off six bottles between them, the restaurant's entire stock.

'It's on old John Ludbrook's account,' Nat reminded them. 'And you deserve it!'

He toasted the team, as one and individually.

'Olivia,' he said. 'You are the goddess of typing. Sarah Jane, without you, my mailing list would be nothing.'

Lizzy felt herself colour crimson when Nat praised her pretty blue eyes. 'Which are so good at spotting a masterpiece!'

Dessert arrived. Lizzy chose sticky toffee pudding with cream, getting some on her finger as she pulled the dish towards her. Quick as a flash Nat grabbed her hand and stuck his finger in her mouth.

'Don't want to waste any,' he said.

Lizzy almost crawled under the table for shame. She was hugely relieved no one else seemed to have noticed.

'How are you getting home?' Nat asked Lizzy as they were collecting their coats.

'I'll get a cab,' she said.

'Where to? Hammersmith, isn't it? My place is on the way there. We'll share a ride.'

They started kissing as the cab sailed past the roundabout at Hyde Park Corner. By the time they got to Nat's flat in South Kensington, Lizzy knew she wouldn't be taking the taxi on.

'Do you have any cash?' Nat asked. 'I left my last tenner as a tip.'

Lizzy duly dug out her last twenty and handed it to the driver.

'Thank you. You're a poppet. I'll pay you back tomorrow.'

Nat took her by the hand and led her into the shared lobby of the mansion block in which he lived. They continued to kiss in the mirrored lift. Nat's tongue flickered inside her mouth like an eel in a bucket. Lizzy smiled at her reflection over Nat's shoulder as he nibbled at her neck. She sighed with delight as Nat slipped his hand up her cashmere sweater and started to fumble with the clasp at the back of her bra.

Once inside the flat they went straight to the bedroom. Lizzy's nerves were as taut as violin strings as her clothes fell to the floor. Would Nat still want her when he saw her naked body? Nat's growl soon told her that he did.

'Oh. Yes,' Lizzy sighed as Nat cupped his hands around her bare breasts and fiddled with her nipples. As he sucked each one of them in turn, he somehow managed to slide her little white cotton knickers down as far as her knees. While Nat turned his attention to Lizzy's buttocks, the knickers dropped to her ankles and Lizzy kicked them off. Now she was completely in the raw but Nat was still fully clothed. He soon remedied that.

While Lizzy arranged herself on the sheets in what she hoped was an alluring manner, Nat divested himself of his tie, his shirt, his trousers and underpants as though the clothes were on fire. There was a brief and awful moment when Lizzy thought Nat might actually be intending to ravage her with his socks still on, but he remembered just in time and pulled them off as well. They went flying across the room. One ended up dangling from the standard lamp.

Nat dived onto the bed, narrowly avoiding head-butting Lizzy in the nose as he did so. Lizzy hadn't really thought about what would happen next. More kissing, she hoped. She wanted to be covered in kisses from head to toe. Top to bottom. Indeed, it seemed that Nat was already very fond of her bottom. It wasn't long before he flipped her over onto her tummy and was bestowing naughty little love-bites to her shapely pink buttocks. So far, so silly. Lizzy giggled as Nat jiggled the spare flesh on her bum. But then things turned rather more serious. He stuck his hand between her legs. She felt his fingers groping for a way inside. And then, suddenly, he lay fully on top of her, squashing her face into the mattress. She felt his erection – which she hadn't really seen yet or got to know – pressing hard against the place where his fingers had been moments before.

'Nat, I . . .'

She meant to tell him but before she knew it, the inevitable was already happening. Lizzy drew breath sharply at the first thrust. Fortunately, there were only five more of those before Nat came with a terrifying bellow that made Lizzy respond with a cry of her own.

'Good for you?' he asked as he pulled out.

Good? Well, it hadn't hurt as much as she expected. And there was no blood. If she was honest, most of Lizzy's enjoyment of the moment had been stymied at the thought that she might leave a dirty red stain on Nat's pure white sheets. But she didn't. She checked. There was no evidence whatsoever that anything monumental had taken place.

Fact was, Nat didn't even know she was a virgin. Lizzy thought he might have guessed, but, if he had, he didn't say anything. He just rolled off her and fell asleep. His face as he lay dreaming was youthful and perfectly untroubled. Unlike Lizzy's.

She lay awake all night, staring at the bare, plain walls of Nat's bedroom (utterly typical for the home of a forty-something divorced guy), replaying the event over and over, wondering and worrying if she had done what was expected. And then, of course, there was the question of contraception. They hadn't used any. Would her local chemist stock the morning-after pill? What were the rules about taking it? How had she got to twenty-six without actually knowing this stuff? How had she got to twenty-six without losing her virginity anyway? She shook her head in disbelief as the disapproving face of her only serious boyfriend came to mind. He had been president of the Christian Union at university and had flat out refused to have sex outside marriage. They broke up when Lizzie was twenty-five. There had been opportunities since but by then Lizzie had decided that getting to your mid-twenties without having done it was just plain weird and she didn't want to have to explain so she avoided the issue. And after all that she lost it to her boss. In just eleven minutes from taxi to finish. Was that it?

Finally, at seven in the morning, Lizzy decided it was time to go.

'See you in the office at nine,' she said brightly. Nat nodded groggily. Lizzy bounced out of bed and headed for the tube and a change of clothes in her grotty flat in Hammersmith. She was borne all the way there on a tide of regret. And so preoccupied was she with her big faux pas that it wasn't until she got to the office that she remembered it was a Saturday.

Chapter Two

'Up.'

Carrie Klein issued her first order of the day.

'Wha . . . ?'

The young man in her bed sat up against the pillows and rubbed his eyes.

'What time is it?' he asked.

'Seven thirty,' she said.

'Seven thirty? But it's a Sunday.'

'Makes no difference to me. I have things to do today and I need you out of the apartment while I'm doing them.'

'Carrie,' Jed opened his arms. 'There is nothing that really needs to be done at seven thirty on a Sunday morning. You need to chill out more, babe. Let me help you. Come back to bed.'

Carrie eyed Jed's firm chest dispassionately. He was a male model. There was no doubt that he was beautiful but lately Carrie had been wondering if this relationship was working for her. It was a funny thing. A female model was the Holy Grail as a partner for a high-flying guy but what high-flying woman should be with a man who pouted for a living?

'Jed, I have a position of responsibility,' she reminded him as he tried to slip a hand inside the folds of her dressing gown.

'I can think of several irresponsible positions I'd like to see you in . . .'

'Not now,' she insisted. Jed never seemed to understand when she was being serious.

Carrie Klein was second in command in the Old Masters department at Ehrenpreis. Of all the auction houses in New York, Ehrenpreis was the newest. Founded in the 1960s, it didn't have centuries of history like Christie's, Sotheby's or Ludbrook's but it had already had a reputation for excellence. Recently, the house had held some very high-profile sales that had set tongues wagging. The older houses at last admitted they had something to worry about.

Carrie had begun her career in Christie's. When she moved to Ehrenpreis aged thirty-one, leap-frogging many of her peers, some of her former colleagues had tried to belittle the appointment, saying that there was no way Carrie would have got such a senior position in any 'proper house'. She was determined to prove them wrong. And that meant working hard. Working on the weekends if she had to. And she did have to.

'Jed, please don't make this difficult for me,' she said. 'I have a big auction coming up next week. There are people I need to talk to. People in different time zones. You do realise that they're already halfway through Monday in Asia?'

'Then call them on their Tuesday. They can wait.'

'They won't wait.' Her mobile phone vibrated to let her know she had voicemail. 'See?' she said. 'I've got to get going.' She tugged on a turtleneck sweater.

Carrie sat down on the edge of the bed and began to roll her stockings up over her long slim legs. Jed moved so that he was right behind her. He started to knead her shoulders and much as she didn't want to, Carrie found herself responding to his expert touch. To supplement his income as a model-cum-actor, Jed had learned the art of Swedish massage. He made home visits to society ladies all over Manhattan and was very much in demand. He had a real talent for touch.

'Jed . . .' Carrie began to protest but now he had moved on from massaging her shoulders to kissing what small part of her neck he could reach. Before she knew what was happening, Carrie lifted her arms and let Jed pull her turtleneck sweater off over her head.

'Oh. All right . . . I guess it *is* the weekend. But just thirty minutes, OK?'

'I can do a lot in thirty minutes,' Jed grinned at her. She knew it.

Carrie let Jed unpin her long blonde hair. She shivered as the silky soft tresses settled on the bare skin of her back above her dove-grey slip.

'Arms up again,' Jed instructed.

Soon her slip was on the floor, too.

'Lie down,' he said.

Carrie lay back on the pillows and tried to look a little more relaxed even if she wasn't exactly feeling it. Jed, who had often told her that he worshipped every inch of her, seemed determined to prove it that morning. He started at her feet.

'You have the most beautiful feet,' he told her as he kissed the arch of each perfectly pedicured foot in turn. Then he placed another kiss on each ankle. He laid a little path of kisses up her shins to her knees.

'Great knees,' he said with a smile.

'Behave,' Carrie warned him. 'You know I'm self-conscious about my knees.'

'They are my favourite part of you,' Jed responded.

'Just keep kissing me.'

Jed moved on to her thighs. He traced a line from her left knee to her hip with his tongue, and then repeated the move on the other side. With gentle hands he parted her legs. He dipped his head and nuzzled the soft triangle of her pubic hair.

'Feeling better yet?' he asked.

'Much,' she said, as she felt his warm breath on her clitoris. 'I might have to let you have forty-five minutes instead.'

'I'll make the most of it,' Jed promised.

But then the telephone in the hall started ringing. Carrie immediately tensed up.

'Ignore it,' said Jed. 'Just ignore it.'

Carrie tried. She lay back in the pillows again and closed her eyes and tried to concentrate on nothing else but the feeling of Jed's tongue on her clitoris, but it was no good. It wasn't working. Soon she was biting her lip with anxiety. She had turned the ringer on the phone beside the bed to silent, but the set in the hall rang out loud enough to keep her from all thoughts of the erotic. And then her cell phone joined in, vibrating urgently on the nightstand.

'Stop!' she pushed Jed away.

'For fuck's sake.'

'I'm sorry,' she said. 'But whoever it is has been trying every way they can to get hold of me. It must be important.'

'What?' Jed snapped. 'What on earth can be more important than letting me pleasure you?'

'Jed, I will make it up to you,' she said as she simultaneously pulled on her dressing gown and checked the messages on her cell phone.

'I don't know if you'll have the chance,' said Jed, hopping out of bed and searching the floor around it for his own clothes.

Carrie nodded vaguely. Already absorbed in her voicemail messages, she didn't hear Jed's threat. She waved him in the direction of the kitchen.

'There's juice in the refrigerator,' she said.

'I'll get some on my way home.'

He left, slamming the door as he went.

Carrie hardly noticed. She was already calling her boss.

'I'm sorry. I would have picked up but I was on a call to Asia,' she lied.

'Don't worry about that,' said her boss Andrew Carter. 'But I need you in the office right away. There's an emergency. You know that small Constable in next week's sale?'

'The one with the sheep in the stream?'

'Exactly. I just got a call from a guy in England, tells me he's looking at the *exact* same painting hanging on the wall in the study of a stately home where he's on a shooting weekend.'

'F—.' Carrie swallowed a swear word. 'And he thinks it's real?'

'He does. And as long as I've known him, he's never been wrong. Where did ours come from?'

Carrie sat down heavily on her sofa as though she were receiving bad news about her health while Andrew ran through the nightmarish details. His informant was one of the UK's most respected experts on the artist in question. If anyone knew the real thing, it was he.

'Shit.' This time Carrie couldn't keep the expletive in.

'Exactly,' said her boss.

Jed's attempt to get Carrie's morning off to a good start was all but forgotten now. She closed her eyes and let the horror wash over her. She had taken on a fake.

Chapter Three

Serena Macdonald could only dream about waking up next to some hot young guy who wanted to give her a shoulder massage. That morning, as had been the case most mornings for the past few months, she awoke to the sound of a small pink puppet making farting noises. She opened one eye to see her five-year-old daughter Katie sitting on the end of the bed, absorbed in *CeeBeebies* on the television Serena had inherited from her kindly brother.

'Morning, Mummy,' said Katie, without turning round.

'Morning, sweetheart.'

'Breakfast?' Katie suggested.

Serena glanced at the clock. It was half past six in the morning. 'Jeez,' she sighed. As an artist, Serena had always considered people who got up before ten deliberately to have lost the plot. But it was Monday. And a school day. And now she was one of those people.

Serena snaked one bare arm out from beneath the duvet

and felt around on the floor for the jeans and jumper she had been wearing for the past four days. There was no way she was getting out of bed without dressing first. It was icy cold in that farmhouse. Cornwall? It may as well have been Siberia.

Serena had grown up in Cornwall. She'd had what anyone would describe as an idyllic childhood but, all the same, she'd been only too eager to leave the county and head for London at the first possible opportunity. She went to the Chelsea College of Art and Design and after that worked in the art departments of a few private schools. And London was where she met Tom, her soon-to-be-ex-husband. Serena often thought about that moment when Tom walked into her life. The second she laid eyes on him, she had a feeling that he was going to play a big part in proceedings from that day forward. How had she failed to foresee that ten years after Tom asked her to marry him (on their first passionate date), he would be shacked up with someone else?

The day on which Tom asked for a divorce was as clear in her mind as the day they met. She'd sensed that something was wrong as he walked into the kitchen. His tie was askew. He looked as though he had been wrestling a tiger rather than pushing paper at his banking job in the City.

'I'll fallen in love,' he said. 'With someone else . . .'

It was the last thing any wife wants to hear.

It got worse. It transpired that the woman Tom had fallen in love with was his boss's wife. Serena was stunned when she discovered her rival's identity. They'd met a few times, at corporate functions and Tom had always been quite scathing about the woman: a social X-ray transplanted from New York who spent her days shopping and meeting her superannuated 'girlfriends' for lunch. Donna Harvey was always immaculately groomed. Hair, nails, whiter than white teeth ... She dressed in that way only American women of a certain social status do. It seemed she had exchanged her jeans for a Chanel suit and pearls the moment she left grad school and would not change out of them again until they were fitting her up for her shroud.

'She makes me feel so unkempt!' said Serena, after one particularly tortuous dinner party. 'You must be so ashamed of me.'

'Nonsense,' Tom had said that night. 'You are a thousand times sexier than she will ever be. I bet she's the kind of woman who takes a shower before and after she shags.'

Well, now he would know for sure, thought Serena bitterly.

Naturally, Tom's boss didn't take the news all that well either. Though technically he couldn't sack Tom for shagging his wife, he made it practically impossible for Tom to stay. Tom leapt at the chance to take redundancy. But there was no fabulous redundancy package. Tom's boss moved back to New York as soon as he could, leaving Donna in the house in South Kensington. Tom moved in.

'We can't afford to keep the house in Fulham, Serena. I'm sorry. I've got no money coming in. We've got to put it on the market. Start looking for something else for you and Katie. You should be able to get two bedrooms in Stockwell.'

Serena quailed at the thought of such a rough neighbourhood. 'You want me to live in *Stockwell* while you're living it up in your love pad in South Ken? For fuck's sake, Tom, ask *her* for the mortgage money.'

'I can't. I'm sorry. It could prejudice her settlement. I'm doing my best.'

'Well, if this is your best ... I hope you can hold your head up when you explain to your daughter that she had to move into some flea-infested pit because you couldn't keep your dick in your pants.'

There was no way that Serena was going to move into some two-bedroom flat on an estate she was afraid to walk through in the daylight but she couldn't afford anything big enough somewhere nice. After viewing a couple of shoe-boxes in SW6, Serena bowed to the inevitable. The only option was to move out of London altogether. She started looking around Guildford, thinking she should try to stay within an hour's distance of Tom so that he could see Katie whenever he wanted. But the sad truth was that, even though he lived just a couple of tube stops away and, in theory, had nothing to do all day in his state of unemployment, Tom wasn't making much effort to see Katie at all.

The final straw came when Serena needed Tom to look after Katie one Wednesday evening while she attended a meeting at the local college where she was hoping to teach a figure-drawing course to help cover the rising cost of groceries.

'I can't baby-sit,' he said. 'Donna's giving a dinner.'

'I'm not asking you to *baby-sit*, Tom. I'm asking you to look after your own daughter. To be a dad, for once.'

'I'm sorry,' he said hopelessly. 'She's invited someone who might be a good contact for me. I can't take Katie. It's just not going to work.'

'Too right,' said Serena. This arrangement wasn't working out at all. There and then Serena decided she would no longer run her life for Tom's convenience. The following day she started browsing the Internet for property in Cornwall.

And then – finally – she had a stroke of luck. Her brother Joe called. His high-flying wife Helena's company were sending her to Hong Kong for a couple of years and he was going too, meaning they would have no time at all to use their house in the country.

'It's all yours, sis,' he said.

Serena and Katie moved to Cornwall just before Christmas. Sure, Tom protested at the thought that his daughter would be so far away but he didn't come up with an alternative. And when the day came for Serena and Katie to hand over the Fulham house to the nice young couple who had bought it, Tom was nowhere to be seen. Donna's concierge service arranged for a removal van to pick up what remained of Tom's chattels and take them to her sterile South Kensington mansion, where even the books on the shelves had been chosen by an interior designer for their covers rather than their content. Tom had told Serena she could keep all the furniture. He even left behind his favourite leather chair. The one he'd bought with his first pay packet. She knew it had nothing to do with being fair however. As she thanked him, Serena could hear Donna's voice in her head.

'You think I'm going to have that filthy chair in my salon?'

That Christmas was not the usual festive occasion. Serena forced herself to go out and buy a tree for Katie's sake. She bought a little chicken rather than a turkey for lunch. Serena had worried that Katie would be miserable spending Christmas day without her father but the ridiculously extravagant gifts he sent seemed to make up for his absence. Katie spent New Year in London with Tom and Donna. Having spent the evening absolutely alone, Serena toasted herself with a cup of tea as the old year turned into the new. Alcohol seemed too risky while she was feeling so very down.

It seemed too much to hope that the New Year would be better but she prayed for it all the same.

About a week into January, one of Serena's new neighbours dropped by to introduce herself. Serena liked Louisa Trebarwen at once. Not least because she brought with her home-made chocolate cookies.

'I'm from next door,' said Louisa.

She didn't have to introduce herself. Serena knew of her already. The house next door was called Trebarwen and Serena had heard plenty about its chatelaine. Louisa lived in the enormous house on her own. She was in her late seventies but still slim, sprightly and very elegant indeed. That afternoon she wore a neat skirt and a Hermès scarf around her neck. Serena glanced down at her own jeans and felt ashamed.

'Is this a good time?' Louisa asked.

'I ... er ... Of course.' Might as well let the woman in now, Serena thought. The house was a tip but it was unlikely to get better. At least she could realistically claim unfinished unpacking as an excuse for the disarray.

But Louisa Trebarwen seemed oblivious to the mess around her. She perched on one of the high stools next to the breakfast bar and chatted about the weather while Serena made tea in the pot she never used.

'What a lovely painting of your daughter!' Louisa admired the little picture on the sitting-room wall. 'Where did you find the artist? I've been looking for someone to paint my two for the past five years. This is the first portrait I've seen that doesn't look as though you had it done by one of those caricature chaps in Leicester Square.'

'Thank you.'

'So, are you going to tell me who painted it?'

'Actually,' Serena looked down at her shoes a little shyly. 'It was me.'

'You painted that picture?'

'I did.'

'Wow. I mean, Helena told me that you had been to art school but . . . gosh. It's like an old master.'

'That was the idea,' said Serena. 'I spent a bit of time in Florence after I graduated, getting to learn the traditional techniques.'

'Well, it was certainly time well spent,' said Louisa with real admiration. 'I'm in awe.'

'Oh, please . . . It's not so good. I knocked it out in a couple of hours.'

'No, Serena. You must not belittle your talent. You really have something. Will you paint my babies for me?'

Serena started to shake her head. It was one thing painting her own daughter for herself but she couldn't imagine painting Louisa's children. She hadn't painted properly in a long while. When she left work to go on maternity leave, Serena told herself that she would soon pick up her paintbrushes again, but the reality was that she simply didn't have time. Before the baby was born, she spent all her time getting ready for the new arrival. And after the baby was born . . . well, finding a moment to sleep became a far greater priority.

Later, Serena had wanted to go back to work but Tom insisted there was no need. He'd had a promotion. He was earning enough to support them both. Besides, if Serena went back to work they would have to get proper childcare, which would all but wipe out the money she earned anyway.

'And I don't like the idea of my daughter being looked after by strangers,' he added. 'That's not going to happen to you.' He kissed Katie on the head.

He seemed to have forgotten about that little promise. How could Serena be expected to support herself without going back to work and leaving Katie in the care of a stranger now?

'I would pay you,' Louisa interrupted Serena's thoughts.

'I really couldn't accept any money,' Serena said, fearing that she would only have to give it back when Louisa saw the result.

'But you must. Serena, I hate to be presumptuous but Helena has told me all about your situation. That terrible feckless husband of yours going off with another woman.'

Serena blushed.

'I know it hurts, my dear.' Louisa placed a hand on Serena's arm. 'It happened to me. And because it happened to me, I know there is no place for moping around. You have to pick yourself up as quickly as you can. And that means earning some money of your own. I am willing to pay you a thousand pounds for your trouble. Please don't turn me down.'

Serena opened her mouth to protest.

Louisa misread her hesitation. 'Was that insultingly low? How about one thousand five hundred? Two?'

'Mrs Trebarwen . . .'

'Call me Louisa.'

'Louisa, I can't take your money. Heaven knows I would love to. I can't deny I need it. But this little painting of my daughter. It was a fluke. I don't know how I managed to get such a good likeness. I'm out of practice. This was my first attempt having not picked up a paintbrush for years. It was lucky. I suppose it helped that I know the subject's face better than I know my own. I promise you would be disappointed if I tried to do portraits of your sons.'

'My sons?' Louisa Trebarwen gave a little giggle. 'Who said anything about my sons? Darling, I don't want portraits of those great ugly lummoxes. They both grew out of their looks a very long time ago. Serena, you'll have to get used to me. When I refer to my "babies", I am talking about my dogs.'

Dogs were an altogether different matter. Serena could easily paint dogs. Later that same afternoon, when she had picked up Katie from school, Serena dropped by Trebarwen House to meet her new subjects. Louisa was delighted to meet Katie and Katie was instantly smitten with Louisa's beloved pets. They were two rather regal-looking greyhounds, called Berkeley and Blackwater Bess.

'I got them from a greyhound rescue charity,' Louisa explained. 'They both raced when they were young but now they've retired they're actually the ideal companions for older people like me. They don't need half so much exercise as you would imagine.'

As if on cue, Berkeley opened his mouth and curled his tongue in an extravagant yawn.

'How would you like to paint them?' Louisa asked. 'You're the artist so I'm giving you free rein.'

Serena thought for a moment. 'How about I paint them together, standing at the top of the steps leading down to the garden with a stormy sky in the background. A cloudy sky would be the perfect way to highlight the sheeny grey of their coats.'

'That sounds wonderful,' said Louisa.

Serena set to work that very day. While Louisa took Katie all over the house and even let her ride the delicate old rocking horse that had carried Trebarwen children since the nineteenth century, Serena got out her somewhat out-dated digital camera and took a few snaps of the dogs. Then she headed outside and took some more snaps of the garden to help her make a start on the portrait's composition. There was little hope that the dogs would stand still on the step for real. It was hard enough to get them to stand at all. They really were the most amazingly lazy creatures.

A week later, Serena had completed a number of preliminary sketches and let Louisa choose the composition she liked best. Then it was time to transfer the sketches on to canvas. Serena asked Louisa how big the painting should be. She would order the canvas online.

'Hmmm. Actually I was wondering if you could paint over this?' Louisa asked as she produced a Victorian portrait of a rather dour-looking man.

'But that . . . I can't . . .'

'It's not a family portrait,' Louisa explained. 'I think I found him at a fete in 1973.'

Louisa quickly became a friend. Serena set up her easel in the drawing room of the big house so that she could look out on the garden as she filled in the background. Louisa was always happy to have Katie around. Katie was delighted to have so many dusty old rooms to roam in.

'I rarely see my grandchildren,' she sighed. 'My eldest son's wife doesn't like me. God knows if the youngest will ever breed. He doesn't seem to be able to commit to any one woman for more than a month. He takes after his father. Couldn't keep his pecker in his pants for a minute, that one . . .'

It was odd but listening to Louisa's stories about her feckless ex-husband was strangely comforting. Serena liked Louisa very much and the knowledge that she too had been a victim of infidelity reassured Serena that it happened to the best of people. It didn't mean that she was a loser.

And so Serena began to feel better. For the first time since Tom walked into the kitchen and announced that he wanted out of their marriage, Serena felt as though she had reason to smile. Katie was happy. Serena had a great new friend in Louisa. And then there was her work. She had forgotten the most important reward of painting: a sense of flow that pushed all other concerns to the back of her mind if only for a little while.

The portrait of the dogs turned out very well. Though she was usually her own harshest critic, Serena allowed herself to be pleased with the result of her hard work. She had been right with her initial thoughts for the piece. The stormy sky was a perfect backdrop for the regally silky grey of the dogs' glossy coats. Serena thought perhaps that even the dogs' faces had turned out better than she hoped. There was individuality to them. Louisa could tell at once which was which.

'I love it,' said Louisa. 'You are an absolute marvel.'

She enveloped Serena in an extravagantly perfumed hug. 'I will hang it above the fireplace right here in the drawing room.'

'Really?' Serena was stunned. That would mean moving a painting of Louisa's two sons as small children. 'But that's such a wonderful picture. Are you sure?'

'Absolutely. I'm bored to death of that old thing. And my beautiful babies need a truly regal setting.'

'Well, OK,' said Serena.

'Help me hang it now,' Louisa asked.

* * *

The following weekend, Louisa's elder son Mark dropped by.

'What happened to the painting of me and Julian?' he asked the moment he stepped into the drawing room. 'Where did you get that bloody awful dog picture? How much did it cost you? Tell me it isn't . . .'

'It's Berkeley and Blackwater Bess,' Louisa told him proudly. 'Since my real children only visit when they want something, I decided to have my new babies on the wall instead.'

'Mother. For heaven's sake.'

'It's rather wonderful, don't you think? The girl who moved into the cottage painted it. She trained in London and Florence.'

'I don't care where she trained. I can't believe you would take down a portrait of your own children and put a picture of your bloody rescue greyhounds in its place!'

'Well, you will be able to put yourself and your brother back up there when I'm gone,' said Louisa. 'And don't worry,' she added. 'The dogs may have replaced you above the fireplace but they haven't replaced you in my last will and testament. Yet. You'll have to keep visiting for a few more months, at least.'

'Years, more like,' said Mark, barely disguising his annoyance. 'I have no doubt that you will outlive us all.'

OLIVIA DARLING

Vintage

**Three women who dare to make it in a man's world.
One sparkling prize.**

MADELEINE ARSENAULT has prepared for this moment all her life. She is determined to rescue the beloved family chateau and prove she's got what it takes to run the most successful champagne house in France.

Former supermodel CHRISTINA MORGAN knows she hasn't got what it takes. But she's sure as hell not going to show it. And with the help of her friends, she'll turn her ex-husband's hobby Californian vineyard into a major player.

Chambermaid KELLY ELSON would rather drink vodka and coke than champagne. Then she inherits a vineyard and suddenly she's thirsty for success.

Watching over them all is MATHIEU RANDON. Super-rich. Seductive. And a sociopath.

Competing to produce the world's best sparkling wine, the three women are swept into a world of feuds, back-stabbing, sabotage and seduction. Have they got what it takes to survive?

Out now in paperback.

HODDER